ONE SHILLING & SIXPENCE.

FOR HONOUR

OR THE YOUNG PRIVATEER

BY E H BURRAGE

FOR HONOUR:
OR, THE YOUNG PRIVATEER.

"YOU GO BELOW, MASSAR DUNCAN," SAID MONKEY JACK, "DAT'S YOUR PLACE

CHAPTER I.

THE FRIGATE AT SEA—FRIENDSHIP AND ENMITY—THE APPROACH OF A FOE.

A STORM at sea! how the wind rushes along, revelling in the havoc among the rigging of fragile ships! How it roars and twists the fleecy clouds into fantastic shapes, driving them across the midnight sky and sweeping down upon the agitated waters of the deep, while men, snug in their homes on land, gather closer to the bright fire, and listen to its hollow voice and breathe a silent prayer for those upon the storm-rocked deep!

Hark! it comes again, bearing with it a semblance of the ocean's roar, and the mind pictures the broad expanse of salt water tossed into mountains capped with foam, and the mind's eye sees some gallant vessels struggling against the elements

now in the trough of the sea, now on the watery hill tops, the captain at his post, with speaking trumpet in hand, and ready sailors clinging to the nearest stay at hand, prepared to do his bidding.

In such a storm, one night in the month of November, 1780, a British frigate, under close-reefed topsails, was beating about the Island of St. Domingo, the waters striking her bows with a sound that rivalled the rolling thunder, and threatened each moment to overwhelm her.

The officers and crew stood calmly at their posts, ignoring the repeated drenchings they received, or coolly giving themselves a shaking when a heavier mass of water than usual fell upon them, with their eyes fixed upon the gloomy expanse of ocean, with its white crests of foam faintly visible around them.

The good ship was in no danger, for she was well handled and sea-worthy, and below in the midshipmen's berth the usual skylarking was going forward on the part of those who were off duty.

The midshipmen's berth of the "Curlew" was not a very roomy affair, and was generally inconveniently filled with mates, midshipmen, and others entitled to use it for a resting-place ; but sailors of whatever degree are not fastidious, especially if they rank on the ship's books as midshipmen.

On this particular night, some of the young dogs were more than ordinarily mischievous, and seemed inclined to use their tormenting powers to the fullest extent. This was especially observable in the very youngest of the party, a lad of fourteen, a laughing, reckless young imp, named Harry Carlton.

"I say, Wantlake," he shouted, addressing a burly sulky-looking young fellow of eighteen, " how are you getting on with that little affair of yours ?"

Wantlake looked up from a book he was reading, and suddenly demanded—

"What affair ?"

"Oh ! you don't know," returned Harry with a laugh, " certainly not. Miss Clara, to be sure—the peerless daughter of our good captain."

A roar of delight escaped from the rest of the occupants of the place, and Wantlake sprang up with an oath. The boy took refuge behind the table and there grinned defiance at the other.

"You keep your mouth closed, will you ?" growled the elder mid ; " your con-

founded chattering makes a lot of mischief."

"Mischief," exclaimed the boy, opening his eyes in surprise, "mischief—I asked the question because I am interested in any case of spoons—I've had one or two little affairs of the heart myself."

The merry faces of those around him, old and young, told Harry that his fun was appreciated, and receiving no reply, he renewed the attack.

"I also asked the question," he said, " because I am much afraid that Harold Greystone is cutting you out."

"Curse Harold Greystone," rejoined the other, " will you shut up ?"

"Directly, old boy ; just let me say this, that Harold is better looking, braver, and never yet showed the white feather."

A furious exclamation sprang from Wantlake's lips, and hurling his book at the head of his tormentor, he darted round the table in pursuit.

It would have fared ill with Harry then but for the interposition of the rest, who stood between him and the infuriated midshipman.

"Don't hurt him," they cried, " he's only a youngster."

"Once and for all," roared Wantlake, "I've had enough of his confounded impudence ; let me get at him, that's all."

"Look here," said Harry Carlton, "I don't want to funk a fight with you, but I like a thing which is fair—you go into training, reduce yourself to my weight, and I will settle this affair in a gentlemanly manner."

The exquisite impudence of the boy exasperated his foe, but delighted the others, who maintained their mediative position, and contrived to shield the lad.

"Sit down, Wantlake," said one, soothingly, " consider his age—wait until you are cooler, and then cob the young rascal."

"A very fine thing for you, Martin," growled the mid, " but what does he mean by the white feather ? Who has shown it, you imp of darkness ?"

"Not Harold Greystone," replied the boy, " he's the pluckiest fellow on board the 'Curlew'—Miss Clara said so—at least she said he was the bravest, and that is the same thing."

Wantlake turned all colours, and a second explosion was imminent when the subject of their conversation came below from his watch.

Harold Greystone was a model young

fellow of nineteen years of age, with a lithe but strong and well-proportioned figure. Drenched as he was to the skin, he was still a handsome youth; nothing could remove that impression from those who beheld him, and as he stood in the doorway, shaking off the wet, with a merry smile upon his face, and the light of happiness in his eyes, he looked every inch the gallant young sailor he was known to be.

"By Jove!" he exclaimed, "what a night, buckets of water from the clouds, and the waves running over us like maddened horses; but, thank Goodness, the storm is subsiding, and Captain Harloch says it will be almost a calm by the morning."

"We have had a storm below," grinned Harry Carlton, looking at Wantlake.

"Now, Harry, Harry," remonstrated the previous speaker; "you have been up to some of your tricks. You are like a young kitten."

"He is a confounded nuisance," growled Wantlake, rising to his feet, "and one of these days he'll get his neck twisted."

"Keep your temper, Wantlake," said Harold; "he is the youngest in the berth, and therefore privileged."

"To insult me alone, I suppose," sneered the other; "why doesn't he put some of his fun upon *you*? you would sing a different song then."

"Not a bit, my dear fellow; I should laugh at the young rascal; but as it is disagreeable to you, I hope he will give up his nonsense. You hear me, Harry?"

"Yes, I hear you," replied Harry, "and if Wantlake is a good boy, I will leave him alone. He must be careful, though."

In the midst of the merriment following this piece of impudence, Wantlake swung himself out of the cabin, and Harold sat down to some cold beef and biscuit brought out by Peter, the cabin boy.

While partaking of it, the full particulars of the late quarrel were explained, and when the part concerning the captain's daughter was alluded to, Harold flushed to the very roots of his hair.

"It was wrong of you, Carlton," he said, "to drag the name of the young lady into a discussion here."

When angry with the boy, he always called him Carlton, and Harry knew it.

He had no desire to lose the friendship of his elder, and therefore apologised after his own fashion.

"I didn't think of it, upon my word, Harold," he said; "I would lay down my life for Miss Harloch if she wished me to, but I feel as if I must aggravate Wantlake, if I die for it."

"Then choose another subject, Harry," rejoined Harold, and nothing more was said about it.

As the captain predicted, the storm rapidly subsided, and nought in the morning remained of the outbreak of the elements but the heavy rollers of the sea.

The frigate dashed gallantly on its way, breasting the waves nobly, and justifying the eulogy of the first lieutenant, who declared "she skimmed the water like a bird."

The men bustled about with renewed vigour, the officers chatted merrily together, and were in the midst of a discussion respecting the probability of their falling in with an enemy, when the man on the look out cried—

"A sail!"

"Where away?"

"Ahead, sir."

The glasses were brought out, and the stranger inspected, but little more than her upper rigging was visible, but it was soon confidently declared that she was a French frigate, carrying many guns, a heavier and larger vessel than the "Curlew" by far.

Captain Harloch at once gave orders for all sail to be crowded on, to give chase, and ready hands swung out the canvas to the steady breeze.

Now all was indeed life and gaiety; one would have imagined that a festivity was approaching instead of a deadly fight, when many a gallant man would be shut out from this bright world for ever.

As they neared the stranger, the opinion first expressed became confirmed, and to the delight of the crew of the "Curlew," the Frenchman kept steadily approaching, as if he ignored his gallant little foe, so eager for the encounter.

The decks were cleared for action, every soul on board was on the alert, and ready for orders. Harold, Wantlake, and little Harry Carlton also stood upright on a dart between two lower-deck guns, prepared to double up at least six foreigners when the opportunity offered.

It was his first scent of battle, and the boy's heart beat fast, but his face showed no sign of emotion, all around him were calm and cool, and he resolved to emulate their example.

Harold Greystone had the command of

a division of guns, and walked to and fro with a step firm and light, expressive of dauntless courage.

While giving a few necessary commands, he was interrupted by Mason Wantlake, who came down from the deck.

"Mr. Greystone," he said, in a soft tone, so that none around them overheard, "will you step into the captain's cabin, and see that Miss Clara is in a position favourable to her safety."

"I?" rejoined Harold, flushing; "by whose orders?"

"Captain Harloch's—you are a favourite of his, you know," said Wantlake, bitterly, "or I should have had the pleasant office. It is hard for her to be aboard at such a time."

"Captain Harloch will leave her at Kingston with his brother; in the meantime stern duty compels him to fight. Private feelings give way at such a time as this. I will do the captain's bidding."

Wantlake went out first, and disappeared; Harold having informed the head gunner of his object for leaving, hastened out, promising to return in a few moments.

Minutes passed—half an hour, and a crash overhead proclaimed that the first shot had been fired, and he had not returned. The men stood ready at their posts, waiting in vain for a directing hand, and strange whispers began to float about.

CHAPTER II.

DISGRACED.

"Mr. Greystone! Mr. Greystone!"

"Not here, sir," replied one of the men, as the second lieutenant appeared in the gun-room.

"Not here?"

"No, sir—he went out half an hour ago, and we have not seen him since."

"This is strange conduct," said the lieutenant, and hurried to the deck to report his absence to the captain.

He soon returned, with Mason Wantlake by his side, and again Harold was called for. Two men were dispatched to find him, but they soon returned, and reported their inability to do so.

"He is skulking," sneered Wantlake.

"Impossible!" exclaimed the lieutenant, "so unlike him—take his post, Mr. Wantlake, there is no time to lose, the enemy is upon us."

Boom! the guns above belched forth their deadly fire. Crash! came a shot from the enemy through the vessel's side, and two gallant tars lay writhing in mortal agony.

Little Harry Carlton saw them, the first time he had beheld man in mortal agony, and turned pale, but he braced up his stout young heart, and piped out to the men the orders he received from his seniors.

The fight was soon at its worst, and all else forgotten. For a time, nobody thought of Harold Greystone and his mysterious disappearance.

Wantlake was ghastly pale, or rather sallow, but he shouted out his orders loudly, and thereby covered the signs of inward quaking.

The shots crashed through the framework of the ship, and splinters flew about, doing deadly and fearful injuries to the men. As fast as they fell their comrades bore them below, where the surgeon and the assistants examined them, and either declared that all was over, or set to work to alleviate their agony or remove a fractured limb.

The enemy was a powerful one, and as the two vessels came to closer quarters the havoc was dreadful; showers of bullets poured through the port-holes, and three of the guns, under the charge of Wantlake, were silent for want of men.

The sailors continued to work the others with their usual cool intrepidity, obeying orders with the alacrity and precision of a true British seaman, but more than one thought within his heart that the "Curlew" was overmatched, and would be compelled to succumb to her powerful foe.

The noise was deafening, and the crash of timber unceasing, but suddenly, above all, up rose a scream of agony, and Mason Wantlake lay writhing on the deck with his right arm broken by a bullet.

He rolled over and over like a trampled worm, and those who carried the wounded below had some difficulty in bearing him away, and when they did so, he was yelling for mercy from Heaven, and weeping like a woman in despair.

The men glancing briefly at each other with contempt upon their faces, but the expression quickly changed when little Harry Carlton stood forward and took the command.

"Steady, men!" he cried, "stand to your guns, we are not beaten yet!"

They laughed, but cheered lustily, and the guns sent forth their iron messengers until they were hot to the touch.

The enemy's fire slackened a little, and a cheer uprose from the deck of the "Curlew."

"Her mainmast's shot away," cried one of the men, looking through the port-hole; "hurrah!"

The very next moment a round shot struck his head from his shoulders, and his quivering corpse was stretched upon the deck.

"Poor fellow," sighed Harry, and a feeling of sickness came over him; but he rallied instantly, and again his youthful voice was heard amidst the din.

"Starboard guns, fire!" shouted the lieutenant, and a terrific iron hail riddled the Frenchman. The fire was but feebly returned, and in a few moments the vessels were alongside, the grappling-irons out, and the British sailors boarded the enemy with irresistible ardour.

A scene of carnage ensued, the foe fought nobly, but stronger arms and stouter hearts decimated their ranks, and the breathless remainder of the Frenchman's crew threw down their arms, and cried for quarter.

All was over, the prize was won, and nought remained now but to count his loss; thirty gallant sailors turned to senseless clay, and fifty moaning and writhing upon the deck and in the hammocks below. A hundred Frenchmen slain, and a long, long list of wounded.

All was over; the officers leant upon their swords to gather breath, and the seamen turned down their shirtsleeves to hide their blood-stained arms, and wiped from their cutlasses the gore of those who now lay still and ghastly in the glorious sunlight.

No enmity now, victory had fallen to the British tars, and friends and foes alike demanded their sympathy: the wounded first to be cared for by the surgeons, the dead next, to be buried reverently beneath the waves, there to lie until the sea shall give up its dead.

When these things were done, and the sailors busy restoring the "Curlew" to its original trim, the thoughts of the officers turned again to the absence of Harold Greystone.

"Mr. Mountford," said the captain, addressing the first lieutenant, "will you oblige me by recapitulating the incidents attending Mr. Greystone's disappearance? With the enemy so near I very imperfectly considered them."

The lieutenant told the story again, and expressed the general opinion when he said "the whole affair is unaccountable."

"Can he have shown the white feather?" mused Captain Harloch.

"Impossible, sir."

"Or fallen overboard?"

"He was on duty below, and voluntarily left his post."

"It must be seen to at once," rejoined the captain; "have the ship thoroughly searched, and bring your report into my cabin."

The two gentlemen bowed, and the captain retired, puzzled and distressed. As he was about descending the companionladder, Harold Greystone, the object of his thoughts, staggered upon the deck.

His face was wild, his hair dishevelled, and his whole demeanour that of a man awakened from a drunken sleep.

"Mr. Greystone," said the captain, knitting his brows, "I request you to favour me with an explanation of your conduct."

"My conduct, sir?" rejoined Harold, vacantly, "I—I—don't know, sir. I thought we were preparing for action."

"We have prepared, fought, and won the day," was the stern reply, "while you have skulked below. Where have you been, sir?"

"I skulked?" returned the youth; I hide when there was an enemy near us? Oh, Heaven! I remember now. Will you hear me, sir?"

"Follow me," said Captain Harloch, and led the way to his cabin.

Harold staggered after him, encountering several brother officers on the way, who turned their backs at his approach, expressive of their opinion of his absence.

Captain Harloch went into an inner cabin, leaving the youth for a few moments alone, who stared out of the stern window with a gaze of hopeless horror and despair.

"Now, sir," said the Captain, returning, "your explanation."

Harold began his story by relating how Wantlake had delivered the message respecting Clara Harloch.

The Captain interrupting him,—

"I gave no such message," he said, "and the gentleman who is supposed to have delivered it to you lies wounded below, and it is doubtful if he will ever recover. Probably you are aware of the fact—but proceed, sir."

Harold drew himself quickly up, a dash

of the old fire appeared in his eyes as he answered,—

"You do not believe me, sir; that I much regret, but I will obey your orders, and conclude my story.

"I was close by this cabin door," he said, passing his hand over his brow, as if to recal events, "when I heard a light footstep behind me. I thought it was Miss Harloch, and turned to deliver my message. A handkerchief, or something of a similar nature, was dashed into my face; it was held there, and my strength was paralysed."

"Go on, sir," said the Captain, with a sarcastic smile, seeing he paused.

"After that I lost my senses," resumed Harold, "and remember no more until I found myself in the purser's store-room, covered with a heap of old canvas."

"An ingenious story!" said Captain Harloch, "and I wish I could believe you, as I am shocked and surprised beyond measure to find an officer of mine away from his post in an hour of peril. Mr. Greystone, are you aware of the penalty in store for you?"

"With what shall I be charged?" asked the youth, in a low tone.

"Cowardice and desertion from your post in the face of the enemy," replied the Captain.

"I know the penalty, sir," returned Harold, bitterly, "it is death. I fear it not; but to die with the brand of cowardice upon my name! Oh, Captain Harloch, how can you believe me guilty of it?"

"I have no other resource," was the sad reply.

"Think, sir," cried the youth, "of my conduct from the first hour I have been on board. "It is true that this is the first engagement the "Curlew" has had since I joined her, but in storms and other perils attendant upon our life, have I for a moment shown a dastard spirit?"

"No, Mr. Greystone; you have been a smart young officer, and I hoped for better things."

"I came to sea for the love of it," pursued Harold, his eyes sparkling and his form erect. "Had I been a coward I might have stayed at home, for I am rich, and have more money at my command than many wealthy men. Why need I then have craved the dangers of a life at sea if I had not loved it? Ask my old messmates of the "Sea-gull," with whom I spent three years, if ever the coward dawned in me,

or if even a lie was ever associated with the name of Harold Greystone."

"All this can be brought forward at your trial," returned the captain, coldly.

"I shall also require the evidence of Mr. Wantlake," rejoined Harold, proudly "he knows the whole story."

"Do you insinuate, Mr. Greystone, that he has victimised you in this matter?"

"No, sir, I assert it. Mason Wantlake is a double-dyed coward and villain—never a friend of mine; he has done this to bring upon me everlasting ruin and disgrace."

"Enough," cried the captain, hotly; "you only add to your infamy." Mr. Mountford, the first lieutenant, at this moment entered the cabin. "Will you place Mr. Greystone under arrest?"

With bent head and almost broken heart, Harold left the presence of his superior officer, and a few minutes later was a prisoner in the purser's cabin, who was slain during the late fight, and two marines placed on guard by the door.

A coward! bitter thought!—he, Harold Greystone, the favourite of the midshipmen's berth, the pet of the men, a skulker, hiding away from the shot of a foe!

The whole land would ring with his infamy, and his death be hailed with joy.

"Thank heaven!" he cried as he sank upon the ground, "my father did not live to see this day. His noble spirit would have broken with mine—a coward—dastard—oh! it is horrible."

The strongest man would have given way under such circumstances, and Harold, lying on a heap of old canvas—the same he had lain under during his hours of stupor—wept bitterly.

He was aroused by a gentle hand laid upon his shoulder, and starting up, beheld little Harry Carlton. He was pleased to see the youngster; it assured him that he was not despised by all.

"They may say what they like," said the boy, brushing away a few indignant tears, "but I don't believe you funked the fight."

"Thank you, Harry," replied the other, gently, "you are a good fellow. But how came you here?"

"They let me do as I like," rejoined Harry, "I'm only a youngster, you know—a sort of dolly for them all, but they will find out their mistake shortly, as soon as another fellow joins, and I am no longer

"YOU JIST ONE MOMENT TOO LATE, OLE BOY."

junior—but bother my affairs, Harold. I want to talk about yourself."

"What do they think of me?"

"Opinion is divided, old chap, but you have the most honest fellows on your side, and you are getting more friends as they grow cooler."

"What of Wantlake; is he better?"

"Oh, yes! he's a duffer, Harold—howled awful—even when the worst was over. The captain has been to see him—I was there."

"Well—what took place?" eagerly demanded Harold.

"The captain asked the beggar if he gave you a certain message," returned the boy slowly, "and the brute denied it."

"The liar!" impetuously said Harold.

"Hush! old fellow—don't talk too loud. I have something more to say to you. Everything is against you—no mistake about that, but it will all come right one day—I'll stake my chance of being admiral against that. For the present you cut it."

"Fly from the fear of an inquiry?"

"Certainly: here's a port-hole; to-night we shall anchor before Kingston, and a boat will be under here just about the middle watch—that's mine—you drop into her and get away."

"That would be a coward's act," returned Harold—"stay," he added, as a thought crossed his brain, and sent his blood like lightning through his veins, "I will do it, Harry; you have the boat there."

"Three taps will be the signal," said the boy, "as soon as you hear them, slip out and be off like a Spanish hulk when our chasers come in sight."

The friends shook hands, and Harry slipped outside, where he had much to do to soothe the feelings of the marines who were angry at his being so long. They had committed a breach of discipline for the love of the boy, but they had considerable respect for their own backs. The cat was in active operation in those days.

The night came, and with it Harry's promised signal. The prisoner had scrawled a note in pencil for the captain, on a leaf torn from his pocket-book, which he folded and laid in a conspicuous position; then slipping through the port, he dropped as quietly as a cat into a boat alongside.

Harry Carlton was there and at once pushed off the boat, and with muffled rowlocks pulled quietly round the stern of the "Curlew." Harold's face was turned towards a dim light in the aft cabin, and he bade the boy halt for a moment.

"Clara is there;" thought Harold, "if I could only see her for a moment!"

As if in response to his wish, one of the windows was opened gently, and a fair young face looked out upon the darkness of the night. The dim light showed she had been weeping, and Harold's heart beat with love and pity.

The boat lay close under the stern, a rope dangled close by, and regardless of the consequences, Harold seized it and climbed to the window.

"Clara!"

"Harold!"

They spoke in almost a whisper, but the tone was full of affection and her arms were thrown around his neck.

"Do you believe this story of me, darling?"

"No, Harold; all the world could not convince me."

"Then Heaven bless you!" whispered the youth; "I can go away happy. I have a mission to perform, dearest; but I shall return, and then this stain will be wiped away. Good bye, darling!"

"Good bye, Harold, dearest!"

One more embrace, and he was again in the boat, and the young middy pulled towards the shore.

"So bad as that?" he whispered roguishly to Harold.

"And, worse, or better," returned Harold, "for life or death, I am true to her; but stay, my dear boy, I cannot take you ashore, you will be missed."

"I have left the 'Curlew,'" returned Harry, coolly; "struck myself off her books, and going in for a little adventure with you."

"They will call you a deserter."

"So they may, Harold, and confound them! I am an orphan, you know, and a rich uncle sent me to sea, hoping some favourable shot might knock my head off. I like the sea much, but like you better, and therefore change my service."

"You shall not repent it," replied Harold, warmly; "give me the oars and steer between the two lights ahead; we can land there."

In the morning Captain Harloch discovered that there were two vacancies in the midshipmen's berth, and he hurried ashore to take measures for the recapture of the fugitives, but not before he had read a note found in the purser's room.

Its contents were brief, and ran thus:—

"I have left the 'Curlew'; but I shall return again, and give the lie to those who call me coward. HAROLD GREYSTONE."

Nothing more; and Captain Harloch, angry at the escape of one whom he deemed a coward, tried every means in his power to recover his prisoner. Large rewards were offered, and strict watch kept on all the avenues of the town of Kingston, but every effort was in vain. Neither Harold nor his friend had been seen or heard of.

CHAPTER III.

THE MASKED CAPTAIN.

SIX months rolled away, and the double war carried on by Great Britain against France and Spain increased in strength. The three nations had each their cruisers of various grades, and privateers innumerable roamed about the seas.

News did not travel so fast in those days, but it became known at the expiration of the time we have named that a strange vessel was out and doing sad havoc among the French and Spanish traders. English vessels it passed at all times, and neither halted nor communicated with them in any way.

The stranger was a rakish craft, schooner-built, and a fast sailer; indeed it defied every effort of the English cruisers to overhaul her.

Strange stories were whispered of her among the seamen; she had been seen off the Carribean Islands one day, and the next she was reported as flying by St. Domingo. Cruisers returning from the African coast declared that they had seen her, and while the story was yet on their tongues, another vessel brought a report of having passed her at the mouth of the Gulf of Mexico.

Sailors before the mast, always a superstitious class of men, declared that the vessel was a phantom; but the officers were wiser, being better educated, and set her down as a piratical craft, which shunned the British vessels because its captain knew the nation's power to punish.

Where the stranger came from nobody knew, but one morning an English trader put into the port at Kingston, and added to the ferment by solemnly declaring that he had not only seen the mysterious ship off the island of Madeira, and been boarded by her crew, but had been taken to the vessel and seen the captain.

"She's a complete beauty," he reported, "rigged to perfection, and carries about thirty guns; all her men are English rigged, and there's middies on board just as we have on our line-o'-battle ships. There's only two things strange about her; the first is that the captain wears a mask and is dressed like a Greek brigand; the second is that there is a confounded nigger aboard dressed like a post captain. I axed the name o' the craft, and larned that it was called the "Crucible." They just overhauled my papers, 'pologized for stoppin' me, and set me afloat again."

The "Curlew" was lying in port at the time, and this story determined the authorities to send her in search of the stranger. She was accordingly fitted out with every requisite, and departed on her mission.

We will leave the "Curlew" now, and transport our readers on board the wondrous "Crucible" as she bears round Cape Verde on her way to Sierra Leone.

All that was spoken of her by the English trader the "Crucible" fully merited; a model craft in every way, hull long and narrow, swelling a little at the waist, masts tall and raking aft, fittings unexceptionable. She was truly a vessel that only required to be seen to be admired.

Straight before the wind she skimmed with the majesty of a swan and the speed of the swallow, her bows contemptuously dashing aside the gleaming water, rising well to the waves and dividing them quietly, as a plough travels o'er a field.

Upon the deck the masked captain lounged easily and gracefully, watching with a faint dawn of smile upon his face a negro dressed in a most outrageous uniform in imitation of an English captain, talking to the ship's carpenter.

Behind, two lads in midshipmen's attire leaned against the bulwarks, pointing to a sail in the horizon.

"Now, Massa Duncan," said the negro, "what you want?"

"To speak to the Captain, Monkey Jack," returned the other."

"Den you can't do it, sar; de capen roomilatin."

"You mean ruminating," growled Duncan, eyeing his dark companion with no great favour.

"I mean jes' wot I say, Massa Gluepot," retorted the nigger with dignity; "don't you be rude to your s'periors."

"My superiors!" sneered the carpenter; "the captain makes a fool of you."

"He no need do dat to you, Massa Duncan—you dat already. Yah—yah—oh! golly!" and Monkey Jack rolled his eyes in ecstacy.

The carpenter, rather a vinegar-tempered fellow, stared indignantly at his tormentor, and made an effort to pass, but Jack interposed his burly frame.

"No, sar—if you hab anything to commoonerlicate it come through me."

"You ain't an officer, are you?" demanded the carpenter.

"No, I am not," replied Monkey Jack; "but I am more—de capen's frend. He buy me orf from slavery jes' when they goin' to roost me for running away. I sabe de capen's life when black debil ob shark come anigh him when bathin'. These muteral bobligations 'twixt us, dat's where it is."

"Mutual obligations!" repeated Duncan, looking pitchforks at him; "you're a mountebank."

"What you call me?" demanded Jack, quickly; "what dat word?"

"Mountebank."

"What's dat?"

"A dressed-up vagabond."

"Oh! is dat all?" said Jack, relieved; "dere's nothin' in dat. I'm a genelman, an' fren' ob de capen, so you mind what you say."

Duncan glared, and endeavoured to force his way ; again Jack checked him. The captain remained quietly looking on.

"You no bus'ness on deck, Massa Duncan," said the negro; "you go b'low and stop dere—dat's your place, Massa Duncan, till enemy punch a hole with a shot—den stick your head in it ; dat's all your dam head fit for."

The carpenter was now fairly boiling over, and a serious outburst would have ensued but for the masked captain, who advanced a few paces and inquired—

"What is it, Duncan ? let him pass, Jack."

"He can come wid pleasur', Massa Cap'en," returned the negro, graciously, "when de order comes from you ; but I stop him acause he smell of glue. Dat very obfensive to real-born genelmen. Yah ! oh lor ! golly ! dat's anoder for him."

Jack retired, chuckling, behind the captain, and there continued his defiance in dumb motions.

"Excuse me, sir," said Duncan, stifling his wrath, "but I made bold to inquire if you intended to engage the enemy ?"

"The Spaniard out yonder ?" inquired the captain, with a careless glance at the sail in the distance.

"Yes, sir."

"Why do you ask ?"

"Well, sir, the fact is, both my mates are down with gun-shot wounds, and I shall want a little assistance. At present—excuse me, sir, we seem to be—to be——"

"Flying from her," interposed the captain, "so I am for the present ; but I shall not lose sight of her. Have everything prepared, and ask Mr. Stanchion to come on deck."

The carpenter gave a sailor's scrape, and retired.

The captain turned to the negro, and added—

"You must not torment Duncan, Jack ; it will end in a serious quarrel."

"He a confoundleded fool, sar," replied the nigger; "he no leave Jack alone. Jack no leave him alone. We moral enemies, sar."

"Mortal enemies, Jack."

"Yes, sar, but if eber he show too much teeth I quash him, sar."

Jack put his foot emphatically upon the deck, and it sounded like the falling of a heavy plank. The masked captain shook his head deprecatingly ; but as Mr. Stan-

chion at this juncture emerged from the hatchway, he turned his attention to him.

Mr. Stanchion was dressed in the uniform of a first lieutenant, a rough, weather-beaten old man, one who had knocked about in the world, but not on the quarter-deck of an authorised man-of-war. He saluted the captain respectfully.

"Mr. Stanchion," said the latter, "I'm going below for a while ; will you take charge of the deck ?"

Mr. Stanchion bowed ; he was evidently not a man who wasted his words.

"Keep the men out of sight," pursued the masked leader, "and quickly substitute the guns with wooden dummies, to give us the appearance of a quiet trader, built to run along these piratical shores—do it quickly, and put on more sail."

"And the same course, sir ?"

"Until I reappear ; we will then wear ship, and run down upon the enemy."

"Very good, sir."

The captain's graceful form disappeared, and Mr. Stanchion, donning a rough jacket over his uniform, bustled about giving his orders. The guns were withdrawn, and the dummies, apparently kept ready for the purpose, substituted.

The broad white gun-line was rapidly painted out, and the glittering figure-head of the schooner smudged, and all the real guns carefully covered with tarpaulins, nettings, and other things available for the purpose.

Monkey Jack was told either to go below or remove his uniform ; but he compromised the matter by covering his shoulders with a piece of canvas, and carrying his cocked hat under his arm.

The middies, too, substituted their gold laced caps for rougher materials, and then lay down upon the deck beside some barrels.

They were a couple of smart youngsters, very young, not more than fourteen or fifteen at the outside, but full of fire and pluck. They were presently joined by Monkey Jack, who squatted rabbit-fashion in front of them.

"More jolly fighten', genelmen," he said, rolling his big black eyes.

"Yes, Jack," returned one; "a big affair this time, I think, something in the piratical line, eh ! Will ?"

"We ought to know by this time, Tom," said the other, with an admiral's air.

"Know," rejoined Jack, ecstatically; "I back you two genelmen agin all the French fleet. What do I say to the Capen but dis? 'Gib me,' I ses, 'Massa Furnace and Massa Steadfast, and I fight forty cussed foreigners.'"

"We are proud of your good opinion," said Will Steadfast, with a merry smile; "Tom and I do our best to deserve it."

"Eberybody tink well ob you," replied Jack; "even dat fool Duncan; not dat you want his good 'pinion," he added, hastily; "but he can't help it. So you tink, Massa Furnace, dat it is a pirate?"

"Will was certain of it from the first. It's a powerful Spanish man-of-war, but there are pirates aboard, I'm sure. You see if I'm not right."

CHAPTER IV.

"FOR HONOUR WE FIGHT."

"ALL hands wear ship!" was piped at this point of the conversation, and looking over the bulwarks, the lads beheld the Spaniard not more than a mile and a half away, bearing down upon them in full sail.

"Right into our jaws," said Will, dancing with glee.

"Hullo!" cried the other mid; "she doesn't like our change of course; too late, my friend, we shall be down upon you in a twinkling."

The Spaniard luffed, and tried to tack across the wake of the "Crucible," but the active little schooner answering her helm, rapidly neared her.

The dummy guns were drawn aside, and the real weapons, double shotted, run out, the lieutenant threw off his disguise, Monkey Jack resumed his cocked hat, and the crew of the schooner gave vent to their feelings by a vigorous cheer.

It was answered by a yell of fury from the deck of the Spaniard, faintly borne upon the breeze; and this was responded to by the masked captain, who sprang upon the deck, and cried—

"The Spaniard is at our mercy. Steady, men! and remember that we fight for the glory of our native land. Give them another English cheer, my boys."

A shout burst upon the air, and a flag ran swiftly to the masthead—a broad blue piece of bunting, bearing upon it in letters of gold, the motto, "For Honour we Fight."

The stranger immediately replied by hauling down the Spanish colours it had carried hitherto, and running aloft a black flag, with the skull and crossbones, the favourite emblem of the pirates of the seas.

The crew of the "Crucible" uttered a shout of execration, the pirates returned a defiant yell.

"Fire, men," cried the masked captain, "aim at her rigging."

Two guns sent forth their missiles, one shot passed between the masts of the pirate, the other caught his mainmast midway, and brought down a shower of sails and rigging upon the deck.

"Dat am good," said Monkey Jack, capering; "spile de beggar's bes' clothes."

The pirate replied with a broadside, the shots rattling among the cordage of the "Crucible," and wounding two of her men.

"She is rather too heavy for us," said Mr. Stanchion, the lieutenant, addressing the captain, "unless we can board her"

"Give her another dose among the rigging," was the reply, "then bear up and board her."

Mr. Stanchion sung out the command, and a well-directed fire played havoc with the pirate's sails and spars; oaths and execrations were borne upon the wind, showing how exasperated the enemy was by the accumulated disaster.

The fire was again returned, but with little effect, the aim being very wild, one shot alone piercing the hull of the "Crucible."

"She is undermanned," said the masked captain; "bring to across her bows, then out with the boats, I will board the fellow myself."

A third iron hail was directed at the enemy, this time of grape and canister, and she lay upon the water a helpless log.

The pirate's colours had fallen, but a few of the most daring fixed the broken spar upon the bows, and there the skull and crossbones waved.

The "Crucible" answered to the helm most gallantly, and rounded the head of the Spaniard about four hundred yards away.

Three boats were lowered, into the foremost sprang the captain, followed immediately by Monkey Jack.

Will Stanchion took command of the second, and Tom Furnace the third.

The boys stood up in the stern of their boats, piping out encouragement to the men, who smiled as they bent willingly to the oars, while the masked captain occasionally uttered a few words to his crew.

Monkey Jack sat upright by the side of his captain, a changed being, very grim and determined, with his cocked-hat drawn fiercely over his brows, and his hand upon the cutlass by his side.

"Jack," said the captain, softly, "what do you think of her?"

"Uncommonly ugly, sar," he replied, "de big ship, but men little, we cut dem up like salt pork."

"I see they are prepared for us," rejoined the captain, then cried aloud, "Steady, men!"

The rattle of musketry followed, but like the firing from the big guns, was very uncertain; two men only in Will Steadfast's boat fell, the rest kept on with the utmost coolness.

The loss of two oars put Master Will in the rear, and when the captain reached the pirate, he was nearly a hundred yards astern.

Up sprang the masked ruler of the "Crucible," followed by Monkey Jack and the men, cutlass in teeth, and arms bared for action.

A host of screaming yelling pirates were ready to receive them; foremost, a tall, brawny fellow, who appeared to be their leader.

"No quarter!" he cried; "down with the accursed race! Death to the British!"

"For Honour and Glory!" shouted the masked captain; "down with the piratical dogs!"

The opposing parties fell upon each other with the utmost fury. The leaders were separated by a mass of fighting men, but in the midst of the din and smoke they could hear each other's voice, and worked their way steadily towards the point from which it came.

The masked captain cut right and left, his blade as swift and almost as terrible as the lightning flash, and the pirates lay upon the ground like slaughtered sheep.

Monkey Jack scarcely removed his eyes from his captain, but followed his every footstep, warding off many a blow when the foe gathered round in numbers.

"Death to the pirates!"

"Death to the British knaves!"

The fight went on without flagging. Tom Furnace and his men leaped over the starboard bow with the agility of cats, and joined the gallant captain and his band; but the men of the "Crucible" were by far outnumbered, three to one at least, and the issue appeared very doubtful.

The two captains at last met, a sudden rush on the part of the British drove the pirates aft, all but their leader. The masked captain had marked him stay and he too remained behind.

For a moment they looked at each other, breathing hard after their late efforts, then the pirate shouted,—

"Come on, you masked dog, and die by the sword of a man who is not ashamed of his face."

The other sprang forward uttering a cry of rage, the pirate drew a pistol, fired point blank at his breast, and the masked captain fell.

Uttering a shout of triumph, the pirate sprang forward, but Monkey Jack, who just disposed of two assailants in the rear, leaped between them, pistol in hand.

"Jes' one moment too late, ole boy," he cried, and fired.

The aim was true—the pirate leaped into the air, and rolled upon the deck a corpse.

"True to your post," said the masked captain, rising slowly. "How many times am I to owe you my life?"

"A t'ousand times wouldn't be too many," replied the negro, earnestly. "You sabe Jack from roasting—Jack true till death. But you wounded, sar?" he added, anxiously.

"A mere scratch, Jack," he returned, faintly; "open my shirt—take your knife and bind up my wound."

Jack tore it hastily open, and there beheld the blood streaming from his leader's side; the bullet, however, had not effected a lodgment, having glanced aside from the lower rib, and after ploughing a deep wound in the flesh, passed out through his clothing.

"Dere no danger," said Jack, rapidly staunching the blood, "but ugly gap for de time. Massa capen get ober it in no time."

"How goes the fight?" asked the captain, whose eyes looked dim and weary.

"Massa Steadfast come aboard," returned the negro, looking up, "and de pirates all a howling wid funk. Here's de 'Crucible,' too, sar, bearin' down; and massa lebtenant gib 'em more pepper."

The captain smiled, and endeavoured to raise himself, but weak from the loss of blood, he fell back upon the deck.

With an effort he passed his hand over the mask, fastened by springs attached to his ears—it was secure, and a faint smile played around his lips.

"Jack," he said, "if I swoon, you know your duty."

"Debel a bit of man shall see massa cap-

MONKEY JACK CAPTURES SNARLEY CROKER.

en's face," replied the negro, "unless he cut Jack into mincemeat, an' Jack berry tough."

"Who is that approaching?"

"Massa Steadfast; he look berry much frightened."

The boy bounded up, and knelt by the captain's side.

"All right, Will," said the leader, faintly, "nothing worse than a flesh wound. Can you get me some brandy?"

"I have a flask here," replied the boy; "but are you sure it is not serious?"

"Certain, Will—ask Jack.

"De wound is berry temprerry," replied the negro, with dignity; "it come round in one wink ob de eye. Jack gib his word, and Jack neber wrong,"

With a happy face the boy arose, and rushed back to his comrades.

The pirates by this time were fearfully thinned, but those remaining fought desperately, fearing that as they gave no quarter they would receive none—nor was it given.

The decks were slippery with blood, and the cutlasses reeked with their deadly work, no longer flashing in the light of day, but dim and gory. Fire-arms were abandoned, for it was now a hand-to-hand battle for life or death.

Step to step, the pirates were driven back, until they crowded in the stern—then the hindermost began to leap into the sea, preferring a watery grave to a death by steel.

A boat fastened to the stern of the frigate, by its painter, rapidly filled, and with the desperation of drowning men who catch at straws, the rope was severed and she pulled away.

Not to escape, however, for those in charge of the "Crucible" marked their flight, and a well-directed shot stove in the frail bark, and scattered the pirates over the glittering waves.

Then transpired a scene of an awful nature. First, the fin of one shark arose above the water and another quickly followed. The wretched men turned towards the ship and swam for dear life.

Two were seized instantly, and as they were drawn under, their screams pierced the ears of their comrades, several of whom lost all heart and strength, and throwing up their arms, disappeared with a look of horror indescribable.

The heart-rending screams of these unhappy men caused a cessation of hostilities, and friend and foe looked upon their struggles together.

Again the fins flashed above the sea, and two more victims disappeared. A general cry of horror uprose, and the pirates upon deck, completely cowed, threw down their arms and cried for quarter.

It was given for the time, and they were driven below and secured. In the meantime the "Crucible" had launched a boat, and the men were busy picking up the few wretches who still struggled for existence.

Half-a-dozen only were saved, and these with about twenty who laid down their arms, were all that remained of two hundred and fifty souls.

The boarders, too, had suffered, seven killed outright, and thirty wounded more or less severely, the captain among them.

He was borne on board, attended by the faithful Monkey Jack, who never left him for a moment; even when under the charge of the ship's surgeon, a Scotchman, whose name was Thornley, a clear-headed young fellow, well up to his work.

He examined the masked captain's wound and confirmed the opinion already expressed by Monkey Jack, much to that wor-thy's delight, who laid it up in store as a future pill for Duncan, his enemy.

The first lieutenant took the command, saw the wounded attended to and the slain buried, and the captain being by this time able to converse freely, he went down for orders.

"Ah! Stanchion," said the captain, "how have we fared in this fray?"

"Seven clean gone, sir, and thirty disabled," he replied.

"A heavy loss. Poor fellows!"

"The enemy is almost annihilated, and the few remaining are completely subdued."

"How came they in possession of such a craft, Stanchion, have you heard?"

"Surprised her at Porto Rico when most of the officers and men were ashore. It was done in the night, and all they found aboard were murdered."

"Terrible."

"One of the fellows confessed it. I just managed to make out his gibberish—these half-castes have a tongue peculiarly their own."

"A cruel remorseless race. And the frigate what shall we do with her? Can we run her home?"

"We might do it, sir," replied the lieutenant, shaking his head, "if the wind holds easy, but we are terribly short-handed."

"Send Steadfast aboard with a dozen men, remove all the arms, and make sure of these piratical scoundrels, bear a hand."

"He is very young, sir."

"Steadfast! oh, certainly, but I have no other trustworthy hand."

"Send Foote, the boatswain, the two together might manage to keep her in our wake."

"Very good, let it be so."

Foote, the boatswain, known as Grim Foote, was a taciturn old salt, with a cherished pigtail of extra dimensions, a foxy old tar, who was just a little too much for the elements, and whom the sharpest squall always failed to catch napping.

Nothing disturbed his equanimity, he rolled his quid as coolly in a storm as he did in port; during an encounter, the shrill hiss of passing shot caused him to hitch his trousers in a thoughtful manner but nothing more, and he walked into a hand to hand fight as if he were out for a stroll.

This was the man who was accompanying Will on board the Spaniard, its name by the way, was the "Don Pedro," and Duncan was also told off to put her into condition for sailing.

Will, Grim Foote, and Duncan were seated in the cutter, and about to shove off when a cocked hat appeared over the taffrail, followed by the dark face of Monkey Jack.

"Hullo, Massa Duncan," he cried, "you goin'."

Duncan looked very scornful, but made no reply.

"When you 'dress ole Duncan prop'ly," continued the nigger, grinning all over his face, "he not know what you mean. Call him Massa Gluepot, and he speak at once."

"You cursed black wretch——" began Duncan.

"Dere, I told you so," cried Jack, delighted, "he know 'im proper name. Yah! oh, Golly! He call himself ship's carpenter, but he's a bery bad bungler; de cap'n know, an' goin' to make him cook's mate—wash de greens, an' stir de soup. Yah! yah!

"If the captain had any respect for his company," said Duncan, savagely, "he would shoot that fellow."

"Don't be a fool, Duncan," interrupted Will Steadfast, "you cannot speak disrespectfully of the captain with impunity. Where would you find another like him?"

"True, sir," replied the carpenter, touching his hat; "excuse me, sir, but that black lubber half maddens me."

"Who you call black lubber?" cried Monkey Jack, who overheard the latter part of his reply; "I 'bout settle you in no time—knock off your ugly head—make bait ob you for de sharks. You call me black lubber! come on deck an' do it again, you 'farnell wood-cutter; you, you, congloberation of all dat's ugly!"

"Push off," cried Will, laughing; "good bye, Jack."

"Good bye, Massa Steadfast," replied the negro; "mind dat Duncan don't drill hole in wrong place in de frigate, an' sink her."

Duncan ignored this parting injunction, but he breathed hard, drawing his breath as if he were taking soup, a sure sign that he was very angry indeed.

"How about the weather, Foote?" asked Will, as the cutter skimmed along.

"Fine for a bit, sir," replied the boatswain.

"Long enough for the run home?"

"Yes, sir, and a day to spare."

Will felt very easy, for he knew that Grim Foote never erred. A short pull brought them to the "Don Pedro's" side,

and hurrying on board preparations for sailing were at once begun.

By the evening all was ready, and the two vessels, under easy sail, bore down upon the burning coast of Africa.

CHAPTER V.

HOME OF THE PRIVATEER—TRIAL OF THE PIRATES—NEWS FROM THE SLAVE LAND.

THE weather held fair, as Grim Foote predicted; and two days later the cruiser and frigate together sighted the feathery palms growing on a long line of shore.

The masked captain at once signalled for the frigate to keep well in his wake, and the old boatswain took the helm. Will Steadfast was upon the quarter-deck, speaking trumpet in hand, a miniature captain.

"'Don Pedro,' ahoy!" sung out Mr. Stanchion.

"Ay, ay, sir," replied Will.

"Prepare to bring to off Deadlock Point for the night."

"Ay, ay, sir," again replied Will, and gave orders to shorten sail.

Deadlock Point shortly after appeared in view, a low ridge of land running out into the sea, the waves dashing upon it, and forming a long line of breakers.

Beyond this was the coast, apparently one vast forest, without a sign of human life, not a house, hut, craft, or form of man was in view, nought but the variegated foliage swaying gently to the soft regular breeze.

The frigate was brought round a short distance from the point, and the anchor dropped in about six fathoms of water; but the "Crucible" kept on, apparently bent upon destruction among the angry breakers.

But there was no sign of apprehension in the faces of either Will Steadfast or Grim Foote, as they watched her course; they knew the road she was taking, and were perfectly acquainted with the fact that in one part of the white foaming water was a path for a vessel much larger than the gallant little craft.

They saw her among the foam, dim and shadowy in the spray for an instant, the next moment she was in the clear water beyond, and turned towards the land.

Beyond Deadlock Point, the mouth of a river appeared, not very broad but very dark, showing it to be of great depth. Up this the "Crucible" sped, the masked privateer in the bows, with Monkey Jack by his side, keeping a careful watch ahead.

A hundred yards from the mouth, the river suddenly turned, massive trees covered the banks on each side, higher than the masts of the " Crucible," and here she lost the breeze, but as the tide was running in, she bore up some distance further until the sea was lost to the gaze, and here the young privateer ordered the anchor to be lowered.

The river here was about the sixth of a mile broad, and the tide having but just turned, the banks lay high above the water. On the western side, a rent in the line of trees showed a small tributary stream, winding a short distance into the interior of the forest.

" Give the signal, Mr. Stanchion," cried the masked captain, and immediately a gun boomed out.

The echoes were yet rolling away in the distance, when a reply came from the shore; the sharp ringing sound of a brass gun, and the tributary stream became instantly alive with boats.

Many of them were ordinary ships' crafts, cutters, long boats, and so on ; but the majority were canoes of various sizes, shaped from a single log, some with only two men, others capable of carrying eight, ten, and a dozen men.

The majority of the men were negroes ; but each craft had one or more blue jacket in command, who steered or directed the movements of their sable companions.

They surrounded the " Crucible," and immediately there uprose a clashing of gongs and music from rude instruments, fashioned from large reeds, into which the negroes lustily blew. The notes were wild, and in some cases harsh ; but the effect, on the whole, was not discordant, although it was weird and witch-like.

In a few minutes it ceased, and a hearty cheer was given by the blue jackets, the negroes doing their best to imitate the cry, the men of the " Crucible " returned the salute, and then the new arrivals clambered on board.

A strange scene ensued, the negroes prostrated themselves before the masked captain, uttering guttural sounds in their own tongue, to which the young privateer replied in a few words.

The negroes after this arose, and retired aft, and the white men advanced hat in hand.

" Comrades," cried the captain, "we have again been successful ; outside the point rides a Spanish frigate, first capt

horde of pirates, then conquered by my gallant men."

A hearty cheer uprose, with a waving of hats; the captain elevated his head.

" You know your task," he continued, " bring her in, and place her with the other prizes in Honour Dock ; as she draws a deal of water, you had better lighten her of some of her guns and cargo. Where is Willis ?"

A broad-shouldered, sturdy son of Neptune stood forward and pulled his forelock.

" Willis," said the young privateer, "you behaved well in the last cruise; to you I entrust the safe keeping of the Spaniard ; do your duty well, and you will not be forgotten. You can break off, comrades. Jack, clear out the negroes, and bid them prepare the big tent."

The sailors mingled with their white comrades, and Monkey Jack, cocking his hat fiercely, strode among the negroes.

" Now den, you dam niggers," he cried, addressing his dark brethren, " de capen hab had enough ob you flisterogomys; yer just clear out at once, and get the big canoe ready for me."

At this moment he caught sight of a brawny negro, with all his apparel about his loins, affectionately licking the edges of the grog tub.

" What you do dere, sar?" he shouted.

The negro made no reply, but continued his occupation, rolling his eyes in ecstacy.

" I bring you out ob dat," muttered Jack, looking around. His eye caught a stout piece of planking, about the length and substance of a cricket bat. This he raised, and crept carefully towards the rum-consuming culprit.

The other negroes watched his movements with suspended breaths, motionless as statues. Monkey Jack got within easy distance of his man, and then—

Up leaped the nigger with a yell, his hand behind him, and a vast amount of the whites of his eyes visible as he rolled them in agony.

" How you like dat ?" demanded Jack, endeavouring in vain to get another blow at him. " You lick de grog tub again, p'raps. Do you tink genelmen will take dere grog out ob dat tub after you ? Now den, darkey boys—all ashore ?"

Capering and grimacing, the whole body of negroes leaped lightly into their canoes, Monkey Jack taking his seat in the largest with the air of a port admiral at least.

They paddled up the branch of the stream,

where, a short distance up, several landing places appeared constructed among the reeds and extending over the swampy part of the shore.

Beyond this was a vast clearing, upon which the various paths from the landing places converged, the naked mangrove stems with their feathery foliage high in the air surrounded the space with a fence of laced vines at all points but the entrance, strong, wiry, and an effectual bar to the approach of man.

A circle of huts lay around the enclosure, the homes of the negroes. In the centre was a vast tent, with three others of smaller dimensions, the large one was the captain's, the smaller were for the white seamen.

Monkey Jack led his dark brethren to the principal tent, and throwing aside the massive folds at the entrance, commanded them to get to work.

"Now, you black debils," he said pompously, "you bustle about and get de table ready, double quick. No skulking or I floberate you. See dis weapon; me catch you idle, and I'm among ye."

He held up the piece of wood with which he smote the surreptitious rum drinker, having retained it for further service, as it had undoubtedly proved effectual in the first instance.

A wondrous activity was immediately observable among the negroes, more especially in the late culprit, who worked until the perspiration stood upon his skin like oil.

The great tent was divided into three portions, a sleeping place at each end, and a dining apartment in the centre.

The latter was sumptuously furnished, a long mahogany table ran down the middle, handsome velvet-covered chairs were ranged on each side, about the floor lay a number of tiger and lion skins, and piles of the same in the corners, and scattered about for those who chose to lounge.

Cool and shady, and surrounded by the grand African forest, it was truly a resting-place for a king.

The table was quickly laden with fruit, wines, and various meats, flesh of the antelope and bison, and bread made from rye; and all was ready long before the masked captain appeared.

He came at last with Mr. Stanchion, little Tom Furnace, and a great portion of the crew of the "Crucible." Entering the tent, he took his seat at the head of the table.

"Gentlemen," he said, "all distinction vanishes here, as hitherto. What is needful for discipline on board is not necessary here. Eat, drink, and be merry."

The lieutenant sat on his right; Monkey Jack, after throwing his cocked hat at a sable waiter who was yawning, on his left; Tom Furnace next, and the men disposed of themselves as they willed.

There was no constraint, every one at his ease, and although the Captain sat almost silently at the head of the table, speaking but a few words now and then to those nearest him, the cool wines were drank, and the merry jest passed freely round.

The virtuous indignation of Monkey Jack against drinking did not extend to himself, for he drank very freely of the fruit of the vintage, and talked and laughed with the loudest.

The sun set, and while its last rays tinged the summit of the mangrove trees, darkness fell upon the enclosure; but instantaneously a score of Chinese lanterns were lit within the tent, adding yet another charm to the scene.

Toasts were drank, songs were sung, Monkey Jack howled a ditty of his own composition — a choice production, you may be sure; it was of enormous length, and when he concluded the masked captain had retired.

This was accepted as a hint, and the company shortly broke up, Mr. Stanchion and Tom Furnace sleeping in the apartment facing the captain's, the men retiring to the tents outside.

Monkey Jack spread a pile of skins, and lay down outside the captain's room, as watchful and faithful as a dog.

At early dawn the enclosure was full of life; and inside the tent all signs of the previous evening had disappeared. Jack was up and at work, arranging the table, in accordance with instructions he had received the day before, for the trial of the pirates who had been captured.

The transparent lanterns were removed, with the other signs of festivity, and a long black cloth spread over the table, trailing a few inches upon the ground, the chairs covered with the same sombre material, and papers, pens and ink spread out.

By the captain's seat was placed a book with iron clasps, heavy enough in appearance for a record of the gloomiest nature, this the negro spread open, and then struck a single blow upon a gong.

The young privateer, his lieutenant, the middy, and a few petty officers entered and took their seats.

The gong again sounded, and the prisoners were led in.

Twenty-six in all, swarthy, sullen scoundrels, ferocious half-breeds from Southern America, men who valued not the lives of others, never showed mercy even to a friend, or spared a foe.

The young privateer entered the opening words of his record relative to the "Don Pedro," and how she was captured, then bade the men give out their names.

One by one they were entered down, and the masked captain formally charged them with piracy on the high seas.

Sullen and half-defiant, they pleaded "Not Guilty."

The man who had confessed, whose name was Luiga Cordello, was ordered to stand forward. As he advanced a low, hissing noise, like that of the serpent, came from the other prisoners.

Luiga hung his head, and bad as the others were, they looked men in contrast with the shrinking wretch; they, at least, were true to their band, bad and wicked as it was—he was a traitor and a coward.

He told his tale,—no need to record it here, it was a story of bold piracy, of a frigate seized in an hour of neglect, of weak merchantmen stopped and plundered on the high seas, of murdered crews, of strong men and weak women walking the dreaded plank, and finding a grave under the green waves, or slaughtered in cold blood.

When he finished, a second shivering wretch, fearing death, stood forth and confirmed the sad account, hoping thereby to save his miserable life.

"What is your answer to this?" the clear voice of the masked captain demanded.

No reply, but scowls more sullen, and brows heavily knitted.

"Prisoners," continued the young privateer, "your silence confirms the story of your confederates. You have been tried, and proved guilty of a series of diabolical crimes, of atrocity incomprehensible to those who have a heart beating within their bosoms. By your hands many helpless men and women have been cut off in the full tide of health; rapine and murder is your trade, and now say why the fate you have dealt so freely to others should not be dealt to you?"

Not a sound, but the eyes of many rolled about in helpless despair towards the waving mangrove trees. There was no escape, for sturdy seamen, cutlass in hand, and a cordon of negroes barred the way.

"I do not take life in cold blood," pursued the young privateer, rising, "and, therefore, you are spared; but you will be fittingly punished. Far away from here lies an island to which you will be conducted, upon it grows no tree, but the soil is fruitful, and thither you will be despatched with seed and implements for agricultural purposes. There you need not starve, but with naught but yourselves to taint with your vices, with no opportunity to renew your ravages, it is hoped that you will become wiser and better men."

The pirates exchanged glances of dismay, and more than one muttered "better die at once."

"It is possible," added the young captain, "that you may be visited by me in years to come—I cannot promise, but if it is in my power I will—and should I find the change desired, you shall be transported back once more among your fellow men."

He resumed his seat, and waving his hand, the pirates were led from the tent with bowed heads and loose slouching limbs, weary of the present, hopeless of the future.

All but the two informers, who remained behind. Turning to them the masked captain said—

"You have been the instruments of your fellow culprits' punishment—to send you with them would be your destruction. I, therefore, retain you here—not as free men but as slaves, bondsmen to Africans I have here, who are freemen. Your ancestors took their forefathers into captivity, and you shall reside here fit emblems of the justice due to your race."

As he uttered these words, the eyes of the captain shone beneath his mask, and his lips quivered for a moment with emotion as he retired. The pirates bowed silently, and following the beckoning finger of Jack, left the tent.

"Dere's your home," he said, pointing to a hut in ruins; "first put dat right, den Jack gib you furder orders."

The pirates looked as if they would have disobeyed him, but Jack drew his cutlass with a determined air, and they crawled across the green sward—slaves to the dark-skinned sons of Africa.

And they had betrayed their comrades for this, had told the dark story of their lives to be rewarded with a serfdom to men whom they had looked upon as the slaves of the earth. It was bitter, it might be justice; but death, captivity on a lone island with their comrades in crime, was better than such servitude.

Scarcely had they retired, when a little negro bounded into the enclosure. He panted for breath, and the dew drops of fatigue hung upon his brow.

A few rapid words in their native tongue passed between him and Jack, and then the faithful servant of the young privateer dashed into the tent.

"Massa capen, massa capen," he cried.

"What is it, my good Jack," asked the captain, looking out between the folds.

"Dem cursed slaves at work again."

"Who brings the news?"

"Swiftfoot, massa capen."

"What says he?"

"King Borabea bring two hundred men, women, child to de coast ready for ship."

"Bid Mr. Stanchion come here," cried the captain, "and go on board with orders to prepare for sailing."

"Yes, massa capen."

"Send out also a cutter for Mr. Steadfast, he will sail with us."

"I will, sar."

"Lose not a moment, Jack, and as you go out, send Swiftfoot here."

Jack bowed, and hastily retired, calling aloud for Swiftfoot as he emerged from the tent.

The negro came, and, receiving his instructions, passed within.

"Swiftfoot," said the captain, as he buckled on his sword, "how many of your nation are captives now?"

"Two hundred," replied the negro, in broken English; "chain—neck and heel—in shanty."

"Is it known when the cargo ships?"

"In day—two day, sar."

"In two days—too short a time; but Heaven send us a fair wind, and we will foil them yet. Ha! Mr. Stanchion, I am glad you are here; are we ready for sea?"

The lieutenant at this moment entered the tent, and replied, quickly—

"Half an hour will put us all square, sir."

"Away, then, at once," cried the captain, "I will be with you directly."

"And the pirates, sir."

"There are men here who will do my bidding," was the reply "We have other work before us; bodies to save from slavery, and souls from everlasting perdition —knaves to thwart and punish!"

"Ay, ay, sir," returned the lieutenant, cheerily, "we are ready, sir, for such good work, both heart and hand."

CHAPTER VI.
THE "CRUCIBLE" TO THE RESCUE.—HAUNT OF THE SLAVE DEALERS.

GALLANTLY the little "Crucible" sailed as soon as Will Steadfast came on board, running out merrily to sea before a brisk breeze. The captain and Monkey Jack were below, and Mr. Stanchion, the lieutenant, held the command, as he knew thoroughly well the point for which they were bound.

The two middies, Tom Furnace and Will, lay under an awning on the after-deck, where the cool breeze fanned the cheeks of the youngsters as they talked low and earnestly together.

"You say it is dangerous work, Will?"

"Very," replied Steadfast, "as sure as my name is Ha— — Will Steadfast."

"It's my first affair of the sort," rejoined the other, "for during the two months I have been with you, I've seen nothing better than sea-fighting—a turn on shore would be an agreeable relief."

He spoke like an old hand at deadly encounters, one tired of the monotony of sea-battles. Will smiled.

"We have a good captain," he said, "and plenty of the best guides; for, look you, he has been a friend to the poor dark savages, and they know it."

"I should like to see his face," mused Tom.

"You never will," quickly returned his friend, "until a certain hour arrives."

"Well, I like mystery, and that is why I joined you in preference to going out in the regular way. I am glad I met you, Will; by the way, is your name Will?"

"What does it matter?—is your name Tom Furnace?"

"There, old boy, you have me—it is not; but about the captain. Why does he wear a mask?"

Will looked steadily out at sea, and made no reply.

"Is he a monster?—pshaw! what nonsense, have you ever seen his face, Will?"

"You must not ask me anything about the captain," was the quiet reply. "I am bound in honour to say nothing. It would only make mischief and do you no good."

"All right, but I can't help being curious."

"I can tell you this much, Tom, that Jack and I are the only two on board who have seen him without a mask. Mr. Stanchion would not know him among a crowd of strangers, were it removed."

"Indeed."

"A fact, I assure you; but he knows the object of the 'Crucible's' career, and ne brought the crew together—sailors like a spice of mystery, you know—and we had the pick of the men from the port we sailed from."

"And that port, Will?"

"Cannot, of course, be kept a secret, as every man on board knows it. Havanna is the place we hail from; you joined at Porto Rico four months after we made our first appearance upon the seas."

"I remember," laughed Tom; "I was roaming about one night when I met you strutting about in your uniform, the size of life, and we struck up a friendship ending in my being smuggled on board."

"And brought out when we were two days at sea; lor! how you blinked when you got among daylight again."

"The captain was rather angry at first, Will."

"Not much, old boy, for he likes a fellow with pluck, and he has a little, oh! just a little."

"I've seen it, and now, Will, I think you might open your heart about Monkey Jack. Why is he always with the captain, and allowed to wear that comical uniform?"

"We were lying off Cuba," Will began, "near a small town with a crackjaw name which I need not trouble you with, when a bumboat man—a coal black nigger, about five hundred shades darker than Jack—came on board, and, as usual, brought a heap of odds and ends of news."

"I know the sort of fellow, Will, a rollicking impudent sort of a cuss."

"Just so, but don't interrupt, Tom. This old nigger went by the name of Crikey, a preposterous name, of course, but an agreeable change from the host of Cæsars and Pompeys who generally visited us. Crikey began his rigmarole, but we noticed that he was uncommonly agitated, all abroad at times, as if he were completely floored about something. The captain stood by, rather an uncommon thing for him to come on deck near a port; but

there he was, and hailing Crikey, he asked him what he had on his mind."

"'Oh! massa—sar,' replied Crikey, 'I berry sore in de tomach, de heart am broken, and Crikey no lib happy any more,'

"'Speak out, man,' said the captain; 'have you lost your wife?'

"'No, massa,' replied the nigger, 'she alibe an' well, too much alibe and well, she trow all crockery at Crikey's head dis berry mornin'; Crikey no griebe when de missus gone.'

"'Then what is it, man?' asked the captain," and I could see, Will, that he was half inclined to smile, rather an unusual thing with him, as you know.

"'De fac' is,' replied Crikey, clutching his woolly hair, 'dat I hab a brodder.'

"'That is no great affliction,' said the captain.

"'No, massa,' rejoined the nigger; 'but my brodder is a slabe, wid a brute ob a massa. My brodder's name Jack—Jack run away; dey follow him up troo de wood, troo de water, wid bloodhounds, and catch him in de marsh. His massa lose lots ob slaves lately, so he say, I make a sample of Jack, an' burn him; dat what he say he do.'

"'Impossible,' exclaimed the captain, and I saw his eyes glistening with anger.

"'It's trufe,' said Crikey, 'and de law berry bad for de black man here; dey burn my brodder Jack by em by, dis berry morning, close by de palm trees on de hill. Lots ob people go to see.'

"'Villanous,' I heard the captain mutter, and after a few moments' whispering with Mr. Stanchion, he ordered two of the boats to be lowered, and away he went with twenty picked men. I was left on board, but I heard several shots fired on shore, and a few moments later the boats pushed off with all the men, only one wounded, and poor Jack, half dead with the sufferings he had undergone.

"Poor old fellow."

"You may well say that, Tom, any man but a Cuban planter would have pitied him, but he soon recovered, and we set sail. Crikey went with us, as it was feared he would be known as the party who had supplied the information, since then Jack has more than once saved the captain's life, and he makes a sort of pet of him, humours him, in fact, and that accounts for his dress.

"And what has become of Crikey?"

"You remember the nigger who was lieking the grog-tub yesterday?"

"He whom Monkey Jack dropped upon so neatly?"

"Yes! that was Crikey—we shall go back to stockade after cutting out these slavers, and then if we get a few days' rest you will see some fun with the two niggers. They are very fond of each other, but Crikey requires to be kept within bounds—he swizzles frightfully if he is not checked."

"Yes! Massa Steadfast, my brodder am a dark guzzler, and Jack cork him up."

These words came from Monkey Jack, who had approached unperceived, and was standing near in full fig.

"I hear your last words, sar," pursued the negro, "but I not listen much. Jack is no eavesflopper, as de cap'en call it."

"Certainly not," replied Will, with a merry look at his friend.

"No, Jack am honourable trufe itself," returned the sable hero, "and so all his family—Crikey too fond ob rum, but Crikey good man in his heart, wurf two hunded tousand Duncans, who at de best am only one wood-cuttin' skunk."

"Your bitter enemy, eh, Jack?"

"He confounded fool. I say to him t'oder day, dat I will fight him duel, de men say dat he ought to fight, but Duncan say no, de cap'en not like it, den I say I fight him wid fists, so."

Jack put himself into a most extraordinary attitude of self-defence, both the lads exploded into a fit of laughter.

"You may laugh, genelmen," continued Jack, with a good-humoured grin, "but Massa Duncan look berry black."

"Did you fight after all?" asked Tom, wiping the tears from his eyes.

"No, nuffin' come ob it; he know bery well, did ole Duncan, dat one blow ob dis my fist, knock him nose orf, shut up him eyes, and flabbergate him all over."

"Of course it would," said Will, rising. "but there is Mr. Stanchion calling me. Good bye, Jack."

"Good bye, Massa Steadfast."

Will advanced to the side of Mr. Stanchion, who was leaning against one of the aft guns, surveying the horizon with his glass.

"What is it, sir?" asked the lad.

"Just take a squint to leeward, youngster," replied the lieutenant, "your eyes are younger than mine. Do you see anything?"

"I fancy there is a sail, sir," rejoined William, slowly sweeping the horizon with the glass; "but it is very indistinct. It's a small craft, if there is one at all. Now it is clearer, sir—yes, I see it well."

Just then the man on the look-out cried—

"A sail, sir."

"Thank you for nothing, you lubber," growled the lieutenant.

"Shall we bear up, sir?" asked Will.

"No! we will ease off a bit. I don't want to be seen," replied Mr. Stanchion; "that's the slaver on her way to receive cargo. We are overhauling her."

He gave orders at once to shorten sail, and in a few minutes the stranger ahead disappeared.

The "Crucible" crawled on until nightfall, when more sail was run out, and on again the gallant craft danced gaily o'er the waves.

Mr. Stanchion, after a careful survey of the sky to see if dirty weather threatened, and finding all well, went below to the captain's cabin, where he found his leader busy with a chart spread upon the table.

"Good evening, Mr. Stanchion."

"Good evening, sir."

"How is all above?"

"Trim and taut, sir, and a merry breeze bowling up along."

"Excellent! You sent me down a report respecting the slaver—has she been sighted again?"

"No, sir. I gave her plenty of time to get clear away."

"Good! Now, Mr. Stanchion, listen to my plans—Here is the mouth of the river, where the slave station is, as you are aware. A short distance up the water rapidly shoals; the slaver, in consequence, must bring to just past the point."

"I see, sir, she will be at our mercy."

"You are correct, Mr. Stanchion, but I want more. To break up the station altogether, and this cannot be done if those on land have warning of our coming. We must steal down upon the slaver and capture her quietly."

"A difficult matter."

"Not at all, we must lay-to in an hour, off here," the captain pricked the chart with the compasses, "and take to the boats —you command them, and by the early morning's light steal quietly in, before, if you can find the river. The rest must be left to your judgment."

"I understand you, sir.'

"I will bring the 'Crucible' up by sun-rise. Be careful how you proceed, and you will have reason to be proud of your work. Keep her on the present tack, and call me when you are ready to depart."

An hour later, the 'Crucible' was hove-to, the boats lowered, and with a few final instructions the lieutenant and thirty men departed in the direction where they knew the land was lying.

It was a service of great danger, but they were men who loved ventures out of the common line, and went away with light hearts and a parting jest to their comrades on their lips.

At first the men conversed together in an undertone, for the discipline of the 'Crucible' was not unnecessarily strict, but the lieutenant at length bade them be silent, and rest upon their oars.

He listened intently, a low murmuring melodious sound ahead fell upon his ears.

"Give way—steadily," he said; "there's land a mile away; steady, my lads."

The boats, with the rowlocks muffled, sped silently over the heaving water, until the white foam of the breaking waves could be plainly seen in the faint light from a glorious starry sky. Then they crept along by the shore like spectres, without a word, without a sound, beyond the faint lapping of the sea against the wooden sides of their frail barks.

They kept on thus steadily until past midnight, when they "spliced the mainbrace" to ward off fatigue, and again resumed work.

Mr. Stanchion remained in the stern, with eyes fixed upon the dim shore. Suddenly he passed the word softly for the boats to bring to. They had reached the mouth of the river, with a current running swiftly in round an abruptly jutting point.

Great precaution now became necessary, and when the boats moved on, two men were placed in the bows of each to keep a watchful look ahead.

The river was broad at its mouth, but narrowed half a mile from the extremity of the point, and the boats of the "Crucible" were carried in with irresistible impetus, the water foaming and hissing as it swept along the land on either side.

Past this the river spread out in the shape of a balloon, and here the water was nearly calm and apparently clear.

"No signs of her," muttered the lieutenant under his breath.

"I think I see her, sir," said one of the men.

"Where?"

"Close under the trees, forward, sir. They've struck her topmasts, and everything is hauled close."

"Right," returned the lieutenant, "I see her now; give way gently."

Keeping well in shore, they pulled round until the slaver-ship was distinctly visible. She lay still and black upon the water, without a sign of life on board; no light or steady tramp of men upon the watch.

"Very strange," muttered Mr. Stanchion; "looks rather snaky, something of a trap, I fear. Get round her stern, my men, and if there are any of her crew on board we shall soon hear from them."

But apparently there was not a soul in the craft, for the "Crucible's" boats crew drew up without being challenged, and the bold lieutenant climbed on board.

The men quickly followed, without a sound, their cutlasses between their teeth, and then the mystery of the strange silence was revealed.

A dozen men lay about the deck in various positions, some on the sails lying in loose heaps, others on the bare deck, and one was lying with his head and shoulders down the hatchway.

"Yellow Jack," muttered several of the men, shrinking back.

"Nonsense," rejoined the lieutenant, with a soft laugh, "they are only dead drunk—secure the lubbers, bind and gag them, then search the craft."

The handy fellows quietly secured the slaver crew, of whom but two showed any signs of returning consciousness, and they only opened their eyes for a moment, growled a sullen defiance, and fell off again.

Below in the cabin they found three more men in the same plight, who shared the fate of their companions, and the whole were finally stowed away in the forecabin like so many well-trussed fowls.

"We have no officers here, I can see," said Mr. Stanchion, after examining them by the light of a small lantern, "the worthy gentry are ashore. However, better the sprats than no fish."

He went on deck and placed a watch, as it was impossible to get her out of the narrow mouth of the river before the tide turned, and having seen all in order for the night, he lay down upon the planking and waited for the morrow's dawn.

The sun rose behind them, throwing the shadows of the forest across the water, and by the first ray he beheld the "Crucible" lying at anchor about a mile from the shore.

CHAPTER VII.

THE ATTACK UPON THE SLAVE HOUSE.—
SNARLEY CROKER, THE SLAVE DEALER.

MR. STANCHION ran a white flag to the mizen peak, the signal agreed upon if all went well with him, and a boat from the "Crucible" put off at once, with the masked captain, Monkey Jack, Tom Furnace, and a dozen men.

Arriving on board the captured craft, the captain and his lieutenant shook hands, the former uttering a few words of congratulation on the happy termination of the venture.

"Any loss, Mr. Stanchion?" he asked.

"Not a blow struck," replied the lieutenant, "we found them all intoxicated, fifteen of the crew; the officers are ashore."

"Any negroes aboard?"

"Not one, but there is little doubt of her being a slaver, she is fitted up from stem to stern for the trade."

"I have no doubt of her," returned the captain; "I shall certainly retain her—an example which I doubt not will be followed by my countrymen at large. Where are the prisoners?"

"Below, sir."

They went down together, followed by Jack, who always dogged his master's heels during any service wherein danger could be apprehended.

The captured seamen, half-castes to a man, lay upon the floor of the cabin, blinking like owls in a ray of sunlight streaming through a port hole.

"Jack," said the captain, "remove the gag from that fellow," pointing to the nearest, a tigerish-looking wretch with a heavy mass of coal-black hair, matted and dishevelled, shading his eyes.

"Do you speak English?" asked the captain.

A defiant scowl flitted over the fellow's face, but he uttered not a word.

The same question was asked in Spanish, and elicited no reply.

"I see how it is, Mr. Stanchion," said the captain to his lieutenant, "this man is deaf and dumb, of use to neither friend nor foe. Jack, have a rope swung out at the yard-arm. Then bring down a couple of men, and swing him off——"

"Pardon me, sir," said the man hastily, seeing the captain was determined, "me spike a leetle Englese."

"Fortunately for you," returned the captain, grimly, "just enough to save your worthless life. Where is your leader?"

"De capitano, sir?"

"You know what I mean. Where is he?"

"Gone up de rivare to de settlement."

"How far is it?"

"Two-tree mile."

"Between two and three miles?"

"Yes, sare."

"How shall I know it?"

"By de piece of bunting hanging from mangrove tree. De settlement up creek dere."

"How many men are there?"

"Only captain and three officers besides nigger."

"Then myself and a dozen would be sufficient?"

"Plenty, sare."

"Very good. Mr. Stanchion, I will away at once, leaving you in charge of the two crafts. Run out at the turn of the tide, and lay to by the side of the "Crucible." If I return not within six hours, string this fellow up and his companions also, for I shall have been betrayed."

The half-castes all intently listened, the fading colour leaving their dark skins a ghastly hue. The masked captain perceived it, and knew the man had lied.

"Perhaps captain had better take more men," said the informant, hurriedly; "dere may be more white men dere."

"Oh! there may be more—how many?"

"Eight white men from Espano."

"Is that all?"

"Every one," replied the man, fervently calling upon a string of saints to bear witness of his truthfulness.

The captain of the "Crucible" speedily made his arrangements, and pushed off with the long boat and cutter, ample provision for the work in hand, but no more than was judicious, as he knew that the natives who were free, and the instruments of the vile traffic, as a rule, defended the cause of the slavers.

Monkey Jack was, of course, of the party, and Tom Furnace, the middy, after much pleading, was allowed to go, the captain having at first intended to leave him behind with the lieutenant.

He was a youngster, and there was to him a strange, romantic appearance about the scenery they passed on their way to the creek.

Numberless birds, most of them unknown, sailed to and fro, dipping their beaks into the cool water, and uttering strange cries as they flapped their wings in angry defiance of the intruders.

Two miles up they saw the piece of bunting hanging from a tree upon the bank, a broad piece of cloth marked with the then almost unknown stars and stripes, the symbol of nationalism chosen by the men who fought for the freedom of the States.

"A desecration," thought the captain, as it met his eye; "it is the banner of freedom, and should never be used by a trafficker in human flesh."

Close by the star-spangled flag they found the mouth of the creek, and headed the boats for it.

Entering it, a glorious avenue lay before them.

Tom Furnace had never seen the like before; the umbrageous screen of mangroves closed overhead, shutting out the sun and strong light as if it were a gigantic artificial arbour.

The water was clear and pellucid as crystal, the beauty and coolness of the place indescribably luxurious.

Above was a perfect web of verdure resting on the trellis work formed by the boughs, the ghost-like crane flitted about, and more than one owl was flying to and fro as if there were no blinding sun hanging in the sky, above the glorious network of nature.

As for the fish, they seemed to choke the creek, rolling lazily about, and ever and anon flashing their silver bellies as they rolled over in wanton sport.

"Glorious," involuntarily exclaimed the middy.

"Dis am not much," replied Jack, contemptuously, "not'ing to my native home, trees ten times big, tousands more birds and fish——"

"Silence, good Jack," interposed the captain; "remember where we are."

"Jack beg cap'en's pardon, and be dumb as ole Duncan when him drunk," rejoined the nigger, who could not refrain from having a blow at his mortal foe.

An impediment to their progress shortly arose, several vast trees on either side had settled over the water, and their dense foliage, together with a variety of creeping plants, formed an impassable barrier.

The quick eyes of Jack detected a path on the larboard shore, which he pointed out to the captain

The boats pulled in, and recent foot marks became visible upon the banks.

The captain gave orders to land, an the boats were drawn in.

Taking his place in the van, he led their on; Jack by his side, tracing out the trai which grew fainter and fainter as the so became firmer, until it disappeared to th eyes of all but the negro, who stalked con fidently, as if a guide was before him.

Suddenly he halted; the captain an the men clustered in the rear.

"No do dar," said Jack, hurriedly "dem very near somewhere, spread about.

Hardly had the words been uttered, an the men began to scatter, when a sharp ringing sound ahead startled them, and perfect shower of bullets rained above an below them.

"Small ship gun," said Jack, who stood with Tom Furnace in the shade of a tree "dey load wid bullets, an' make pepper po of him."

A heap of brushwood lay a few moment before in their path, but this was now swep away, revealing a small brass gun, being reloaded by a couple of half-caste sailors.

"Stop a binnit," muttered Jack, "me berry soon stop dat."

Gliding swiftly behind the trees, he suddenly ran out among them, shouting—

"'Go home wid you, you copper-colour niggers," and fired two shots in rapid succession.

One of the men fell, but the other fled into a string of bushes, from whence a dozen muskets immediately rattled. Jack's cocked hat fell off, and he staggered back.

"Are you hurt?" cried the captain, springing forward.

"Get back, massa cap'en," cried Jack, recovering, "me not hurt—two holes in hat—oh! wurra, wurra, dat am a shame."

As the enemy was invisible, and their strength not known, the captain again retreated to his place of shelter, to arrange in his mind some plan of action. The tars, too, were stowed away, all but the poor fellow, and he lay perfectly still, with a bullet through his heart.

Rapid as thought in action, the masked hero decided to advance ere the enemy gathered too much courage, and rushing forward he cried aloud,—

"Forward, my men; out with the hor nets."

Again the muskets rattled out their fire from the bushes, and two men rolled upon the earth. Jack, too, threw up his hea

THE NEGROES' REVENGE.

as if a wasp had stung him, and cried, " dat bery near spiling my flisyogomy," but kept on by the captain's side.

The bushes concealed a stockaded enclosure about forty yards square, and here was gathered a tall gaunt man of the true Yankee type, and about fourteen men of various nations, ferocious ruffians every one.

Want of discipline and confusion had caused them to empty their muskets together, and ere they had time to reload, the captain of the " Crucible " and his merry men were over.

The desperadoes were all armed with boarding pikes and cutlasses, and for a time fought ferociously, but pluck and persistence told, and when half of their number were slain, the rest turned tail, the tall Yankee leading the way.

From the moment the invaders entered the stockade, Monkey Jack had fixed his eyes upon this man, but the struggling mass was between them, and the negro in vain endeavoured to reach him.

When the American retreated, Jack uttered a howl of rage, rivalling the cry of a hyæna, deprived of his dinner, and running round his panting comrades, darted after him.

The masked captain shouted for him to

return, but his faithful servitor, for once, disobeyed his commands, and continued in pursuit.

"What madness!" cried the captain, "they will fall upon him in a body—forward, men."

The slavers had cast away their guns to a man, and had therefore nothing but their cutlasses—the Yankee excepted, who wore a brace of pistols. The Englishmen at once dashed forward in pursuit.

It was a vain one, however; a hundred yards away every sign of Monkey Jack and the enemy was lost in the forest.

"A curious freak of Jack's," said the captain, in a vexed tone. "The scoundrels have fled, and in such a place as this further pursuit would be useless. What can have induced him to go?"

They shouted aloud, pistols were fired, and every device resorted to for the next ten minutes, but no responding shot or shout answered them.

Just at this moment, one of the men, who had been prowling a short distance away, ran up crying—

"Here's a shanty, hard by, crowded with the dark skins."

This aroused the captain from his vexed mood, and he bade the man point out the way.

He led them to an open area, some hundred yards in diameter, the soil appeared to be mixed with loose stones, and white ash, and trampled hard and flat. In the centre stood a long, low, one-storied building of mud, thatched with the leaves of the broad palm, and from this came a most unearthly groaning and screaming, dreadful to hear.

In the centre of the hut was a small wooden door, and this ready hands and feet burst in, the captain and Tom Furnace foremost.

A fearful sight presented itself. More than a hundred negroes were huddled together, chained by the neck and limbs. The only light to the building came from the door, and the further corners of the hut were wrapped in gloom.

Crying out in anger, the ready men dragged out the poor wretches, hacking at their manacles with their cutlasses like madmen, until the loud voice of their captain recalled them to their senses.

"You have better weapons than those for such work," he cried, and every man drew from his waistband a short strong file, with which he had been provided.

Quick work then, and the clanking chains fell rapidly, and one by one the negroes, men, women, and children, some but little more than babes, stood erect free.

When they found their liberty, they did not sing, or dance, or shout, the poor wretches were too much broken for that, but they lay upon the ground and sobbed out their thanks in an unknown tongue.

Two men were despatched to the boats, and they soon returned with two large bags of biscuits and a small keg of rum. The latter was mixed with water, and there by the hut, food and drink were served out to all, white men and black, rescuer and the rescued.

Sweet liberty! how little do we, in our dear native isle, truly appreciate the priceless boon.

The humble but much needed repast over, the cutter with half-a-dozen men was despatched to the "Crucible," the captain and the remainder keeping guard over the body of unhappy natives who clustered together on the ground and patiently awaited the fate in store for them.

"Tell Mr. Stanchion," said the captain to Tom, who had command of the cutter, "that I shall remain here until I know something of the fate of Jack, and ask him to be so good as to send me a small sleeping tent. You can return with it and bring Steadfast if you wish it."

Tom replied that he did wish it, and bade the men give way.

Evening was at hand, when he returned with his chum by his side in the stern sheets, both uncommonly down in the mouth on account of Monkey Jack, whose loss was great indeed.

They had brought the tent with a fresh supply of ammunition and food for three days. Also half-a-dozen hatchets for felling trees, so that the men might construct a shelter for themselves and the negroes.

A busy scene followed the return of the lads, the sun was sinking low, and soon it would be night, dark as pitch in the forest of cashaw trees and mangrove jungle.

First they pitched the captain's tent, and by a neat contrivance swung a hammock near the centre. Sentries were then posted around, and the men busied themselves with erecting a rough covering to keep off the deadly night dews.

The shanty, reeking with its late unwholesome occupation, was unfit for a resting-place, but the negroes lay outside its walls and slept like tired children.

A dozen stakes with a thatch of broad fern leaves suited the requirements of the sailors, and shortly after sundown all but the sentries were sound asleep.

A host of chattering paroquets, seated on the branches surrounding the enclosure, aroused them in the morning; a hasty breakfast was partaken of, and men despatched in various directions to search for poor Jack.

They came back, one by one, without any news of him, and the day crawled on with the captain and the mids still in suspense.

The hot noon-day sun straight above them rained down its streams of fire, and all but the masked captain lay beneath the shade, and he was seated inside his tent gloomy and sad. The negroes lay like logs of ebony under the trees, happy and contented.

A sentinel paced to and fro, overcome with heat, and dozing as he went. Tom and Will lounged among the verdure, dreaming of Paradise.

What voice is that which breaks upon the stillness?

All knew it well, and every man is upon his feet—we include Will and Tom among the men, to suit their manly aspirations.

"You long cuss, you want too much dragging, but I'd drag you for eber rader han gib you up."

Then Monkey Jack emerged from the trees, hauling the tall Yankee with his powerful arms.

Such a cheer arose. but it was mingled with laughter, although there was a tear in more than one eye. Jack was certainly a favourite.

"Dere," he cried, dragging his captive before the masked captain, "I get you home at last."

"What is the meaning of this?" asked his master, contending with mingled emotions. The Yankee had been sadly mauled, and looked very much like a ruffled bird, and Jack was sodden with perspiration, and appeared completely worn out. Altogether they presented a strange picture.

"De meaning?" responded Jack; "do you not know him, massa?"

"I cannot say that I remember him at this moment," was the reply.

"You not know him?" repeated Jack, excitedly, "not ynow de biggest rogue dat er run about in a pair of breeches?"

"I certainly recognise him to be an unmitigated scoundrel!" replied the captain;

"his presence in this place and calling pronounce him to be so."

"But you not know dis to be de great villain, Snarley Croker?"

"Snarley Croker!"

"Dat am him, de 'Merican scoundrel who came to Cuba to settle, an' buy Jack dere, den chop him about like log of wood, and when Jack run away hunt him wid bloodhounds and say he roost him."

"My last interview with this gentleman," returned the captain, "was so very brief, that I at first failed to recognize his features. But I remember him now."

"Glad ob dat, massa cap'en," said Jack, "now I bring him here you tell me what to do wid him."

"We will see presently. Ho! there—secure this fellow."

The tars, who had hitherto kept at a respectful distance, now advanced, and a cord was passed deftly round the arms and legs of the sullen, silent Yankee.

The negroes, who had been aroused by the noise, sat on their haunches eyeing the captive, and shortly a whisper passed round while the expression of their faces became absolutely diabolical.

They knew the author of their sufferings, and woe to him should he fall into their clutches.

"Now, Jack," said the captain, when the prisoner was removed, "tell me what you have been doing the last four and twenty hours."

"Me see dat scrushinatin' scoundrel," returned Jack, "and me see him turn him tail, so I follow quick, as flyin' fish afore de shark. I hear cap'en call, but I say I come back by and by, and bring de long snake of de Yankee."

"You must obey my orders, Jack."

"Allers, arter dis, massa cap'en, but dis time my feelin's too much. He try to make cook meat ob me, so I foller him and other rascals until they tire, one arter de oder, and I jes' give dem a little poke wid my sword, an' dey lay quiet for eber."

"That is, you killed them."

"Dead as a crane wid his head shot away by cannon ball, but de 'Merican keep on, him got long legs, but Jack's much stronger, and come up wid him at last. Gorra! I not stab him, but I gib him one thump on de back ob de head, and down he go."

Jack smote his palm with his iron fist, and grinned like a victorious prize-fighter.

"All ob a heap he lay," he resumed.

" and I take away him arms, he kick, I gib' him 'noder blow, an' den he lay still. We bof got tired, so I sit down and tie his arms, so, elbers togedder nearly, an' he howl like wile cat.

" All dat night, massa cap'en, I sit by him, and neber move, but in de morning I say to him, ' you jes come back wi' me': he say, ' I see you scolloped and biled fust '; I say, ' I scollop you, Massa Croker, if you don't come.' He then get on his feet, and swear orful, call me a ' farnal nigger,' wid great rudeness ; but I make him come along until we near here, den his bonds break, his arms get free, an' he try to run ; but I down upon him, like female fieliphant when de young is stolen, and bring him here."

" And a good piece of work, Jack."

" Berry good, massa cap'en, you ought to make me admiral arter dat."

Jack grinned, showing two complete sets of ivories, and the same faint smile dawned upon the captain's face, but it was a sad smile withal.

" I cannot make you an admiral, Jack," he said, " but I can make you my friend."

" Better dat dan all de admirals about;" cried Jack, kissing the extended hand of the captain. " Confoun' eberyting an' eberybody body but massa cap'en and his fren's."

" You would make the world a blank, Jack," rejoined the masked leader, rising. " Now, what shall be done with the Yankee ?"

" I not know," replied Jack, shaking his woolly head until his hat fell off. " Him berry bad now, and I ought to kill him at fust, but not now."

" As you will, Jack," said the captain, retiring within his tent; " he is entirely in your hands."

Jack walked away meditating, until his eyes fell upon his rescued countrymen, with whom he at once mingled, embracing and fondling them as if they were cubs of his own.

CHAPTER VIII.

THE SLAVE DEALER'S DOOM.—THE VILLAGE IN THE FOREST.

HE was evidently not of the same tribe, for their tongue was strange to him; but niggers, like Frenchmen, introduce a vast amount of gesticulating into their conversation, and language is almost superfluous.

Something in their ways made him un-

easy, but it was not until the day was nearly spent that he sought his leader, and gave vent to his suspicions.

" Massa cap'en," he said, " dem niggers up to some game."

" Surely, they would not fall upon their friends," was the hasty rejoinder.

" No, sar; but dey gib dat 'Merican pepper, if he get among dem."

" Have him removed for the night to the opposite side of the enclosure."

Jack saw this was done, and with two sailors kept guard over him.

Fatigue overcame the negro, and the warm still night soothed the sailors into slumber. When the trio awoke at dawn, the Yankee was gone.

Monkey Jack was fairly overwhelmed with consternation and rage. He had on the previous evening seen the Yankee slaver, Snarley Croker, securely bound, had laid down beside him with two additional guards, and yet the scoundrel had contrived to get clear away without a sign.

" Dis aboot de mose scrumptinating ting I eber met with, sure," he said, addressing the seamen, who were equally bewildered and dismayed.

" There warnt even a rustle from the cuss," muttered one of the men.

" You berry bad watchmen," rejoined Jack, eyeing them with disdain, " or you conflounded traitors."

" That obsarwation b'longs as much to you, Jack, as to us," retorted the previous speaker.

" You no Jack me," replied the nigger, very upright and stiff in a moment, " I Massa Jack from common men."

" Ax yer pardon, Mister Jack," said the man, with an irrepressible grin, " if your honour overlook it this time we'll be werry careful in future."

" I must see the cap'en," muttered Jack, turning away, " afore I go on him trail again. But I go, dat's sartain."

The young privateer was grieved and angry to hear that Snarley Croker had effected his escape; but as words of reproach could not restore the scoundrel to his power, he contented himself with bidding Jack to do his best to investigate the mystery.

The negro settled his cocked hat with a determined air, and returned to the place where his prisoner had slept.

Just there the ground was very hard, and one would have thought the detection of footsteps impossible; but Jack followed a trail invisible to all but himself to the fence of cashaw trees and then he stood erect, a dozen sailors who had followed him curiously clustered near him.

"Dere one ting no man can hide," said Jack, "dat's his footmark—and when 'tis cussed nigger, t'under storm can't wipe it out. De Yankee snake hab been carried orf by two niggers."

"How do you know that?" asked Will Steadfast, who came up at the moment; "come, Jack, give us a lesson."

"Dere's signs known to proper niggers, such as myself, as no white man see. Dere's marks of two nigger walking berry heaby, so dey carry someting; dere's no marks of old Croker's feet, so dey carry him."

This opinion, uttered with the air of a great philosopher, met with approval, but Will struck in,—

"May not these marks perceived by you have been made yesterday?"

"Yesterday!" repeated Jack, with contempt, "you young an' ignorant, Massa Steadfast, although you good gentleman. Yesterday! no, dese 'ere footmarks just tree hours two minutes old."

"Oh! Jack, that won't do."

"It's palpitable fac', Massa Steadfast. Now I go on de trail, who go with me?"

Will volunteered of course, and all the men were eager to join.

"Not so fast," said Jack, "too many brofs spile de cook. I don't want hundred lubbers blundering about; I take tree men and massa Steadfast."

"And my chum," added Will. "Here he comes."

Tom Furnace came bounding up, and his services were accepted. Prior to starting, Jack went back to his captain, to whom he imparted the arrangements made.

"Take care of the youngsters," said the masked hero, "I cannot afford to lose them."

"Jack bring 'em back, massa cap'en, or he don't come himself."

The negro returned to his post, and with the two middies and three sailors, went upon the trail.

There was a deal of pomposity, natural to the sable leader, betrayed in all his movements, but he was evidently possessed of extraordinary powers in tracing the progress of the two negroes and their burden.

In the depths of the wood, where the ground was covered to a great depth with decayed vegetation, he sped on at a rapid pace, but sometimes they came to an open where the ground was harder, and then his progress was slower; but he never halted for more than a moment, or ceased talking for an instant.

"Here, you see," he said, "dey stumble ober a fallen trunk in dere hurry to get away—and dey wipe orf de moss wid old Croker, at which him swear orful; den here dey felt tired, and lay him down; dere's de heel of his boot, an' here he scratch de ground wid his hands acause him berry savage, and no help himself."

"If you young genelmen," he continued, "will look at dat mangrobe tree, you see a dull mark, dere one nigger lean to shift de part of ole Croker him carryin', t'oder one lay down his feet, and here be rogue's boots again. Oh, golly! yah! dey hab struggle here, but Croker double up in no time."

The signs of the scuffle were nothing more than a few disarranged leaves on the even surface of an open space of ground, but Jack spake with such confidence that his hearers could not but believe him.

Thus they travelled on until the sun was a third way in the heavens, and a halt was called for refreshment.

Rations had not been forgotten, and the huugry pursuers made a hearty meal.

"I say, Jack," cried Will, "what is the idea of those fellows carrying off the Yankee?"

"It is not because dey lub him," was the evasive reply.

"We know that; but give us the real reason."

"Dey know him, Massa Steadfast and Furnace, dat him be a uncommon diblocally willan, and dey say to demselves dat we take him orf, and hab revenge."

"You should have warned the captain," said Tom, reproachfully.

"I warn him, sar, all I know," replied Jack, offended; "I no know de langwage ob de niggers, but I see enuf to tell cap'en dat dey mean mischief. So de cap'en tell me to keep look out, but de niggers too much for me, for de time."

"I beg your pardon, Jack," rejoined the boy, "I ought to have known that you would do all that could be done."

Peace was made, and after a little further rest, the forward movement resumed, Jack insisting upon silence, and, marvellous to relate, setting the example by gliding in between the trees as quiet as a serpent seeking its prey.

There is something overwhelming in the solitude of a vast tropical forest unknown to all but those who have roamed there, and sat beneath the vast spreading trees, and listened to the strange cries of birds and beasts muffled by the dense foliage around.

The harsh notes of the screeching parrot are softened down by distance, and mingling with the soft hum of myriads of insects, become a pleasing portion of Nature's musical chorus, and while the upper branches of the gigantic trees rustle in the wind, the lower ones, sheltered from rude Boreas, hang lifeless and still in the cool shade.

It is this very stillness which awes the stranger, he hears the familiar rustle of the branches, yet every leaf around him is motionless, his eyes failing to penetrate the dense clusters on the lower stems.

Jack stopped once, and pointed to the ground, uttering softly, "De lion, him no far away," and the lads involuntarily glanced around with looks of apprehension.

"You no be afraid ob him," continued Jack, "he run away like ole boots in de daylight—him berry much coward when de sun shine."

After this he spoke no more until the trees grew thinner, showing that they were nearing the verge of the forest or an open glade of more than ordinary dimensions. Here he halted, and whisperingly bade them await for his return.

Jack fell upon his hands and knees, progressing with the agility of a monkey. In that position he would have been an edifying sight to Mr. Darwin, had that gentleman of the ape theory lived and been present at the time.

His absence was brief, not more than a few minutes, ; and he came back hurriedly, his eyes rolling with excitement.

"Forward!" he said, softly, "you hunks dere behind, de ole willan am 'ere—oh! golly—Yah! such a sight for dem as lub him."

The whole party stepped cautiously forward, the sailors, with the happy indifference of their class, removing their shoes, and treading fearlessly among the fallen leaves and foliage.

Suddenly Jack raised his finger, and pointing to a cluster of acacias, growing luxuriantly in the form of a fence, whispering, bade them creep up and look through.

The flowers and foliage hid everything beyond from view, but lying down they could obtain between the stems a glimpse of the space beyond.

It was a scene startling to the strongest man: the place was a large opening in the forest, rugged and almost bare of plants and herbs; in the distance, the sun's rays fell upon a row of rude huts built of mud and thatched with palms, but there were no signs of life apparent, all seemed emptied and deserted.

Midway was the sight which caused a feeling of horror to spring up in the bosoms of the lookers on.

Bound to a huge stake, and surrounded by a heap of inflammable wood, was the form of Snarley Croker, the slave dealer; and he was alone—staring at the distant huts, with the hopeless expression of a man who knew the world was lost to him.

"Where are the niggers?" whispered Will.

"No know," returned Jack; "dat why me so cautious; dere may be t'ousand more somewhar by, and dey go fetch them; dat's why me so causterous."

"Cautious, Jack—that's the word."

"Causterous my word; Massa Steadfast use which him please."

"Very good, Jack; but let us remember that poor devil there; we must not allow him to be burnt alive."

"Hush, Massa Will!" returned Jack, bending close to the ground. "I hear de tramp of men—one—two. Gorra, massa, dere's on'y two as bring him!"

Two negroes appeared at this juncture, emerging from the wood on the right, each bearing a flaming torch in his hand.

"Forward, men!" cried Will, assuming the lead; "save that wretch. Don't go round; cut your way through the fence. Follow me!"

The two negroes heard the cry, and turned upon the spot where the sailors were hacking the foliage furiously with their cutlasses the looks of startled wild beasts, but the next moment they rushed down upon their victim, and fired the pile.

Snarley Croker heard the cry too, and responded with a heartrending shout for help.

"Help! Hold, for the love of Heaven; I am not fit to die!"

That cry rang in the ears of his listeners for many a long day—by some it was never forgotten while they lived. Cutting and slashing furiously, they made a gap sufficient for the passage of their bodies, and rushed through, Monkey Jack the most eager of them all.

"Help—help!"

The screams of the wretched man were

THE YOUNG PRIVATEER. 31

fearful; the delay entailed in forcing the passage was fatal to him. Fast and furious arose the flames, high in the air, and twining around his body like serpents.

The two negroes waited but to see that the work was effectual, and then, uttering horrible yells of triumph, sprang into the wood and were seen no more.

In vain the sailors sprang fearlessly forward, and, reckless of their own burns, dashed the blazing logs aside; in vain Monkey Jack and the middies strewed it right and left, and seized the burning logs with their hands and cast them aside; the mass was too great and too well laid. The flames gathered stronger around the doomed man.

"Save me!" he cried piteously, tossing his head, the only part of his frame not securely bound, violently to and fro; "don't let me burn before you! Oh, God, have I sinned against you for this? Help—help! Oh, mercy—mercy! I am not fit to die! I am not fit to die!

That was the burden of his cries, "I am not fit to die!" Nor was he. A man violent at all times, and indifferent to the sufferings of others, he had passed a life of cruelty and brutality, and, now that keen suffering had fallen upon him, he learned how bitterly the delicate form of a tortured man can feel—and learned the fact too late.

"Don't stop, Massa Steadfast!" yelled Jack, begrimmed with smoke and scorched by the fire; "dere's no man bad enuf to burn! Don't stop, Massa Will, for the lub of all dat's good!"

In vain—the dry wood, interspersed dry leaves and long grass, raged on; soon the form of the captive became dim in the smoke, his cries grew fainter and fainter, at length dying away in one long last groan of mortal woe.

His head fell forward on his breast, the hair of his head crisped up and fell away, his face blackened, the skin cracked, and curled up, and the Yankee slaver was no more.

"No use, Massa Steadfast and Furnace," said Jack, halting, "it all ober wid him. De niggers lay de fire too well, and Snarley Croker roasted as he would hab roasted me; but I sorry for him—berry sorry. Wurra, wurra—de def is drefful!"

Now that all hope was gone they let the fire rage, and it soon expended itself, sinking down into a heap of glowing ashes, with the half-burned stake and scorched remains of the slaver a ghastly picture in the centre.

The sensation of their own burns diverted the party from the sad sight, but these Jack quickly relieved by the application of bruised herbs gathered in the margin of the wood.

Their wounds attended to, they inspected the rude village, examined the huts within and without, finding in them all signs of a struggle, but nothing alive.

"Dis is de village," said Monkey Jack, in explanation, "dat Snarley Croker—Wurra! how bad him die—de village dat Snarley Croker come to in de night, and wid his men clear out all de niggers, man, woman, and little piccaninny. Dey go round fus' one place, den anoder, until dey get all and chain togedder; den drive 'em down to shanty—Wurra! de ole job berry bad, berry bad indeed."

It was true; the little colony of black savages found chained in the shanty had indeed been wrested from the huts around, and thither the slave-dealer had been borne to expiate his crime after the manner designed by the rude, ignorant beings he had outraged.

There, in the centre of the homes—rough, but the homes of living creatures still—he had paid the penalty of his crimes, and in a way he but a few short months before had chosen for another, and that other his helpless slave.

A dreadful death—an end of torture, but he had always lived amidst sorrow and pain of his own rearing. Seeds of hatred he scattered broadcast, and in the final harvest he, the cold-blooded, cruel slave-dealer, was gathered into the barn.

Such things have been, even in the time of your fathers, dear readers, and in some of the far-off nations bordering on the Andes the old cruelties still languish, but of all sins mankind have been guilty of, and their name is Legion, not one has brought down upon the heads of the promoters such dire suffering and loss as the crime of traffic in human flesh.

It is a tree which blossoms freely, and its fruits are cruelty, remorseless hate, and ungoverned revenge.

CHAPTER IX.

THE RETURN HOME—HONOUR BAY—CRIKEY'S REBELLION.

ERE the little party left the village, they buried the remains of Snarley Croker to shield his blackened corpse from the birds and beasts of prey already giving signs of approach.

Specks high in the air were declared by Jack to be vultures, and a dismal howl from the forest he announced as the cry of "dat 'fernal sneak de jackal," so with compassion they did all that could be done, and hid the slaver under the earth.

The journey back was easily performed, the broad trail they had left being an unerring guide to the negro, who strutted between the mids, chattering like a parrot. Jack had a very loose tongue, and unless under extraordinary pressure it would not keep still.

They reached the spot where the shanty stood late in the afternoon, and there another surprise awaited them, the tent of their captain had disappeared, and the captain too was gone.

"What! dat is most scrutinating now," exclaimed Jack, "where am massa cap'en, and de men? dere on'y two left, and dey snoose under de tree. Git up, you lazy hunks, where de cap'en?"

The men awoke and hastily arose, touching their caps to the middies, and one presented a note to Will.

"From the captain, Mr. Steadfast," he said.

The youth opened it, read the lines carefully with a surprised expression of face, ending with a whistle of dismay.

"Here's a pretty go!" he exclaimed, "come here, Tom, just read this."

"An' me too, Massa Will," suggested Monkey Jack with a broad grin.

"Yes," said Will, "you may read it."

"P'raps Massa Furnace read it out?" rejoined the negro, "he got berry nice voice, an' it sabe me using my speckler."

Jack had the eye of an hawk, and his allusion to spectacles was a joke of course.

"Say you can't read," said Tom, folding back the paper, "and don't humbug."

"I read some tings," replied the negro, with a certain dignity his quaint dress could not hide, "Massa Furnace read de t'oders —dere," he added, pointing to the forest, "is Jack's book, and he read it berry well."

Tom felt the reproof and apologised, then he read aloud as follows:—

"DEAR WILL, I must away at once, on an important and unexpected mission; for once going without my faithful friends."

"Dat me," interrupted Jack, with a grin; "I'm de fren's."

"Of course you are," agreed Tom, to make amends for his late rudeness, an continued his reading;—

"'I have left you seven men, and wit the three you have you will be able to wor the slaver back to Honour Bay. Go ther and await my return. Leave Jack to di pose of his countrymen.—Ever yours,'—

There was no signature, but a seal at th bottom bearing the words "For Honour. upon a miniature flag. Tom folded the le ter and returned it.

"Better go at once," he said, "that is you are ready, Will; of course you are i command."

"I flatter myself I am," replied Wil "Now, Jack, what is to be done with you countrymen?"

The poor wretches were still sittin patiently by the fence, confident of thei rescuers' kindness.

Jack proceeded to explain what wa necessary to be done.

"Dey must go home," he said, "tain berry far, and dere too many nigger aboo Honour Bay now. Me gib em de word t march."

"If any wish to go with us let them d so."

"I ax 'em, massa Steadfast, but I tir dey like better to go home, 'cept dat woma dere, she in lub wid me, and I tink I'll ha a wife."

The monstrous grin on Jack's face sen the lads into a fit of laughter, in which mos of the sailors joined.

"Are you mad?" said Will, "think o Crikey."

"Now I tink ob Crikey an' his missus,' rejoined the darky, slowly, "I tink I ha no wife arter all."

"Dismiss the poor devils then, and let us get on board."

Monkey Jack settled his uniform, put on his best air, and addressed his sable country men thus,—

"You niggers can cut away like ole Duncan when I offer to ring him nose. Dere's all your homes ready for you, and we not make slabes ob you; we gib you free dom an' a bag ob biscuit, and de sooner you are gone de better. I tink ob habin' a wife once, but I 'member Crikey and den gib it up. Don' make a row, but go like good piccninnys."

Although they understood not a word he said, his signs were comprehended. The meek, patient creatures as they seemed, had yet one and all connived in the slave dealer's death, and seen him quickly but

[for]cibly seized as he slept, and borne away gagged and helpless. So far can a wrong bring out the deadly passions of hate and revenge.

They filed out through the bushes, prostrating themselves for a moment before the middies and sailors as they passed, one of those in the rear shouldering the bag of biscuit pointed out by Monkey Jack.

When they were gone, the dark shanty was fired, and all hastened on board the slave craft, where they found the five other men getting ready for sea.

She was a beautiful vessel, named the "Defiance," her hull was beautifully moulded, a superfine run, perfect bows, and sides as round as an apple. By the time the middies came on board, the topsails were sheeted home and hoisted, and after a quick clattering of the windlass, she glided out of the little bay before a smooth breeze.

The voyage back was effected without incident of any note. Will Steadfast knew the course, and in two days they made Deadlock Point, and ran into their hiding place in the river.

As the captain was not on board, they made no signal, but the middies, leaving the "Defiance" in charge of the men, all trustworthy we may be sure, went ashore with Monkey Jack, and walked to the stockade.

As they neared the enclosure, the home of the masked captain, a strange confusion of voices fell upon their ears—singing, shouting, and laughter, with a jingling of bells, and light beating of gongs.

"Dat am Crikey up to someting," said Jack, "an' him berry drunk for sartain."

"But he could not make all that row," rejoined Furnace.

"No; but him get de niggers to help. Now he sing."

The words of a song, or rather negro ditty, literally and fairly howled, came floating towards them :—

> Of all de Cuba bumboat men,
> Dat's up to ebery game,
> Dere's one dat lick de biling lot,
> An' Crikey is his name.

"I say so," said Jack, looking very fierce, "Crikey am a disgrace to de fam'ly. He's ass, fool, rogue. I berry quick stop him singing."

"No hurry, Jack," interposed Will, "let us have a look at them."

Here the song broke forth again :—

> De gals do lub him lubly face,
> De smile upon him sweet,
> Dey wink and cry, "Oh! Yah! Yah! Yup!"
> As him walkin' down de street.

A chorus, consisting of the last line repeated a score of times or so, followed this precious outburst of melody, and while it was at its height, the unexpected arrivals stood in the entrance of the stockade.

There, under the shadow of the captain's tent, a score of niggers were assembled, seated on the ground, with Crikey in the midst, perched on an empty barrel. As the master of the ceremonies, he had clothed himself in various garments belonging to the young privateer, and was, furthermore, in possession of a grog tub, which he guarded carefully. Each of his comrades had the half of a cocoa-nut shell; he was in possession of a large drinking cup.

Crikey had evidently been very liberal in dispensing the good mixture to himself; but, judging from the appearance of the rest, their supply had been limited.

"Now dat song is ober," said Crikey, "I gib you a toast, and toast mean de health of genelman. In dis present company dere am one s'perior to the ole bunch ob yer, and dat is de chile who sit on dis barrel, an' we drink him health. Long life to King Crikey, who am—. Hullo! what de debil dat?"

"It am me," cried Monkey Jack, who had dethroned his brother by a violent application of his boot, "you—you—porrykpine—you—you—lost chile—you ruin de fam'ly name. I blush for you—."

"You jist kick your brodder again," returned Crikey, sparring wildly among his sable brethren, who were completely overcome by the unexpected arrival of Jack, "strike him again, and see what he do."

"I strike de lot," replied Jack, producing a stout stick, and forthwith charged into the midst of the festive group, "dere's one for you, Joe—dere's a wipe for you, Pompey—I see if you drink the cap'en's grog when him away. Dere's someting to make it nice—not de sugar you expec' though. How you like dat, you cannibrills?—I'm round about your hunks."

They scattered about the stockade, Crikey disappearing altogether, and Jack, after a little ineffectual dodging, gave up all further attempts at castigation for the present.

Will and Tom, who had remained hidden, to enjoy the scene, now advanced to the side of the panting Jack.

"Dat's how to put 'em right. Golly! how dem did spread," he gasped; "I jest 'ave anodder one at Crikey. den I stop."

"You've have punished them enough, Jack?" laughed Will. "Get us something to eat, for I'm as sharp as a wolf. Where are the men?"

"De white sailors down at Honour Bay, Massa Steadfast, dat why dese dam niggers cut dere little capers. I make 'em cut caper and get de table ready."

"Honour Bay," said Tom Furnace, when the middes were alone within the tent, lounging on a pile of skins, "that is another of your mysteries. I have never seen it."

"It need be no mystery to you," returned Will; "when we have pecked I will take you over. We call it sometimes Honour Dock, but just as often Honour Bay—it doesn't matter which."

"Now, den," shouted Jack outside, "are you comin' dem dishes for the officers?" I make you move d'rectly."

A nigger, bearing a silver dish of stewed prickly pears, came into the tent with a jerk, leaving the middies to infer that he had received a little assistance outside. And in this way about a dozen appeared in succession, all rolling their eyes until nothing but the whites were visible. Then Jack entered.

"All ready, genelmen," he said.

"Take a seat, Jack; you must be hungry too."

"Tank you, I will. Now, you niggers, cl'ar out; what you stop here for?"

They disappeared with the celerity of black spirits, and the three companions devoted the next quarter of an hour to the consumption of the fruit and meat before them.

The middies then left Jack to his various duties connected with the stockade, and walked out of the enclosure.

"We can get to the bay by land," said Will, "it is not more than half an hour's stretch for us. What do you say?"

"Land by all means—if the path is clear."

"It is, Tom, to those who know it."

"By the way, Will, I wonder where the captain is."

"He's gone on something very important. I never knew him to leave Jack behind until now. I have been, and you too, but that was not often."

"I should like to see his face," mused Tom.

"Don't you be an idiot. Upon my word," exclaimed Will, indignantly, "you're as curious as a girl."

"It's all very well for you, Will, but you know him."

"And knowing him, Tom, I warn you not to be an ass. Look! there's a beautiful snake."

They halted to watch a green serpent, of a species unknown to them, slowly winding its way up the trunk of a palm. It had evidently been startled by the boys' arrival, as it more than once turned its head towards them and hissed. Finally it crawled into the feathery foliage of the tree, and nestled there.

"Very pretty," Will remarked, "but I like them best at a distance. Let me see—I have lost my way. No, here's the mark; do you see it, Tim?"

"I can't say I see anything out of the usual way."

"The broad arrow by the root of the tree."

"Oh! it's plain enough."

"Now it's shown you," returned Will; "but it's safe enough with white strangers; they seldom look beneath their noses; from the blacks we have nothing to fear."

"I suppose there is something in that."

"Everything, Tom. Look between those two trees. What do you see?"

"A sheet of water—blue enough to be salt."

"It is salt. What do you see beyond?"

"A long huge mass of rocks."

"That's Honour Bay. Come into the open. Look to the left first, Tom: those rocks are in the sea, stretching from two points of land, and, as you may imagine, it makes this sheet of water, half-a-mile across, a lake. It has but one outlet—there, do you see it?"

"Yes, but not to seaward."

"No, it runs into the river. Now, turn to the right: steady—what do you think of that?"

"Jemini!" cried Tom, "how on earth came all those vessels here?"

"Prizes of the captain's, Tom—nine in all. There are two French privateers, four Spaniards of various sizes, and three slavers. The one we have outside will be the fourth of the class. There's our friend the 'Don Pedro.'"

"I see her; but why, Will, are they stowed here?"

"Curious again, old boy?" rejoined Will, with a smile; "but you must remain so for the present."

"Who on earth would suspect there being here?"

"That's just it, Tom,—nobody! In the first place, the river would be passed unheeded or ignored by half the navigators: and secondly, the passage to this bay is almost hidden, even to those in the river, and yon tall rocks prevent the vessels being seen from the seaward, and so they lie snug enough until they are wanted."

"I can't make it out," said Tom, thoughtfully; "it is the strangest thing I ever heard of. Is the captain going to start an entire fleet to capture the world—or what is it? Can't you tell me just a leetle bit, Will?"

"Nothing more than wait and see."

"There seems to be a lot of fellows on board."

"Each craft has a few hands to keep her in order—nothing more. Now, back we go, Tom; and be grateful for your peep at Honour Bay."

CHAPTER X.

CRIKEY'S GOOD NAME.

BOOM! the sound of a gun to seaward startled the lads, they both listened intently.

Boom! another came, ere the echoes of the first had died away.

"The captain!" cried Will; "Let us skurry back. Now, Tom, buckle too!"

They threaded the mazes of the wood at a sharp trot, reaching the stockade out of breath, panting like a couple of dogs after a severe chase.

They met Monkey Jack, bareheaded, and rushing to and fro in a state of wild excitement, yelling and shouting, after a dozen flying niggers.

"Now, Jack, what's the matter?" demanded Will.

"Oh! Massa Steadfast," cried Jack, with tears in his eyes; "Here's doleful job! Massa capen come back, and he signal for me and dem niggers to go on board, but I can't go. Oh! Massa Steadfast, here am a doleful job!"

"Why can't you go, Jack?"

"Acause," screamed Jack, dancing to and fro, "some teif steal my cocked hat! Oh! wurra, wurra; here am a job!"

"Go without it, Jack," suggested Tom Furnace.

"And show up afore ole Duncan like common nigger?" rejoined the darkey, "No, Massa Furnace, I no do dat: die fust!"

Just then Crikey came sauntering by, with an impudent grin on his face. Jack saw the expression, and, interpreting it, sprang upon his brother.

"You gib me my hat," he cried, "or I make crow meat ob you!"

"What dat you talk about, a hat?" returned Crikey, wriggling out of his grasp; I never wear hat in my life."

"But, you tief, you tole mine!"

"Dat am one big lie! Me tole your hat? Oh, Jack, you kick your brodder, den take him good name!"

Crikey pretended to shed tears, but he could not quite conceal the grinning expression of his lips. Neither of the middies said a word.

"I gib you warnin', Crikey," said Jack, "dat I hab my hat, or I down upon you like a load ob beef. Dere's the cap'en ag'in," he added, as another gun resounded. "My hat, you confusitate willan; I command you to gib him up!"

"I repudlehate your orflority," replied Crikey, with intense scorn, "eber since you kick me orf de tub where I stand up and tell dem niggers to lub de cap'en for eber."

"But you won't repudiate my authority will you, Crikey?" asked Will.

"Dat berry different ting, Massa Steadfast. I do what you want, quick as lightning."

"Then bring Jack's hat immediately."

"I will, Massa Steadfast," replied Crikey. "Who want his ole hat? It on'y fit to bile de kettle wif. I bring him at once."

Raising a large stone lying near the tent, he brought forth that article of attire, crushed flat, as if it had been passed a score times through a patent mangle. Advancing with defiant strides, he threw it at his brother's feet.

"You be tankful," he said, "dat Massa Steadfast speak for you, or you would hab no cock hat for a moon—p'raps two moon."

Jack made no reply, but occupied himself by attempting to restore his pet chapeau to its original form. Having got it into something like its old shape, he with the middies hurried down to the creek, where the large canoe with a dozen negroes awaited them.

"Crikey my brodder," said Jack, as he took his seat, "if not—if not I put him under dat same stone and make flounder ob him."

Will winked at his brother mid, and bade the negroes give way. Urged onward by their swift paddles it quickly reached the mouth of the stream where the "Crucible" lay with its captain impatiently awaiting their coming.

CHAPTER XI.

NEWS OF THE "CURLEW."—A FRESH PIRATE AFLOAT.

"WHAT has detained you, Mr. Steadfast?" asked the young privateer, who stood in the gangway.

"I was down at Honour Dock, sir," replied Will, as he leaped on board. He wisely abstained from relating the cocked hat incident, as it might have got Jack into trouble.

"Come below, I want to see you alone. Mr. Stanchion!"

"Here, sir," cried the lieutenant, coming forward.

"Run in with the tide and put everything square for the night. I shall sleep on board. When you are ready come below to my cabin."

"Very good, sir."

"Now, Mr. Steadfast," said the captain, "I am at your service."

When they arrived below the captain carefully closed and barred the door. Then he sat down, and removing his mask, revealed a handsome face beaming with exultation.

"Will," he cried, seizing the boy by the hand, "I have news for you."

"Good?"

"Ay! my dear friend, I could not wish better. The story is short, listen. In his Majesty's service there is a certain vessel of war, the frigate 'Curlew.'"

"I've heard of it," rejoined Will, with twinkling eyes.

"It has a captain named Harloch, who has a daughter, and for some months past she has been on board."

"Ay, ay, sir," said Will, as the captain paused.

"This girl," pursued the young privateer, "I have heard is fair, and in consequence she has lovers; one was—no matter what, he is not near her, the other is a villain."

"Three weeks ago," he continued, "the 'Curlew' captured a pirate, and, imprisoning the crew below, a number of men with this villain lover were sent on board to take

her to Kingston. Scarcely had he taken command, when the captain learned that the scoundrel had that day grievously insulted his daughter."

"The double-dyed villain," ejaculated Will.

"Captain Harloch signalled the pirate to bring to," the young privateer went on, "and went on board. The dusk of the evening was falling at the time, and what transpired could not be seen from the deck of the 'Curlew.' I thank Heaven it could not."

"He did not—not kill the captain?"

"No, Will, but high words ensued, and he struck his superior officer. The captain would have cried for help, but the scoundrel stopped his cries and bound him fast for a few minutes. His next step was to release the pirates, with whom it is presumed he had been communicating, and then, setting Captain Harloch free, he bade him return to his ship.

"There was nothing else to be done, the pirates outnumbered them ten to one, and this traitor declared that a single shot from one of the men would ensure the death of all. For the sake of his men Captain Harloch consented to retire peaceably, and he left the accursed ship."

"But could he not signal to the 'Curlew?'"

"No; it was growing dark, and the clouds were gathering in the sky, A part of the 'Curlew's' crew, put on board the pirate, were also disaffected, and joined the traitor. The rest were crowded into the captain's cutter and returned with him."

"Surely he might have struck a blow?" said Will.

"Captain Harloch thought he could reach the frigate in time to punish the traitor with good round shot; it was the wisest plan, for they must have been slaughtered had they resisted."

"I see—the situation was awkward."

"As soon as the cutter was pushed off, the pirate made all sail, but the frigate remained lying to for its captain. By the time it was possible to make those on board understand the true state of affairs, it was dark, and the pirate being a swift sailer, far away. The 'Curlew' followed, but quickly lost her; and in the morning the sea was clear—not a glimpse of the vile craft could be seen."

"Oh, Will," continued the young privateer, "Heaven pardon me for calling this good news, but think of the main issue of

"DAT YOU JACKY?" CRIED CRIKEY, APPEARING FROM A HOLE IN THE MIDST OF THE CARGO.

it—Mason Wantlake is a pirate on the high seas, a felon and a traitor to his country."

"Has he been found?"

"No, no, Will, that task is mine. I that have hunted other murderers and villains will now hunt him, heart and soul; tomorrow we will away with a strong crew, and well provisioned for many months at sea; and when I capture this last monster, my task is done."

The light in his eyes showed the fire in the soul of the young privateer, and found a reflection in those of Will Steadfast.

"A speedy capture of the scoundrel, say I," he shouted.

"And captured he must be, not slain," replied the captain, replacing his mask. "I think I hear Mr. Stanchion's step—admit him, Will."

Will obeyed, and the first lieutenant entered. As the business on hand was of a dry technical nature about charts and so on, the middy intimated his desire to go on deck, and received an affirmative nod in reply.

There he found Tom Furnace ablaze with curiosity, burning to know what was in store for them. The 'Crucible' had been brought into the river, and boats were plying to and fro with provisions, heaps of it lying on deck preparatory to being stowed away.

"The news, Will—the news if you love e !" was Tom's first exclamation.

"More fighting, my boy."

"Where ?"

"Uncertain yet. We are going to hunt one of the darkest scoundrels on the face of the earth."

"Hope dat not me," interposed a doleful voice, and they became conscious of the presence of the delinquent, Crikey. Tears were in his eyes, his woolly hair seemed limp, and his whole appearance most dolorous.

"It certainly is not you," replied the lad, "what put such a thing into your head ?"

"I'm most outragelrous scoundrel on two legs," said Crikey, wiping his eyes, "I hide Jack's hat and make him sabbage."

"It was very wrong," rejoined Tom.

"A criminal offence in the eye of the law," added Will, "now what form will your repentance take ?"

"Me no understan', massa."

"Do you wish to make it up with Jack?"

"I do, Massa Steadfast, most surfanly —me downright blessed miserable."

"I'll see what I can do, Crikey, there's Jack in the forecastle, go to him."

"He berry soon smash me."

"Nonsense. Jack !"

"Yes, Massa Steadfast."

"Come here."

Crikey stowed himself away behind one of the guns aft as Jack walked up, unconscious of the presence of his unnatural brother.

"Now Jack," said Will, "do you know what is the first principle of a good man ?"

"No, Massa Will, can't say I do; it not anyting to eat ?"

"Not by any means—every good man should forgive his enemies."

"Den me no right to pitch inter de pirates an' Frenchmen, Massa Steadfast."

"Oh ! yes we have; they are the enemies of our country, Jack, not our own."

"Dat am a difference, but not much."

"But there is a difference, Jack, and you must act upon it, you must forgive your brother."

"Forgib Crikey ! arter him bury my hat ? No, Massa Will, don't ax me dat; I scrunch him, I hab him sent away from de stockade."

Crikey trembled in his hiding place ; listening keenly, however, to the further pleadings of his advocate.

"You must overlook it, Jack ; the poor fellow is very miserable and very sorry."

"If him sorry let him say so, and al ober it am."

"He is here to do it. Come forward Crikey."

The dark hat-destroyer crawled out o his hiding place, looking rather slily at his dignified brother, as he said—

"Me berry sorry, Jack, dat I mean enuf to hide dat hat, but if it be berry dirty I wash it for you."

The middies turned away, stifling their inclination to laugh. In a few minutes the brothers followed them, and declared that all differences were settled.

But they did not say that it had been arranged between them that Crikey was to go the next voyage, that is, start with them on the morrow.

"Better not," said Jack, "de men say one nigger enuf, ole Duncan ses it too much. P'raps de young genelmen tink so to. Me hide you until a day out, den I come and let you out."

This was the programme, and accordingly, during the bustle on board, Jack stowed Crikey away in the hold with a few biscuits and a bottle of water, where he was destined, as our readers will see, to cause a slight sensation.

Stern earnest work was evidently in store, for a large quantity of ammunition from a hidden depot on land was stowed away, and throughout the night the negroes laboured hard, their chattering never ceasing during the long dark hours.

Monkey Jack never thought of rest, but bustled about among his countrymen, urging them to increase their efforts, and to lose no time.

"'Member," he said, "we go out to fightin' an' hard work, while you niggers lay under the mangrobe and palm-tree, countin' your toes, an' snorin' like pigs. So cut about, and bring up de food for de fightin' men. Wurra dere, Pompey, you run ag'in' me once more wid a bunch ob greens, and I bait a shark-hook wid your carcus. De debil in some nigger I tink. Dey run again' genelman as if he am common dirt."

This was the general style of address kept up without ceasing until the sun arose, when all that they needed was aboard, and in a great measure stowed away.

Mr. Stanchion appeared early on deck, and the masked captain quickly followed. They went round together examining the guns, and conversing in a low tone.

"A larger vessel would be more suitable, perhaps," said the captain, as they halted aft, by the wheel: "but the pirate has not only to be sought, but we have other things to avoid. Ships generally sail—the 'Crucible' flies."

"Well, sir," replied the lieutenant, "your judgment is always the best."

"Except in downright seamanship," returned the captain, "and for that I have a lieutenant worth half his Majesty's navy. You could sail blindfold over the seas."

"Much obliged for your good opinion, sir," rejoined Mr. Stanchion. "Shall we weigh?"

"At once. I perceive your ready eye has marked a welcome breeze springing up from the south. Get her out, then join me at breakfast."

The anchor was hoisted, the white sails spread, and the Crucible set out upon a long voyage of wondrous daring and adventure.

CHAPTER XII.

ANOTHER ENCOUNTER WITH THE SHARKS OF THE OCEAN.—A FIGHT IN A FOG.

THE young privateer kept the source of his information a secret, but it was evidently of a reliable nature, for he kept on a steady north-east course, bearing towards the mighty Gambia during the first day and night.

This time was a busy time for the men, for there was much to do on board in righting the ship, and thus it happened that nothing of an unfriendly nature transpired between Duncan, the carpenter, and Monkey Jack, these worthies having respective and absorbing duties to perform.

On the morning of the second day, just as the sun fairly arose above the restless waves, a sail was sighted, and the news being conveyed to the young privateer, he came instantly on deck, the ever ready Monkey Jack following him half a dozen seconds later.

Mr. Stanchion was standing forward, watching the stranger through a glass.

Will Steadfast stood near him anxious for his report.

"What is she like, Mr. Stanchion?" asked the captain.

"Rather suspicious, sir," replied the lieutenant; "too low in the hull and rakish in her rigging to be honest. She is bearing down upon us."

The masked captain took the glass tendered him, and gazed steadily at the approaching craft.

A brisk breeze was blowing, and the vessels rapidly neared each other.

In five minutes the young privateer closed the glass with an air of satisfaction.

"A shark," he said; "may be the one we seek, crowd on all sail, and bear down upon her. Clear the decks for action, but conceal your movements as far as possible, our old tactics, Mr. Stanchion."

"Very good, sir."

The first lieutenant immediately proceeded to carry out his orders, and the men, among whom the intelligence of a promised fight spread with electrical velocity, tumbled over each other as they clambered on deck in their haste to reach their posts."

Monkey Jack, who plumed himself upon his nautical knowledge, at once expressed his opinion of the enemy to Will Steadfast :—

"Dat's a pirate," he said, "sure as my brodder Crikey—is—oh, golly—as sure as him is my brodder—but he is de ass ob pirates, for he takes us for quiet merchant ship, with lots ob grog an' ladies on board."

"He may have done so," rejoined Will, who was still watching the craft, "but he has found out his mistake, and is sheering off until he makes certain of our strength."

The young privateer had also perceived the movement, and ordered the "Crucible" to be brought dead before the wind, and away went the lively little vessel, cleaving the ocean as if the water was no more than air, bearing in a line across the bows of the stranger.

The two ships were now sufficiently near to make out each other's colours by the aid of glasses, and the dreaded skull and crossbones was distinctly perceived at the masthead of the stranger. The "Crucible," which had hitherto borne nothing but a plain piece of blue bunting, ran up her gold-lettered banner with its motto "For Honour we Fight!" and a hearty cheer from the crew rolled over the ocean.

The pirate, having apparently satisfied himself of the mistake he had made, brought his vessel round and beat a retreat, showing that part of his craft proverbially associated with a "long chase."

"A swift vessel that, sir," said the lieutenant.

"And well-manned," returned the young privateer ; "he is giving us a stern chase, but I doubt his capability of showing us a clean pair of heels."

Pursuer and pursued kept on their way for some two hours, and to an inexperienced eye the "Crucible" would not have appeared to have gained an inch, but the old salts on board knew better, and Grim Foote gave a decided opinion as to the time they would overhaul the chase.

"If the breeze lasts," he said, "we shall be alongside afore mid-day grog sarving, but that I'm doubtful on ; there's a calm for'ard somewhere, or I'm a Dutchman."

Duncan, the carpenter, who was one of his auditors, asked him how he knew or guessed at such a thing.

"By 'sperience, lad," returned Grim Foote ; "I ain't in a persition to tell you how I know, for the signs are too cur'ous for me to put into words ; but to a man as knows 'em, they're in the sky, and upon the salt water."

"I can't see anything," said Duncan.

"Who de debil 'spect you to do it ?" broke in a hated voice, that of Jack. "What de wedder to do wid you ? You de wood-cutter ob de ship—dat's all."

"I'm not a cussed nigger," growled Duncan.

"No ! dat's what you wish yourself," replied Jack, drawing himself up ; "but dere ain't a nigger tribe in de ole ob Africa as wouldn't blush to hab such a scarecrow among dem, Dere ain't a flannibal tribe dat would scondlercend to pick your bones."

During this delivery, Monkey Jack gradually elevated his voice, and the conclusion was at the highest pitch expressive of contempt and indignation. The young privateer whispered a few words in the ear of Mr. Stanchion.

"Silence—forward !" shouted the lieutenant.

This command checked the reply of the angered Duncan, who disappeared down the hatchway, muttering anathemas against the whole of the dark descendants of Ham.

Monkey Jack, recalled to himself, resumed his post beside his captain, with his hat fiercely cocked in defiance of Duncan and every foe.

The prophecy of Grim Foote, the boatswain, was realised within two hours of the time of utterance ; the pirate was the first

to lose the breeze, and the "Crucib[le] rapidly overhauled her until within a m[ ] when she, too, lay still in the midst of calm.

With a bitter heart the young privat[e] paced the deck for a few moments in silen[ce]

He believed that the man he sought w[as] on board the ill-looking vessel, lying bu[t a] short distance away, but he saw that [to] attempt to conquer her by boarding wo[uld] be almost madness, for her decks we[re] literally alive with men.

He had resolved to fight her with l[ ] guns, but as the vessels lay he could bri[ng] none to bear upon her with effect, and t[he] delay might last until night, with that breeze and escape.

He summoned his trusty lieutenant [to] his side, and said—

"That craft, Mr. Stanchion, must n[ot] escape, but I am loth to risk the lives [of] my good men without a fair chance of vi[c]tory. But I must have her."

"We must wait for a breeze, sir."

"Wait, wait," impatiently exclaimed t[he] captain, "do you know, Mr. Stanchio[n] "what it is to suffer a great wrong, to b[e] an outcast from all you hold dear, and wi[th] the means of redemption almost withi[n] your grasp, to know that it may slip awa[y] perhaps for ever ?"

I have suffered," returned the lie[u]tenant, quietly, "although I've almost ou[t]grown it ; sorrow and trouble brought m[y] first grey hairs."

"Did you ever long for revenge ?"

"I did so for years, sir, and was disap[ ]pointed in the end."

"Look yonder, then," said the maske[d] captain, pointing to the pirate craft, "o[n] that vessel stands, I believe, my cruel, re[ ]morseless foe. He has outraged all man[ly] feelings, he has outraged his country's laws, and he who has suffered by him and hi[s] country alike cry out for the capture o[f] the villain."

"You may be wrong after all."

"True, but I must lose no chance ; whe[n] that fatal flag is raised in our sight it mus[t] not be allowed to flaunt in the breeze again No, Mr. Stanchion, at any risk I will board her."

"Give me the task, sir," said the lieu[ ]tenant, warmly.

"No, Stanchion, no ; I would have n[o] other hand than mine secure the knav[e] Call the men aft."

The crew were called, and came, forming a semi-circle round the two officers.

"My men," said the captain, in a clear ringing voice, "I intend to cut out yon skulking scoundrel; it is a work of great danger, even success means a great loss for us, failure a total annihilation. Who volunteers?"

There was an immediate rush of the whole crew, petty officers, and middies, all prepared and anxious to fight for their heroic leader.

"I am gratified by this proof of your devotion," he said, gently; "but I cannot take all, nor will I favour any, choose half of you to go with me."

They retired to draw lots, all but the middies, who had no occasion to do so, and Grim Foote, the old boatswain, who remained in foot of his captain, bowing and pulling his forelock.

"What is it, Foote?" asked the privateer.

"Axing your pardon for a liberty, sir," rejoined the boatswain; "but may I give 'pinion on this little matter?"

"The cutting out?"

"Yes, sir. If we goes now we shall be riddled long afore we touch her sides, not s I or any man aboard is afeerd on it, but if a man can do the same work, without losin' his life the work is jest as good, and all the better for the men."

"Certainly; what do you propose?"

"You see, sir, the calm will last all night, that I'll bet my life on, and there'll be a fog airly in the mornin', I'm ekally sartain o' that, sech bein' the case, we might creep up just afore sun-rise and drop upon 'em unawares. It's only my 'pinion, captain, and I axes pardon for givin' it."

The captain's spirit chafed at the thought of delay, but he abhorred a useless sacrifice of men; and having a strong faith in the boatswain's weather-gazing powers, he, after a brief conference with Mr. Stanchon, decided upon pursuing the course advocated.

So, they lay quiet throughout the day, watching the enemy, who returned the compliment, and fired blank guns as signals of defiance.

"All in good time," muttered the privateer, "your guns will sing a different song to-morrow."

Shortly after midnight a fog, as predicted by Grim Foote, settled upon the sea, at first floating lazily about, but accumulating fast, all objects a few yards distant became obscured.

The boats of the "Crucible" were then lowered, and the chosen crews took up their stations. The rowlocks were muffled, and each boat was tethered to another bow and stern, so that none might go astray.

The captain, in the long-boat, headed the whole, and away they went in ghostly procession towards the spot where they hoped to find the pirate.

The young privateer carried a dark lantern, which he occasionally flashed as a guide to the boats in the rear. Will Steadfast sat by his side, with the rudder lines. Monkey Jack lay coiled up at his feet, with a mighty naked cutlass in his hand.

The men pulled for half an hour, and then, in obedience to a signal, all lay upon their oars. The privateer listened intently. From the left came a hum of voices, and the trampling of busy feet upon a vessel's deck.

Now, certain of his course, the masked captain steered the long-boat, bearing round towards the point from whence the sounds arose.

In a few minutes the hull of the pirate cruiser loomed faintly before them, invisible to all but the keen eyes of an experienced sailor.

Again the lantern flashed, and the boats, five in all, drew up alongside—creeping slowly towards the doomed vessel.

They touched the larboard side almost simultaneously and immediately a cry of alarm arose from the deck, and the execrations of men awoke the stillness of the night.

The masked captain mounted the ship's side, cheering on his men. Several heavy guns of the pirate were fired in wild alarm, and a shower of shot and bullets rained upon the still water. Five of the "Crucible" men were blown to atoms, the rest reached the deck in safety, favoured by the mist.

A scene of fierce courage and wild ferocity ensued, the pirates mustered strongly, and fought desperately, but as the young privateer plied his deadly weapon, a finely-tempered blade, which pierced a man as if he were made of paper, he thought that their numbers were few in comparison to what he had anticipated.

It was not easy to judge, however, for no man could distinguish friend from foe except by their voices; and the "Crucible's" men wisely kept up a succession of cheers such as only the British throats can give.

The pirates threw up rockets, but they disappeared without giving more than a momentary flash, and the sound of their rising was lost in the clash of weapons employed in the deadly conflict.

Hot blood ran upon the decks, and Will Steadfast slipped and fell, the next moment a pirate fell upon him with his breast gashed by the masked captain's sword. The man was dead, but he lay heavy upon the breathless lad; the life-giving fluid poured out, giving Will a bath of blood.

A deadly, sickly sensation came over him, and overpowered by the weight of the ruffian's corse, and the horror of his position, he fainted.

During the first part of the encounter, the pirates held their ground, but as their numbers thinned, their hearts sank, and they retreated towards the after deck, where further confusion awaited them.

A body of their comrades held in reserve, mistaking them for the attacking party, fired into them and rushed into their midst with the utmost fury. In vain the unhappy wretches shrieked and implored; blinded by the smoke and mist, and maddened by the uncertainty of their position, the pirates cut down their comrades like sheep.

English arms and weapons did the rest; they were driven back step by step, until they reached the hatchway, down which many fell and lay in a helpless heap below.

Mercy to such wretches would have been without avail; pistols were fired upon them by the men of the "Crucible" until the wretches were fairly riddled, and lay clustered together in the agonies of death.

Still there was fighting going on—a few of the pirates cut and slashed in the mist utterly regardless of friend or foe, and only intent upon their own worthless lives. One by one, they were slain, and as the last rolled upon the deck, the mist slowly uprose, and revealed the rising sun in all its glory.

The crimson-tinted sea was outdone by the gory deck, where lay a hundred men with gaping wounds, in pools of blood. Eleven of the "Crucible" men lay dead, as many wounded, and two missing, supposed to have fallen through the portholes during the struggle, for they were never seen or heard of more.

Close by one of the guns stood the masked captain, with his faithful attendant, Jack—both in a state of exhaustion from their recent efforts.

"All's ober," said Jack, "de ship is won, massa cap'en."

"Not over," hoarsely rejoined his leader, "find me the captain of this craft—dead or alive."

A wounded pirate lay near, with a broken arm doubled under his body. He heard the remark of the privateer, and, despite his agony, smiled.

"You will not find him, my friend," he said.

The youthful hero turned upon him quickly, and asked what he meant.

"He is not aboard," replied the fellow.

"Has he fled from my sword?" demanded the privateer, scornfully.

"Nothing of the sort," replied the pirate, shuckling, "exchange is no robbery. He's gone to cut out your craft."

An exclamation of surprise sprang from the masked hero's lips, and acting upon the first impulse he gave the man the lie.

"You deceive me, dog; the villain skulks."

"Is that skulking?" cried the man, exultingly, as the noise of combat fell upon their ears." "No, it's tit for tat. I care not now, we are amply avenged."

He turned slightly over, and with a grim smile upon his face breathed his last.

Forgetting his private wrongs, the captain turned all his thoughts to the "Crucible."

The mist still enshrouded the gallant little craft, but it was fast clearing, and the news having been circulated among the surviving men, they crowded forward, awaiting the curtain of fog to rise.

They could hear the shots, and by-and-by, a gun belched forth its flame, the mist uprose, and the whole scene lay before the anxious spectators.

The pirate boats, four in number, very heavily manned, were gathered round the bows of the vessel, and the men climbing like cats up her sides, but only to be hurled back into their boats, writhing in mortal pain.

One tall figure was prominent above the rest; thrice it led the way, and was thrown back upon the men behind, to rise again unwounded and with renewed vigour.

Suddenly several men were seen to rise upon the bulwarks of the "Crucible," and hurl something into the boats below. Two immediately sank.

"Hurrah!" shouted one of the spectators; "they are staving the boats with round shot."

"But why do we idle here?" cried the captain; "follow me, my men. Jack, you here, and Will. Where is Mr. Steadfast?"

"All over with him, sir," returned one the men; "he's lyin' under a piratical chap—there, sir."

Jack rushed forward, and cleared the lad of his encumberance. He was pale and cold, and apparently lifeless.

"I leave him in your charge," said the captain, with a sigh. "Poor Will! Look to him Jack; time is precious—I must get back to the 'Crucible.'"

He gently pressed the boy's hand, and sprang into a boat alongside; half of the men imitated his example; the rest he commanded to remain in charge of the pirate.

Ere the captain reached his ship the contest was over, and the pirates defeated. Mr. Stanchion, begrimed with smoke and bespattered with blood, welcomed his leader back.

"They made a mistake," he said, "when they hoped to surprise the 'Crucible.' I was prepared for them."

"But the captain?" exclaimed the young privateer.

"A tall young fellow, I think, was the man," returned the lieutenant. "Where is he?"

"Cut and run, sir," interposed Grim Foote; "while we were a hollerin' about victory, he sneaked round the starn, and made a bolt of it."

He pointed to a small boat in the distance, pulled by half-a-dozen men, and a tall fellow standing in the stern sheets steering.

"A glass," cried the captain, hastily.

One was given him, a brief glance sufficed, and dashing the instrument upon the deck, he paced to and fro, overcome with anger and vexation.

"'Tis he," he muttered, "and I away on a fool's errand. Oh! would I had been here. Mr. Stanchion, can we not follow?"

"In what, sir?" asked the lieutenant; "there is not a cat's-paw of air, not enough to move a feather, and every man is pumped out. I will man a boat if you wish it."

"No, it would be folly," returned the other; "long before we could reach the knave, he will be safe in one of the hiding-places along the coast."

"You are right, sir."

"Have the ship cleared," concluded the captain; "serve out a double allowance of grog to all. See that the wounded are well cared for, and bring me a list of the dead."

The first act of the lieutenant was to signal those on board the pirate to tow her alongside, and this being done, all the wounded, friends and foes, were put on board the "Crucible," among them, Will Steadfast, who had been unconsciously wounded during the scuffle, but not dangerously.

The loss of blood and the crushing weight of the huge pirate had, however, weakened him so much, that he was fairly entitled to be placed upon the sick list, which was done, with two nurses, Jack and Tom Furnace, to minister to his wants.

CHAPTER XIII.
DUNCAN FINDS HIS TROUBLES INCREASED.—A DISCOVERY.

IN the course of the day a fair wind sprang up from the south, and the "Crucible" followed upon the track of the boat in which the pirate captain had escaped. The pirate, with a few hands on board, was dispatched to Honour Bay, with instructions to sink or run her ashore if attacked by any of the proas known to infest the coast.

Fifteen men were struck off the "Crucible's" roll, and buried with fitting ceremony beneath the blue waves. This done, the good ship resumed its old appearance, the decks cleared of all signs of disaster, and its willing crew as light-hearted as before.

This was not because they were callous, a sailor's life gives but little time to mourn; he who is slain leaves a vacancy in his mess, and nothing more, the stern duties of their daily lives demand all the energies and thoughts of those he has left behind.

Will progressed fairly, and on the following day he was brought on deck, and laid beneath an awning. While dozing there, he became a listener, at first an indifferent one, but afterwards an amused one, of a confidential communication made to Grim Foote by Duncan, the foe of Monkey Jack.

"Have you had much acquaintance with niggers, Mr. Foote?" asked the carpenter.

"Wal," replied the boatswain, "considerin' I've lived among them in the swamps, I may say I have."

"And how have you found them?"

"Found 'em?—black enough wherever I've been," was the reply.

"That isn't what I mean. Haven't you found 'em cruel and treacherous?"

"Can't say I have; no more nor white uns."

"Ah! then you don't know 'em," returned the carpenter, drawing closer; "they can't be trusted."

"Well, we don't trust 'em here," gruffly rejoined the boatswain. "What are you drivin' at?"

"Monkey Jack," replied the carpenter, "that's what I'm drivin' at."

"He'll drive you," said Grim Foote, with a grin, "if you ses much to him."

"Ah! he's a bad un," sighed Duncan, hypocritically; "he's up to somethin'."

"Out with it."

"He's goin' down into the hold about every three hours. Ah! he's up to no good."

"In the hold," exclaimed the puzzled boatswain; "wal, he sartainly ain't no business there."

"I want to make sure afore I blows on him," said Duncan; "but I think he means to fire the 'Crucible.'"

"Fire the —— pooh!" returned Grim Foote; "don't talk like a ass."

"I'll watch him to-night, and give in my report," replied the carpenter; "not a word till then."

"I'm mum."

They each went their way, leaving their youthful listener to follow out a train of thought broken by the appearance of the dark individual in question, who came up to inquire after his patient.

"Gettin' berrer, Massa Will?"

"First rate, Jack," replied the lad. "I say, old fellow, how you smell of the hold."

"Smell ob what, Massa Will?"

"The hold."

"Dat am a joke, Massa Will; p'raps you smell ob de deck—yah! golly—had you dere!"

"Had me where, Jack? don't be stupid, but tell me why you are so often in the hold."

"Trufe," said Jack, with a virtuous air, "am always de best. I got Crikey dere among de bales, and tings, and he eat as much as big-jawed pelican, and drink as much as de blubber whale."

Will was amused with this piece of intelligence, but being pressed he promised to keep it a secret for the present, at the same time forbearing to inform the nigger of the discovery Duncan had made, as he anticipated some fun would arise therefrom.

At dusk, Jack with his pockets we[ll] laden with eatables, stole softly below, un[con]conscious of the near presence of his enem[y] the vituperated Duncan, who, with a lan[tern] wrapped up in a pea jacket, followe[d] closely at his heels.

"I'll have him now," muttered the worthy, "once find out his game, and i[f] it's anything serus, there'll be somethin[g] hanging at the yard-arm."

The latter words he unconsciously ut[tered] tered half aloud. Monkey Jack halted i[n] the darkness and called aloud:

"Anybody dere?"

No reply, but Duncan breathed shor[t] and quick. The quick ears of the negr[o] heard this also, and he muttered to him[self] self:

"Some ob de company following m[e] p'raps ole Duncan, now I sell him."

Jack reached the hold, dropped upo[n] his hands and knees, crawled behind som[e] barrels and bales, and there lay quiet.

Duncan was close behind, but the silenc[e] threw him off the track, and he stood fo[r] some minutes in doubt.

"Confound the fool," he though[t] "where's he got to? I can't see an inc[h] before me, and I don't hear him."

A voice broke in upon his meditation[s] an unnatural, half-smothered bellowing o[n] his left, probably meant for singing:—

Crikey am de chap dey lub,
Dey smile upon him sweet,
And ebery one cry, yah, yah, yup,
As him goin down de street.

"He's got away under the cargo," though[t] Duncan; "I can have a light now."

Throwing off the pea jacket, he held th[e] lantern aloft; naught but the various bale[s] and barrels in the hold were visible.

"Let me see," murmured Duncan; "th[e] voice come from there—no it didn't—an[d] yet—dashed if I know where!"

Once more the musical bellowings brok[e] in upon his meditation:—

If you wished to lib a happy man,
And hab a pleasant life,
Just gib a good ten feet clar
To poor ole Crikey's wife.
She lubs to trow de crockery
And break up all him pans,
And den de broken pieces shy
At him, or any oder mans.

"The brute's got among the bales[,]" muttered Duncan, "to drink hisself blin[d] and howl hisself mad—Hark! there—"

"Dat you, Jacky," cried Crikey, a[p]pearing suddenly from a hole in the mid[st] of the cargo—"you berry late, ole ma[n] dis evening."

"Who the deuce are you?" demanded Duncan, staggered by the appearance of the naked nigger.

"Dat what I ax you?" rejoined Crikey, who, dazzled by the light of the lamp, could not make out his interlocutor.

"What are you doing there, you black imp—who are you?" roared Duncan.

"Dat's my brodder," said Jack, rising from his hiding-place, "you call him imp again, you farnal ole figger-head. Crikey —come out to your brodder."

Crikey obeyed with alacrity, leaping into the gangway with the agility of a monkey.

"Take dat lantern from him, Crikey."

It was snatched in a moment from the hands of the stupefied and enraged carpenter.

"Now, Crikey," said Jack, placing himself in the path of retreat, "I'm jis goin' to punish de spy. Look arter my hat and coat, and pick up ole Duncan when him go down flop."

"What—what do you mean?" gasped the alarmed captive.

"Dis," returned Monkey Jack, rolling up his shirt sleeves. "I shall spile your flisiognomy for a month; but I'll fight fair, so stand up, ole Gluepot; it ain't no use hollerin,' for dere's not a man can hear you. Yah! am you ready?"

Crikey stood by, rolling his eyes in a frenzy of delight, until recalled to himself by the voice of his stern brother, who asked him "how he could punch ole Duncan if him wobble de lantern?"

Duncan was not exactly a coward, but he knew the enormous strength of Jack, and, like a prudent man, endeavoured to come to terms.

"Jack," he said, eyeing the brawny arms of the negro, "why should we quarrel— why not be friends?"

"Fren's," repeated Jack, with infinite contempt, "me hab anyting to do wid you —on'y fit to cut up sticks to bile de kettle wid. Crikey, hold up de lantern. Now, ole Duncan, dere's one for to begin wid."

It was also sufficient to finish with, for the wretched carpenter was sent away into the darkness with magical celerity.

"Dat's a good un," said Crikey, with a critical air; "he hab to shift wid one eye for a day—two days."

Although his enemy had disappeared, Monkey Jack kept up his pugilistic attitude, sparring wildly at the empty air, and urging the already defeated Duncan to renew the fray.

"Jes' one little more blow," he urged, "It is no use lay howling dere—what, you no come?—den I come to you."

"Jack," pleaded Duncan, who sat by a barrel with a hand upon his eye, "I ax your pardon,"

"An' Crikey's too, ole Duncan?"

And Crikey's too," repeated the carpenter, "also the whole biling o' niggers under the sun."

"Den I forgib you," rejoined Jack magnanimously. "Dere's on'y one ting more for you to do; you say to de capen that you lub my brodder Crikey so much you stow him on board."

"I'm —— if I do," growled Duncan.

"Den you please stan' up and have a leetle more fight."

"I suppose I must," groaned Duncan. "Let me get out of this place, and I'll say anything you please."

"Take Crikey by de arm, like genelman, den."

With a muttered reverse of a blessing upon the head of his tormentor, Duncan complied.

Jack resumed his hat and coat, and holding the lantern aloft, led the way to the upper deck.

CHAPTER XIV.

DUNCAN INTRODUCES A NEW MESSMATE.—A VAIN SEARCH.—THE LONE MAN OF THE OCEAN.

"GOT Massa Duncan now," thought Jack;" "make him bile ober wid passion. He berry much like to make pumpkin squash ob me."

If Duncan's face was an index of his real feeling, he certainly was in the humour to pound Jack to a pulp, grind him in a mill, or slay him inch by inch, in a manner worthy of the Inquisition, but he wisely held his peace, and followed his leader, leaning upon the arm of the grinning Crikey.

"Now, you jes' halt here one moment," said Jack, stopping at the foot of the companion; "dis am a 'portant sleremony, and must be done reg'lar. Crikey, if your fr'en' Duncan mobe one inch, gib him a blow big enuf to keep up de fam'ly name."

"I knock him troo de ship's side if he on'y wink too much," replied Crikey—"I dance a hornpipe all ober him body—I crack him thick head like egg-shell. Golly! dat's what I do, Jackey."

Jack, assured that he might safely leave his prisoner in charge of his brother, stepped on deck, his broad black face one vast grin of ecstatic delight.

The two middies, Grim Foote, and Mr. Thornley, the surgeon, were conversing to leeward; the masked captain and the lieutenant were together by the binnacle.

Monkey Jack, without perceiving the latter, strutted up to the others, his hat at an angle of forty-five, his arms akimbo, and his dark eyes rolling.

"Gentlemen," Jack began, "you know Massa Duncan allus say him hate cussed nigger—call dem smutty hunks, sons ob Satan, and oder confounded names?"

"His remarks on your race are not, as a rule, very complimentary, I must admit," rejoined Mr. Thornley, with a smile.

"Dey berry rude, massa Thornley," returned Jack, "but he make joke all de while; he lub nigger from de werry bottom ob his heart."

"Mr. Stanchion," whispered the young privateer, with a side glance at Jack, "I think it will be wise to leave our friends to a piece of sport, evidently at hand. It won't do to openly countenance it, and it would be unwise to check it."

"Jack is as good as physic to the men," replied Mr. Stanchion, as they moved away; "and I agree with you, sir, it is well to be blind at times to what stern natures look upon as rank folly."

Monkey Jack heard their steps as they walked aft, and for a moment felt confused at having appeared before his captain with his dignity laid aside; but he quickly resumed his usual style, and remarked:—

"Dere he go—de best an' noblest genelmen in de world, he say to himself, does de eapen. 'My fr'en' Jack,' he ses, 'up to some lark wid old Duncan, an' I leab him to it;' dat what he ses."

"You were saying something about Duncan loving the nigger," hinted Will Steadfast.

"Jes' so, Massa Will an' genelmen. I say ole Duncan lub the nigger, an' I probe it. He not satisfied wid habing dis child on board, but he stow my brodder in de hold, an' dey now below enjoyin' demselves, like two piccaninnies wid a jampot."

"You are joking!" "Nonsense!" "Draw it mild, Jack!" exclaimed his hearers.

"It's all fac'," returned Monkey Jack; "you keep quiet and see. Duncan comin up now to interjuice Crikey to the company. Now, den," he shouted below, "you two lubbing frens', come up, an' show your flisiognomys."

It was a beautiful moonlight night, not a cloud in the sky, and every object around clearly to be seen, when, therefore, the faces of Crikey and Duncan appeared above the hatchway, their expressive countenances stood out distinct and bold.

Crikey's mouth was in a state of alarming expansion, revealing two rows of glistening teeth; Duncan's, on the contrary, was firmly compressed with the corners drawn down, in the shape of a horseshoe.

Both their eyes were rolling, one with delight, the other with rage, anger, and despair.

"Dere's de two chiles," grinned Jack, "lubbing each oder; arm in arm, genelmen—so I tell no lie."

The auditors could not trust themselves to reply, and Jack went on,—

"Now, Duncan, ole boy, jes interjuice that genelman to de officers here."

"I can't and won't, I'm——" began Duncan.

"Crikey," exclaimed Monkey Jack, "hold my hat, an' jest pick up ole Gluepot when I floor him."

"Don't be passionate, Jack," hastily interrupted Duncan, "I'll—yes—I'll do it. This is Mr. Crikey, gentlemen."

"A good fam'ly nigger," added Jack.

"A good family nigger," repeated Duncan.

"An' one I hab scrutinating lub for."

"And one—no I'm——if I can," cried Duncan, goaded to madness. "I won't stand any more of it.

So saying, he dived rapidly below the deck, leaving his audience in a state of high enjoyment.

"Dat a good 'un for de wood-cutter," grinned Monkey Jack, "he shine uncommon small arter dis."

"But Jack," said Will, drawing him aside, "how will the captain take this? he objects to have any negro beyond yourself on board."

"I put him right," returned Jack, confidently, "I see him laughing wid Mr. Stanchion. I go at once."

Jack accordingly walked respectfully up to the young privateer, and touched his hat.

"Well, Jack."

"Massa cap'en, I take a great liberty," returned Jack.

"You generally do," muttered the lieutenant.

"What is it?" asked the privateer.

"I bring my brodder, Crikey, on board."

"That was very wrong," rejoined the captain, gravely; "you know my opinion of negroes in general."

"Always in the way, like monkeys and wild cats," muttered Mr. Stanchion.

"Massa cap'en," replied Jack, with tears in his eyes, "I berry sorry dat I offend you, but I trow Crikey oberboard an' go myself rader dan offend you."

"Well, well, Jack, we'll say nothing more about it," said the masked captain, "send him below, and let him keep there as much as possible. He can help the purser and cook."

Jack immediately returned to the spot where Crikey was standing, and addressed him thus:—

"Crikey, I jes' get inter trouble 'bout bringin' your ole hunk on board; de capen berry angry, but he says you can stop if you keep b'low. You jes' show your ugly head above de hatchway, and I knock it orf."

His brother, having received this parting injunction, hastily retired, and Jack sought his hammock to sleep away the grief aroused by the apparent anger of the young privateer.

We will not dilate upon the sufferings of Duncan, when the story became known to the whole ship's company; suffice it to say that he was rarely seen when off duty, during a week following, and at the end of that period the joke became stale, and he resumed his old place among his messmates.

The "Crucible" meanwhile sailed along the coast in search of some sign of Mason Wantlake, the pirate, but found nothing to reward them for their trouble, and in the end they returned once more to the open ocean.

"Such a scoundrel," said the young privateer, "is sure to find a place of refuge and plenty of friends to set him up again in his nefarious pursuit. We will watch and wait, Stanchion,—watch and wait."

For two months the good vessel sailed northward, halting for awhile by the mouth of the River Senegal, where a slave ship was lying, waiting for a cargo.

As she refused to come out, the boats were sent to take her, but the owner, a desperate man, blew her up ere they could board, and took refuge on shore.

As pursuit was needless, the boats were signalled to return, and the "Crucible" steered towards the Cape Verde Islands, intending to touch at St. Jago.

Three days out the man at the masthead perceived something, apparently an empty barrel, bobbing about on the ocean. Having given notice of it, the captain came on deck with Will Steadfast, and surveyed the black speck lying about six miles away.

"It's a boat," said the captain, "the remnant of some lost vessel. She may carry some perishing wretch, and Heaven forbid we should go on our way indifferent to his fate."

The helm was accordingly put up, and they made for the floating object. It proved to be a boat, as the captain surmised, and in the bottom a man, apparently dead, was lying.

But Mr. Thornley made a rapid examination, and declared that he was living, but suffered much, but with care might be restored.

They bore him to the "Crucible," one of the men mechanically carrying his cap. As he passed the young privateer, he carelessly threw it upon the deck, so that he might assist his comrades in getting the unfortunate man below. The captain raised the cap, and read the letters on it,—

H.M.S. "Curlew."

"Restore that man," he said to the surgeon, who was bringing up the rear of the procession, "then ask a boon, and be it what it may, it is yours."

CHAPTER XV.

THE FATE OF THE "CURLEW."—MASON WANTLAKE'S TRIUMPH.—JACK'S ARRIVAL.

IN two hours Mr. Thornley reported the man in a fair way of recovery, and by the evening he was in a fit state for interrogation. The young privateer requested him to attend at once upon him in the cabin, and dispatched a similar order for the attendance of Will Steadfast.

The man came, a fine strapping fellow, despite his sufferings. He had been warned by the surgeon not to be surprised by the appearance of the captain, and advised to be as ready as possible in his answers.

Will and the privateer were ready to receive him—both masked—Will wearing, in addition to the black velvet covering his face, a jacket similar to that worn by his captain.

"You belong to the 'Curlew?'" asked the privateer.

"Ay, your honour; or p'raps I ought to say I did," replied the man, "for the 'Curlew's' struck out of the log, she will never float again."

"Wrecked or captured?" hastily demanded the interrogator.

"A bit of each, your honour," returned the sailor, "I can spin the yarn if you've the patience to listen, sir. 'Taint a long 'un."

"Go on: be as brief as you can."

"The 'Curlew' was commanded by Captain Harloch," the man began, "and we were cruisin' orf Sierra Leone in sarch o' privateers, when a job happened as caused a little sorrer on board. A mid, one night upon gettin' his stificate, bein' put aboard a prize, fust struck the captain and then got clear away to go into the black trade."

"Slave dealing?"

"No, your honour, the skull and cross-bones. Well, there was sommat more than this that riled Captain Harloch, for he have been uncommon active to be sure in sarch o' that pirate cruiser. Some on us thought that his purty daughter was mixed up in it, but that's as may be, men afore the mast ain't no right to know o' such matters; anyhow, the cap'en were down upon the chap uncommon sharp, and didn't seem to rest day nor night.

"We never overhauled that craft, but five days ago we sighted a black flag flying at the fore of a rakish-looking cruiser skimming like a bird about the mouth of the bay lyin' south o' Cape Blanco. Your honour might be sartain that every eye was on her, and with a fresh wind from the sou'west we bore down.

"But lor, sir, that craft didn't seem to draw more than a canoe, she went close in among the rocks and reefs, ontil nothin' but her masts were visible; and the breeze now rollin' up uncommon stiff Captain Harloch decided to sheer off.

"As soon as we were hauled to the wind we double reefed the topsails, but the werry sky seemed to scowl upon us and heavy clouds floated about like black bags o' wate and a sea comed up in a moment as it wer settin' the vessel dead on a lee shore.

"I won't trouble your honour wi' all tha we did. Captain Harloch did all a seama could do, but the sea broke over us as w lay in the trough o' the sea fearful, doubl breechings were rove on the breechings but we lurched so that one broke loose an nearly stove her side out.

"We naturally thought all was over the rain was fallin'; and the wind blowin such a sight o' spray from the sea tha nothing could be seen fifty yards ahead and we knew that the Cape couldn't b lyin' fur away.

"Suddenly, the wind dropped, the rai was over, and the clouds broke awa showin' patches of blue sky. There warn' a heart as didn't in the fust moment say; prayer, but Lord forgive all on us, for i turned to summat else when we saw th Cape not a quarter o' mile away, and a long row of rocks lifting their ugly head out of the water about fifty yards on our lee

"Every soul knew then that nothin could save her, but every man kept at hi post, quietly shuffling orf his toggery, so that he might have a chance to reach land

"The 'Curlew' struck, and the heavy sea still runnin' heeled her clean over or her beam ends. Her starboard guns stared for a moment at the sky, then broke from their tackle and pounded her lee side to matchwood.

"More than one man met with an awful death, but them that survived rallied to the voice of the captain, and stood ready to cut away the heaps o' rigging hanging about her, for when she struck the masts went by the board.

"At fust, sir, we thought she would have sunk at once, but the carpenter crawled on deck and told us that she was fixed on a rock shaped like a spike, which had stove in her side and went clean across the cabin. This turned out to be true, and as the sea was fast settling, we hoped by patience to get all ashore.

"But, sir," continued the narrator, impressively, "our danger worn't over. Toward sunset there was an easy sea runnin' and we were makin' the boats, at least such on 'em as were left, ready to go ashore, when the cap'en spied the pirate sneakin' out like a rat from a hole.

"He came on, his colours flyin', until within easy distance, and then, a bright

TOM FURNACE DEFENDS MONKEY JACK.

upon him, he opened fire on the helpless 'Curlew.'

"What could we do? Nothing. There she lay upon the bare rock, for the tide had run out, with her keel clear from stem to stern, and every gun overboard or useless. So the black scoundrel riddled her until her hull was like a honeycomb, and then sailed away. He knew better than come to a hand-to-hand fight.

"Then Captain Harloch, with his purty daughter nigh him, speered at the pirate, round the 'Curlew's' starn, and then I heard him say to the lieutenant,—

"It is as I feared, that villain Wantlake is our aggressor."

"Them's the words he used, and I may as well tell you that this Wantlake was the mid as struck the captain and seized the prize."

"I supposed so," said the privateer, with a quiet smile, "but proceed, my good fellow. What became of Captain Harloch, his—his daughter, and the crew?"

"They got ashore by degrees," returned the sailor, "but as there were only two boats left it was a long job; they warn't all ashore until the next mornin'. During

5

the day we worked back'ards and forrards, gettin provisions ashore, and now I comes to the reason o' my bein' alone adrift."

"Phil Maystone, the captain o' the fore-top, and four men went aboard at midnight. I was one on 'em. We landed on the rock, and, as we thought, made her fast and took the oars with us, layin' 'em on dry land. There was a strong current running, and, just as we started away, it dragged the boat from its moorings. I saw it goin', and, shouting, jumped in. This drove her clear o' the rock, and away she went, with a strong tide settin' south. I'd no oars. I can't swim. so I went away with nobody to help me but Heaven. As for my mates, they hadn't got over their surprise afore I was too fur away for them to help me.

"I don't know how long I've been alone, sir. I know I suffered hunger and thirst until I fell down, as I thought, and hoped to die, and when I came round I was snug in a hammock on board this neat little craft."

"What is your name?" asked the young privateer.

"Turner, sir."

"Then list to me, Turner. If you are willing, you can act with my crew; but I won't press you. Will you join or not?"

"What's the natur' of the sarvice, sir?" asked Turner, giving his trousers a hitch.

"To hunt down this pirate villain!" cried the masked captain.

"Then I'm in, sir," rejoined Turner, with an oath; "and when we overhaul him, I'll be the fust on board, with your honour's permission."

"Well said," rejoined the privateer. "Now go to your mates, but be not too curious respecting anything you hear or see. Rely upon this at all times—the 'Crucible' is honest."

"I'll swear to that," replied Turner; "your woice have got the true ring. I seem to have heerd it afore, but where on airth it was I can't say."

"Again, be not too curious. One question more—What will Captain Harloch do on land?"

"He's goin' to form an encampment with the men until he can make some arrangement to get away. He hopes to sight another cruiser, the 'Bulldog.' She's ex-pected to pass there on her way to the Canaries."

"Thank you, Turner; you may go."

When the sailor was gone the masked privateer rested his head upon his hand and remained for some time buried in deep thought.

Will, removing his mask, sat watching him in silence.

"We must make for Cape Blanco at once," said the captain, at last; "there shall we find the new nest of this double-dyed villain. I told you, Will, he would soon find friends and be afloat again."

"But there you will meet with Captain Harloch," suggested Will.

"That must be avoided for the present," was the reply; "but there lies our place for work, and thither I will go. You, in the meantime, must be put upon the sick list."

"Sick list!" ejaculated Will; "I am well enough."

"But you forget Turner."

"Put him on night duty; I couldn't stand being cooped up here."

"I can do that, certainly—Who's there? he asked, as somebody knocked at the door."

"Me, massa cap'en," said the voice of Monkey Jack.

"Come in!"

The faithful fellow entered and made a profound bow.

"Massa Stanchion wait for orders, sar."

"I will be with him in a moment; re-main here, Will, until I have made ar-rangements respecting Turner."

He hastened from the cabin, leaving the middy and Monkey Jack together. The nigger was in a state of great excitement, he evidently had some news to impart.

"Oh! Massa Will, he said, "de most scrumptuous fun."

"Where, Jack?"

"In de galley—Crikey an' Duncan hab a big fight. Crikey on'y one eye left to see wid, ole Duncan got none!"

"But surely," cried Jack hastily; "there has been none of that horrible gouging."

"Lor, no, Massa Will," laughed Jack: "it proper fight, and ebery eye a 'spectable bung up."

"Fair fisticuffs."

"Dat's it, Massa Will."

The captain's return checked further disclosures, and Monkey Jack accordingly departed, bestowing upon Will a wink of the most subtle meaning.

The "Crucible" reached Cape Blanco without any mishap, being wafted there by fair weather and a steady breeze. But one vessel was sighted, apparently a trader, who sheered off with wonderful celerity, being doubtful of the "Crucible's" nature; and once when they neared the coast a couple of proas put out with murdering and plunderous intentions, but a single shot disabled the foremost, and the other, taking her in tow, beat a hasty retreat.

It was a lovely evening when they hove in sight of the cape, where the gallant frigate lay with her copper glistening in the light of a setting sun.

As they drew nearer, the work of the pirate became visible, shot-holes showing the sky behind her hull.

Sea birds in thousands rested, flew, and floated about her, and the cut and torn ropes hanging over her side swayed to and fro, moved by the gentle wind.

"A sad sight," murmured the young privateer, "poor old 'Curlew,' your race is indeed run! Mr. Stanchion."

"Sir."

"Bring to as soon as you can find a bottom, and man the cutter; I shall visit the wreck before it is dark."

"Very good, sir."

When all was ready and the cutter prepared, the captain stepped in.

He looked around for Monkey Jack, but he was nowhere to be seen.

"No matter," he murmured; then aloud, "give way, my lads."

When the cutter was half-way towards the wreck, Monkey Jack suddenly rushed upon deck in a fever haste.

"Massa Stanchion," he cried, "is de cap'en gone?"

"He is, Jack."

"Confound it! dat all de fault ob Crikey, he hab anoder little bit ob fun wid Duncan, an' get anoder bung up. Den I put beef in it, and while I do it de cap'en's gone. Blow Crikey's eye."

While Jack fretted and fumed, the cutter was cleaving the water towards the huge frigate, lying on the bare rock.

The captain sprang ashore as soon as they touched land; all was grim and desolate excepting the multitude of birds wheeling and screaming around as they rose up from the shattered hull.

"Stay here," said the captain briefly, "and wait for me."

He walked to the wreck, and clambering up her side, crept across the deck, and went below.

Everything was in confusion; barrels, boxes, ropes, hatchets, and a vast quantity of provisions strewn about.

These the privateer passed by, and went at once to the midshipmen's berth.

He examined the lockers, and found all of them open but one.

This was locked, sealed, and labelled,—

"Harold Greystone,
"Coward and Traitor.

"In this locker lie his clothes, books, and papers, to remain untouched by honest men, until the coward shall reappear."

"He will come one day," murmured the privateer, "and ask for these; if left here they will perish. I will secure them for the coward. I may be present when he returns to his judges. I want Will here. The cutter shall go back for him."

The young privateer reappeared on deck and bade the boat return for his friend.

The men pushed off at once and pulled towards the "Crucible."

The masked captain returned to the berth, musing o'er the sad fate of the gallant "Curlew." As he re-entered, a light flushed before his eyes, and half a dozen men held him fast.

He took a rapid survey of his captors, and saw they were remorseless scoundrels —pirates of the ocean—and foremost was the man he had sought so earnestly, Mason Wantlake, scowling upon him.

"So my fantastical captain," cried the ex-middy, "I've nabbed you neatly. I knew your cursed craft as soon as she brought up by the point, and remembered what she did to my gallant 'Defiance,' but I little thought her captain would drop so neatly into my mouth like a ripe plum."

The privateer made no reply, but his eyes shone like diamonds beneath his mask, and his hands worked convulsively in the grasp of the ruffian who held him.

"A captain of so smart a craft," pursued Mason Wantlake, with a sneer, "should have better eyes. He should have seen the masts of the 'Riversnake' lying beyond the rocks, and my boat drawn up by the stern of this old hulk."

Still the masked captain made no reply, his brain was busy revolving the chances of escape.

"Let me see the gentleman to whom I owe so much," said the pirate, raising the mask. "By the light of Heaven—YOU here."

"Yes: do you know me, villain?" rejoined the privateer sternly; "do you remember me—dog?"

"Perfectly," returned Mason Wantlake, recovering himself. "Here, my lads, secure the dog to this ring, replace his mask, and leave us together."

The pirates re-covered our hero's face, bound him strong and fast to the side of the berth, and left them alone.

Mason Wantlake seated himself opposite his prisoner, gloating over his prize, as a miser over his treasure.

"You here," he repeated; "had I asked a boon from Heaven I could not have asked for more."

"Such boons as you seek do not come from Heaven," replied our hero; "good deeds and you are things apart."

"Perhaps so. Shall I speak your name?"

"As you will—it matters not."

"I hate it much, it is poison in my lips, but I will do so—Harold Greystone. You say that good deeds and I are things apart; it is true. I hate good, and revel and glory in a crime."

"Stale news, Mason Wantlake."

"But true, Greystone. I always hated you, but never so much as now. The lovely Clara, if she keeps her word, will live and die a maid; for hark you, Harold, she told me that she loved you, and bade me trouble her no longer. I tell the story to you, so that you may carry it into eternity——"

"You will murder me!—I thought so," interrupted the young privateer, calmly.

"I will," replied the pirate, "but not as common natures kill. You shall not die by bullet or by steel, but live enough to feel the torture of a lifetime. Men in mortal agony have lived a lifetime in a moment, and fifteen minutes shall be an age to you. See here."

He rose up from the barrel, and rolled it to the far end of the berth; five others lay there.

"These barrels," he said, with devilish coolness, "are full of powder, and were about to be removed by my men when you arrived so timely. I will use them for another purpose. Watch me, Harold, and bid adieu to this bright world."

He drilled a small hole in the head of the cask, and fixed a slow match there. Then opened a lantern left by one of his men, and ignited it.

"The match," he said, as if lecturing on the subject, "was made to burn for fifteen minutes; it may be a trifle more or a trifle less. I do not warrant it. About that time your friends of the 'Crucible' will be treated to a pyrotechnic display of an unusual nature. Now, let me look to your bonds. Excellent. Harold Greystone, fare ye well, and a pleasant journey—aloft."

Mason Wantlake raised his hat with cynical politeness, and sauntered out, with a Satanical smile upon his dark face.

Left alone, Harold Greystone—there is no further occasion to conceal his name—made a violent effort to obtain his release, but the knots were tied by practised hands, and the rope refused to yield.

"And shall I die thus?" he murmured, with the dew of agony upon his brow, "die with my name yet unredeemed from the stain of cowardice."

He glanced at the match, it was slowly and steadily burning, throwing off a spark occasionally as the fire encountered the grains of saltpetre. The match was but three inches long—three inches of saturated paper between him and a violent death.

He was no coward, but the desire for life wrung a cry from his lips—the cry which springs so readily from the lips in the hour of distress.

"Help!"

"Hark! there is a shouting outside and a clashing of swords, mingled with the oaths of angry men. Friends are at hand.

"Help, help!"

An answering cry comes back, and Monkey Jack rushes into the cabin, saying—

"Massa cap'en, dis chile am here jis when him wanted. Oh! Wurra, wurra, what hab dey been up to, de skulkin' tiefs?"

"Cut these cords, Jack," said the young privateer, calmly, "waste no words, for each moment is precious."

"Dere dey are, Massa cap'en," returned Jack, slashing them asunder, "now I cut back to dem piratical skunks."

"Are they still here?" cried his captain.

"Yes, sare."

"Give me your sword, Jack, they have stolen mine, and retain the pistols for yourself."

Forgetful of his late danger of the burning match, Harold rushed forth, followed by his sable attendant, but was again too late. His foe had succeeded in escaping towards the shore, leaving half his men writhing upon the rock at the feet of the panting crew of the "Crucible's" boat.

CHAPTER XVI.

THE LAST OF THE "CURLEW."—THE LITTLE
CAMP ASHORE.

"GONE," cried our hero, in agony, "once more the villain has escaped my clutches. To the boat," he continued, remembering their imminent peril, "a minute longer here may be fatal to us!"

Without waiting to learn why, the men obeyed his voice and leaped into the boat. Jack and the captain followed.

"Give way, my men."

The next moment the boat glided into the deep water, and a few sturdy strokes pulled it out of danger. Harold then bade them rest upon their oars.

"A slow match is burning beneath the decks of yonder vessel," he said, "fixed to a barrel of powder. A few moments hence and every plank will be torn asunder!"

"It blow dem wriggling pirates to smifereens," murmured Jack, "sarve dem right. I wish dey get blowed up twice."

"The wounded men!" exclaimed Harold, "in the excitement I forgot them. I would not have an enemy die such a death."

"Shall we pull in, sir?" asked the stroke oarsman, readily.

"Alas, my good fellow, it is too late—see there."

The "Curlew" suddenly parted amidships, a dense spire of flame leaped straight upward, a vast volume of white smoke surmounting it, and a terrific report followed, rolling away in numberless echoes over land and sea.

Stunned by the noise and blinded by the glare, the men sat motionless in the boat, watching the great white cloud rolling about the rock until recalled to themselves by the patter of falling spars and broken timbers into the sea.

Then bending to their oars, they sped across the agitated sea towards the "Crucible."

The young privateer stood up in the stern sheets watching the spot where he had so lately been in peril, until the fleecy clouds floated away, showing the rock grim and bare in the twilight.

"'Curlew,'" he said softly, "fare ye well, a good ship and true, although an abode of sorrow to me. Senseless mass of wood and iron as ye were, your fate shall be avenged. Farewell!"

Monkey Jack allowed his leader to resume his seat and indulge in a few moments'

reverie ere he broke the silence, but, as we know, he could not be silent for long, especially when he wanted to learn something:—

"Dat a good ship gone," he said.

"A glorious one, Jack," replied the young privateer.

"Massa cap'en know it, p'r'aps."

"I've seen her, Jack, more than once before. How came you so opportunely to my rescue?"

"Me gen'ally poppertoon," rejoined Jack, seizing upon a new word; "when I find de cap'en gone, I kick up a bobbery, and say I die ob grief, ontil Massa Stanchion call me cussed troubleson nigger, an' tell me to take de jolly-boat. So I hab it lowered, and come wid some men. On de way we meet de cutter, dey say dey go for Massa Steadfast, and leab you, sir, on board ob the frigate. Den I feel berry bad, as if you in trouble, an' tell the men to pull like one clock."

"You had a presentiment, Jack."

"No, Massa cap'en, I bring not'ing but cutlass an' pistols."

"A presentiment, Jack, is a foreboding, a fear that something is about to happen."

"Den I hab dat, orful bad, all ober my hunks; so I tell de men to pull. We reach de rock: up came the pirates. Fust I t'ink dey hab killed massa cap'en, so I slosh among dem frightful, ontil I hear your voice, sar; den I rush down hatchway, and dat all."

"Once more your debtor, Jack: shake hands, old fellow."

"Dis de happiest moment ob my life," murmured Jack, as he complied: "berrer even den when I see Duncan's eyes close up by Crikey. Bof times scrumptious, but dis beets t'oder into fits, massa cap'en, my fr'en'."

"For life, Jack!—here comes the cutter, with Will aboard."

"Jolly-boat, ahoy!"

"All right, Will," cried the privateer, "all safe and sound."

"Thank Heaven!" returned the lad, as the boats drew up alongside; "we feared that you were lost. Who blew up the frigate?"

"Thereby hangs a tale, Will," replied Harold, "and it shall be told over a bottle of wine after dinner. All well with the 'Crucible'?"

"All well. Mr Stanchion discovered a vessel lying close in to-day."

"A pirate, Will; the one we seek. If a sharp watch is kept he cannot escape."

The return of the party, with their beloved captain safe and sound, elated every man on board the "Crucible." Nor was their joy lessened when he stepped on deck and ordered a double allowance of grog to be served out, to celebrate his happy rescue.

In a few plain words he told the story, and Monkey Jack was immediately a hero.

Mr. Stanchion openly apologised for having a short time before called him a "cursed troublesome nigger," and the crew carried him twice round the main deck on their shoulders—a style of ovation very agreeable to Jack's love of popularity.

"I'll drink a grog wid you," he said, to the men, "den I go b'low wid genelmen like myself—massa cap'en, an' so on. Dis am a night ob liberty, an' Crikey may come on deck; hab him up an' gib him his grog."

Crikey was accordingly hauled up, a large bandage on his head concealing the latest handiwork of the outraged Duncan, and partook of his grog with a will.

Jack went below to the aft cabin and joined his more aristocratic friends, while in the forecastle merriment was the order of the evening, although a strict watch was maintained, and nothing in the form of duty neglected.

A bright particular star was Crikey among the rough tars; he talked, he laughed, he sang and danced, until the moon paled before the sun's first ray, and then he rolled down the hatchway, and upon a pile of sails went peacefully to sleep.

Happy be thy dreams, thou joyous Crikey !

The earliest sea-gull screaming o'er the sea found Monkey Jack, Will Steadfast, and Tom Furnace upon deck, for they had important work in hand.

It had been arranged overnight that Monkey Jack should go ashore, and endeavour to find out where Captain Harloch and his men had made their encampment, and at their earnest solicitation, the two middies were allowed to accompany him.

"I bring 'em back, genelmen," he said, "I know de woods too well. I no blunder upon any man, for I see footmarks wheresomdever dey may be. If I don't bring dem back, genelmen—you—you may hang my brodder, Crikey."

This liberal offer was, amidst much laughter, closed with, and the trio were ordered to be ready by early dawn. The mids scarcely slept a wink, but Jack snoozed away the time, and awoke at the right moment, with the certainty of a man accustomed to do so.

"On de plantation," he remarked, when complimented on this virtue, "dey used to come round wid the cow-hide, an' one cut wake a nigger up for a week—I had enuf for lifetime, so I wake reg'lar."

A lug-sail was fixed to the jolly-boat, for Monkey Jack had decided upon landing a few miles down the coast, and with half a dozen men to bring her back, they departed, amid a general shouting of good wishes from all.

The masked privateer was there to bid them adieu, and his last words were to Jack.

"I can trust in you at all times," he said; "so bring back the lads."

"May dis nigger hab his ugly head knocked orf if he don't. Good-bye, massa cap'en, and don't let dat tief steal away."

He pointed towards the spot where the pirate lay, and joined his youthful adventurers already seated in the jolly-boat.

They had nought but their brandy flasks and a day's biscuit for provision, for Jack had assured them that all the food they required he would find on the plain or in the depths of the forests, but they were all well armed, and each carried sixty rounds of ammunition.

The boat landed them at a well-wooded point selected by the negro, and after a hasty adieu, the adventurous trio plunged straight into the forest.

With an ever-ready eye and ear, the negro led the way, stalking between the trees in silence for at least five minutes. At length he halted beneath a banana tree.

"Genelmen," he said, "we safe unuf here; dere's not a white man or nigger who come dis way; dere not'ing to show ob dem; and, I should say, genelmen, dat you are de furst picaninnies dat eber come dis way.

"Can it be possible?" exclaimed the breathless boys.

"It's trufe," returned Jack earnestly; "I say dat no man eber put him foot under dese trees afore. Now, genelmen, we look for proper place to lib in while we stop here."

Turning sharp off to the left, he walked on silent as before, until they came to the end of the forest, terminating in a long grove of cocoa-nut trees, stretched along the shore.

"Here we lib," he said, pointing to the beach; "we jes' six mile from where we land; dere's turtle for meat, nut for fruit, and plenty o' oder tings for bread."

"And water?"

"De sea for a wash, cocoa milk for drink."

"Glorious," cried the lads.

He then took them down to the bay—a beautiful semicircle of green sea water, clear as crystal, its surface darkened by small crisp waves, forming a glorious covering to a forest of coral, clearly distinguishable beneath, every fibre visible.

Jack took them to a small jutting rock, and bade the boys lay down and look into the crystal depths. They did so, and beheld the bottom alive with shoals of fish, sporting in the warm rays of the sun, or motionless in the many shades cast by the coral.

Below all, a beautiful ground of silver sand, spotted with transparent pebbles, and white gleaming stones.

"What tink you ob dat?" asked Jack, softly.

"Fairy land," replied Will, enthusiastically, "the home of a sea-god."

"If mermaids and water sprites exist," rejoined Tom Furnace, "that would be their home,

"This scene," said Will, "tells me more of a great guiding Power than a thousand lectures from a thousand men."

They went back to the grove, where Jack speedily dislodged sufficient fruit for their repast, and there, in a spot to which no temple could compare, the boys lay upon the luxuriant turf, and satiated their appetites, while listening to Monkey Jack's recital of the glories of his native land.

After the meal they strolled along the shore, until a small cave or grotto was discovered, washed out by certain tides, so Jack said, of which there was no danger for many months to come, and there they took up their abode.

"Seven days' leave, have we?" sighed Will, "I could live here for an age."

"Massa Will sing anoder song afore de week's up," returned Jack.

And the sable hero was right.

CHAPTER XVII.

DISCOVERY OF THE SETTLEMEMT.—JACK MEETS WITH A FOE.

THE lads and Jack slept quietly through the night, awakening in the morning with a delightful sensation of freedom. Tom and Will rushed down to the beach and plunged into the sea; but they did not go far away, as Jack had warned them that "confounded shark hab their lily white limbs in no time, swallow them jes' like pill."

They came back without having seen the remorseless monster of the deep, and partook heartily of a breakfast prepared by their faithful sable friend. The meal over, Jack proceeded to business, the why and wherefore of their being there.

"Dis berry nice life," he said, "but massa cap'en 'spect me to work—an' you too, young genelmen. So I give you now de progum ob our life ashore."

"The what?" exclaimed Will, winking to Tom.

"De progum, Massa Will."

"Programme, Jack!"

"Dat's it, sar. I say progum fust jes' to see if Massa Will know dat word. Glad him do. Yah! oh! golly!"

"Get along, Jack. One of these days when you roll your eyes like that you will never get them back again."

"Nigger eyes," returned Jack, complacently, "not common eyes, dey go quite round.

As he was anxious to know what work was in store, Will did not attempt to contradict this remarkable assertion, but begged his negro friend to proceed.

"De cap'en," pursued Jack, "say to me, 'Jack, my fren,' he ses, 'you jes' take your hansom' limbs on to de land, and see whar de wrecked cap'en an' crew ob de English vessel am lyin', Also find out,' he say, 'jes' whar dem pirates skulk, an' jes' how many dar am about."

"Not many signs of them here," interposed Tom.

"No! Massa Tom," replied Jack, "we find 'em few mile away, troo de mangrobe tree, an' 'cross swamp, whar none but nigger know him way. White man go down souse, mud cober him up, an' neber see him more."

"Do I understand you to say that you have put a swamp between us and our enemies, impassable to them, but an open road to you, and, therefore, to us?" asked Will.

"Dat jest it," rejoined Jack; "we lib here snug as flea in my best Sunday jacket, until we cross de swamp to see whar Cap'en Harloch an' his men am."

"Not forgetting Mason Wantlake and his piratical crew?"

"No, sar, me 'member dem werry particular, for dem nasty skunks to run agains'; so, genelmen, when you ready we make a move. As soon as we find out whar dem are, we make signal off de point, an' go on board agen."

Both the lads made a mental vow that they would have some fun first, and having settled their dress and weapons, they now declared themselves ready to follow wheresoever Monkey Jack might lead.

They went back to the forest, turning towards the north in a direction inclining to the reef where the "Curlew" came to her untimely end.

The trees at first were literally alive with parrots and monkeys, but as they penetrated into the deeper shades the squalling and chattering almost ceased.

Jack told them that the birds and monkeys loved to gather by day on the verge of the forest, but at night they sought places of shelter in the interior out of the reach of all danger except that arising from the regular beasts of prey.

His keen eyes distinguished, and his ready tongue described, many of these resting-places as they advanced, the roosting branches of the birds, and the hollows where the monkeys congregated, in some places, as he declared, by hundreds.

Many other things he also pointed out, but as they are not to the purport of our story, we will get along quickly until a sudden halt was called by Jack.

"Now, Massa Will and Massa Tom," he said, "you see no danger dore."

"None," Will replied; "the wood is certainly thinner, and there are more plants and creepers between the trees."

"Dat whar de nigger shine," returned Jack, in high glee; "now, Massa Will, walk along dat tree, on de roots, den put one foot on de ground—hold tight to dat lily branch above."

Will stepped lightly along a heap of gnarled roots, seized the branch indicated, and pressed his foot upon the soil.

It sank to the depth of several inches, and as he hastily withdrew it, black water followed and filled up the impression of his foot.

"Dere's a man-trap for you," laughed Jack; "you step bof feet on it at once, and you hab no branch to hold by, Massa Will, and down you go, fus' ober boot, den de knee, den de hips, den up to de troat, den eyes, nose, an' mouf, and Massa Will smoddered as sure as Duncan a big fool."

"Horrible!" exclaimed Will, with a shudder, as he rejoined his companion.

"It looks firm enough," said Tom.

"To white eyes," rejoined Jack, "but not to troo-born nigger. It jes' dry on de top, no thicker dan silk hank'chief, but I see de water underneaf, an' know dat sartain death am dere to any man who go upon it squash, slave cap'en sometime get catch dat way."

He furthermore explained that the morass was caused by a fork of the river, which penetrating into the wood lost itself among the trees formed this deadly swamp.

It seemed that he had worked his way round to the mouth of the river, where the pirates were supposed to be concealed, and the English sailors to have taken up temporary encampment.

"We cross now," he said, in conclusion, "young genelmen, follow me."

The trees, as we have hinted, were not so dense in the narrow as in the other parts of the forest; but they were sufficiently close to allow of the branches intermingling, and in many instances to be interlaced so thickly as to leave in doubt the stem from which they sprang.

Jack's path over the morass was the branches thus entwined.

Mounting a tree he led the way across a vast bough with the agility of a monkey, and seating himself upon the next tree encouraged his young friends to follow his example.

"No hurry, Massa Tom," he said; "you slip, and down you go into de swamp; dat's it, take hold ob de lily branch, now de oder, and here we are."

"Rather hard work," laughed Will, as he sat down to rest by the side of the negro, "are there many roads like this Jack?"

"Many, Massa Will, but we no use dem 'cept in 'stremities."

"'Stremities."

"Yes, when de slaver come, or tribe too big to fight, den we use dem."

"I see, except in extremities. I've got my wind, Jack, on we go again."

"Slow 'an sartain, Massa Will, dere's plenty ob time."

They progressed in this fashion from tree to tree, halting now and then to rest, for nearly two hours, when Jack, suddenly swinging himself from a bough, dropped upon the ground and declared they were safe.

The novelty of this mode of travelling had worn off, and the lads were glad to be once more on terra firma. Will uttered a whoop of delight.

"Dat enuf to bring ten thousand rogue upon us," said Jack, in agony; "oh! Massa Will, do 'member we on the enemy side now."

"Beg pardon, Jack; but it was so delightful to feel the ground again."

"You shout again, Massa Will, and you no feel it much longer."

The trio partook of a hasty meal, and a council of war respecting the next movement was held. Of course, Jack proposed and carried everything, although he allowed his young friends to have their say upon every point.

"I go away alone fust," said Monkey Jack, "but I find you hidin'-place where I leab you for one, two hour——"

"I thought we were to go with you," grumbled Will.

"To much danger for three," said Jack, gravely, "You genelmen came out for fun —you hab it. I cum out for work—now I begin. Me make you snug little place, den go; but I be back afore sundown."

Selecting a cluster of tall plants, he skilfully bent their tops over until a roof was formed, leaving an opening on either side. Over this he threw some creeping plants which he cut for the purpose to conceal the entwining, and to give the whole as natural an air as possible.

"De creepers look fresh for hours," he said, "long enuf for me to cum back to you, genelmen; so good-bye. I cum back soon troo dem trees dere—one wid de big knot, and t'oder wid de branch struck by lightning."

He pointed to two trees standing side by side, one blasted by the electric fluid during a late storm, the other with a monstrous excrescence growing out of its side. Having shaken hands with the lads, and warned them not to leave their hiding-place,

Monkey Jack stalked away, and was lost in the surrounding foliage.

Tom and Will crept into their hiding-place, shaped after the style of a gipsy's tent, and each hugging his knees they grinned at each other in inexpressible delight.

"Prime!" ejaculated Will.

"Beats all the palaces of the world into fits," said Tom; "what plant is this? The leaves are magnificent."

"Don't know, Tom. I say, this ground is very soft; the shade is lovely, and I am rather tired after the monkey work this morning, suppose we have a snooze?"

"Just the thing," replied Tom; and the boys, without bestowing a thought upon danger in any shape or form, stretched themselves at full length upon the moss, and lulled by the buzzing of innumerable insects flitting round their habitation, fell asleep.

There we must leave them, and follow Monkey Jack upon his expedition. The negro's unvarying instinct kept on in a straight direction until the fast-thinning trees warned him of his approach to the outskirts of the forest.

Not a sound or movement escaped his vigilant eyes and ears, as he skirted an open space of ground where a large fire had recently been burning, and fragments of food strewn about showed that a feast of a rude description had lately been partaken of.

"White men," muttered Jack; "but wedder pirates or sailors? dat's de point."

After a keen survey of the wood around, he concluded that he was alone, and boldly advanced into the open. Close by the ashes of the extinct fire, lay a torn ribbon with gilt letters upon it.

"War ship," said Jack; "pirate skunks not proud nuf ob dere name to wear it. Now for de trail."

He soon discerned the footsteps of a party, consisting, probably, of about a dozen men, and from the way that one occasionally strayed from the group, Jack concluded that they were in a merry, rollicking mood; indeed, at one place he discovered signs of shuffling feet, as if a sailor had attempted to perform an English hornpipe.

"Sailor all ober," grinned Jack; "dey no care for any danger, but larf, an' sing, an' dance, jist like piccaninny, wheresomeber dey may be. Me hear dem d'rec'ly, I swear."

Keeping on at a swift pace, he rapidly overhauled the party, men of the "Curlew," laughing and chattering merrily, as if they were in port at home, and not in the midst of an African forest, surrounded by cruel and remorseless enemies.

Gliding from tree to tree, Jack kept up with them unperceived, no crackling twig nor rustling leaf informed the sailors of his presence. Like a dark shadow he glided unheeded in the rear.

They travelled thus for a mile or more, the gallant tars rollicking, reckless, and indifferent; their watcher, grim and resolute, with all his mirth laid aside for a more fitting opportunity.

"Who goes there?"

It was the voice of a marine, pacing to and fro, that broke upon the stillness. One of the foremost sailors replied—

"St. George and our good captain."

This was the pass-word, for the marine replied—

"Pass, St. George and our good captain, and all's well."

The sailors passed on, but Monkey Jack, lying behind a clump of bushes, meditated upon his further course.

"Can't pass that fellow," he thought, "so I go round, I suppose; den, perhaps, I fall on 'noder red sailor. I put him orf de scent, den follow up smart."

He disembedded a fair-sized stone from the earth, and hurled it dexterously between the trees, a dense bush of ivy on the left. The marine, who was pacing to and fro, hallted, and cried again—

"Who goes there."

No reply came, of course, but the leaves still oscillated from the blow they had received, and at a distance had the appearance of a living body crawling behind it. The man boldly and promptly advanced, thrusting his bayonet among the rich green leaves.

Jack, acting upon this advantage, glided swiftly and silently past the post of the sentinel, and pursued his way, keeping a line of trees between him and the marine, who resumed his post, cursing an imaginary wild animal he supposed had disturbed him.

The negro had not much further to go; fallen trees soon obstructed his path, and the voices of many men soon fell upon his ear. In five minutes a clearing in the forest was revealed, with a number of busy men, occupied in constructing a fence around a cluster of habitations, rudely but substantially constructed of fallen trees cut into suitable lengths, and thatched with broad leaves.

Two men, sailors, were busy sawing up a huge log on the edge of the clearing and near these Jack lay down to listen for information. Presently they halted from work, and one, a weather-beaten old tar, turning a quid in his cheek, remarked—

"I likes a spell o' this, Bill; it's a change from reefing an' splicing."

"If we don't get too much on it," growled the other. "I heered the captain say that we might be here for months afore a frigate touched in sarch on him and that's why he want such a snug little cabin built for him and Miss Clara."

"She's a lovely crittur, Bill; lord, when her eyes look at me, I'm speared right through."

"Your's ain't the figure-head for lovemaking," laughed Bill, "an' this ain't the place for it neither."

"Right old man; where ha' Muddle an' his mates been this mornin'."

"Out a-hunting arter the wild pigs; they've just come in with two as fat as butter, made my mouth water."

"Yes! I heard 'em give the word; it ain't altered, is it?

"The word? no mate; it'll stand for a week, as some o' our men are down by the coast, keepin' a look out; it's dangerous work, though, for you know them pirates are pretty thick. I'm sartain, as the captain says, they're on'y waitin' for another lot, or until they're strong enough to attack; but we've got enough perwisions from the ship's stores to last three months, and it'll take a strong lot o' pirate swabs to break through us. Miss Clara ain't no cause to be afeared, and she knows it."

Jack waited to hear no more, but crept cautiously away; he had fulfilled his mission and learned that Captain Harloch thoroughly acquainted with the dangers of the coast, had resolved to intrench himself a short distance inland, to await the coming of a ship certain to be sent upon his track as soon as it was known that he was missing, keeping a quiet watch meanwhile from the shore for any chance vessel passing that way.

Around the woodland camp was a cordon of sentinels, marines accustomed to that class of duty, and Monkey Jack had no little difficulty to escape their vigilance.

but he managed it by pursuing similar tactics to those he observed before, and hastened to rejoin his young companions.

"By jingo," he exclaimed, halting, "me almost forget pirates, dere certain to be harabouts, I jes' hab one little run dis way afore I go back."

He was not far from the boys' hiding-place when he made this resolution, but resolving to go alone he set forward at a swift pace towards the sea.

Jack reached the outskirts of the wood without perceiving any signs of the enemy, and rapidly scanning the open ground, was about to give up the task for the day, when a massive built ruffian stepped from behind a tree with a musket in his hand.

He was clad in rough sea-faring costume, with a fur cap upon his head and long jack boots upon his feet. In his belt he carried a knife and pistols, altogether a most formidable ruffian.

Clubbing his musket, he dealt the unsuspecting negro a violent blow upon the skull, and brought him to the earth.

He was preparing to repeat the blow when a third figure, that of Tom Furnace, appeared upon the scene, and striding quickly over the prostrate form of Jack, he presented a sword at the ruffian's breast.

CHAPTER XVIII.

JACK'S OPINION OF NEGRO ANATOMY.—WILL STEADFAST MISSING THE FIGHT AT SEA.

THE pirate, with an oath, rushed upon the lad, but Jack, who was not much hurt, having simply fallen from the weight of the blow, caught the ruffian by the heels, and hurled him to the earth with terrific force.

After the fall he neither moved nor spoke, his heavy breathing being the only sign that he still existed.

"Dat enuf for him," said Jack, rising; "tank you, Massa Tom, for coming in de nick ob time."

"Quite an accident, Jack," laughed Tom. "I got tired of being in our hiding-place, and came out for a stroll, lost my way, and found you here. What's to be done with this fellow?"

"Kill him, Massa Tom."

"No, no, not in cold blood."

"It more marciful, we must tie him up to tree—p'raps he stop here week—no one come—starve—die ob thirst—vulture pick him eyes out—wild hog bite him legs."

"It will give him a chance of escape, if nothing more," said Tom, firmly; "let him have it."

As the pirate showed signs of returning to life, they dispossessed him of his weapons, and by the time his eyes opened he was firmly bound to a stout young tree.

He stared suddenly at the negro and middy without uttering a word, but Jack, having secured him, had something to say,—

"Now, mass pirate," he began, "you be berry tankful dat dis young genelman spare your life. I settle you at once but for him, but he say no kill in cold blood, so I spare you—you hear dat?"

"You speak loud enough," growled the fellow.

"So we spare your life," continued Jack, "and leab you here; you keep quiet jes' one hour and den open your ugly mouth much as you like, jes' whisper one leetle word afore an' I come back and knock your head orf."

"It's nigh sundown," said the pirate; "if I'm left here after dark I shall be pulled to pieces."

"Dat your bisness," replied Jack, indifferently, "you hab a leetle chance ob life, it better dan none, be tankful. Massa Tom, we go now."

As Tom went by he marked the despairing glance of the pirate's eyes. He could not leave the man to such a fate, so pressing a finger upon his lips, he thrust a knife into the man's hand, and followed Monkey Jack.

A good deed, done at a moment of impulse, but destined to bear good fruit.

"You don't appear to be much hurt," said Tom, as he walked rapidly along.

"Me! whar?" asked Jack.

"The blow on your head, Jack—it fell heavily."

"Massa Tom, said the negro, "me tell you somefin' dat all de world don't know. It no use knocking nigger on de head; you may make hole in it if you can, but he no care for dat; you may crack it like old earthen pot, but him no wus. De man who hit nigger on de head is conflounded ass."

"It is considered to be a very sensitive part of man, Jack."

"Berry likely, Massa Tom, but not ob nigger; he diff'rent to rest ob de world. I b'live him lib jes' as well widout as wid it."

"What is the part to attack, then?" asked Tom, laughing.

"Dat I no tell any man," said Jack, "if it eber it come round to ole Duncan he settle me in no time."

"But I won't peach, Jack."

"Wall! I tell you, Massa Tom, but if eber you tell, you no friend ob mine. De only part of nigger dat hab any feeling is de shins."

This important secret, communicated in a thrilling whisper, Tom promised faithfully to keep from all but Will, for whom he obtained permission to share it. Jack then entertained him with various anecdotes of the power of a negro's head when used for battering purposes, which we fear to repeat lest our readers should entertain doubts of our veracity."

Tom told him that he had left Will lounging in the hiding-place just aroused from a nap, and that he (Tom) had started out for a few minutes' stroll, and as he said before, lost his way.

"Luckily for you, Jack," he said, "I came up at the right moment."

"But it berry wrong for you to come out," replied the negro, gravely, "so many ugly tiefs about here. How you know if Massa Will no come out too an lose him him way. Den what shall we do?"

"Don't think of it," hastily rejoined Tom, "here's the bushes. Good Heaven, what is this?"

The hiding place was broken open, branches and leaves strewn about, with other signs of a fierce struggle. Jack and Tom stood staring at the place aghast and dismayed.

"Poor Massa Will," moaned Jack, the tears rolling down his cheeks, "de pirates hab him, sure enuf. Dey fall upon him him too many—but him fight well, an look here Massa Tom, see dat pool ob blood."

He pointed to a dark circular patch at the foot of a tree. Tom knelt down, touched it with his hand, it was, as Jack suggested, blood, and the gory stain upon his fingers sent a shudder through his frame.

"Poor Will," he cried, burying his face in his hands, "murdered, what a miserable wretch I was to leave you. Jack," he continued, turning upon the negro, "you can follow them, lead on."

"Too late, massa Tom," rejoined Jack; "dere go de sun, and de eyes dat can see trail in de dark was neber known."

As he spoke, the whole scene darkened, and a veil of gloom seemed to fall upon him. Almost instantaneously the cry of day-birds ceased, and the harsh cry of the jackall fell upon their ears.

"Nuffin to do but to wait for de morrow," said Jack; "we hab night afore us but it not berry long dis time ob year."

"It will be an age to me," muttered Tom.

"It no use dryin' up, massa Tom," rejoined the negro; "p'r'aps massa Will alive arter all, an' pirate on'y hide him, den we find him, and let him out. Yah! jes' so, massa Tom."

He tried to speak gaily and hopefully, but his sorrow overmastered him, and he sobbed aloud.

"It—go—berry hard," he moaned, "if I catch—pirate—arter dis. I—I—roll him out—flat."

The intensity with which he uttered this threat would have warned any listener, who was likely to fall into his power, to give Monkey Jack at all times a very wide berth. There was no doubt of his having ample vengeance upon those who had deprived him of the companionship of Will Steadfast.

"Massa Tom," said Jack, wiping his eyes, "all dis no use—all de blubberin' in de world won't bring him back. We sit down now, an' wait till de sun show him red nose agen, den we go to work."

Sleep was not to be thought of, so they sat down, the negro with his hand upon the lad's arm, to assure him of protection, and thus, speaking occasionally in whispers, they passed the night.

Above, through the intertwined branches, a few stars gleamed; these Tom watched as they travelled on their course, until they grew faint, and disappeared before the orb of day. Then came the light filtering through the trees, revealing the many wonders of nature around him—the giant trees, the gorgeous flowers, and the infinite variety of herbs, many of them unfolding their leaves, like conscious beings, to meet the morning sun.

"Which way, Jack?" asked Will, springing up.

"To de sea; pirate skulk along shore," replied Jack; "here am dere footmarks, we follow dem clearly."

With his unerring instinct, the faithful negro followed the trail of the ruffians. He occasionally uttered a few words, but in an undertone. From these Tom gathered that the pirates were in considerable force,

A COMBAT TO THE DEATH.

eir numbers augmenting as they pro-
essed, as if they had picked up sentinel
mrades on their way.

The marks led direct to the coast, but
e open space where Jack had received a
ow the day before was avoided, the trail
ading round the outskirts to the foot of
giant rock rising some three hundred
ove the sea.

It was a huge mass, broken on the sur-
ce, rough blocks affording hiding-places
r men, a dangerous place to seek in the
ce of an enemy, particularly at daylight.

Jack and his companions lay ensconced
in the foliage below, eyeing this uncom-
promising termination to their journey.
There could be no doubt that in some part
of it the pirates lay concealed, for on either
side the shingle was without a sign of life.

"Dat de rascals' home," said Jack.

"An ugly place," rejoined Tom; "shall
we venture?"

"No use, Massa Tom, what we do; if
we try, but run again a bullet, which de
rascals send at us——"

"But think of Will?"

"I tink ob him, and dat why I don't go."

"They may be murdering him."

"Dey do it afore now or not at all. Wait a leetle while, Massa Tom, p'raps we see somebody, at present dey all hide."

"Do you hear that, a gun, Jack?"

The familiar sound came rolling towards them at that moment from the sea, and, as if by magic, the crown of the vast rock or cliff became alive with heads, while the forms of many men were seen scrambling over the surface to reach their comrades.

Where they came from it was impossible to say; to Will they seemed to spring, like the gnomes of the fairy tale, from the earth; indeed many of them were ferocious and ugly enough to be anything.

"Dere anoder," cried Jack, as a second gun resounded, "and dat's a 'Crucible;' I swar, dere anoder, dat de music we know, Massa Tom."

"They are fighting behind this massive rock," cried Tom, fidgetting with excitement, "what a beastly nuisance, Jack?"

"We see 'em if we creep round rock," rejoined the negro; "follow dis chile, sar, and all de 'Crucible' up to, we shall see."

On one side the massive rock overhung the sand, and by keeping close to it the two adventurers were hidden from the host of pirates crowding on the summit, all gazing out to sea.

There two vessels were running, side by side, towards the mouth of the river, about two miles away to the north, exchanging rapid shots. The "Crucible," with her blue bunting floating before the wind, could not be mistaken, but the other was a stranger, and Tom was certain he had never seen her before.

"She carry no colours," said Jack, alluding to the stranger, "dat bad enough. Ah! dere dey go—de cruel black flag."

"Bravo 'Crucible,'" shouted Tom, forgetting where he was, as a well-directed shot carried away the mast with its sombre banner; "there's another raking shot—good again, 'Crucible.'"

The gallant little craft, commanded by Harold Greystone, the masked captain, now weathered the stranger, and compelled her to go upon another tack. This, owing to the damages she had received, she was indifferently able to perform, and the consequence was that the "Crucible" drew up, and poured in the contents of the whole of her starboard guns.

CHAPTER XIX.

WILL STEADFAST TURNS UP AGAIN.

"OH! golly," said Monkey Jack, caperin "dat bury de rascals under de riggu massa cap'en make it berry warm dis time

"The piratical scoundrels are taking their boats," rejoined Tom, "what a nun ber of them."

"Dey swarm here, Massa Tom, lil flies on big honey pot."

Half-a-dozen boats laden with me were lowered from the pirate, that vess being apparently in a sinking conditio and made towards the shore.

The pirates had found that there wi little hope of escape, but they would n surrender, probably anticipating the fat they fully deserved.

"That's another hornet coming hom to its nest," muttered Tom; "stoppe just in time by the little 'Crucible.'"

The noble little craft was now ver near the shore, and in danger of gettin upon one of the many reefs aboundin there. The captain, perceiving the dan ger, shortened sail, and sending a boat t board the deserted pirate, continued t fire upon the crew making for the shore

The first shot fell short, sending up vast column of water and scattering spra over the nearest boats. The pirates ut tered a yell of derisive defiance.

The second shot turned their defian cries into screams and curses. It cut th largest boat in twain, scattering the mei upon the bosom of the deep.

Regardless of the entreaties of thei drowning men, the others pulled for thei lives, urged almost to madness by the sho which skimmed the water on either side

A second boat was struck, and its oc cupants immersed, but the other four suc ceeded in landing down the beach, where they defiantly waved their weapons unti a round shot ploughed up the sand ai their feet, cut two of them to pieces, and scattered the others right and left.

Those upon the summit of the rock had meanwhile, been shouting encouragement to their comrades, and now that many of them were ashore, hastened down to join company.

Concealed behind a boulder, Jack and Tom Furnace beheld them fraternise, and from their despairing gestures concluded that the lost pirate vessel had a valuable cargo of plunder, which they deemed wonl sink with the vessel.

But here they were mistaken; more men were sent from the "Crucible," and were seen to work the pumps; the shot holes were got at and plugged, and the maimed vessel, with what sail she could carry, stood out to sea with her conqueror.

Then arose from the pirates, who had eagerly watched these movements, a chorus of shrieks and blasphemies, engendered by the loss they had sustained, and the mortification of knowing that the fruits of their criminal labours had been plucked from their grasp.

They danced like madmen in their agonised disappointment; drew their knives, and flourished them in the air; fired their pistols at the retreating "Crucible" in impotent rage; and did a score other things, equally absurd, in a wild and frenzied manner, as if they were indeed demented.

The pirates—those from the ship and those from the rock—gradually grew cooler, and lay upon the sands in groups.

Tom, who had for the moment forgotten his friend, suddenly remembered him with a feeling of reproach.

"Jack," he said, "we are forgetting Will."

"Poor Massa Steadfast; me fear him dead," sighed Jack.

"Don't croak like that, old hoss," broke in a cheery voice, and Will himself stood before him.

"It's not your ghost—is it, old fellow?" gasped Tom.

"Ghost be smothered," returned Will, "it is I, safe and sound. If you open your eyes another hair's breadth, Jack, you will never close them again."

"Massa Will," said the negro, taking his hand, "you knock me clean ober for de moment—First, I tink you dead, and dat your spirit, den I tink you alive, but no see how you came har, so I jes' completely flabberglasted, and dat's de solemn trufe."

"As for how I came here," returned Will, "that's a subject for a story, not a long one, but too much to tell here; how long I have been here, I can tell you at once—ever since the pirate skunks rushed down the rock to meet their rascally skunks of comrades."

"Make de bolt when dey turn dere back, Massa Will?"

"Not exactly that, Jacky, old hoss; but we can't stop here, those fellows will soon be returning."

Crawling close to the rock, the trio worked their way back to the bushes unperceived, and struck into the forest.

As Monkey Jack resolved to return across the swamp, Will reserved his story until safe within their temporary home by the coral reef, and despite Tom's entreaties, laughingly refused to say a word on the subject.

"It was an adventure, I assure you," he said, "and my life was saved by a very intimate friend."

"Not a pirate, I hope," rejoined Tom.

"At present, he is not," replied Will, with a merry twinkling in his eye; "what he may become I cannot say."

"But if he is not a pirate," persisted Tom, "how could he save you there?— how could he be present?"

"He was not there."

"Not there?"

"No, and yet, Will, this friend of mine saved me."

"Mystery on mystery," exclaimed Tom; "now be a brick, and tell me what you mean."

"Not until we are safe in the coral grotto," replied Will.

They went back over the morass as they came, finding the journey upon the second occasion easier of performance, passed through the intervening wood, and returned to their late haunt by the crystal pool. It was yet early in the day, but as none of the friends had really slept throughout the night, they lay down under the shade of a tree, and were soon wrapt in sound slumber.

Will Steadfast will tell his story when he awakes, like a young giant refreshed.

CHAPTER XX.

WILL STEADFAST'S STORY. — THE CAPTAIN ASHORE.

As soon as the three friends had recovered from their fatigue, Will was called upon to relate his story—how he fell into the power of the pirates, and how he miraculously (as it seemed) escaped.

"A strange story, but not a long one," Will began; "but the strangest part of it is, Tom, that to you I owe my life!"

"That's all bosh," returned Tom Furnace. "How can it be so. I've not set eyes upon you since I saw you lying under the bushes, yonder, when I set out for a stroll and lost my way."

"Nevertheless, Tom, you saved me: an

compose yourself to listen patiently for a few moments, and if Jack will cease rolling his eyes in that fearful way I'll begin."

"Fire away, Massa Will," rejoined the negro. "I berry quiet, and screw my eyes up tight."

"Very good, Jack. Now, then, for the most veracious account of my adventures: After you left me, Tom, I continued to lie upon my back, half awake and half asleep, dreaming of Old England and all I left behind me—all my uncles, aunts, and pretty cousins, with whom I used to be such a tremendous favourite—ahem! You may smile, Tom, but it's a fact.

"Well, as I was saying, I was dreaming of these old friends, when I became conscious of a pair of very ugly eyes fixed upon me —eyes, my boys, enough to freeze the very marrow of your veins! At first I thought they belonged to some dread monster of the forest, but on closer inspection I observed the outline of a nose—ugly, but still human—in close proximity to them. Then I saw a mouth, and finally, as horrible a countenance as I ever wish to see again.

"Now just mark this, Tom, and you, too, Jack. I'm not a funky one, am I? and you won't think I'm fibbing when I tell you that I kept cool through it all, will you? No. Then on I goes; and mark what follows:

"The ugly fellow looked at me. I looked at him.

"'How do you do?' I asked, as politely as I could, and the unmannerly wretch answered with an oath, and a request in rough but true English for me to 'come out of it!'

"'I'm very comfortable here,' I replied.

"'By the stars!' he growled, producing a pistol about the size of a bow-chaser; 'I'll riddle you, if you're not smart.'

"I saw that he was terribly in earnest, but I was resolved not to be taken quietly, so I sprang up, out with my pricking-iron, and made a thrust at him. He blazed away; the bullet grazed me; see, here, it cut my cap, and then I closed with him.

"We rolled about a good bit, but he was too much for me, and others arriving, I was bound hand and foot, and carried off, picking up a lot of other skulking hounds upon our way.

"They took me to their home, that little lump of rock, which, I assure you my dear boys, is completely honeycombed with galleries and chambers, where the pirates live. Jack, if you insist upon rolling your eyes, I must give up."

"Massa Will," rejoined Jack, apologetically, "I stop 'em now; dey not move for a month."

"Thank you," replied Will Steadfast, "the expression was too much for me. But to proceed: They carried me up the rock, and thrust me into a cell about the size of a purser's cabin, and left me there to 'moody meditation fancy free.' There I remained many hours, long hours, dear boys, and then I heard the sound of a shot from seaward, and the pirates buzzing about like a nest of wasps poked up with a stick.

"One of them, the leader, a certain Mason Wantlake," continued Will, with a significant expression of face, "looked in upon me, and kindly acquainted me with his intention to blow my brains out if his consort, the vessel then being attacked by the 'Crucible,' was sunk.

"I thanked him for the information, and expressed an earnest hope that both he and his consort would be under the sea without delay. He scowled upon me like the brigand he is, and scampered away.

"I suppose I must have been alone about twenty minutes, listening to the bark of the 'Crucible,' and the growl of the pirate, when the door of my cell opened, and another unwholesome pirate entered, that is, he looked as bad as the rest, but he proved, as you shall see, a very decent sort of fellow.

"'You've friends in the wood?' he said, abruptly.

"'I have,' I replied.

"'A middy and a cursed nigger?' he said.

"'No,' I replied, for I would not stand by and hear Jack called a cursed nigger, 'one is a middy and the other a very good fellow.'

"'It does not matter much,' he said, impatiently. 'Now you just cut and run. You will find them at the base of the rock; and tell the young 'un that one good turn deserves another. He saved my life a few hours ago, and I've saved yours. Now we are quits; but if we meet again, look out for squalls.'

"I cut clean away, you may be sure," concluded Will, "and found you as he mid. So you see I am indebted to you for my life, for the pirate was captured, and I believe Wantlake would have blown my brains out. And now tell me, Tom, how it was."

"The fact is," replied Tom, "that Jack tied him up to a tree, where he must have perished; but I quietly gave him a knife, and I suppose he severed his bonds and got away."

"Undoubtedly. And the result is that I am alive and well, instead of being a 'foul unhandsome corse!' Jack, there's a moral for you!"

"A what, massa Will?"

"A moral—a lesson showing you how a little act of mercy may bear good fruit."

"Me berry glad it hab," replied Jack; "but me gib you a moral ob my own: Suppose you sabe all dem pirates' lives, what den? Will dey be all tankful?"

"I fear not, Jack."

"How many would, massa Will?"

"Perhaps not one in twenty, Jack."

"Dat about it, massa Will. Den how am I to 'scriminate 'tween dem? No, genelmen—me berry glad massa Tom fall upon lucky pirate; but whenever I meet one ob dem are skunks I scrunch 'em."

"As you will, Jack," replied Will Steadfast, smiling; "but make sure that I'm not in their clutches first. Now, what's the 'progum,' Jack?"

"De progum, Massa Will, is back again to the 'Crucible.'"

"So soon?"

"At once, sar. I got all de inflammation de cap'en want; so I go back."

"I should like a long stay here," sighed Tom, looking at the sceue beyond the grotto; "but duty before pleasure."

"We not stop here long, anyhow," said Monkey Jack, emphatically. "De pirates rummage 'long here, and make it berry hot."

"They'd never cross the swamp, Jack."

"No, Massa Tom; but dey come round in boats by de sea."

"True, old boy—your instinct is worth ten times more than ours. How about the signals?"

"I hab dem here," returned Jack, producing half a dozen rockets without the sticks, from his pocket.

His first care was to remount them on straight willow-like wands, which he cut for the purpose from a tree close by, and fix them in a position of advantage for discharging.

He chose a jutting point of the rock near the coral creek for a double purpose—it answered the purpose of a look-out point by day, from which he could see and give timely warning of the pirates' approach, and at night it would be favourable to the firing of the rockets, and enable them to be clearly seen at sea.

The "Crucible lay in the offing, while her late capture was gone, probably sent forward to Honour Bay, there to await the final disposal of the masked privateer, Harold Greystone, with which our readers will shortly become acquainted.

Tom and Will joined the negro at his look-out, and although none of them had a glass—an omission on the part of all, which they keenly regretted—they felt certain by the manner the "Crucible" was drawing in, that they were perceived.

"As we are to go," said Will, "we won't wait for night. Wave your cap, Tom—that's it—now I'am certain she perceives us."

"And see, they are lowering a boat. After all, I shan't be sorry to be again on board."

"But jes' look to de right," interposed Monkey Jack, "dere's a nice little lot ob dem cussed skunks comin' dis way."

He pointed to quite a little fleet of pirate boats sweeping round a point near, bent upon getting between the cutter coming from the "Crucible" and the shore.

Undaunted, the boat with its dozen oarsmen pulled towards the rock, and the middies soon perceived the form of their beloved captain in the stern, accompanied by Grim Foote, the boatswain.

"Rash!" muttered Will Steadfast, "but like him—a bold, noble fellow."

The pirates were now nearing fast, some evidently straining every nerve to touch the rock before the little cutter—while others pulled a little out to sea, as if to intercept her should she endeavour to return.

So eager were they in pursuit of their smaller foe, that they failed to heed the movements of the "Crucible," which was creeping in under shortened sail, and deliberately cutting off the pirates in their turn.

"Boom! a loud report rung out, and a shot skipped over the sea, scattering spray in all directions.

The pirates now saw their danger, and endeavoured to return, but the "Crucible," running down faster, poured in shot after shot, scattering confusion and dismay among them.

A cheer rung out from the little cutter, and Harold Greystone, standing erect, waved his sword in defiance of the foe, who was pulling wildly towards the shore to escape the flying missiles of the "Crucible."

"O, golly," cried Jack, capering, "Massa Stanchion de boy to pepper 'em, next to de cap'en. Dere go one boat smash; now dem dirty debels get a good wash."

"Many appear to want it," rejoined Will; "look at their cowardly friends, not one of them halts to pick the poor wretches up."

The pirate boats were indeed pulling in for the shore, regardless of the nature and position of the landing.

Two drove upon a reef, and immediately capsized, but most of the men managed to reach the shingly beach. The others landed in safety, and the men took prompt refuge in the woods to escape the rapid firing of the gallant privateer, which had anchored within three hundred yards of the shore.

One pirate boat alone drew near the cutter, but as the occupants perceived that they could not overhaul her, they too, at last turned towards the shore.

A shot struck the water close to the stern, sending a mass of water over the men; a tall fellow at the helm, who had hitherto kept his face muffled, sprang up and shook his fist at the privateer. The action revealed his face, and immediately the clear voice of Harold Greystone rung out—

"Give way, my men. I must have that fellow."

The pirate heard him, and shouted in reply a few words of defiance, to which the masked captain rejoined.

"Halt, coward, and meet me hand to to hand."

"I fight no dog who wears a mask," returned the pirate, Mason Wantlake, "I show my face in the light of day; off with that velvet, Harold Greystone."

"I will," replied the young privateer, as the boats drew nearer, "when the hour comes, and when it does, look to yourself, Mason Wantlake."

"Why not now?" shouted the other, tauntingly.

"Can you ask," returned Harold, "and yet why do I ask such a thing of you? With real shame, well-merited shame, upon every feature, you care not to hide. That once branded on mine was done by a traitor's hand, but while the stain is there I care for no man to see it."

"Ha! ha!" roared the reckless pirate, "good, Harold, good."

"Laugh on," sternly replied the young privateer, "you have but little time left for mirth, your hour is near."

"Bah," cried the other, "what can you do?"

"Wring a confession from your coward heart."

"Ha! ha! good again, Harold Greystone; no torture in the world could do it."

"We shall see," said Harold. "Give way, men, yon dog will prove the richest prize of all to you."

In a few moments the two boats, about a hundred yards apart, rounded upon the shore of the little bay where Will Steadfast and his friends had taken up their home. Both crews sprang out, and Harold was joined by his three friends, who had followed him along the reef.

The pirates at once followed the example of their comrades and took to the woods, their leader beckoning to the pursuers mockingly to follow them.

Exchanging a hasty greeting with the trio, Harold rushed forward, followed by all his devoted adherents. He was swift of foot, and rapidly outpaced all, and disregarding their entreaties, he followed in the wake of Mason Wantlake, who, with one of his men, kept straight away, the rest having scattered in all directions to foil the pursuit.

Half-mad with apprehension, Monkey Jack followed his young leader, imploring him to stop; until a huge ruffian crossed his path, and his further progress was delayed by the necessity of fighting him.

Will, Tom, Grim Foote, and the crew of the cutter were divided into pursuing parties, the young middies and the boatswain following in the wake of their captain, until they too encountered a portion of the flying foe, upon whom they fell with the utmost fury.

The masked captain kept on, blind to his own danger, and resolved to secure his enemy, or slay him outright.

Suddenly Mason Wantlake said a few

words to the man by his side, and they both turned upon the young privateer.

Not a word was said on either side, for all were panting with the severity of the running; but the keen blades glittered as they entwined, and the turf was trampled by their active feet.

The masked hero swiftly parried half-a-dozen furious thrusts, but the odds were heavy, for both his opponents were well skilled in the weapon they used, and he had to exert his whole knowledge of fencing to shield himself from death.

Cool and wary, Harold Greystone contented himself with acting on the defensive, until the unknown pirate, a huge fellow, succeeded in puncturing his shoulder.

The wound was not deep, but it exasperated the youth, who leaped aside, made a false lunge, thereby throwing off the ruffian's guard, and then drove the bright keen blade through his heart.

The pirate fixed upon him a ghastly stare, made a feeble effort to raise his weapon, swung round upon his heel, and fell dead.

"Now, Wantlake," cried the young privateer, "we are alone, man to man. Have a care to shield your traitorous carcase."

Trampling to and fro, they lunged and guarded with lightning-like rapidity, the fire of their swords matched by the gleaming lustre of their eyes.

Hand to hand and foot to foot they fought, the one to satiate his hate, and the other to avenge his dishonour.

In height they were well matched; but the pirate was the stronger—he was older and more burly in form, and the weapon he wielded was heavier by far than the light weapon borne by Harold Greystone.

The young privateer fully understood and appreciated these disadvantages; and there was another danger in store for him, the blood was flowing fast from the wound in his shoulder, and he was growing faint.

"Shall I fall and die with the stain of dishonour upon me!" he thought—"O! wretched fate."

"He is wounded," thought Wantlake; "let me play with him a little while, and he will fall easily into my power."

Acting upon this thought, he retreated step by step, while Harold, conscious of his dimming sight and failing nerves, followed him up and thrust with the fury of despair.

His wound sent forth an increasing jet of blood, which ran over the gold lace of his jacket, and fell drop by drop upon the moss covered ground. The pirate smiled as he saw, and retreated further away.

"You have lost your skill, Greystone," he said jeeringly; "I could drill a dozen holes in your mountebank jacket, if I so willed it."

"Do it, you cur!" panted our hero, "die, or fight like a man, not run like a beaten hound."

"I prefer playing with my fish before I land it," replied Wantlake, coolly; "besides, I have no desire to kill you—just yet—you will become insensible, *mon cher*, in a few minutes, and I will make you prisoner. My men will be very glad to get hold of the man who has cost us so many lives."

"They are a ruffianly crew," rejoined the masked captain.

"Their trade would not suit drawing room dandies," was the reply. "Steady, Greystone, you are getting weak on your pins; why, man, you bleed like a pig!"

"Coward!" muttered Harold, staggering back and leaning upon his sword. "Strike, ruffian; you have destroyed my good name, now murder me."

"All in good time," returned Wantlake, laughing; "steady, man, you are not in a ball-room, and needn't waltz. Ha! already—now, my friend, I have you."

Harold Greystone had fainted, and for a moment his foe stood over him with upraised sword as if he would have completed his work; but acting upon a design he had formed in his mind during the last few minutes, he raised the inanimate form and bore it into the forest.

Half an hour later his friends, headed by Monkey Jack, having slain or beaten off the foe, arrived upon the spot, where the signs of a struggle and the dead body of the pirate told a dismal tale.

CHAPTER XXI.

THE CAPTAIN MISSING.—TRACKING HIM TO THE PIRATE'S HAUNT.—MASON WANTLAKE'S REVENGE.

"DERE been a fight here; berry serus," said Monkey Jack, running over the ground like a hound upon the scent; "one—two—three foot—and dat one de cap'en. Ha! here one runaway, not de cap'en's; where dat one got to?"

Jack rapidly skirted the ground where the encounter took place, but, of course, found no signs of his leader.

Halting, he thought for a moment, and then the truth burst upon him.

"Massa cap'en killed or wounded," he said, wringing his hands; "and oder pirate carry him away. Wurra! wurra! dis wus dan all—dis berry bad indeed."

Will Steadfast and Tom, surrounded by the men, stood gazing upon Monkey Jack, who capered about with grief.

His actions were very grotesque, and at any other time would have brought a smile to their faces, but they were sad and silent, and could only exchange looks of apprehension and grief.

"What is to be done, Jack?" asked Will.

"Get de men ashore from de 'Crucible,'" replied Jack. "den follow up——"

"And fight it out," rejoined Will; "back to the boat."

They hastened again to the beach, but here a new and terrible disappointment awaited them.

The boats had disappeared, and the "Crucible" had drawn out a mile further from the shore.

"We will not dally here," said Will, assuming the lead, as he was entitled to do; "how many do we muster—Tom, Jack, Foote, and seven men, with myself, eleven in all. Who volunteers to rescue our good captain?"

All held up their hands, and Will rapidly continued,—.

"Jack, lead the way, track the footmarks of that ruffian, we will know our captain's fate ere the sun dips into the sea."

"Hurrah!" shouted his listeners, in chorus.

"Ready hands and willing hearts will win him back to us," pursued Will, warming with his theme; "not a moment is to be lost. Follow Jack, and silence, now, if you please."

The negro tightened his belt, settled his hat upon his head, and forthwith proceeded on the track of the pirate chief and his victim.

Our readers are fully acquainted with the black's extraordinary instinct, and we will therefore abstain from giving a full account of their journey through the wood until they came to a point where Mason Wantlake had been joined by many others.

Here Jack halted, and after a keen survey of the ground, declared that at least fifty had fallen in with their leader, and proceeded with him into the interior of the forest.

With vast odds like these, additional precaution became necessary, the more so as Jack informed them that they were not far ahead, in fact, he said, had they followed in the first instance instead of rushing down for assistance from the "Crucible" they would have recovered their captain, dead or alive, before his captor had met with the great body of his comrades.

Confounding his want of judgment, Will Steadfast bade Jack continue the pursuit; but the negro insisted upon going alone, as the day was far advanced, and the pirates would in all probability not travel very far.

"I see jes' whar dem rascal camp," he said, "den I come back, and we drop upon dem in de night."

Without waiting for an approval of his plan, the negro sped away, and the tired sailors lay down to rest.

Will, Tom, and Grim Foote sat together, with their backs against the trunk of a mighty banana tree, gloomy and silent.

Jack came speedily back with the news that the pirates had settled down for the night by the side of a spring, and that the masked captain was in their power, alive, but wounded.

This news gave his listeners new life; their captain was not dead, and it should go hard with them if they failed to rescue him.

Naturally, all were eager to advance at once, but this was overruled by Will Steadfast, who held a short conference with Jack, and declared night to be a more fitting time.

We must leave them for a time, and see how it fares with our bold young hero, captive among a horde of ruffians.

Recovering from his temporary insensibility, he found that he was carried on a rough sort of litter by four men, and a number of others were around him.

Fortunately, his wound was roughly bandaged, but his limbs were strongly bound, and resistance or escape for the present hopeless.

By his side marched Wantlake, who occasionally turned exultant looks upon his captive, and once he spoke.

"I thought you went up with the 'Curlew,' he said; "but I thank the Fates for reserving me this hour."

"A higher Power than the Fates you thank is reserving another hour for you. Beware of that!" replied Harold.

"You will not live to see."

"Perhaps not; but your punishment will be the same."

"You canting hound!" sneered Wantlake; "you branded coward!"

"Give me a weapon," replied the young privateer, calmly, "then face me if you dare, wounded as I am."

"Bah!" exclaimed the other, "I am not such a fool. I have a very different treat for you in store."

"It matters little," said Harold; "it can but end in death."

"It will not end there," hissed the pirate, "for mark you, my old comrade, I intend you to wander for many years to come; a curse to yourself, and a thing to pity. Ah! your face may blanch. I can see that part beneath your mask turn pale. A thing of pity, I say, shall Harold Greystone be."

"What would you do?"

Wantlake whispered in his ears. The form of the masked privateer visibly trembled.

"Surely you would not be so pitiless?" he said.

"I can, and will," cried the pirate; "put down your burden, men, we will rest in this glade to-night, and hold high revelry o'er this bold young captain."

The men laid down the litter, and proceeded to assist their comrades in preparing for the night. Mason Wantlake threw himself upon the turf beside his captive.

"Greystone," he said, "you asked me a few moments ago if I could be so cruel, and I told you I could. Cruelty I love and revel in—have done so from a child."

"You are a merciless scoundrel."

"Yes! I am," coolly rejoined the other. "I would not exercise it for any one, much less for you. I know that I am cruel, remorseless, pitiless, but never so pitiless, remorseless, and cruel as now—shall I tell you why?"

"Consult your own desires," rejoined Harold, coldly.

"I will," returned the pirate. "Harold Greystone, you robbed me of the girl I loved, and made me what I am."

"Had I never lived," replied the young privateer, "she would have despised you as she does now."

"It's a lie!" furiously cried the pirate, striking the earth with his clenched hand; "until you came on board the 'Curlew,' all went well with me. I was the favoured knight, and made happy by the sunshine of her smiles. You came upon me like a cloud, and then what was Mason Wantlake? A thing to look coldly on, and pass coldly by. It was all Harold Greystone—Harold Greystone, and none but he, to attend upon my lady."

"Wantlake," said Harold, after a pause, "your life has been one great mistake. Clara never loved you; she saw your boorish devotion, and was kind, until your mad conceit prompted you to insult. After that you were of necessity a stranger. The trap you fell into was of your own making."

"Greystone," returned the other, in tones of concentrated passion, "I know you lie. I have been bitterly wronged, and I will be bitterly avenged. My life may have been a mistake, as you arrogantly observe, but there will be no error in what I am about to do. My revenge shall be full and complete."

"Dastard," exclaimed our hero, with a curling lip; "you taunt a helpless man?"

"I know, Harold Greystone," he replied, "but your mock notions of honour trouble not me. I have promised to send you forth into the world an object of pity to all. I will do it, Harold Greystone; I will revive an old custom, and will slit that delicate nose, and cut off your ears, and I will put out your eyes! Yes, I, Mason Wantlake, the Philistine, will destroy the eyesight of my puny Samson."

As he uttered this diabolical threat, the scoundrel leant over, and turned back the mask of his victim. He looked upon the face he hated with his whole heart, hoping to see some sign of fear, but the look of scorn he encountered compelled him to avert his gaze, and replacing the covering over Harold's face, he sank back into his old position.

"You are a good actor," he said; "you can hide the flutterings of your coward heart."

"I have no flutterings to conceal," replied our hero; "if my pulse is quickened, this wound upon my shoulder is the cause. I do not fear you. Do what you will, I can only despise one so base and vile."

"We shall see," muttered Wantlake, rising—"the time is near—we shall see. Now, my hearties," he added addressing his men, "bind this lady-bird to yon tree."

Half a dozen ruffians raised Harold from the ground, and bound him fast to a stout young palm, whose graceful foliage, rising above the surrounding trees, was gilded by the rays of the setting sun.

Already the shadows of evening were gathering in the forest, and the pirates had prepared a huge fire to ignite, when darkness set in—opposite this Harold was bound.

When that was done, Wantlake bade his men gather around. They gathered together in a group fronting the pile. The young pirate then addressed them.

"Freebooters of the Point," he began, "we have here captive a little fly that has buzzed about our ears for the past few months. He has destroyed our gallant little 'Defiance,' captured our consort, the 'Hornet,' and by foul means made many vacancies in our mess."

A murmuring passed among the men, and the shadows of the night grew deeper.

"Many around me," pursued Wantlake, "miss the familiar face of a father, brother, or some dear comrade. Where are they? —lying at the bottom of the sea, food for fishes—sent there by whom? The man that stands before you."

A growl escaped the throats of the gang of ruffians, and the shadows of the night grew deeper still.

"To him we owe our losses," continued Wantlake, "him we may thank for comrades slain—and now that he is here, what shall be his fate?"

"Let him die," shouted the barbarians.

"Die!" repeated Wantlake. "No! that were poor revenge. Cut off the dog's ears, slit his nose, put out his eyes, and turn him adrift, a warning to all who cross our path."

A hoarse affirmative shout uprose, and darkness fell around them.

"Fire the pile," cried Wantlake.

As he spake, a terrific hissing noise fell upon the pirates' ears, and a long train of fire darted through their midst, blinding several, and scattering the rest.

Like all cowardly natures, the ruffians were superstitious, and many fell upon their knees, while others stood paralyzed, glaring at the darkness around.

Again came the awful sound, and a second train of fire passed through them, and horror-stricken, they turned and fled.

Our hero was as completely dumfounded as the rest, the phenomena was of such an incomprehensible nature, but the solution was soon given him, for his bonds were cut asunder, a few words whispered in his ear by Will Steadfast, and he felt himself borne away on the shoulders of several sturdy men.

Recovering from his surprise, he could make out the forms of about a dozen men, headed by Monkey Jack, gliding like shadows between the trees. Looking down at those who bore him, he made out Will Steadfast and Tom Furnace, one on either side.

Will drew near him and took his hand, Harold cordially returned it, but as he judged imperative silence was necessary, uttered not a word.

Thus in silence the party walked for an hour or more, when the murmuring of the sea was heard. Then Will spake softly.

"Are you wounded?" he asked,

"Slightly," replied his captain.

"We feared the worst."

"But you acted for the best, Will," returned Harold, laying a hand upon the boy's shoulder, "how did you find me?"

"Jack did it," said Will, "and he must tell the story."

CHAPTER XXII.
MONKEY JACK'S STORY.

JACK led the way to the grotto where he had been staying with the mids, and entered it in silence. The party followed, a torch was lit, and then Jack gave vent to his feelings.

"Massa cap'en," he said, wiping his eyes with the sleeve of his coat, "I berry glad, I tingle all ober, I altogedder exscrutinated with joy, I cry like a big fool."

"Jack," said our hero, toking his hand, "a few more fools like you around me, and others may have all the wise men the world ever knew."

After this, he exchanged hearty greetings with all those who had shared in his rescue, and some of the men went out to gather brushwood to make a resting-place for the captain.

Soon the whole party were gathered in a circle in the interior of the grotto, more torches were lit, and garments hung over the entrance to hide the light. These precautions taken, the captain asked for the story of his rescue, by whom and how it was performed.

"Jack will tell the story," said Will, "he knows all about it."

"I'm not good at lannygoats," Jack began.

"Anecdotes, Jack."

"Lannygoats, massa cap'en, but I hab a shy at dis one. When you, sar, run away like deer I follow berry quick until I hab force to stop and kill two chuckle-headed pirates, den I lose you ontil I come to de spot where you fight one—two pirates."

"That is where I overtook the greatest scoundrel of them all," said Harold; "go on, Jack."

"When I see blood about," continued the negro, "an' turf squashed, I say de cap'en killed, an' I howl like picanniny dat steal de sugar, an' get hard slap on him tender part. But den, Massa Will and Tom, and all dese grinning children here, say go an' get de 'Crucible' men. We come to de shore, but de oars gone, a great hole punched in de boat, and not'ing was left but for us to come after you, massa cap'en, as we were."

"Boldly done, Jack."

"Massa Will take de lead, like true young middy; den he say, 'Come on this moment, an' squatulate de ole bilin' lot ob warmints,' but I say, 'No, Massa Will, follow dem, and down upon dem in de dark.'"

"Very prudent, Jack."

"It am so, sar; so I jes' make out whar dem pirates stop for de night, den I bring up all dese children, one at one time, and we all get snug among de bushes, to see what dem up to."

"But how about those mysterious streams of fire, Jack?"

"I come to dat, dis moment, sar; Massa Will say to me in whisper—tickle my ear he do, so close him speak, an' he say, 'Jack, you hab some rockets in your pocket?' I whisper back, and tickle him ear, and I say, "Massa Will, I hab', den he say agen, 'You jes' shoot one straight at dem beggars, bend down dat ting, so it go prop'ly, dat skeer dem more dan anytink,' so I stick de rocket in de ground sloping, and I bend down stick ober it, I do anoder de same, and den me shoot one."

"It startled me, Jack," laughed the captain; "no wonder it alarmed those cowardly ruffians."

"I see de rocket shoot," grinned Jack, "an' give gib one feller sech a crack on de jaw as make him teeth rattle like bag ob bones. Down him go, and oders dance 'bout like Cuba bumboat men when dey swindle ole ship's crew. So I send second rocket, dat make 'em dance more, den we cut de ropes dat was round you, sar, an' come home here, sar, widout speakin' one word, so dat de skunks not know whar to foller."

"Thank you, Jack," said Harold, "I am much indebted to you and all my friends here. Trust me, this night's work will not be forgotten."

"And now my story done," rejoined Jack, "me gib a bit of advice. De 'Crucible' de bes' place jes' now. In anoder hour or two we hab all de bilin' ob pirates skulkin' along de coast. Me go out, see if they show light anywhar."

Jack accordingly departed, the torches were extinguished, and the rest of the party adjourned to the open air.

It was a glorious starry night, such as you and I, dear reader, never see in this cold clime, and the room was just showing her round large face from the sea, while ever and anon a meteor flashed across the sky, and faded out for ever.

The silver-tinted waves lapped the shore so gently that no foam lay upon the sands; not a breath of air ruffled the foliage of the forest, not a cry broke the stillness of its gloom.

About a mile from the shore they could see the faint outline of the "Crucible" at anchor, her naked spars and rigging intersecting the stars like a monstrous cobweb, while from her hull lights momentarily gleamed, as signals to the hoped-for friends on shore.

Looking towards the narrow reef, they could see the form of Monkey Jack, crawl over it like some monstrous insect, his cocked hat forming a powerful resemblance to the head of a gigantic beetle. They saw him halt for a moment at the head, and then a rocket darted upward towards the gleaming stars.

Instanter a boat was seen coming over the gentle waves, propelled by powerful arms. It passed the point, entered the little bay, grated upon the beach, received its willing passengers, and returned to the gallant little craft lying at anchor in the moonlight.

CHAPTER XXIII.

THE STRANGE VISITORS. — THE SHOT AT MIDNIGHT.

THE return of Harold Greystone and his comrades to the "Crucible" was, in a measure, enforced—the enemy was too powerful for the little party, and prudence prompted a retreat.

What of that? Wise and great generals retire before impossible odds, but where reinforcements are at hand, they "have another shy," and probably thrash their opponents.

But the visit had not been without its useful results; the young privateer had learned a little of the strength of the pirates; Monkey Jack knew a little more, and Will Steadfast could furnish him with a vast amount of information.

The sum and substance of that information was this :—

Massa Wantlake was in possession of a stronghold, with at least three hundred men at his beck and call.

He was also connected with a vast gang of sea-robbers, who had stations all along the coast, and although the gallant Harold had destroyed and captured several, there were many more roaming about or in their secret harbours.

The vessel last captured, as witnessed by Monkey Jack and Tom Furnace, was one of the piratical fleet who, all unsuspecting, was boldly entering the bay when the little "Crucible," mistaken by the captain for Wantlake's ship, fell foul of her, and brought down her colours.

He furthermore learned what our readers are already of, that Captain Harloch, late of H.M.S. "Curlew," was, with his fair daughter, entrenched within the wood awaiting help from a cruiser expected at the point, and this fact was a double source of perplexity to our gallant young hero.

He wished to rescue the captain from his present predicament, but he was not strong enough, and he wanted to see the issue of events, but the contact with a Government vessel, probably of a heavy calibre, would be disastrous in every way to his projects.

"Not yet," he mused, as he restlessly paced his cabin; "my time has not yet come. Oh, Heaven! send the day quickly that sees the restoration of my good name."

Will Steadfast knew much of his captain's affairs, and he, too, was puzzled to d a satisfactory course to pursue

To fly now would leave a path open for the escape of Wantlake and his crew; to remain there might place the little "Crucible" in the power of some English man-of-war.

"I'm hanged if I can tell what the captain will do," he said to Tom Furnace, to whom he had been rather confidential on the subject; "we can't run, and we can't cut that fellow out, for the rock is honeycombed for musket, and they've huge masses of stone, placed on the balance, ready to topple over, which would crush a hundred men. But as for leaving without having another shy at him, that can't be thought of. I'm completely bothered."

Nor could Tom help him out of the difficulty. As for Monkey Jack, he was downright absurd when he proposed " to lick de big English ship. Massa cap'en lick anyting, double 'em up like ole hat."

"He will never fire at a British craft," rejoined Will gravely; "he is no traitor to his country. He wars with pirates and he fights For Honour."

All this transpired within two hours of their return to the "Crucible," and dawn was breaking as Will gave forth this decided opinion upon the captain's course of conduct.

As soon as the sun was above the sea, Will swept the horizon with his glass; not a sail was in sight.

"Thank goodness," he exclaimed, "we shall not have to run just yet."

"Neber see de day
Dat ' Crucible ' run away,"

sang a voice close by, and Crikey crossed the deck with a coffee pot for the captain.

Will and Tom smiled, but Monkey Jack took offence at his brother's singing.

"You open your ugly mouf on deck agen," he said, "and I'll hab it corked wid a big bundle ob oakum."

Crikey grinned from ear to ear, but disappeared down the companion ladder without a word. Below they heard him singing—

"A little ship upon de sea,
　Was waitin' for de foe
Axing him to come an' fight,
　And dat foe say ' No, no.'
But still him hide behind de rock,
　And wink him wicked eye,
And say, ' When it again am dark,
　To run I'll hab a try.' "

"Crikey is quite a poet," said Will, smiling.

"Him catch it ob t'oder bumboat men," returned Jack, indignantly, "but I soon

LYING IN WAIT.

lick it out ob him. He be. de fust ob our fam'ly dat am conflicted so."

Will endeavoured to point out that it was rather an accomplishment than otherwise, but Jack would not have it so.

"It low habit," he said, "and I take it out ob him."

With this intimation he dived below, and a very warm colloquy indeed ensued between him and his worthy brother, which, however, subsided before the going down of the sun.

The day proved an uneventful one. The enemy did not show from land, and the sea gave up no cruiser, so Harold and his men had a lazy time of it. Nevertheless, everything was prepared to run in closer or out to sea at a moment's notice,

The night was destined to be more eventful; but ere we record what passed we wish to have a few private words with our readers.

This is a sea story—well and good; but in narrating the events of our hero's carreer we have purposely avoided hampering these pages with technical sea terms, incomprehensible to most landsmen.

We could, if we would, pen every word

of command uttered, and write learnedly, after the fashion of the literary small fry, of cleats, combings, jib-booms, davits, cat-heads, and so on, very clever, no doubt, but very confusing to the young mind, who reads for amusement, and not with the intention of qualifying himself for second mate to the forecastle cook. We have, therefore, cast aside many sea terms to make this little narrative as clear as possible to old and young, who live on land and love the briny waves.

To resume:

The night, we say, proved to be eventful; the moon rose early, and for a while shone undimmed by a cloud; but towards midnight some ugly little "rags" crossed the sky, hurrying from the nor'-west like messengers of bad tidings.

Grim Foote said they had something bad behind them, and Grim Foote was right.

Everything aloft was stowed away, and preparations were made for the anticipated squall.

Every eye was fixed upon the cloudy messengers, increasing every minute in number, and none thought anything, or very little of their enemies on shore.

They, however, were on the alert, and a number of them, in boats, were stealing towards the "Crucible," with muffled oars.

Faster and faster rose the clouds, and crossing the face of the moon, darkened the ocean.

Nearer and nearer came the boats with their villanous crews.

Will Steadfast and his chum, both off duty, sat by the bulwarks, talking, as youths delight to do, of daring deeds and longing for well-earned fame.

"I'm getting awful strong," said Will, playing with his sword, "and I am a match for many men."

"So you are, Will," replied Tom gravely, "but you want weight. Hallo! did you hear that?"

"Where, what?"

"Something touched against the ship's side."

"Hush, I hear it now."

Both the lads turned over, and knelt, listening. At that moment the clouds parted from the face of the moon, and the forms of two men climbing over the bulwarks were revealed to the lads.

"Like your impudence," said Will, split-ting the foremost ruffian's skull with sword. "To the rescue! help! an attack

Over the vessel's sides a host of ruffians poured; but the "Crucibles," hearing the boy's shout, rushed upon deck, the young privateer and his sable attendant foremost

The attacking party numbered fifty men, perhaps, and there were more coming, as Harold, who cast a swift glance towards the shore, could see.

Waving his finely-tempered sword, he rushed upon the foe.

"Forward, my men!" he shouted "down with the dogs! remember, a prize for every pirate slain. Forward, my gallant fellows! cut them down!"

His call was obeyed readily, pistols flashed, and clashing sabres sent forth myriads of sparks as the two throngs met.

Half-blinded by the smoke and noise the two mids kept close to their gallant leader, and cut and thrust like men; Jack just behind, intent upon the safety of the three whom he loved more than all the rest of the world.

The pirates seemed to be without a leader, at least no one thrust himself into that prominent position, but the truth must be confessed they fought well.

It was dogged, brutal courage; but there was no flinching. Hand to hand foot to foot, they fought and fell.

Harold caught sight of Mr. Stanchion plying his sword as a reaper does his scythe, and shouted to him to look out for the other boats.

The lieutenant sprang into the bows, and saw them hastening towards the shore.

This conduct was at first inexplicable, but the cause was soon apparent. Looking to windward, he saw a white wall of foam stalking down upon them.

A terrific hurricane was approaching.

Everything was ready; the storm-sails of the "Crucible" were set, and the lieutenant rushed aft. Grim Foote, who had also seen the danger, was at the wheel. So far all well.

The fight, in the meantime, went fiercely on—the pirates believing in approaching help, the others fighting with all their heart for life and liberty. Hand to hand, foot to foot, for life or death.

The squall came down, struck the "Crucible" with irresistible force, and drove her on her beam ends.

Friends and foes tumbled together in a confused mass, many receiving accidental wounds as they fell, and half-a-dozen, rolling through a porthole, disappeared in the foaming sea, and were never heard of more.

The "Crucible" righted, and Grim Foote, at his post, put her straight before the wind.

Up sprang the combatants, and in the dim light renewed the deadly strife.

The elements fought and hissed, and screamed and roared. The hoarse shouts of men, the clash of sabres, the noise of pistols, was lost amidst the din, but men fell and rolled upon the deck in the agony of death, their last shriek drowned by the roar of the wind and water.

Yet another horror! A flash of lightning rent aside the dark clouds, revealing the faces of the angered men, with eyes flashing and lips compressed, as they parried and cut like maniacs.

No quarter!—what wretch had voice enough to plead for it? A shrill trumpet would have been sounded then in vain.

Thinned in numbers, bewildered by the glare of the lightning, hopeless of escape, the pirates lost all heart; the "Crucibles" saw it and cut them down like sheep.

A few, some three or four, preferred a watery grave, and sprang overboard, the rest died by pistol or sword, the last falling by the keen weapon of Harold Greystone.

Through all he had kept up his cries of encouragement, useless as we know, but in the heart of the combat he thought not of the storm; now it was over, he clung to the mainstays, and looked around him.

What a scene of terrible grandeur.

The lightning glared unceasingly, revealing the huge waves as they uprose, foaming and roaring on either side, and the deck strewn with men, dead or in their last agonies.

He looked around for his friends. Will and Tom were safe, clinging to the tackle of a gun, but poor Monkey Jack lay stretched upon the boards, motionless.

"Poor Jack," he exclaimed, and then, as the Prince of Wales spoke of Falstaff, he added, "I could better have spared a better man."

The next moment he asked himself where a better than Jack could be found, one more faithful, honourable, and true, and then he made an effort to reach him.

It was strange that during the heat of the combat he kept his feet, but now that the excitement was over, he could barely make his way to the side of poor Jack; but so it was, and it was only by clinging to every available support that he eventually succeeded.

Will and Tom, watching his movements, perceived the cause of it, and speedily joined him, all lamenting the fall of their ebony favourite.

Harold, kneeling, felt his heart. It beat still. He thanked Heaven for that, but poor Jack was grievously wounded by a severe sabre cut across the head, and a pistol bullet lay in his shoulder.

How it was done none of the actors could tell; but, while the wind howled and the lightning flashed, they got Jack below, and placed him under the charge of Mr Thornley, and then returned on deck.

The wind by this time had lulled, and the thunder ceased to roar, although the distant lightning still illumined the sea, and the waves rose as high as ever, lifting their white foam-crested heads almost mast high.

Harold succeeded in reaching Mr. Stanchion's side, and being able at last to make himself heard, inquired how many men of the "Crucible" had fallen.

"Cannot say for the moment, sir," replied the lieutenant, "three went overboard I know—poor Turner of the 'Curlew' was one—I saw his face as he went through the porthole—just as the squall struck us."

"Poor fellow," sighed our hero, "he has had his share of perils at sea. How nobly we have ridden the storm."

"The 'Crucible,'" cried Mr. Stanchion, enthusiastically, "can weather anything," and he was pretty right.

One would have thought that they had endured enough for one night, but the perils of the hours of darkness were not yet over.

Close on their weather bow a large vessel suddenly loomed, showing many teeth— or guns, my young friends—as she bore down upon them.

Heedless of the heavy sea, she fired a gun as a signal for the "Crucible" to display a signal or heave-to.

The "Crucible" declined to do either.

She kept on her way, edging off from the unwelcome stranger, who, however, would not be thus curtly cut.

Another gun was fired, and a shot danced across the bow of the privateer.

"Thank you," muttered the young captain; "but you must send something nearer than that ere I heave-to. Will, do you know her?"

"It's the 'Bruiser!'" replied the mid. "I know her well, and her captain, old Stiff; he is not to be trifled with."

"We'll have some fun with him nevertheless," rejoined Harold; "he cannot damage us much with such a sea running."

He gave orders for the "Crucible" to be put dead before the wind, thereby showing the stern of the craft to the frigate—and then instructed the men to hang out a couple of lanterns in full sight of Captain Stiff, who was watching the lively little craft with angry eyes.

"A pirate!" muttered that worthy officer, "give her another shot, Mr. Llewellyn."

Mr. Llewellyn obeyed; but it flew wide, and the "Crucible" impudently putting on more sail, skimmed the waves like a bird.

"Whoever that fellow is," growled Captain Stiff, "he's a good plucked one. Can we carry more canvas?"

"I fear not, sir," replied the lieutenant.

"Then he'll give us the good-bye, Mr. Llewellyn, and see, the saucy knave hangs out a couple of lanterns; keep in his wake we'll overhaul him in the morning."

But he did not; the gleaming lanterns died out and in the surrounding darkness, and in the morning Captain Stiff had an interesting view of a clear sea.

"A cursed clever fellow," he muttered.

"A phantom craft," said the men; "for take her size, and the canvas she put on, it was impossible to live in such a sea."

Our readers know who was right.

CHAPTER XXIV.

THE ILLNESS OF MONKEY JACK.—THE STRANGE ISLAND.

FOR many days Jack lay in a precarious state; the heavy cut he received across the head entirely upset his theory of the strength and durability of the skulls of his much maligned and unfortunate race, but the shot wound rapidly healed up after the bullet was extracted.

The captain came often to see him, but he was unconscious of the visits, and raved of piccaninnies, the forests of his native land, his troubles as a slave, and of his 'beloved master," mixing them together in a strange jumble, as minds diseased are wont to do.

Will and Tom helped to nurse nigger as he was; and, when reason returned, sat by his side reading aloud, or talking of his exploits past, present, and to come, in fact, doing all they could to cement the love Jack already bore towards them.

Two others on board were also keenly interested in the recovery of the captain's favourite; all were more or less so, but these demand special notice. They were Crikey and Duncan, the ship's carpenter.

The latter bore but little love for Jack, and he regarded the prostration of the sable hero with a feeling akin to joy; indeed, he went so far as to earnestly hope that the nigger was about "to slip his cable," but he kept that hope within his breast, it was more than for his life's sake he dare do.

As for Crikey, his grief was all-consuming, and he went about shedding an incredible quantity of tears, singing, in a hysterical manner scraps of "poetry," and blundering so frightfully in his duties that he and the cook were at perpetual war.

"Confound your thick hide," roared the cook, "what are you doing now?"

"I berry much done up," replied Crikey, "an' I spill de brown gravy."

Poor ole Jack, him on him bed,
An ugly cut upon him head.

"Dash your brother's head!" growled the cook, "you spill another thing to-day, and I'll lay you up for a week."

Nevertheless, Crikey continued to mourn, sing his scraps of versification, and break things, until the cook was on the verge of insanity, and sounds of strife hourly arose from the little den in the forecastle where the food was prepared.

Having taken the necessary observations, the masked hero and Mr. Stanchion ascertained that the storm had driven them nearly three hundred miles in a nor'-westerly direction.

"It will be useless to return to Cape Blanco," said our hero—"at least, for the present. I shall return to Honour Bay by a circuitous route, to escape our friend, the "Bruiser," and there fit out another craft. I shall put you in command with Furnace, and we can sail in company. Let Wantlake then look to himself."

Such a proposition, of course, delighted the lieutenant, and he hastened to put the ship upon her course, while the captain went below to visit Monkey Jack.

With regard to Clara Harloch and her

father, our hero was much disturbed, but he knew that there were stout English hearts around them, and but for some untoward event, would remain in safety until help arrived, either from a British cruiser or himself.

Mason Wantlake, he knew, would fly the place, or at the most, make one effort to capture Captain Harloch and his daughter, but the arrival of the " Bruiser," which was bound for Cape Blanco, would limit the operations of that young gentleman, and compel him to fly.

So for seven days the " Crucible" sailed homeward without encountering anything worthy of recording, and at noon on the eighth day the man at the masthead cried, —

"Land, ho!"

In a few minutes it was visible to those on deck, rising like a cloud out of the sea —an island apparently about fourteen miles long.

It was unknown to all on board the "Crucible," nor was it down on any of the charts. The fact was our hero was sailing out of the usual track, and had fallen upon one of those islands which are dotted about the vast watery expanse, ignorant of the other parts of the world, and themselves unknown.

Although time was precious, Harold decided to touch there—water was running short, and a little fresh meat, if animals could be found, would be very acceptable.

Drawing nearer, they could see narrow belt of yellow sand where the waves fell and scattered foam, running from end to end without any break of huge rocks, so common to the isles of the Atlantic. Behind, the country appeared to be a vast unbroken wood of giant trees, some rising like huge spires, others slim and topped with broad leaves glistening with gold and silver tints as they moved in the sunshine.

"One of those Edens without its Adam and Eve, I suppose," said Harold.

"Not so, sir," rejoined Mr. Stanchion. "I can see a number of creatures moving on the beach."

Harold too the glass, and as his craft drew nearer he perceived that there were many score men and women on the beach, scampering to and fro in a state of intense excitement. They were naked, and seemed to be very stunted in form.

As they drew nearer the beings on shore became plainly discernible. They were indeed a wretched race—none more than five feet in height, with huge heads, and unnaturally broad chests, like the mannikins who guard the gates of the sultan.

As soon as the "Crucible" dropped anchor and a boat put off, containing our hero, Will, Monkey Jack (now recovering rapidly), and a dozen men, they scampered into the bushes like startled rabbits, and the beach was clear.

Harold stepped ashore, and Jack, with difficulty—for he was yet very weak— followed. Several of the men accompanied them—the rest remained with Will in charge of the boat.

Advancing to the bushes, Harold espied a solitary native standing about a hundred yards beyond, with his body half turned, ready to fly.

Our hero made signs of friendship, the savage remained immovable; then Harold held up a yellow silk handkerchief and waved it. The colour and material roused the curiosity of the native, and he drew a few steps nearer.

By degrees, they enticed him to within a dozen yards, but there he remained immovable, blinking his large eyes and rolling his matted head.

He was a ghastly sight, a veritable boguey, more horrible than any ever described by nursery maids when they wish to freeze obstreperous youngsters into silence.

Short, stunted, bow legs, arms of an unnatural length, chest broad and muscular as a giant's, features ugly and repulsive to a degree, distorted by vile arts, and made more repulsive by fish bones through his lips and nostrils, were presented to the astounded visitors, who stood as if they could not realize the sight, all but Jack, who had probably seen men as horrible in the inner wilds of sun-scorched Africa.

There he stood blinking, until Harold tossed the handkerchief to his feet, this he picked up and examined as a miser would the unexpected discovery of a bag of gold.

Then he made signs for other portions of our hero's apparel, but the young privateer shook his head, and pointing to the trees and a few wild hogs in the distance imitated the act of eating.

The savage nodded his head, and went through a pantomime of an extraordinary nature, twisting, turning, rolling on the ground, and finally staggering about as if he bore a heavy burden.

It was all incomprehensible to our hero; but Jack put an interpretation, correct, as usual, upon it.

"Him go dis berry day," said Jack, "him an' all him people to hunt de hog. To-morrow dey come and bring enuf to fill ship."

"He did not seem much astonished," rejoined Harold; "fear was the cause of their retreat."

"No, massa cap'en," said Jack, "they see ship and white man afore."

"Very seldom, I should think, Jack."

"P'raps so, massa cap'en; but I say dat dey hab seen white men, and know the taste of 'em; dem's cannabrills."

"Impossible, Jack," exclaimed his startled leader, as he resumed his seat in the boat.

"It's trufe, sar," replied Jack, "I know a cannibrill's mouf, Massa Will jes' de sort dat dey like, young an' tender, dat rascal pick him bones in no time."

"Still you may be wrong, Jack."

"May be, sar, but what I say is dis, you bring the big gun in de long-boat, and when dey show dere teeth to-morrow, as dem sure to come, let fly among 'em, sar. Dey berry bad lot, I'm sartain."

Harold fully appreciated the sagacity of Jack, and resolved to take all needful precautions for the morrow.

He decided upon landing in the long-boat, with a howitzer loaded with small shot, and upon the first sign of mischief, to give the natives a taste of its qualities.

As soon as this resolution was known, every man wanted to be of the party, to "see the fun;" but as all could not go, lots were drawn, and the lucky fellows spent a happy evening, anticipating the morrow.

The mids received an intimation that they might accompany their captain, and Jack, being one of the "inevitables," promised them a rare treat.

"When dey show dere teeth," he said, "we jes' gib 'em one pepper, den follow dem up wid cutlas an' pistol. Dey berry bad lot, and we extarmilate 'em, genelmen."

During the day the natives kept out of sight, and our friends kept on board. Although loth to sacrifice the time, Harold remembered the old adage about all work and no play, and wisely resolved to give his crew a holiday.

Not a sign of a canoe had been seen, but the young privateer knew well that its construction was an instinct with the savage, and that many were doubtless stowed away about the coast. A watch was therefore kept all night, but nothing appeared, although Mr. Stanchion fancied he saw many light craft skimming about near the shore.

In the morning, however, the sea was clear, and, breakfast over, the long-boat, with its howitzer ready loaded, put off for land.

But for his love of adventure, our hero would have turned his back upon the island. The matter of provisions was not so urgent, although fresh meat and fruit would be welcome. But, as we have said, he loved adventure, and was resolved to make further acquaintance with the strange race he had fallen upon.

As soon as the boat touched land, their strange acquaintance of the day before appeared from the bushes, and prostrated himself upon the sands. A score or so of his countrymen, as ghastly as himself, quickly followed, emulating his example.

"Dey got no hogs, sar," whispered Jack; "jes' what I say—dey dam rogues."

"We will give them a little time," replied the young privateer; "this may be one of their usual ceremonies."

"But dem all got ugly wood knives ready, sar," urged Jack, "and dere eyes roll like sabage tiger."

"I mark them," returned Harold. "Will," he added in a whisper to the mid, "have the match ready; when Jack and I break away, fire straight at the beggars."

While he was speaking, a horde of natives arrived upon the scene, prostrating themselves in an abject way, but none brought either hogs or fruit, and they were creeping nearer. By ones, by twos, by threes, the dark-skinned monsters came, each bearing a wooden knife, fixed in a belt of grass matting, but no signs of the provisions demanded.

Harold watched their approach with curiosity—it was indeed a strange sight—at least two hundred of the savages had appeared, all crawling on the sand, headed by the fellow who wore the yellow handkerchief upon his arm, the gift he had received the day previous.

He was several yards in advance of his brethren, and our hero advancing touched him with his foot. The savage raised his face.

A sign from Harold warned him to come no further; and the savage, rising to his feet, uttered a few words in a deep guttural tone to his brethren.

They arose and drew near to him in a dense cluster; half the crew of the long-boat, who were ashore, gathered around their captain.

"Jack is right," thought Harold, "these beggars mean mischief."

Behind him, Will Steadfast and Tom stood by the howitzer, with the slow match burning in their hands, the rest of the boat's crew sat, cutlass and pistol in hand, ready to leap ashore "and have a shy at the warmints," as some of them said.

Leaning easily upon his sword, our hero awaited the further movements of the savages. Their leader, he with the yellow handkerchief, soon began to dance in a wild weird fashion, without shifting his ground, Those near him took up the step, the others followed until all were skipping and leaping, working themselves into the needful pitch of frenzy.

Presently he began to sing, or rather growl; the others took up the song, and the air was filled with a sound like that of a number of beasts in pain.

"Maybe a ceremony only," mused Harold; "these strange tribes have strange ways."

"But he was quickly undeceived, for suddenly the chief halted, and, uttering a wild scream, drew his knife. Immediately a host of these rude weapons darkened the air.

Harold knew that danger was at hand, and, rushing forward, he sent his slender weapon through the heart of the traitorous chief.

Then, retiring as quickly as he came, he made a sign of retreat; the men of the "Crucible" parted asunder, and the howitzer belched forth its host of missiles into the thick of the horror-stricken savages.

It was the first time such a sound had ever fallen upon their ears—a sudden eruption of the earth could not have had a more startling effect; and when the survivors saw some fifty of their friends writhing upon the ground in every stage of agony, they turned and fled.

Angered and disgusted by the premeditated treachery, Harold, with his friends and a portion of the crew, followed them, but the wild, deformed wretches, having a knowledge of the intricacies and hiding-places of the wood, melted away like snow before the sun, and soon Harold pulled up.

"Scattered them," he exclaimed, with the slight smile so rarely seen upon his face.

"Yes, massa cap'n," replied Jack, "dem berry quick on dere legs—dey like lilly-de-flisps."

"Will-o'-the-wisps, Jack," explained Will.

"Dat de chap," grinned the negro—"Will-dam-wisps."

"Jack," interposed the captain, "I should like to know more of this strange race. Can you trace them to their lair?"

"Me track anyt'ink to anywhar," replied Jack, with an air of pride.

"Then lead on at once."

Jack promptly obeyed, and stalked on at the head of the party, his hat at its favourite angle, and his arms swaying like the sails of a windmill. The wood was to him full of beaten tracks, and within half-an-hour he brought them to an open spot, where a strange, uncouth scene met their view.

CHAPTER XXV.
SCENES ON THE CANNIBAL ISLAND.

A STRANGE scene!

A large, open space of ground, upon which was arranged several circles, one within the other, of large, white stones, and upon each stone a skull facing inwards, grinning at each other in ghastly merriment.

In the centre was an altar, rudely built of rough stones, but maintaining the appearance of design, for the summit was a series of steps, upon each of which stood many gold vessels of very antique form.

The marvel of these was that their workmanship was perfect, and bore the imprint of Spanish workmanship of the sixteenth century.

To say that our hero and his friends were profoundly astonished is to say little, for all were dumbfounded at the sight, and stood for some time motionless, glancing alternately from the circles of stones, with their ghastly burdens, to the rude altar, with its golden burden.

"We must have touched on the mainland," said Harold, breaking the long silence. "This is the home of some barbarous tribes upon the coast."

"Not a touch ob nigger in him," repined Jack; "no nigger build place like dat; he make it better or him leab it alone."

"But the cups?" said Will.

"From a wreck, probably," returned Harold; "if we skirt the coast we shall find some remains of it."

The savages had disappeared entirely, leaving no trace, a fact which did not trouble our friends much, who were watching Monkey Jack.

That worthy negro was going round from cup to cup, examining the interiors with a curious expression of countenance, in which fear and horror were mingled.

"What is it, Jack?" asked Harold.

"O! massa cap'en," replied the negro, "dese fellows worse dan any sabage—worse ten times dan niggers—worse dan de ole ob ole Africa put together; they hab killed white man, dey eat him body, and fill de cups wid him blood."

He turned several of the vessels over; at the bottom lay a dark congealed mass of the peculiar tint so familiar to them all —it was indeed blood, and if confirmation was wanted of its source, the grinning skulls supplied it.

"What monsters roam o'er the earth's surface!" thought Harold, "what are my sufferings to those endured by the victims here, and my wrong-doings compared to such as these?"

His ruminations were interrupted by a savage screech or cry, and a perfect shower of short spears or darts rained down. One of the "Crucible" men fell, and writhing violently on the ground, cried out that the darts were poisoned.

"It burns—it freezes—Oh! what misery is this: help—help—water—water!"

The words died quickly away as he was numbered with the past. Harold crying out to his followers to avenge the death of their comrade, rushed in the direction of the missiles, and found a host of the savages flying from their pursuers.

Swift of foot, they sped in all directions, leaving no trace to ordinary eyes, but Jack in front, talking as a hound would yelp, followed them close.

They found and destroyed many of the wretched creatures, some were under bushes, others hidden in holes in the earth, which showed signs of being their only home; a few stood boldly wielding a feeble spear until the brittle steel pierced their dark skins, and they fell as mute as a fox when the hounds complete their work.

There was something so inexpressibly horrible about these wretches, that most of the pursuers felt a repugnance to touch them, and viewed them as we should look upon some coarse specimen of mammalia wallowing in its slime.

Thus following, and slaying when possible, the young privateer and his little party went straight across the island, and sighted the sea upon the opposite side.

Here the mystery of the cups was accounted for. Upon the beach, thrown up far beyond the reach of the sea in smooth weather, lay an old Spanish galleon. She must have lain there for more than a hundred years, for huge masses of sea-weed almost hid her time-eaten timbers, and from the shore side many hardy plants, such as thrive in sandy soil had taken root.

The hull, for of course it was nothing more, was, with the exception of one huge rent in the side, intact, and around it was placed two circles of stones, in the same fashion as those arranged in the enclosure.

It was evident that the savages regarded the ship as a god, and worshipped it after the manner of their rude ways, and the awful rent, illustrative of the doom of its crew, had never been penetrated.

The sand and sea weed had gathered around, but no foot of man trod there.

A strange feeling came over our hero as he surveyed the wrecked symbol of the bygone power of Spain; and, absorbed in the thoughts arising in his mind, he forgot the real object of their pursuit, until recalled to himself by Monkey Jack.

"De flannibals, sar," hinted the negro, "run like one-two people; dey soon git clar away."

"Let them go," replied the young privateer, "here is something more worthy of our notice. Here we may find some relic of the Spanish dons worth seeking.

"Lead on," said Will Steadfast, in a mock tragic tone, "I'll follow."

The young privateer clambered over the sea-weed and sand, and peered into the opening of the ship's side.

As he did not enter at once, Will inquired if any of their friends were there.

"No," replied Harold, drawing a pistol from his belt; "but there is a vast assemblage of self-invited guests."

He fired into the opening, and immediately a cloud of bats of all forms and sizes arose in the air, and staggered about in the sunshine.

"One more shot," said our hero, "and I think we may enter."

He fired again, and a second, but small, body arose, squeaking and flapping their wings.

Harold stepped lightly within, Monkey Jack and the middies following, while the men clustered around the orifice surveying, with curious glance, the interior of the ill-fated vessel.

It was the main cabin, probably that devoted to a man high in authority, for the fittings, torn and decayed by the elements of time, still showed remnants of their great beauty.

A long table lay in the centre, as it had been overturned when the ship struck, and close by the rent, where the rock had pierced her side, lay at least a hundred flagons of gold and silver, just as they had fallen at the time when the sea cast the huge mass of wood work upon the sands.

Around the side of the cabin, arms in great variety still hung, huge two-handed swords, arquebuses, pikes, and a number of other weapons of the age when men fought hand to hand; but the chief thing that rivetted the eyes of all was a long chest at the far end, which had the appearance of being a store for treasure, "savoured strongly of gold," as Will said.

It was securely locked, and the weapons they bore were unsuited to forcing the fastenings.

Harold, therefore, resolved to dispatch a messenger to the "Crucible," and get Mr. Stanchion to bring her round, and send the necessary implements on shore.

Jack volunteered for this service; in fact, insisted on performing it.

"I laugh at all de flannibals out," he said; "dey berry good at a skulk, and hide away like rogue piccaninnies, but I gib 'em some trouble to find me, when dey tink to catch dis chile."

So Jack went, and the rest of the party camped outside the wreck to await the arrival of the "Crucible," the men indulging in their propensity for yarns, Harold and Will conversing in whispers.

"In about a month?" said Will, in continuation of a topic under discussion.

"In a month, Will," replied the young privateer; "by that time I hope to appear before my accusers, and cast the name of coward in their teeth. No captain of the fleet ever had such a string of prizes as I possess."

"Not one," rejoined Will, with brightening eyes; "fancy the moment when the 'Crucible' shows up in the port with all her big captures in her wake. The song sung by many of our old acquaintances will change."

"It will be a proud moment," returned Harold, "but we must leave nothing to chance, nothing to the mercy of men in office. Pardon for us both (Heaven save the word); then you and I, Harry Carlton, otherwise Will Steadfast, can return."

"I am in no hurry," rejoined Will, with a smile, "I love a life of adventure."

"And ours will not end with our return to the admiral," said Harold, "but when that is over, and my mask laid aside, I intend to have a cut at the Algerian pirates."

"I shall be glad, Harold, to see the sun shine upon your face again," said Will.

"But it shall not, with my sanction," replied the young privateer, "until my dishonour is disproved. I swore it, Will, and I will keep my oath. I, so nice in honour, so proud of my good name, could not show my face to man while there was one who could say, 'Thou art a coward.' No, Will, while that stigma rests upon me, I keep this covering o'er my face."

The time passed rapidly away, and in a little more than two hours the gallant little "Crucible" came bowling round the headland and anchored about a mile from shore.

A boat put off with Monkey Jack, and Grim Foote, with weapons to force the locks. When they landed, the young privateer bade them get to work at once, as the evening was drawing on.

It was, indeed, drawing on, and strangely too, the sky was clear of cloud, but of intense coppery hue, and the sun lay in its midst like a huge fiery ball, magnified by the atmosphere to six times its usual dimensions, while its edges appeared to be many, as one sees it sometimes when reflected in gently rippling water.

Above the sea a number of birds wheeled and flew screaming, halting in their flight and tacking in a strange unnatural manner, while every few minutes huge fish leaped from the water, their thousand scales catching the rays of the setting sun.

These various phenomena had been observed by Harold for some time, and he knew they portended some violent outburst of nature, a hurricane or thunderstorm; but when the boat from the "Crucible" touched the sands, he drew Grim Foote, the boatswain, aside, and asked that old weather-gager his opinion.

"Well, sir," replied the old salt, " 'tain't easy to put the looks o' the sky into words, but a sun like that allus means mischief; whenever he swells hisself out, he means to kick up a row."

"Can you tell me from what point the danger is to be apprehended?" asked our hero.

"I can't zackly, sir," was the reply, "but I'm inclined to think it 'll be a sort of general affair—land and sea—above and below——"

"What do you mean?"

"This, sir," replied Foote, in a confidential whisper, "that we'd better get aboard and run out to sea, for that sky means a volcanic eruption."

"In this latitude?" asked our hero.

"Bless you, sir," replied Grim Foote, "we're right in the line of it—them wolcanis go like belts about the earth, breaking up here and there, just when you least expect it, but you knows 'em when they do come."

"Not a word of this to anyone, Foote," said our hero, hastily; "but quietly get them on board for the night. I do not wish to alarm the men."

"Most on 'em knows it by this time," replied Foote, "for we've talked it over on board; but you ain't got a funky lot, sir—they knows their duty, and they wouldn't do anything to shame you."

So saying, the boatswain touched his hat and sauntered towards the wreck as leisurely as he would have walked to the grog-tub at mid-day when there were no signs in the heavens of an awful impending danger.

Then, under his superintendence, the chest was broken open and found to contain a vast quantity of doubloons, bars of silver and gold, and other treasures.

These, with the drinking cups and most of the arms hung around the cabin, were put on board the little craft; and as the sun dipped beneath the waves she spread her canvas out and glided slowly away from the island, doomed to a terrible fate.

CHAPTER XXVI.

THE FATE OF THE ISLAND.—THE FRENCH PRIVATEER.

As the sun disappeared, a low wailing sound swept o'er the ocean, dying away in the far-off east, like the sighing of an Eolian lyre.

There was something inexpressibly painful in the sound, and every listener on board the "Crucible" felt strangely touched and in the eyes of many, tears arose.

The young privateer, surrounded by his attached friends, stood on the after deck, watching the sails as they rose and fell with the dying wind.

"We are losing every breath of air," he said.

"In a few minutes it will be a dead calm," replied the lieutenant.

And so it was—the canvas rose and fell for a little while, but at length hung idly against the masts, without a sign of motion.

The "Crucible" swung slowly round, and floated with the current towards the island.

"Heaven have mercy on us," thought Harold, "if Foote is right, in half an hour we shall be on the shore."

They sounded the depths, but although within a couple a miles of the shore, could find no bottom. There was no hold for the anchor, and the men grouped together on the forecastle, whispered forebodings of their end.

No sound awoke the stillness but the occasional footsteps of one of the officers crossing the deck, and the cry of sea-gulls, as they flew wildly to and fro. The sun was down, but it was not night, for a lurid fire hung in the sky, and the waves gleamed with an unnatural phosphorescent light.

Thus, in the strange light of that awful eve, the "Crucible" drifted back towards the island.

Harold thought of the powerful lines of Campbell, "On the Last Day":—

> "And ships were drifting with the dead,
> To shores where all was dumb."

He called Will to his side, and asked the lad how he felt.

Will replied,—

"I am not afraid to die, but I never thought of such an awful ending as this."

"Then you feel that death is impending?"

"I do, Harold."

"And I also, dear Will; and judging by the faces around all apprehend the same. Foote, summon the men aft."

The boatswain complied, but it was done quietly, and the men stepped lightly over, as if they feared to waken some sleeper.

They gathered round their captain, and the gallant little craft glided on.

The sky deepened in colour, and the light on the sea grew brighter, while huge fish occasionally broke the surface, and scattered the spray about like a shower of fire.

Harold having looked a few moments upon the quiet group before him, in a quiet, clear tone, wherein many emotions were mingled, began :—

"Men of the 'Crucible,' I have called you together for a few moments, to say a parting word, for I need not disguise my feelings further. There is some awful convulsion of nature impending, and we may be suddenly removed from this world—blown like a straw from its surface.

"We have sailed together many months," he continued, "upon a mission of my own. Some of you have suffered, others have died, but you have gone on with unswerving faith, and stood by me in the hour of peril. Men of the 'Crucible,' are you content to die without further knowledge of me? Do you desire to see this mask removed?"

An old tar stepped forward promptly, and touching his forelock, replied,—

"We don't want to pry into your affairs, sir; you're a good plucked 'un, and we'd follow you anywhere, mask or no mask; them's my feelin's, and I speaks for my mates. I'm——"

A low murmur arose from the men. It would have been a ringing cheer, but for the ghastly nature of the scene.

"I thank you all," rejoined our hero; "and now, men, to your posts, and you that will, lift up your hearts to the Great Power above—there is need of it, my comrades."

The men retired. and the principal personages of the "Crucible"—its captain, Jack, the middies, and Mr. Stanchion—clustered round the binnacle. All was silent, and silently the little craft floated on its way.

The sky deepened, and a few stars came out, but the sea was like a huge mass of molten silver.

Suddenly the wailing cry swept o'er the ocean again, and a brilliant flash shot athwart the sky.

A low, rumbling sound came from the depths of the sea, and the water heaved. It was as if a huge monster had turned in his hiding-place below.

Harold extended a hand to Mr. Stanchion, and then shook hands with the rest of his friends. This done, they turned their faces to the west.

A strong light arose in a moment, lit up the whole sky, and disappeared; and once again the awful, rumbling sound rolled beneath them.

The sea became strangely agitated; fish now leaped out by thousands, and columns of water were projected an immense height into the air; but afar off, in the west, they saw the most awful phenomenon of all.

There the sea had arisen like a wall, and was stalking down upon the island, now but little more than a mile upon their lee.

Unbroken it advanced, capped with foam, and the sounds under the earth increased.

"O! Heaven! look there!" cried Harold, breaking the silence on board.

He pointed to the island; it was slowly heaving up, while smoke and fire darted from great rents in the earth. The current was turned aside from its course, and huge rollers bore the "Crucible" from the doomed island.

The huge mass of earth rose higher, parted in twain, and the broad wave which had been stalking down from the west, struck the shore and poured into the rent.

Then ensued a scene of awful grandeur, which no pen or tongue could describe.

In after years, when the men of the "Crucible" told the story, they declared that the air was full of fiery serpents, and the sea turned to blood.

But this more learned men declared to be the result of electricity—the serpents great bands of lightning, and the blood-red sea the reflection of volcanic fires.

The men remembered the island going down, and the waves closing over it, with a deafening sound; and they remembered the swift journey when the vessel was borne along at a maddening pace by the hissing, foaming, and shrieking waters.

Still the noises and sights were so rapidly changed and intermingled with others that they were utterly confounded.

Some were blinded by the glare, others stunned by the noise, and lay upon the deck as if dead, while the young captain and his officers remained by the binnacle, offering up silent prayer for their safety.

When night changed to day they heeded it not, until the glorious sun suddenly aroused them all as if from a dream.

The terrors of the night had fled, and there was a gently-rippling sea spread around them.

Harold was the first to be aroused, and he found himself lying upon the deck, but the last thing he remembered was his turning to look upon Will Steadfast, who was standing by his side.

Stay!—there was a thick, sulphurous haze which came over them, and then he remembered a feeling of somnolency, and the truth was clear.

The "Crucible" had been carried through a poisonous exhalation from the eruption, and every soul on board had been stricken down.

His first care was to arouse his lieutenant and officers. This was quickly done, as they were just recovered, and several of the men were upon their feet, but they staggered as if intoxicated.

Mr. Thornley, the surgeon, was soon amongst them, and to Harold's infinite relief declared that all would recover in a few days, although some were horribly weak.

"We must have shot through the mist like an arrow," said the surgeon; " a minute in the midst of that poison would have killed us to a man."

Congratulations were exchanged by all on board, Monkey Jack going around to all and expressing his delight at their fortunate escape. He was even complimentary to Duncan, who lay upon the deck still in a weak state, but the compliments were of an equivocal nature.

"I even glad to see you alive," he said, "and dat someting berry 'stordinary—for you sartainly am de cursedest hunks that eber biled down de glue."

Then he remembered Crikey, and dived below in search of him, but at that instant Crikey appeared from behind some barrels, where he had lain unheeded, and asked for his brother.

"Any ob you chaps," he said to the sailors, "see my brodder, Jack?"

"Gone below arter you," replied one.

"Gone arter me? So—dat's good.

> " Jack no forget him brudder,
> P'raps him nebber git anoder
> If poor ole Crikey die."

"Whar dat chile, Crikey?" broke in the voice of Jack, " he not below. O! you filthy brute, you gib Jack such a fright.

I good mind to tickle your dam hide, you 'farnal nigger."

Crikey grinned facetiously, and held out his hand.

"Gib it de grip, Jack?"

"Not me," rejoined the offended Jack, "I take de trouble to rummage b'low for you, and you grinning on deck. It not brodderly, sar, it not fren'ly, sar, it dam—un—un—constitoostional, sar."

Crikey, unmoved by this address, only murmured.

> " Jack no forget him brudder,
> P'raps him nebber git anoder——"

The sailors roared with delight, so easily can men forget trouble when the sun shines.

"Your 'farnal poetry," said Jack, "will bu de ruin ob you. Git below, sar, and don't let me see your ugly hunks on deck for a munf at least."

By that time, the routine and discipline of the vessel had been resumed, and the man on the look-out gave the warning cry of a sail.

Immediately all was bustle and life cu board, the sick forgot their suffering, and every eye was turned towards the horizon, from whence a ship, under a press of canvas, was approaching.

"A Frenchman," said Harold; "now, Stanchion, we will wipe away the horrors of last evening by having a brush with this fellow. Let the men have their breakfast, we have time enough, and then clear for action."

The influence of the bright sun, and the prospect of a fight, had such an enlivening influence upon the men that some positively danced, and all was life and gaiety on board.

Breakfast was served out with plenty of coffee, and a slight suspicion of rum, for many of the men still suffered from the events of the previous night, although they hid their weakness under a smile, and in half an hour they were in full view of their foe, and all ready for the " brush."

The Frenchman came on gaily, colours flying.

The " Crucible " ran up the Union Jack with the blue banner and its motto underneath, which seemed to puzzle the " froggies," as the sailors called them, for Harold could make out his foes eagerly examining his bunting, and talking to each other with an immense deal of gesticulation, as Frenchmen are wont to do when aroused or excited.

The two enemies were creeping up to

EVIL WORK.

each other in a triangular course, before a light wind from the south, and each moment brought them nearer to each other.

"I'll have the first shot," thought Harold; "Mr. Stanchion, see if you can reach that fellow."

The roar of a gun followed.

The shot fell short, but it sent the spray over the Frenchman.

An answering gun from the enemy sent a shot through the "Crucible's" rigging, close to where our hero stood.

Turning to the lieutenant, he said, calmly,—

"The Frenchman has heavier guns, we must run in and board him. We have the wind, and can beat him hollow with our canvas."

CHAPTER XXVII.

THE BATTLE.—THE BURNING SHIP.

A SHIP has often been spoken of as "a thing of life walking stately o'er the bosom of the deep," and the simile is justifiable; but never so much so as when two vessels are approaching each other with the obvious intention of meeting in strife.

Then, as the stately hull and graceful

sails sweep down, does it seem as if the wood and canvas were really imbued with the spirit of life, and the moving specimens of humanity upon the deck appear to be but so many minor assistants in the impending struggle.

As the Frenchman neared the "Crucible," the gallant little privateer prepared for the encounter; all her guns were double shotted, and half the crew armed in readiness for boarding.

"I'll not fire another shot," said our hero to his lieutenant, "until I am under the shadow of the Frenchman; then one broadside, a run close in, and board. The rest must be left to our weapons and good right hands."

Mr. Stanchion said nothing, but his looks implied that it was a hazardous venture, and his looks were interpreted by his young captain.

"You think she is too heavy for us?"

"She is very heavy," replied the lieutenant; "her guns are almost double the calibre of ours."

"The greater glory won when we run our colours to his masthead," replied Harold, coolly.

The lieutenant shrugged his shoulders, but, like a good seaman, continued to give out his instructions with the sang froid of a brave man; and the gallant "Crucible" bowled merrily towards the foe.

The Frenchman appeared to treat his foe very lightly, and, although within range, abstained from firing a shot until not more than a hundred yards intervened between the two vessels; then he poured in a heavy broadside, and the privateer reeled under the blow.

The next moment the voice of Harold was heard ordering the helm to be put up, and the foes met with a crash.

Grappling irons were out and fastened with incredible rapidity; and as a swarm of Frenchmen rushed aft, about fifty men of the "Crucible" leaped on board.

When they caught sight of the masked youth, who led on the boarding party, a cry passed from mouth to mouth that they were attacked by pirates, and this lent courage, if it were needed, to the invaded. They rushed forward with a cheer, and an indiscriminate fight ensued.

The Frenchmen were, in fact, taken by surprise. Judging from the size of the craft, they anticipated that a single broadside would send her to the bottom of the sea; but although many a yawning hole in the side of the "Crucible" attested the accuracy of their aim, none were below watermark, and she floated as well and as freely as ever.

Attended by his faithful sprite, Monkey Jack, and followed by his lieutenant and the two middies, our hero rushed into the midst of his foes, and stimulated his men to victory by the vigour of his own attack.

All the great guns were deserted, and the weapons used were small arms and the cutlass, both useful weapons at close quarters.

The smoke soon became blinding, and the clash deafening. Men rolled upon the deck, and gave up their spirit with—the truth must out—a curse. Struck down in their prime, with the life-blood at full flow, they writhed upon the blood-stained boards, and cursed their untimely ending.

The French captain, in the full belief that he was attacked by the bloodhound of the sea, fought with the fury of despair, and urged on his men with cries that there would be no quarter if they succumbed; and calling upon them by all that Frenchmen held dear, to conquer or die.

He had more men than Harold, but hand to hand a sturdy British tar always was, and always will be, let us hope, more than a match for a single Gaul. This the French captain knew, although he would have died rather than admit it, and therefore he fought with the utmost fury—the fury of despair.

Noise, smoke, dust, and the clash of steel—so the battle went, now turning in this direction, now inclining that; favouring the Frenchmen one moment, our friends the next, while the deck grew slippery with blood, and the air burdened with the cries of the wounded and dying.

At length the bulldog courage of the assailants was in the ascendant, and the Frenchmen driven back from the aft to the main deck, each step of the retreat marked by the fall of a friend or foe.

The French captain fought his way to our hero, and crossed swords with him, but the light, flexible weapon of Harold twirled round his coarser blade, and whipped it from his hand overboard into the sea.

"Sacré," he muttered, "this English boy is possessed of the devil."

Harold could not hear the words, but he marked the expression of the Frenchman's face, and smiled.

"Monsieur," he said, politely, "has lost his weapon, will he retire and seek another?"

"I am overpowered by the condescension of Monsieur," replied the other, bowing; adding to himself, "this is no pirate, but why wear a mask?"

He was left to work out the problem in his own mind; for Harold, disdaining to strike an unarmed foe, moved away, and joined the general throng of combatants.

Monkey Jack had also performed prodigies of valour, but he was not so merciful as his leader, and the man who proved to be his inferior fell—not that Jack was particularly bloodthirsty, but he hated everything French, and abhorred every other nation except that to which his idol, Harold Greystone, our hero, belonged.

While keeping an eye upon his leader and engaging with the foe, Jack became conscious of being himself honoured with an attendant in his rear, one who followed him step by step and to all appearance struck blow for blow.

For some time he was foo much engaged to take notice of this familiar, but at length during a temporary lull in the fight he turned and saw, Crikey.

I dare say you might have knocked down Jack with the proverbial feather had anybody been there provided with the feather to do it. As it was he reeled under surprise as he perceived the half naked form of his blood relation armed with a ship's cutlass cutting and thrusting with all the ardour of a practised hand, one accustomed to boarding vessels and sea fights from his youth up.

"Golly, Crikey, what brings you here?"

"Jes' see you thro' it, Jacky," grinned Crikey; "you not got all de pluck ob de family, ole boy."

"You'd better go back to de 'Crucible,'" said Jack, anxiously.

"Not widout you," was the reply; "no Jacky, you an' I lib or die togedder."

At this moment several of the foe resumed the attack, and Jack had barely time to cast a droll look of affection upon his brother ere he was again in the midst of the fight. Wherever the captain went —there was Jack, and wherever Jack was —there was Crikey.

The French captain had obtained another weapon somewhere, and was again urging his men to clear his deck of the pirates, but weight and muscle with pluck were triumphant, and victory with the heroes of the "Crucible."

Half the boarders had fallen, and seventy sons of Gaul lay stretched upon the deck; the rest, numbering about thirty, exhausted with their efforts, threw down their weapons and cried for quarter.

They did not hope for it, but to their astonishment it was given, this was all common seamen desired, but the French captain, with a despairing cry, rushed upon the forecastle, sprang upon the bowsprit, and presented a pistol at his head.

Harold sprang towards him, but it was too late; a report, a white puff of smoke, and the figure of a man with his head shattered rolled into the sea.

It was an act eminently French, and it was immediately emulated by two other men, who leaped over the ship's side, and found a watery grave with their leader.

The rest were immediately driven below and measures taken to prevent a repetition of such rash and unnecessary acts.

The next act was to call the muster-roll of the "Crucible." It wanted twenty-five —twelve dead and thirteen missing; a heavy loss for the little craft, and one that gave our hero cause for deep anxiety.

"We must get back to Honour Bay with all speed," said Harold to Mr. Stanchion, who was wounded, but refused to absent himself from duty.

"The wisest course, sir," he replied.

"Can we take the captive?"

"Both will be short-handed," replied the lieutenant, hesitating, "very short-handed, but the weather seems set fair, and if we keep in company it might be risked."

After some discussion it was decided that the mids, with Grim Foote and what men could be spared, should take possession of the prize, and that certain men of the French crew should be released, to assist them in navigating her.

The arrangements were speedily made, the wounded cared for, the dead buried, many, many fathoms deep, and at sunset the two vessels, under easy sail, bore down for Honour Bay.

The sun went down with a fair sky full of promise of fine weather, and the moon uprose with an unclouded face, reflected in a million broken portions in the bosom of the deep.

"The moon rises fair, Mr. Stanchion," said Harold, as he walked the deck.

"As full of promise as the face of a bride," replied the lieutenant.

"Where is our prize? I do not see her."

"More to leeward, sir; there she is, in a line with that solitary piece of cloud."

"I see her now," rejoined our hero; "she carries a strange light,"

"I have perceived none, sir."

"Look at her bows, Stanchion; she carries two."

"I see them now, sir, but very faintly."

"And there's another, and another at her waist. What is the meaning of this? They grow brighter. Now there are more. I cannot understand it, Stanchion."

"I can, sir," returned the lieutenant, gravely; "she is on fire."

"Let us bear down upon them," cried Harold, impetuously.

"No, no," said the lieutenant, "it might involve us in one common destruction. They have boats, and they do not signal danger."

"Throw up a rocket, and hang out lights."

"I will, sir, and keep within easy distance. She is afire, fore and aft."

The Frenchman was, indeed, in a blaze, the fire seemingly spreading from stem to stern with lightning-like rapidity. Forks of flames leaped through the hatchway, curling around the masts, and flapping up the rigging, but no gun or rocket was fired as a signal of distress, nor could the anxious watchers detect the movement of any human being on board.

"I cannot understand it," muttered Harold, pacing to and fro, anxiously followed by Jack, whose dark face was a rough reflection of the grief of his captain. "Mr. Stanchion, let us send off a boat."

"She carries a magazine," rejoined the lieutenant, "and the fire will soon reach it."

"But think of those on board."

"Doubtless on their way towards us, but rendered invisible by this great glare."

"May be so," said our hero, "but I cannot divest my mind of fear, some treachery, some evil piece of work."

"But those who worked it would not remain quietly on board," returned Mr. Stanchion; "believe me, sir, she is already abandoned, and perhaps they are making a circuit to avoid the inevitable explosion. Small boats are easily lost to the view at night."

Harold could not but acquiesce in this idea, but he felt, in some unaccountab[le] way, that the fire boded no good to h[is] friends on board, that it was the work [of] the enemy, and the funeral pyre of t[he] friends he had left in charge.

"I cannot leave them to their fa[te] Stanchion," he said, and the flames ro[se] above the masts of the doomed vess[el] "put up the helm, at all risks."

"Too late," interrupted the lieutenan[t] "there she goes."

The decks of the vessel parted asunde[r] a bright jet of blinding flame leaped ou[t] the decks rose high in the air, a stunnin[g] report ensued, and all that was left of th[e] Frenchman dropped, in the form of mi[l]lions of sparks, slowly into the sea.

For a moment those on board the "Cru[]cible" stood aghast, the sudden glare an[d] darkness which followed made them fee[l] as if the light of day was suddenly shu[t] out, and the end of the world had come.

But, like men accustomed to violen[t] changes, they rapidly recovered, and si[g]nals were put out to guide the boats the[y] supposed were on the sea.

In vain they shortened sail, and th[e] glare of the rockets dimmed the lustre o[f] the moon.

No hailing voice or noise of oars in row·locks responded.

The night bore away, and the gre[y] dawn came, showing a clear sea, restles[s] under a morning breeze.

Harold, who had remained on deck, the[n] went below.

His emotions he concealed until alone, and then, throwing himself upon a couch, he wept for all who were lost, but espe·cially for Will Steadfast, whom he had known as Harry Carlton.

CHAPTER XXVIII.

THE "SEAGULL."—A PIRATE'S MERCY.

BOWLING before a swift breeze, a well-built merchantman, homeward bound, skimmed over the waves some fifty miles north of Cape Blanco. The captain, a sturdy old man of sixty years, walked the deck with an air of satisfaction, for he had, as he hoped, passed through the re·gions of danger, and was as good as in the sight of the white cliffs of old England.

"We have to cover a lot of salt water yet," he said, to a knot of passengers near him, "but from here, straight away to old England, the home of the brave and the free, our cruisers are as plentiful as black·

berries, and we shall meet with nothing to drive even the roses from the cheeks of the ladies."

Scarcely had the words escaped his lips, when the man in the fore-top, cried—"A sail!"

"Well, what is she?" asked the captain, in an assumed indifferent tone.

"I can see her!" returned the mate, who was watching the stranger with his glass, "but I can hardly make her out—schooner built, I think."

"What's her course?"

"North west by north—same as ourselves."

"Then she gains upon us."

"Hand over hand, and has not yet mounted her topsails and top-gallants—Ah! there they go."

Our captain looked grave, and a number of ladies and gentlemen passengers clustered around him.

"Nothing to fear," he said, a little hastily, "one of our cruisers, perhaps."

"She had set her squaresail now," sung out the mate, "and has changed her course."

The captain mounted the rigging, and eyed the approaching vessel keenly. Having apparently satisfied himself, he went below into his cabin, and sent for his mate, a young fellow on the hopeful side of thirty.

"Dalton," he said, "I rather expect that fellow's a pirate?"

"I feared it, from the first," replied the mate quietly. "What is to be done—run for it?"

"That won't help us much," replied the captain, shaking his head; the 'Seagull' is a good ship of her class, but she ain't much use against these low-rigged devils, who infest the sea."

"Shall we heave-to, sir, and fight him?"

"Fight!" snorted the captain, "what with? our fists?—we've only a rusty carronade and two six-pounders. Fight! I see the grin in the fellow's face as we do our puny bit of pepper. No, Dalton, we can't fight."

"But we can't give up without a blow," hinted Dalton, respectfully. "Think, sir, we have ladies on board——."

"True, true," sighed the captain, "for us it wouldn't be anything worse than death. For them—poor things—but there, Dalton, I can't think of it. What is to be done?"

"Do a dummy piece of business, sir?"

"How do you mean?"

"Try to look what we are not, sir," replied the mate. "Assume a warlike look if we have it not—cut up a spare fore top-gallant mast, and paint a bit like guns—clear the deck of all but seamen, and try to look as fierce as possible."

"Do your best, Dalton," sighed the captain, "not that I've much hope, and keep straight before the wind—we may meet a friend before we are overhauled."

The crew were soon busy, in obedience to his orders, cutting up the spare mast, and painting it to resemble guns; but after all the representation was only tolerable, and caused some misgiving as they were run out in the sight of the stranger, who was coming down upon them fast.

The real six-pounders were posted, and the crew gathered in knots to discuss the approaching danger. As for the passengers, they were below, all in a state of agitation and fear.

Among them was a tall grey-haired man, who had probably seen the sunlight of half a century—a man of striking countenance and noble bearing, one who seemed to have been born and lived a ruler in his land.

Although the captain of the vessel had kept the nature of the stranger, as he imagined it to be, a secret, the passengers had not failed to mark the various preparations and draw their deductions accordingly. The result was that the ladies were half beside themselves with fear, and the men, for the most part, in a state of nervous anxiety.

The grey-haired gentleman alone preserved his usual demeanour, casting glances, half amused and half contemptuous, upon the male speakers, who talked of the approaching schooner in a quivering voice, with bloodless lips.

"We can but die," he said suddenly, "many of us have seen a fair share of life, why should we howl about the few summers before us?"

"My lord," said one of his listeners, a fat old fellow, evidently a prosperous merchant, "we cannot all look so lightly upon life and death as you do."

"But," rejoined the other, half savagely "it bores me to listen to you. What hangs upon your lives? The fate of the world, a nation, or even a town. No! a few years of eating and drinking, nothing more."

"I have a wife, my lord," said another, trembling.

"Then if your fears prove true," replied

he who had been called a lord, "blow her brains out, and die fighting, like a man."

There was a strange recklessness in his tone, and yet it was not brutality, he spoke like a man who was jaded and worn out with the world, as one who had lost faith in all that belongs to it, and his looks bore out his words.

One of the passengers who had stolen out and crept up the companion returned at this moment and said that the stranger was close upon them.

"She is a pirate," he added, "and her decks are crowded with men. It's all up with us," he concluded, despairingly, sinking upon a couch.

The ladies, six in number, gathered around their friends and clung to them with the energy of despair. Most of the poor things were young, and life was sweet to them.

In the meantime the captain had called the men together on deck, and addressed them in a short pithy style, such as goes to the heart of your real tar.

"Lads," he said, "the stranger shows no colours and means mischief. We must fight; our weapons are weak, but our hearts are strong. Think of the ladies below and your precious ones at home. My lads, I rely upon you."

They gave a sturdy cheer, but behind it there was little hope of escape. The stranger was nearing fast, and still showed no colours, and they could plainly see that her deck was literally alive with men.

In the breasts of a few lingered a belief that the schooner would take alarm at the sham guns and sheer off, but she came steadily on, and at length fired a signal for the merchantman to heave to.

The captain cast a despairing glance to leeward, no sail in sight, no hope of a friendly intervention.

"Dalton," he said to his mate, "it's no use firing our pop-guns. Our only chance of life is to bring to. It may pacify that murderous villain, for a murderous villain I am assured he is."

But Dalton would not hear of yielding without a blow, and proposed that they should await the boarding of the pirates, then attack them with cutlass and pistol, with which all were furnished.

"As for our sham guns," said Dalton, "the fellow laughs at them. He has seen through the ruse from the first, and here's a hint we must attend to."

A shot crashed through the sides of the ship, and from below came the screaming of women and the oaths of men.

"Batten down the hatches," cried the captain, "we shall have them all on deck in a moment. There comes Lord Sandcroft."

The cool, grey-haired passenger at that moment appeared, but the arrival of the other passengers was prevented by the hatches being secured.

"My lord," said the captain, respectfully, "the safest place is below."

"At such a time," was the cold rejoinder, "I prefer the deck. Men should fight not skulk; can you lend me a sword?"

"Resistance is useless," hesitated the captain.

"Are you an Englishman?" demanded his lordship, sternly.

"I am, my lord."

"Then show the courage of one, and run up your colours. Why are they struck?"

The captain still hesitated, but the mate, relying upon the protection of his lordship, gave the necessary orders. A ball of bunting flew to the mizen peak, lingered a moment, then floated out, and showed the British Union Jack.

The stranger replied this time by showing the colours of the Columbian Republic, and sent another shot into the bows of the merchantman.

The mate took the command in hand and replied with a six-pounder. Then the schooner, drawing nearer, opened fire with all her guns, and an iron hail fell upon the rigging, cutting the stays, and speedily reducing the merchantman to the condition of a helpless log upon the waters, and she fell away broad side before the wind.

From the cries issuing from below, those on deck judged that a heartrending scene was being enacted, and, indeed, the passengers, terrified by the firing, and otherwise made acquainted with their fate, were reduced to the lowest depths of despair.

Dreading death, yet fearing to live, the ladies moaned and cried like suffering children, and the faces of the men—men who had lived a peaceful commercial life —were blanched with fear and horror.

Suddenly they heard hoarse shouting, and the trampling of feet above; pistols were fired, and swords clashed, and the wretched occupants of the cabin knew they had been boarded.

The combat was of brief duration; the

WALKING THE PLANK.

hatches were re-opened, and a crowd of villainous-looking ruffians of all nations rushed into the cabins.

The passengers anticipated instant death, but they were seized and dragged on deck, where a scene of horror awaited them.

A dozen men lay stretched upon the deck in the various attitudes of a violent death, with little ghastly streams of blood flowing from their gaping wounds.

Among them lay the captain of the merchantman, his head cloven by a hatchet—a fearful sight.

The leader of the pirates stood by him with that weapon in his hand.

He appeared but little more than a youth in years, but his face was stamped with the vices of a depraved maturity.

Around him stood his crew, many of them holding a prisoner, Lord Sancroft, wounded and bleeding, being held by two powerful ruffians.

"Is that all, Halkett?" asked the pirate chief.

"Every soul on board, sir," replied a burly ruffian, who carried a lady in his brawny arms.

"'Tis well," replied the pirate; "keep your prisoners close; we will attend to the crew first. Bring out a plank."

"A promenade?" grinned Halkett.

"Yes!" replied the young pirate—the treacherous Mason Wantley.

CHAPTER XXIX.
A PIRATE'S MERCY.—THE REMNANTS OF A WRECK.

ENOUGH has been told of Mason Wantlake, the pirate leader, standing upon the deck of the captured "Seagull," to assure our readers that but little mercy could be expected from him, and the strangers, his captives, looked at his stern, ferocious face, and read no mercy there.

The captain of the "Seagull" lay dead, shot through the heart by Wantlake as he leaped upon deck; but the gallant tars, ill armed as they were, had not given in without a struggle, and several pirates lay motionless upon deck, struck out from their villanous muster roll for evermore.

For these a terrible vengeance was about to be performed, such as only an evil mind could conceive, and fiends incarnate execute.

Mason Wantlake had all the prisoners arraigned, whose number and station were as follows:—

Thirty-one of the officers and crew of the "Seagull."

Nine passengers, five male, four female.

Lord Sancroft and four merchants, homeward bound, comprised the former, two of the latter had husbands on board, the others were the daughters of a widower, Mr. Nesbitt, who, having made a fortune abroad, was returning with his children to dear old England to pass the remainder of his life at ease.

Wantlake surveyed them, from the cool, collected Lord Sancroft to the cowering cook's mate, with a grim smile, and in a loud voice bade them attend to a few words he had to say.

"Five of my men," he said, "have fallen in the execution of their duty, and their death must be avenged. A life for a life is but poor justice according to a freebooter's opinion. I demand eight for one."

He had numbered his prisoners, and thus artfully included them all in the sentence, for a sentence of death his words portended.

Lord Sancroft, with a strange look upon his face, watched the speaker.

"Five times eight are forty," pursued Wantlake. "How many prisoners have we here?"

One of his men said the number was forty.

"Ha!" he cried, with a sarcastic smile, "see how the fates uphold our laws. Forty lives are due for our comrades' death, and forty prisoners are here!"

" Am I included in the list?" asked Lord Sancroft, quietly.

Wantlake, for, the first time, turned his looks upon the noble captive, and then turned deadly pale.

The sword he held fell from his grasp, but quickly recovering, he raised it from the deck, and rejoined—

"You here, my lord?"

"I am here," was the cool rejoinder, "your captive, mad fool. Outcast heir to my great name."

"Heir to your name?" gasped Wantlake.

"Yes," sternly replied Lord Sancroft; "my eldest boy was drowned at Oxford, my second fell a victim to a fever, and my third and youngest is lost, gone, Heaven alone knows whither, and you are the next of kin."

"Next of kin?" repeated Mason, with a bewildered stare.

"The next," cried his lordship; "but you will never bear the name or walk over my broad lands. You are a doomed man, while yet the bloom of youth is on your brow. At home you are marked, your crimes are known, and you can only return to mount a scaffold."

The young pirate, with cold drops of agony upon his brow, looked at Lord Sancroft with the air of one who suddenly learns that he is doomed to an awful fate, and utterly oblivious of all around him pursued the conversation as if his noble captive alone stood upon the deck.

"I never dreamt of this," he muttered.

"Dreamt," repeated his lordship, bitterly; "what have you ever dreamt of, but the gratification of your own base passions? They took you from the quiet parsonage of your father, and sent you to sea. There they led you on until you are Wantlake, the pirate, the abhorred. Wantlake, the murderer, with a price upon his head, set as they set it upon the footpads, forgers, and murderers at home."

The young pirate listened with increasing confidence to this harangue; it gave him time to recover himself, and when it concluded he forced a laugh from his lips,

"I have set my life upon the cast," he cried, recklessly; "I have lost much of the blessings of namby-pamby life, but I have gained more by the choice I have made. There is no life like the rover's, what say you, my lads?"

His men uttered a loud ringing cheer.

"Do you hear that, my lord?" cried Wantlake; "is there a sound to match it? The hounds in the field send forth music and gladden the heart of the hunter, but what hunter ever rode to such music as that? Away with your house and lands and give me the ocean for an estate. My lord and uncle, you have called me a murderer, now see how I can kill, of all here none but you shall live, and the mercy I give to the women there is that they shall die with the men. Now, mates, bring out the plank."

A shudder ran through the captive seamen, they dreaded the short and awful journey before them, the passengers cowered on the deck, weeping and embracing each other in their agony.

"You will slay them?" demanded Lord Sancroft.

"Would you have them live?" rejoined Wantlake, significantly.

"Better not, perhaps," muttered his lordship, looking at the brutal faces around him, "better not."

"This mercy is granted on your account, my lord," said Wantlake mockingly; "you will please to remember it when my country holds me prisoner and tries me for my deeds."

"Trust me," replied Lord Sancroft, "I will remember this scene at a fitting time."

"Many thanks," said the pirate, in the same sneering tone, "but we delay the performance. Now, my lads," addressing the crew of the 'Seagull,' "who volunteers to be first explorer into the unknown future, you must all go, and whether first or last is only a question of a few moments?"

The young mate stepped forward.

"I will lead the way," he cried, "and in bidding farewell to you now, tell you that we shall meet again. Where and when your conscience tells you. Comrades and friends," to the seamen and passengers, "a brief adieu. Come, one and all, and let no blanched cheek delight that scoundrel there."

The young fellow, with his handsome sunburnt face and curly hair waving in the breeze, stepped across the plank; it tilted in the air, and precipitated him beneath the surface of the blue waves.

A terrible cry arose from the ladies, and the men moaned, but the mocking laugh of the young pirate checked the outburst, and they steeled themselves to undergo their fate.

"Number one," said Wantlake; "he leaves some foolish mother, perhaps, to mourn his loss; but the fool should rejoice, for he has gone to a better world with all his virtues thick upon him."

The blasphemous wretch laughed aloud, and his men roared in concord. In the midst of the uproar, a second man, the boatswain, a rough old salt, who had spent fifty years at sea, stepped upon the plank.

"It don't much matter to me, mates," he said; "I'm only cut short a year or two, but I'm sorry for some as I see here, who've hardly set sail afore they've grounded on that villanous rock." He pointed to the pirate leader, and with a "good-bye, mates," followed his young officer.

So, in sad procession, followed the rest of the crew, each accompanied into eternity by the cries and tears of the frail women, who knelt sobbing on the deck.

When the last had disappeared, the waters closing over him, as if to hide from his view the scene of agony on board the "Seagull," the pirate leader, Mason Wantlake, turned to the passengers, and bade the foremost follow the seamen.

He was a man unaccustomed to the physical hardihood of adventurous life. He had passed his days in mercantile pursuits, and the thought of a sudden and violent death, familiar to those who live a life upon the sea, was strange to him, and, falling upon his knees, he implored for mercy.

"I am an old man," he cried, "and a rich one, name any sum you please; take my bond, and I swear by the light of Heaven it shall be paid."

"Perhaps," sneered Wantlake, "and the messenger tracked to our haunts. No, no, we trust no man living; the sea keeps the secret best."

"I have a wife and children expecting me," moaned the wretched passenger. "For years we have been separated, and our re-union has been the object and aim of my life. I have worked, toiled for it, dreamed of it night and day."

"Walk," brutally rejoined the young pirate, "quick, or you shall have assistance."

The miserable man staggered to his feet, and cast a wild, despairing glance upon the sea.

"I begged mercy for those dear to me, not for myself," he said slowly; "their misery be upon your head."

Wantlake smiled contemptuosly, and pointed to the plank.

At that moment a loud cry escaped the lips of some of the pirates standing aft, and several were observed eagerly pointing out to sea.

"What is it?" demanded Wantlake, striding towards them.

"A boat," returned one of the men.

Gliding with the stream, a few yards abaft the "Seagull," was a boat, and such a boat, with such occupants as is seldom seen.

Standing erect, and swaying with every motion of the boat, were three gaunt figures —an old man and two youths, who feebly waved their arms, and opened their mouths, as if they would have spoken, but no sound came forth.

Their cheeks were pale, and the skin clung to their bones; their forms were atteauated to such a degree that clothed skeletons would have rivalled them in substance, and the current bore them on like the spirits of those who had suffered and died at sea.

For a few moments the pirates looked upon these strange apparitions with fear, and more than one man trembled, for he deemed them to be a sign, warning the murderous wretches of an impending doom, but the voice of their leader recalled them to their senses.

"Shipwrecked tars, my lads; out with a boat, and help them."

Bad as the pirates were, they had one little tender corner of their hearts left, where dwelt a sympathy for castaways. It was a fate that might be theirs to-morrow, a fate more terrible than death by drowning or the sword.

Their prisoners were forgotten, and twenty ready hands made ready a boat, and pulled towards the castaways, who, with their dumb motions, still glided on at the mercy of the wind and tide.

But strong arms and willing hearts outstripped the wind and tide, and overtook the boat; and arms still stained with the blood of the slain, bore them as tenderly on board as a mother carries her babe.

Few could have believed that these brutal wretches had one spark of sympathy in their souls, but the castaways had aroused their dormant hearts, and for a while their coarse natures were flooded with the tenderness of a woman.

Nor was this the only good derived from the strange appearance of the three unfortunates. The passengers were for the time saved; and, forgetful of their impending fate, lent a willing hand to succour the old man and the two lads, whose opportune arrival had spared them from an awful fate.

An old man and two lads saved by the bloodthirsty pirates of the ocean!

Who shall say then that man can so far fall as to be utterly lost? There is no desert without its oasis—no heart without its little spot of human sympathy.

CHAPTER XXX

WE RETURN TO THE "CRUCIBLE."—CRIKEY HAS A DREAM.

"DE berry best ob picaninnys, bof ob dem; dey true grit, real genelmen, bof, to de backbone. O, wurra, wurra, what shall we do widout 'em, sar?"

The speaker was Monkey Jack, and he was addressing his captain, Harold Greystone, who leaned, with a mournful air, against a gun, listening to the bewailings of his sable attendant.

"Bof gone," moaned Jack, wringing his hands, "and ole Foote—true sailor, ebery inch."

"A loss, indeed, Jack," rejoined our hero, in a sad tone. "Is there no hope of their having escaped, Mr. Stanchion?"

The lieutenant was passing as he spoke, and halted to reply.

"None, sir, that I can see; if they had put off with a boat, they must have seen our lights. An easy sea was running, and everything in their favour."

"True," returned Harold, sighing, "poor Harry—true and noble friend! the purpose of my life I heed but little now."

"Perhaps dey lib arter all," said Jack, wiping his eyes. "Cat hab nine lives, so hab picaninny. Jack Tar and Massa Steadfast and Furnace as good as two sailor, each ob dem, so dey hab eighteen lives."

"Had they fifty, Jack," returned the captain, "I fear they have lost them all. I do not see a single loophole for escape, everything is against them. They are the victims of treachery, and have been murdered."

"But what of the captive French crew?" asked Mr. Stanchion. "If our friends have perished, what has become of them?— what have they gained by their treachery?"

"It's all a puzzle," returned our hero, "and the solving is yet to come."

"The sea holds the secret of ten thousand problems more wonderful than this," said the lieutenant, "and will not yield them up."

Mr. Stanchion returned to his duties, and the masked captain paced to and fro, while Jack thought of his young friends, and ever and anon wiped a tear from his eyes.

Poor Jack! his skin was dark, but his

heart was white, and beat as warmly as that of a better man in the world's eye.

He knew little of the sophistry of the educated portion of humanity, and, when tears arose to his eyes, he wiped them away, he did not drive them back.

The "Crucible" sped on her course back to Honour Bay; loitering about would have been in vain, and every gust of wind wafted Harold Greystone farther away from the spot where he had last seen his friends.

The sorrow of his heart was great, and much as he had toiled and fought for the restoration of that treasure, his reputation, he cared little for it now; Harry Carlton —brave Harry Carlton—noble, unselfish Harry Carlton, lay beneath the restless waters of the wide Atlantic, and, without his boy friend, what was life or reputation.

All on board had cause for sorrow.

Grim Foote had many friends; he was a taciturn, and, withal, rather unsociable old man, but he was honest and faithful, and had wronged no man.

There were the men, too, put on board the prize to navigate her home, and each one had his chum, who mourned his loss.

Therefore, it is no wonder that the "Crucible" sped across the ocean like the bearer of sad tidings, in silence and in sorrow, and that private hates and jealousies were for the time forgotten.

Duncan was at peace with Crikey and Jack.

Crikey and Jack had no thought of hatred towards Duncan.

As for Crikey, he sang fragments of songs of his own composing, all in a funereal tone, expressive of his sorrow, in which he bewailed the loss of the two bright-eyed lads, who had gone down with the Frenchman, and the altercations between him and the cook increased in power and number.

"But what care Crikey?" thought that sable gentleman; "de ship hab nobody on board but de cap'en and Jack worth shell ob cocoanut, so let him holler until he blow up, and den holler again—if he can.

This contempt of the cook was so apparent that even Jack, who seldom troubled himself about domestic matters, observed it, and, mindful of his brother's future, he drew Crikey aside, and gave him a few words of warning.

"You cussed fool, Crikey," he said, "why do you quarrel wid de cook, when you comfor'ble? Do you want to go aboard de bumboat, and sell de pines to dam young rogues dat neber pay?"

"Me bery much miserable," returned Crikey. "I t'ink so much of the picaniny reefers, dat I t'ink ob not'ing in de kitchen, and last night I dream ob dem."

CHAPTER XXXI.
CRIKEY'S DREAM COMES TRUE.—ANOTHER HORNET'S NEST.

"You dream of the picaninnys?" said Monkey Jack, eyeing his brother savagely; "what ob dat?"

"Eberyt'ing," returned Crikey, drawing himself up; "wheneber I dream at Cuba dey sw'ar by it, 'cos if it not come true it berry nigh."

"What whar your dream?" asked Jack waiving that question for the time.

"I dreamt I was in de fo'castle," Crikey began, "washing de vegritables for dinner, but de dinner must hab been berry late, 'cause it was dark."

"Any time do for dream dinners," interposed Jack, "dey do you no good, a lily fly starve on dem."

"Wal, it were dark," pursued Crikey, "so berry dark dat de werry greens war black, and de sea and sky like a lump ob ink, but I could hear de wind howl, and de sea wash agin de sides ob de ship, squash, like a cart runnin' ober de shingle."

"Any fool dream such stuff as dat," interrupted Monkey Jack; "if you dream not'ing better dan dat, shut up."

"I does," returned Crikey, emphatically: "while I was washin' dem greens in de dark, I heard a most scrutinating cry, right in my ear, dat make me jump, and it cry "Fire!' I lef' off washin' dem greens, Jacky, and jes' cast my biggest eye around; dere was no fire, debil a bit, but de sky was black, and de sea was black, jes' like a lump of ink, and," here he encountered the exasperated eye of his brother, "I went on washin' dem greens."

"Ob all de——," began Jack.

"Dry up for one moment," interposed Crikey, "and listen to your brodder. No sooner do I begin to wash agin dan I hear de same voice in de same ear, and agin it say 'Fire!' Den when I look round dat time, I see mighty big ship upon de sea, wid de fire all ober her, in de hull, and among de sails; and I hear men screamin' so bad dat I tremble like runaway nigger when him cotched, and I call out for help.

"But nobody come, and dere seem to be not a single soul on board but myself. And de burnin ship come nearer, and de flames git higher an' higher until dey lick the clouds, and when dis ship git close I see Massa Will and Massa Tom on board, and ole Foote standin' at de wheel, cool as lump ob ice, and Massa Will cry out, 'Follow dis ship, an' you will find us,' and den I was woke up by de cussed cook kickin' me in de ribs, and say I obersleep myself."

"Dat berry good story," said Jack; "but not one of de sort to wash; you 'scuse yourself from a long sleep by tellin' conflounded lies to de cook, and den you come it wid your brodder. I blush for you, Crikey!"

"It's trufe," returned Crikey, as he dived below, "and when you see de burnin' ship, you ax my pardon."

Whatever Jack thought of this story he kept to himself, and for two days the "Crucible" kept on her way, a gloomy time for all.

All but Crikey believed the two lads to be lying at the bottom of the sea, "food for fishes;" but he, firm in the faith he had in his dream, believed them to be living, and that they would be found.

It was on the eve of the third day that signs of Crikey being in the right became apparent.

The sun set in a sea of golden cloud, the tints rapidly faded, and the stars peeped out, but still around the west hung a halo of fire.

So uncommon was the phenomenon, that the men on watch kept their eyes fixed in that direction, and Mr. Stanchion sent down for his night-glass to see if he could fathom the mystery of the unwonted light.

Harold came on deck with it, and the two watched the strange halo for some time. At length the masked hero spoke—

"What do you think of it, Stanchion?"

"A vessel on fire," was the reply.

"Another scene of wreck, robbery, and ruin," muttered our hero; "cast off a bit, Mr. Stanchion, and bear down upon it."

"A ship on fire." The worst expression of such an awful disaster spread from mouth to mouth, and the men came tumbling up on the deck, among them Crikey, half beside himself with excitement.

"Follow him up, follow him up, sar," he shouted, "and you will find Massa Will and Massa Tom. Follow him up, sar."

"Is this poor wretch demented?" asked Harold.

"You mean mad, sar?" rejoined Crikey.

"I do."

"No, sar; but I dream of dis ship, a voice say in my ear, 'follow up dis, you will find Massa Will and Tom.'"

And then, in an excited manner, he poured out a rough and garbled account of his dream, capering about like a mountain goat, and flourishing a stew-pan he had been cleaning, when the cry of a ship on fire was first raised.

"O! massa cap'en," he concluded, tearfully, "I born fool, but I dream true allers did; ax Cuban bumboat men, dey know; ax Jacky. No, don't ax him, sar, for him nebber b'lieve in trufe. O, yah, what you kick your brodder for?"

Monkey Jack, arriving in the course of this speech, had fallen foul of Crikey, and inflicted the chastisement thus objected to, and now stood forward to explain the cause of his disbelief, but the captain bade him stand aside for the present, and addressed Mr. Stanchion.

"The meanest people often possess strange gifts," he said, "and there may be something in the dream of this rude creature. Put on all sail for the burning ship."

But the wind was light, and the "Crucible" could make but little way during the dark hours, although the burning ship was a beacon to guide them on.

Just before dawn the flames began to sink, and as the sun rose, a solitary ball of black smoke floated across the sky, apparently all that was left of the ill-fated ship.

But there was more, for an hour later the man on the look-out reported some object, what he could not say, floating idly with the current.

"Port your helm! square away the yards!" shouted Mr. Stanchion.

This order was promply obeyed, and the ship was presently steering back for the spot that had been their starboard quarter, with her yards slightly braced up on the starboard tack.

The masked captain stood with telescope in hand, and by his side was the faithful Monkey Jack, who, with his big black eyes, anxiously scanned the sea.

"The man must have been mistaken," said the captain, turning to Monkey Jack. "I can see nothing. Here, take my glass, Jack, and see if you can make anything out of it."

"T'anks, cap'en," returned the negro

ATTACKING THE PIRATAS ON SHORE.

raising his hand to shade his eyes, "Niggers' eyes better den all the telescopes in de world. Dere's nothing." he continued, aster a minute's silence, " dere's nothing bigger den a flying fish. De —"

What Jack would have said was cut short by a cry from the man on the lookout, who called the captain's attention to a speck on the water ahead.

This time the man was right; and in a few minutes it became distinctly visible from the deck.

"It am a man on a log of wood," said Monkey Jack.

"It is," returned the captain, "and, perhaps, a messenger thus sent by Providence from the burning ship. Heaven only knows what tale of horror this man has to tell."

"The "Crucible" was quickly have to, a boat lowered, and manned in a few moments, and on its way to rescue the hapless being who was lying on the log, with his feet in the water, to all appearance dead.

The boat was soon seen returning, and the officer who had been in charge of the boat clambered on deck, followed by four sailors, bearing in their arms the inanimate body of a sailor.

The clothes of the unfortunate creature were much burnt, his hands clenched and face distorted, telling of the fearful agonies he had suffered.

The men bearing the body laid it carefully down upon the deck, and the sailors gathered round it in silence.

"There has been foul work here," said the captain. "See, the man has been wounded in the thigh. Is he dead?" he went on, turning to Jack, his voice trembling.

"I tink not, cap'en," said that faithful negro, placing his hand upon the man's heart; "I tink not, but he berry nigh it. Him heart do just beat, but dat all."

"While there's life there's hope," said Harold. "Bring some brandy; we may save him yet, and track these villains to their lair."

Some brandy was procured, and poured down the unfortunate man's throat, and to the intense relief of all, after a few minutes he sighed, and opening his eyes, looked round with astonishment and fear.

He attempted to speak, but his swollen tongue and lips refused to perform their functions, and he again fainted.

"Take him below," said the masked hero, "and do you, Jack, watch and attend to him, and as soon as he survives sufficiently to tell his story, send for me."

In about half-an-hour Jack re-appeared on deck and informed Harold that the man was much better and wished to see him.

The masked hero went below, and the men gathered round Jack, and put numerous questions to him, all of which that sable gentleman answered by shakes of the head.

"What's the use of asking him?" said Duncan, the carpenter, who was standing near; who do you think would tell a nigger anything?"

"What you say, you screw-driver?" exclaimed the exasperated Jack, assuming a pugilistic attitude. "Say dat again."

A battle royal would undoubtedly have ensued, but Mr. Stanchion put in his appearance, and quelled the disturbance by ordering Duncan below.

Shortly after Harold appeared on deck, and calling the lieutenant, said,—

"My worst suspicions are confirmed. The man who now lies wounded and burnt below is the only creature saved from a ship, which was burnt, and whose crew has been brutally murdered by the villains who infest these seas, and for whom we are in search."

"How did this man escape," asked Mr. Stanchion.

"By a miracle," returned Harold. "He was wounded and left to perish on the burning ship, but preferring the less painful death, he threw himself into the sea, but not before he had been burnt on the hands and feet, and his clothes almost reduced to tinder."

"And has he any idea," asked Mr. Stanchion, "of the direction the pirates took?"

"Yes," returned Harold. After firing the vessel, the pirates returned to their vessel, and he has every reason to believe that they will land. He will appear on deck in about an hour, and point out the exact spot where this outrage was committed,"

"What number of men do you intend to land with?" asked the lieutenant.

"Thirty," replied the masked captain, "and let every man have twenty rounds of ball and powder."

Mr. Stanchion retired, and Monkey Jack approached and stood before Harold in silence, waiting for orders.

"You will accompany me to-night," Harold said. "I intend to attack the pirates——"

"De debils!" interrupted Jack.

"On land," the masked captain went on; "therefore hold yourself in readiness."

"De sooner de better, cap'en," said Jack, fixing his cocked hat firmly upon his head. "Jack feel berry uneasy about Massa Tom and Will; but we find dem all safe and sound, cap'en need hab no fear ob dat."

"God grant we may!" exclaimed Harold, fervently; "but now I would be alone."

About an hour after this, the man saved from the ill-fated vessel appeared on deck, and informed the captain that he knew they were near the spot where the burning ship had sunk, and that he was certain that the pirates had landed.

Floating masses of charred timber told the truth of the first remark, and a boat, by the captain's order, was lowered to reconnoitre the shore, commanded by Mr. Stanchion.

After an absence of about an hour, he returned, and reported that they had pulled within a few yards of the beach, had heard the sound of men's voices, and seen the gleaming of fires through the trees.

"No time is to be lost," cried Harold,

after listening attentively to the lieutenant's report. "Man the boats, and let nothing be forgotten. Remember our lost comrades, and remember we fight 'For Honour.'"

The men saluted the captain in silence, and, in a few minutes, all was in readiness.

Each man was armed with pistols, cutlass, and musket.

And Monkey Jack, who dogged the captain's footsteps, was armed to the teeth.

The manning of the boats was done smartly, and with the utmost quiet; and, in a quarter of an hour the gallant party left the "Crucible."

The oars were, at a signal, dipped noiselessly into the water, and the boats clove their way through what seemed a sea of fire, so phosphoric and brilliant were the furrows caused by the bows, when quickly impelled by the stout arms of the oarsmen.

It was a dark still night.

Not a breath of air was stirring, and scarcely a ripple disturbed the surface of the ocean.

No moon or stars shone to light the gallant party on their way to the scene of approaching conflict, and not a word passed in the boats.

All was darkness, and Nature seemed hushed into unnatural stillness.

In about half-an-hour they neared the beach, and having landed, proceeded towards a light, which could be distinctly seen flaming up between the trees and giant shrubs that grew thickly within a few yards of the beach.

Those who have never been in tropical regions can form no idea of the rank luxuriance with which trees and shrubs grow in these islands.

To the brilliancy and varied tints of its foliage, no words can do adequate justice, but they form a picture that an artist would delight to paint.

Forms of men could be seen flitting backwards and forwards, casting giants' shadows upon the surrounding trees, and every now and then a hoarse burst of laughter or string of curses echoed through the air.

The boats were gently grounded, and the men having landed, proceeded to examine their weapons.

The muskets were all loaded, and the party divided into two sections, one headed by Harold, and the ever-faithful Monkey Jack, and the other by the lieutenant, Mr. Stanchion.

CHAPTER XXXII.

THE ENCOUNTER.—A RELIC.

A WISE and prudent commander, however personally brave, never rashly risks the lives of his men; and as our hero was no exception to the rule, he drew up his men by the bushes fringing the beach, and sent Jack forward to reconnoitre.

He thoroughly appreciated the incomparable sagacity of the negro, and confidently awaited his return.

Jack crept away as softly as a patch of mist stealing over a moor, and the men of the "Crucible" lay down to rest prior to the struggle, Harold alone remaining erect, watching the gloomy scene around.

A night dark as Hades, with nought to relieve the pitchy blackness but the faint glimmering of the light between the trees, and the silence unbroken save by the distant murmuring of the pirates' voices.

Not a breath of air fanned the drooping leaves hanging listlessly on the stems, and the flowers hung their heads sickening under the rank, impure atmosphere laden with disease and death.

Such a night as this makes men pant and think of cooling, and more than one gallant tar, lying on the sands, turned his thoughts to the time of his youth, where the rivulet bubbled past the cottage door.

Thus in the darkness and heat they lay dreaming until the voice of Jack, speaking softly in their midst, recalled them to the reality around them.

"Dere am precious lot ob dem, sar," he said, "and dey berry merry."

"How many, Jack?" softly asked the captain.

"'Bout hundred, sar."

"Did you recognise any?"

"I tink I know some ob dar hunks," replied Jack; "but I not sartain—dey move 'bout too much, and many ob dem double drunk."

"The easier will be our victory, Jack."

"Hope so, sar; but pirate drunk fight like a good man mad, and him chop about awful; dey all look as if dey see red."

"What of that, Jack?" asked Harold, settling his accoutrements preparatory to moving in.

"When white men or nigger see red," explained Jack, "it make him wild beast. He see like dat when de blood am shed, and den him heart go pit-a-pat—pit-a-pat; he see de deep cuts, an hear de man cry our, and de shout ob de victim; dat de time he see red, and he forget all but de lub ob killin' him fellow-man."

He had spoken in an undertone, but every word was clearly heard, and more than one of his listeners involuntarily shuddered.

They remembered "seeing red" in the heat of battle, and in many a riot on shore.

As for Harold, he had not yet arrived at the awful lust for blood which a life of adventure raises in the heart of man; but he knew that Jack was right in theory, and heartily hoped that the day might never dawn when he should see in that way the fatal colour.

"I can fight," he thought, "for honour, life, and liberty; but I have no wish to run-a-muck in the midst of even the basest of my foes."

This thought passed through his mind as he crept towards the scene of the pirate's revelry, Jack foremost, a pioneer to the destruction of villainy.

The light became brighter, and presently small shafts fell upon the glistening of the naked cutlasses of the sailors, and the fine supple blade of their leader; then, for a moment, he turned, saw in the dim light that all were ready, and gave the order to advance.

"Onward!" cried the masked captain, waving his sword; onward, my brave fellows. Success is certain. Down with the villains."

A cheer burst from the noble tars, which awaked all the sleeping echoes of the forest, causing the birds and monkeys to scream and chatter.

The pirates, cursing and yelling, rushed forward to meet the attack, but a withering volley, delivered into their midst, made their ranks waver, and several already lay dead or dying on the ground.

But still they stood their ground, led on by a man who appeared to bear a charmed life. In the thickest of the fight was he, and above the clashing of steel, and report of musketry, his voice could be heard calling on the villains around him to stand their ground.

In the darkness a number of the pirates dashed past the invaders, to intercept the landing of the others' boats, and concealed themselves behind a mass of water weeds. The boat's crew of the "Crucible" came on, unconscious of their danger, until a shot from the hidden pirates betrayed their position. Then the gallant tars opened fire upon them, and pulling ashore they drove the enemy before them with great loss.

Now and then the clear ringing voice of Harold could be heard uttering the favourite cry of "For Honour."

The fighting was very severe, and the pirates showed the greatest daring, coupled with the utmost recklessness, and as the foremost of their ranks fell by ball or steel, their places were filled up immediately.

The position of the party from the "Crucible" was most critical, as the odds were three to one, and retreat, where they overmatched, was almost out of the question, for no hope of mercy could they expect from the villains, but there was no such thought in the breast of any man there.

Now the pirates are driven back, but, reinforced by fresh men, those who had remained on outpost duty, rallied and made a desperate onslaught, driving the crew of the "Crucible" back as far as the beach, uttering most fearful yells of fury, but suddenly the voice of Harold was heard above the clamour, and the next instant the gallant party charged, clutching their cutlasses with grim energy and prepared for a final effort, or, at least, to die hard.

The pirates wavered before this charge, and one gigantic fellow, with a most fiendish and repulsive countenance, falling beneath the finely-tempered blade of Harold, the men cheered and pressed on, driving the pirates before them.

This turning of the tables infused new spirits into the men, and cheer after cheer echoed through the woods as the crew of the "Crucible," now exultant and confident of success, rushed forward to meet the pirates; but they did not await the charge, having had apparently enough, but fled, pell-mell, into the wood, heeding neither the entreaties nor threats of their leader.

The men of the "Crucible" stopped, and stood, leaning panting on their swords.

Victory was with our hero and his friends; but for several minutes they remained in a state of utter exhaustion, panting like hounds after a severe chase. At length our hero spoke.

"We have disturbed the nest, and slain many of the hornets," he said; "the rest are scattered too much for us to follow.

Have a look round, my men, see what spoil is to be had, and draw back to the 'Crucible.'"

"Here's a cap, sir," said one of the men.

"Nothing in that," returned Harold; "there should be a score."

"But this, sir," urged the man, "is a middy's cap; and, excuse me, sir, I think I knows it."

The tone of the man's voice attracted our hero's attention.

He was standing by the fire, and held in his hand a cap with a gold band so familiar to those at sea.

Harold took it from his hand, and, bending down, looked at the lining.

There, by the glow of the fire, he read, in bold characters, "Will Steadfast."

CHAPTER XXXIII.

A MESSAGE FROM WILL.—THE VAIN SEARCH.

HAROLD felt as if he had received a message from the dead. The cap was, indeed, Will Steadfast's. The name he had, in an idle moment, elaborately written inside was all-sufficient evidence for our hero; but how came he there?

Surely there was something miraculous in his escape from the burning vessel—and was he alone, or had Tom Furnace and Grim Foote likewise survived?

Anxious to solve the mystery, our hero asked Jack if it were possible to follow the pirates who had fled. The negro looked very doubtful.

"Night berry dark," he said, "pirate know him way, and no such fool to make fire again."

"True, true!" muttered Harold, pacing to and fro in restless agitation.

"And if massa cap'en take Jack's word," pursued his faithful attendant, "him put dis fire out; pirate skulk back, p'raps, and make cold meat ob some harabouts."

Harold accepted the advice, and gave orders for the scattered remains of the pirates' fire to be trodden out, resolving to wait until the dawn ere he followed his foes.

The dark hours passed slowly to our hero and his impatient men, who all longed to have another brush with the enemy—all but those who had fallen in the combat and would never fight more.

At length the dawn appeared, and the leaves, silvered by the early light, rustled in the wind. The booty of the camp, principally gold and silver drinking cups, was placed under the charge of two men; and then they followed the trail.

In an hour it was broad and clear, then it appeared that the pirates had collected together prior to departing in various directions. This Monkey Jack explained and pointed out that the remaining portion of the band had split up in various parties and gone hither and hither.

This Harold suspected to be a ruse, designed to put them off the scent, and he believed that the pirates had again assembled together at some chosen point. Determined to fathom the subject, he was about to proceed, when Jack's keen eye discovered a folded paper amongst the bushes.

"What dis hyar?" he muttered, "dis lilly bit ob paper folded like lub-letter—here it is, sar."

Harold eagerly seized the missive, a leaf torn from a pocket-book, and folded and directed "To any honest seaman who may find it."

"He opened it eagerly, and recognised the writing. It was Will Steadfast's, hurriedly scrawled, but retaining its peculiar characteristics. It ran thus :—

"Three of us—Tom Furnace, Foote, and myself,—having escaped from awful perils at sea, have fallen into the hands of Mason Wantlake, the pirate. He will not slay us, nor tell us what fate we have in store. He has other prisoners also, we believe, but we have not seen them. This letter is written with others, and dropped with the hope that some good friend will come to the rescue.—WILL STEADFAST."

"All saved!" murmured the masked hero, "all saved!"

"What you say, sar?" demanded Jack, all ears.

"They are alive, Jack."

"Massa Will, Tom, and ole Foote?"

"All, Jack."

The delighted darkey, overcome by his feelings, there and then turned a complete summersault, alighting on his feet, uttered a wild whoop of delight.

"They are prisoners still," said Harold, musingly, "and prisoners in the hands of a cruel man—"

"We hab 'em away, sar," replied Jack, confidently.

"Forward, Jack," cried the captain, and the party moved on. They followed the trail for an hour, until they reached a spot where the pirates had reassembled, thus confirming the theory of the masked captain. So far so good, but the next discovery gave rise to some perplexity.

The pirates had again divided, but into two parties only, and gone away in opposite directions.

"Now, Jack, put your brains to work," said Harold. "Which of these parties has the prisoners?"

Jack looked keenly at the trails, and then replied,—

"Bof ob 'em, sar."

"Both, Jack; are you certain?"

"I certain, sar, as we am here," was the reply; "some ob dem carry prisoners; oder prisoners pushed and dragged along; look, sar, har de marks."

This was very annoying, and increased our hero's anxiety. What could he do? His little party was not numerous enough to divide, and, if he ventured on that step, one might be lost. In the verdant maze, he had to rely upon Monkey Jack, and that worthy could not be divided.

"Must trust to chance," he thought, and, after a moment's hesitation, chose the trail on the right hand.

Onward again, through the dense foliage, through glades, and, by a circuitous route, to the sea-shore.

Nothing there but footsteps down to the sea, and the mark of a boat lately grounded there.

Harold looked out seaward for the "Crucible," but she was not in sight. They had reached the opposite side of the island.

Far away to the west was a sail rapidly receding from view, the sail of a pirate schooner, scudding along before a stiffish morning breeze.

"Back," cried our hero, "and try the other trail."

They did so, and found it led to another part of the island, and to the shore again, where the deep indention of a boat's keel was again visible.

"They but separated to seek their boats," cried Harold, half beside himself with fury and despair, "and while we frittered away time in following their footsteps, they have been putting the blue water between us."

There was no help for it. They recrossed the island, and re-embarked with the little booty they had, and with the sole satisfaction that the expedition had lessened the number of the hornets of the ocean.

The "Crucible" rounded the point of the island, and during the day kept upon the course the pirate had taken, but night came, and the sea was clear before them.

The next morning broke with no better result, and at noon a slight fog rolled by, obscuring the horizon, and as the hours rolled by it deepened.

The "Crucible," however, was kept on her course, with a good look-out, and cleared the mist, while the sun had yet a third of her course to run.

As soon as the mist was cleared, a vessel hove in sight, one of those crafts which apparently "sneak" over the sea, as a cunning fox slips to cover when the hounds are nigh.

Harold Greystone, who was below, immediately came on deck, and rapidly scanned the stranger.

She was a stranger to him, that he could see at a glance; but that she belonged to the class of vessels he was sworn foe to, he was equally certain, and as one prey had escaped him, he bore down for the other.

The masked captain raised his glass, and directed it to the stranger.

Calling the lieutenant to his side, he said—

"What do you make of her, Mr. Stanchion?"

"It is difficult to say," returned the lieutenant; "but I am of opinion that she has a closely-packed living cargo on board."

"Your opinion is my own," replied Harold. "See, she has perceived us, and is slipping away towards the westward."

Every possible inch of canvas was crowded in pursuit, as it was evident that the slaver had seen the "Crucible," and had no wish to come into close quarters.

A gun was cast loose, and a shot sent across the slaver's bows, and at the same moment the glorious ensign of St. George flew aloft, followed by that bearing the captain's motto, "For Honour we Fight."

The slaver returned the shot, and changing her course a point or two, made off with all possible speed, closely followed by the "Crucible," who was now within shot of the slaver.

Monkey Jack had armed himself for the fight, and looked anxiously after the fleeing vessel.

His brother Crikey was also armed and on deck, having received permission from Harold to take part in the fight.

Apparently he looked upon it in a festive light, as he capered about the deck,

"SPARE MY CHILD!" THE WRETCHED WOMAN CRIED.

brandishing a cutlass, uttering spasmodic cries of delight.

"O, yah! O, golly!" he cried, "Crikey show brudder Jack how to fight. Brudder Jack be nowhere. Crikey 'tend on cap-'en after fight, wear cocked hat, and brudder Jack clean de greens."

"What's dat you say?" cried Monkey Jack, "I clean de greens? Jes' you mind what you to your s'periors."

"S'periors!" sneered Crikey; "jes' you wait till de fight is ober, den hear what de cap'en say. He say that Crikey wurf ten ob his brudder."

Monkey Jack, whose temper was fast giving way, still continued the conversation with becoming dignity.

"What you know ob fightin'?" he said, "wait till you see de decks run wid blood, den you cry for mercy."

"Why me more den you?" cried Crikey, defiantly; "me like you, base born nigger, but——"

Here his sable brother lost his self-control, and rushed towards his unnatural relative, who fled below.

How Monkey Jack and Crikey behaved in the fight will be told hereafter, but we will leave them now, and return to the masked captain, who was addressing the sailors.

"My men," he said, "we have some tough work to do, but I fear nothing, as I know you will all do your duty like men, as you have done many times before, and help me to thrash that enemy who is now carrying a cargo of human beings."

A loud ringing cheer rang out from the throats of the seamen fore and aft, and they all declared themselves ready for work.

Scarcely had the cheer subsided than the portholes of the enemy were opened, a burst of white smoke flew up, and several round shot hopped along the surface, stirring up the water with whizzing splashes.

One of these only struck the "Crucible," but this brought the excitable Crikey on deck, cutlass in right hand and pistol in left, eager for the fight.

"Silence, fore and aft!" cried Harold.

Mr. Stanchion repeated the order, which the captain had just above given.

The awful moment was approaching; no word, laughter, or jest could be heard.

The men at the guns looked eagerly through the ports; the men on deck kept their respective positions, and stood like statues; and the features of Monkey Jack and Crikey would have done an artist good to behold. So fixed, so determined, yet, withal, so comical.

But suddenly the silence is broken by Harold's voice—

"Starboard guns! Fire! fire!"

The guns bellowed out, and the smoke cleared off, showing that great damage had been done in the enemy's rigging; but the next instant the enemy returned the broadside, and several shots struck the "Crucible."

One passed over Crikey's head, shrieking as it went by, but that sable individual merely tossed his head, as if in contempt, thereby winning the good opinion of his brother.

"Dere 'll be some work for ole Duncan, I'm t'inkin'," said Monkey Jack. "O, golly!" he cried, as another shot struck the "Crucible," "ole Duncan will want anoder man tc help him to plug up de shot holes. Crikey!"

"Yes," cried his brother. "What you want?"

"How you like dis?"

"Berry good sport," replied Crikey, indifferently; but the next moment he changed his tune, for another shot struck the bulwarks of the "Crucible," and a huge splinter struck down poor Monkey Jack.

With a cry of rage and sorrow, very much like the roar of a wild beast, Crikey threw himself beside his brother.

"O! Jacky, Jacky," he moaned, "dis am awful. Don't roll your eye so, but tell me, am you berry much hurt?"

"What's this?" hastily interposed the masked captain, "Jack wounded?"

"Not much, sar," gasped the sable hero, "jis lilly splinter in my side—O, golly!—yah!"

"You are seriously hurt," returned Harold; "two men here to take him below. Tell Mr. Thornton to look well to him."

But little need of that. Jack was too much of a favourite to be neglected, and so the surgeon said when he received the message. Crikey helped to carry Jack down and waited to learn if the wound was serious.

"Jes' look you here, Crikey," moaned Jack, trying to rise, "your place is on deck."

"I only want to see how you am."

"Your place is on deck," persisted Jack.

"Jes' one moment."

"You go up dis minute," cried Jack, "an' look arter massa cap'en; anyt'ink go wrong wid him I knock orf that 'pology for head you wear. I do dat like one o'clock, ole Crikey."

"Come—come," said Mr. Thornton, with a smile, "we are not so bad; you may go, Crikey, your brother will get over this."

Reassured, Crikey retired, and the surgeon proceeded with his examination. The wound was in Jack's side, a nasty jagged rent, deep and dangerous, but not necessarily fatal.

"You can bear pain?" said the surgeon.

Jack nodded.

"Then screw your courage up, old fellow," rejoined Mr. Thornton, and proceeded to remove the splinter from the ghastly wound of poor Jack.

It was a terrible ordeal; but the negro bore it patiently, his agony unexpressed save by the compressed lips and drops of sweat upon his forehead. When it was over a soothing draught was given him, and Jack fell into a gentle sleep.

Crikey, meanwhile, had returned to the deck, where all the eager excitement of a chase was going on. The stranger had sheered over a point or two, endeavouring to give her stern to the "Crucible," but the gallant little craft was not to be shaken off, and was overhauling her very fast.

Harold and Mr. Stanchion, the lieutenant, stood up by the wheel, directing the movements of the two men; then pursuer and pursued had ceased firing, and it was evidently the intention of the privateer captain to run down the stranger and board her.

"She's a slaver, I am certain," said our hero, "although she is fitted out for a privateer. What colours are they running up now?"

"United States," rejoined the lieutenant.

"What move is aboard now?"

"Keep on until we overhaul her," said Harold. "I am not to be deceived by such a shallow ruse. She is a slaver, if nothing worse."

"But we cannot touch her if she is an American," urged the lieutenant.

"I am not bound by the ordinary treaties of my countrymen," returned our hero; "American, French, or Spanish, the crime is the same in my eyes, and by the Heaven above me, I will do my best to crush it out. Run out a bow-chaser and give her another shot."

During this colloquy, Crikey had remained amidships in a state of doubt and hesitation. When Jack gave him the injunction to hover around and guard his beloved captain in the hour of need, Crikey fully determined to obey him; but at the same time a dark and deadly thought entered his mind.

He thought of the cocked hat.

Thought of it with a feeling of desire, and he longed to wear it; and if he ever was to do so now was the time.

But how was he to obtain it?

Jack, he knew, would never willingly allow another to usurp his hat, and that the wearing of it would be the greatest liberty any one could take, as far as he (Jack) was concerned; but Crikey would not wholly abandon the idea; he thirsted, longed for its possession, if only for an hour; and at length he resolved to make himself master of the treasure.

He crept softly below. Jack lay in his hammock asleep, the gaudy hat lay near him in a locker, and Crikey stole like a shadow across the cabin, feeling and fearing like a thief at midnight.

It was done—he held possession of it—and retreating rapidly rushed upon deck. There he assumed the symbol of his brother's greatness, and took his stand behind the captain.

"I feel anoder nigger," thought Crikey, "I hab a cut among dem chaps when it come to de fight."

Harold did not perceive him, he was too engrossed with the chase, now scarcely a hundred yards ahead, with every stitch of canvas set.

"We must pursue our old tactics," said the masked captain, "maim his rigging."

"Ay, ay, sir," returned the lieutenant, and immediately passed the word to the gunners to "blaze away at the fellow's canvas."

The deep booming sound of the guns was soon intermingled with the sharp crackling sound of falling spars. The oaths of those on board the flying vessel were also plainly heard in the short lulls between the firing.

They knew that the end was near, and then in their mad frenzy carried out a terrible vengeance upon the helpless cause of their disasters, the negroes in the hold below.

The shrieking manacled men and women were dragged up on the deck and ruthlessly cast into the sea. Husbands, wives, and children, clung to each other in the agony of the moment, and shrieked for mercy. Was it accorded them? No, savage blows and fierce oaths were the only answers they received, and a brief struggle with the rolling waves ended their misery.

The poor wretches were but untutored savages, but the love of life was strong within them, and they had near and dear ties after the fashion of their race, and, therefore, they cried for mercy when rude hands dragged them from the hold. Instinct told them the doom in store.

The crime was perceived on board the "Crucible," its officers and men could see the dark forms of the miserable slaves as they were hurled over the side and fought for awhile for dear life, they marked the fin of the deadly shark as it rushed to and fro revelling in a glutting of blood, then arose a cry of vengeance from the gallant tars.

"Run alongside," sang out the clear musical voice of our hero; "no quarter to the murderers."

Crash! the two vessels were side by side, and the grappling-irons fixed. Then an irresistible torrent of angry men poured over the side, and the carnage began.

No quarter—no mercy—hand to hand the combat raged, and keen cutlasses plunged deep into the flesh, and men fell dead, or rolled about the deck, and shrieked in mortal pain.

"Death to the slave-hunters," cried the men of the "Crucible;" but their opponents uttered not a word, fighting like the mute fox among the mangling hounds for dear life.

The fearful slaughter of the helpless slaves had roused the black blood of the men of the "Crucible," and for a time their gentler natures were laid aside. Blood gushed from deep ghastly wounds, and dyed the deck, and the crew of the slaver thinned fast.

"Death to the slavers," cried the men, and the carnage went on. Blood everywhere, on the hands, the faces, and the clothes of the men; on the deck and rigging; the very air seemed infected with it.

But was not the cause of the slayer just?

Ask the poor slave, the only one left of all their human cargo! He, having no weapons, bit and tore at the wounded slavers like a mad dog; dragged them, wounded and shrieking, to the portholes, and thrust them into the sea, truly mad with the hate he bore for his oppressors.

Harold, for once, was pitiless; the dying shrieks of the negroes rang in his ears, and he plied that keen weapon he bore with fatal and unerring effect—dealing death with every thrust.

And Crikey, he, too, was busy, the sight of his suffering countrymen drove him to frenzy; and when the slaver was boarded, he dashed to and fro, cutting and thrusting fiercely. He was irresistible, and he cut them down as a mower prostrates the wheat of the field.

And when all was over, when the deck of the slaver held nought but the conquerors and the dead, Crikey came a little to himself, remembered Jacky's cocked hat, and clapped his hand to his head.

It was gone.

All other woes fell before this. What should he say to Jack when he was restored to health, and the loss became known? How deny his guilt, when his face would betray it every turn of his life? —it could not be done, and Crikey, throwing back his head, gave vent to his grief in a dismal howl.

CHAPTER XXXIV.

THE "BRUISER."—THE NIGHT VISITANT.

HIS MAJESTY'S ship, the "Bruiser," a fine frigate, was bowling along before a stiff breeze, at the rate of seven knots an hour.

The captain sits upon the binnacle, watching the sun, which is setting in a bank of lurid red clouds.

The officer's face wore an anxious expression, and turning to the first lieutenant, standing a short distance from him, said,—

"I do not like the appearance of those clouds. They betoken rough weather in store."

As if in confirmation of his remark, a gust of wind whistled through the rigging, and a heavy sea struck the side of the frigate, with a sound like that of a peal of thunder.

At the other end of the deck stood a fine looking gentleman, also in the uniform of a captain, upon whose shoulder was leaning a beautiful girl—Captain Harloch and his daughter, rescued from the pirates' lair, and from a terrible death, by the gallant crew of the "Bruiser."

Standing around are several men, whose faces bear the traces of recent suffering. This is the remnant of the crew of the "Curlew."

"Clara," said Captain Harloch, "the evening grows cold, a rough night is coming on, and——"

"I shall be in the way," laughed Clara, as she disengaged her arm from his shoulder, and walked towards the companion ladder. "Very well, I will go below."

The men saluted her as she passed, for she had won the hearts of the rough honest sailors.

Captain Harloch joined the captain of the "Bruiser," who was still seated on the binnacle, night-glass in hand.

"Captain Harloch," said he, rising, "yon clouds puzzle me. I have commanded this vessel for more than twenty years, and have seen many strange sights, but these clouds seem to have something supernatural about them."

They were indeed strange masses of vapour, for, now the sun had gone to rest, they appeared like huge masses of rock rising from the sea.

Some of them had inky, black spots on them, as if indicating the presence of monster caverns, while others were snowy white, hanging in shreds.

The scene was weird in the extreme.

The stars came out and twinkled uncertainly in the sky.

The sea was luminous, and running high.

Explosions of lightning burst from the strange-looking clouds, and the wind moaned in an unnatural manner.

Suddenly the stars disappeared, and the air was filled with a white and almost impenetrable mist; the wind rose and lashed the sea into immense foaming billows.

The men on watch were apparently taking little notice of this strange scene, but buttoned up their coats, and walked to and fro, probably thinking of those far away, wishing their watch over.

Every now and then sounds of laughter, a fragment of a song came from below, these were soon drowned by the howling wind and rushing of the waves.

And thus the twilight gave way to darkness—a darkness that shrouded all.

Even the ship's lamps were of little avail, for they shed but a feeble, dim light, and the hitherto luminous sea turned pitch black, save where it was lashed into foam by the rising hurricane.

Captain Harloch and the captain of the "Bruiser" maintained their positions; the captain of the "Bruiser" giving such orders as were necessary, but no conversation of any import passed between them.

The mist flew past in clouds, clinging to the rough jackets of those on watch, who every now and then shook themselves, like huge retrievers after a bath.

Suddenly a strange sound broke the stillness of the air.

It was like the sound of a human voice—or, rather, like the echo of one—but from whence did it come?

At one time it seemed to hover in the air, now near, and now far away.

Captain Harloch heard it, and called the captain of the "Bruiser's" attention to it.

"A vessel must be close at hand," said the captain of the "Bruiser" in reply; "but I can see nothing; my glass is of no avail in such a mist as this."

"We may be mistaken," said Captain Harloch, "but no," he continued, as the mist cleared off, "see, we are not alone."

The captain of the "Bruiser" glanced in the direction indicated, and saw running parallel, at about two hundred yards' distance from the "Bruiser," a schooner, hull low in the water, and topsails alone reefed.

"Ship ahoy!" he cried, raising the speaking trumpet to his lips; "what ship's that?"

No answer.

"What ship's that?" the captain repeated.

Still no answer.

The schooner was now hidden by the tremendous billows, but the next instant she rose triumphantly, still keeping pace with the "Bruiser."

"Heave to, or I'll sink you," cried the captain, now thoroughly roused.

Still no answer, save a sound like a mocking laugh.

"What do you make of her?" asked the captain of the "Bruiser" to Captain Harloch.

"A privateer, I should imagine, by her silence," returned Captain Harloch.

"If she will not speak," said the captain of the "Bruiser," "we must."

Orders were now given for the guns on the starboard side to be loaded.

"Give her a shot across the bows," cried the captain, and the next instant the gun pealed out, and a shot tore above the water towards the mysterious stranger.

CHAPTER XXXV.

THE END OF THE SLAVER.—JACK DISCOVERS HIS LOSS.

CAPTAIN HARLOCH hastened below to assure Clara that there was no danger, but the girl's face blanched as she spoke.

"A strange ship," she exclaimed.

"Yes," returned Captain Harloch, "but I must go on deck. Fear not. I will return in a few minutes."

As he left the cabin, Clara buried her face in her hands and exclaimed,—

"Can it be he, and in danger, too?"

As Captain Harloch stepped upon deck, a shot from the schooner tore through the rigging.

"Curse his impudence," cried the captain of the "Bruiser," "give him a broadside."

Broadside followed broadside, but still the schooner rode on, neither lessening nor increasing the distance, and so through the live-long night.

. . . .

The "Crucible" was growing short of men. The various encounters the noble little vessel had been in had thinned the crew until barely sufficient were left to work and man the guns. This Harold knew, and wisely resolved not to attempt to take home the slaver as a prize.

He would have gladly done so as another leaf in his wreath of victory, but it was impossible, and he therefore gave orders for her to be scuttled.

Prior to the carrying out of this command, the men made a fearful discovery, one that revealed to our hero and his friends a new phase in the atrocities of the slave trade.

The men found that the bow anchor had been run out to the full extent of the cable, but the water was too deep for it to touch the ground, and it hung a dead weight upon the vessel. This struck one of the men as being very significant, and the masked captain being communicated with, he gave orders for it to be raised.

The men went to work, and slowly the cable came up from the deep. Barely a fathom had been drawn, when the ghastly forms of two negroes—bound to it—appeared above the surface.

A cry arose from the men leaning over the bulwarks, and curses both loud and deep escaped them. They cut the poor wretches adrift, and the cable was drawn higher. More negroes, old and young, in all the ghastly contortions of a violent death, appeared, sixty in all, sent thus diabolically to a fearful end.

Sixty negroes tied in brutal sport to the cable by the wretches now still in death. The murderers had their reward.

There may be some of our readers disposed to doubt the performance of such an atrocity, but the writer begs to assure them it is true, a common trick at one time on the part of slavers when pursued, to rid the ship of the cargo, and yet leave no strong swimmer for the glasses of the pursuer to spy, or blood to tell of murder that is done.

Harold did not regret that no quarter had been given. No! merciful and kind as he was in his heart, he felt that mercy and kindness would have been thrown away upon such men.

They scuttled the slaver, after removing whatever might be of value or service, marine instruments, provisions, and so forth, and then drew away to watch the end of the accursed vessel.

It soon came. Slowly, slowly she became deeper in the water, until her sides were little more than a black line upon the ocean, then with a sudden motion like that of a frightened steed, she lifted up her bows, pitched forward and went down to join the countless other wreck rotting at the bottom of the sea.

"So perish all slave-dealing knaves and their vile craft," said Harold, as the last eddy was lost amid the waves. "Mr. Stanchion, that is all we can do until we recruit; crowd all sail for Honour Bay."

And he went down to muse over the fate of the lads in the hands of the pirate. The discovery of Will's cap had awakened in his breast a hope that they might be living, more than a hope, a certainty it was at first, but it was followed by a suspicion that the cap had fallen into the possession of the outlaws, and been cast aside as a thing of no worth.

Yet how came it there?

On the other hand it couldn't have been there unless the lads had escaped from the burning ship, and if they had escaped, why had they not followed the lights of the "Crucible," she had hovered about

A SHOT FROM THE "BRUISER" SHATTERED THE GOBLET IN MASON'S HAND.

spot while there was a chance of saving life, and at the morning's dawn the sea was clear.

It was a mystery not to be fathomed, alas! by the means at present at his command; so he was returning to Honour Bay.

"There," he thought, "the 'Crucible' shall be refitted and re-manned, and I will never rest until I know whether dear Harry and his chums are alive or dead."

Nor was he the only anxious person on board,—Crikey thought hourly of the lads, and Jack in his delirium raved of them.

And Crikey had a second cause for anxiety and grief.

Where was the gilt-laced hat of Jack?

He knew how dear it was to his brother's heart, and it was not a thing that could be replaced by any of the sailmakers or work-

10

men on board; it was not like a pair of trousers that could be replaced at will.

No! and Crikey between his two sorrows went nearly distracted.

Three days passed, and Jack got the better of his delirium, possessed of an enormously strong constitution his wounds rapidly healed, and injuries that would have resulted in the death of most men only weakened him for the time.

He lay in his hammock, looking through a port-hole at the sea radiant with the evening sun, when Crikey came down to pay his usual visit when the main labours of the day were gone.

"Dat you, Crikey?"

"De same chile, Jacky."

The words of the reply were right, but the tune was wrong, and Jack looked earnestly at his brother.

"You not well, Crikey?"

"No, Jacky."

"What am de matter wid you?"

"Don't know, Jacky; but it am a sort o' kind ob cur'us feeling runnin' all round de back ob dis chile, and out ob de roots ob his ha'r."

The rejoinder was gravely given, and Jack listened to it attentively.

"You see de doctor, Crikey," he urged.

"Not all de doctors in de world do me good, it complaint ob de mind, Jacky."

"Dat dam poetry sof'en your brain, Crikey."

"I gib it up munfs ago. How am you to-night, Jacky?"

"Better, ole boy—I tink ob gettin' up."

"Don't tink ob dat," cried Crikey, alarmed; "dere plenty ob time for dat."

Jack looked suspiciously at his brother. What was the meaning of this unwonted agitation; Crikey felt very pale, and really his skin seemed to be several shades lighter.

"I am goin' to get up," persisted Jack, firmly, "so you jes' gib me dem are stockin's—de doctor say I git up if I wish."

Crikey reluctantly handed up the foot-coverings, and then Jack demanded his breeches These he donned slowly, for he was very weak—then his coat, and finally came the anticipated. terrific question:—

"Crikey, where am my hat?"

Crikey's knees smote together, and he avoided his brother's eyes—affecting to look out at sea, he stammered—

"Your hat—Ja—Jacky?—what hat?"

Jack stared at his brother, and thought he must be dreaming.

"Did you eber," he asked, slowly,; "eber see dis chile in more dan one hat?"

"O! dat hat," rejoined Crikey, making a feeble pretence of looking about. "I don't see it harabouts."

Jack looked at him with a curious light growing in his eyes, catching every furtive glance of the wretched culprit, feigning to seek the lost treasure. Suddenly, as Crikey passed him, he seized him by the throat and pinned him against the ship's side,

"Crikey," he said, hoarsely; "where am dat hat?"

"'Strue's my livin'," gasped Crikey, "I dunno."

"But you hab had it."

"I only war it one hour," moaned Crikey, "and—and—"

"You lost it," thundered his brother.

"I did," sighed Crikey; and Jack, with a moan of horror, staggered back. For a time he remained the picture of abject despair, while Crikey stuttered out the story of his loss.

"I thought, Jacky, dat—dat—de hat bring luck in de fight—and—and I put him on and foller up de cap'en, den we get into de row, and I pot a nigger, shove de cutlass bang troo him, den anoder nigger gib me a prod in de back, and anoder nigger knock orf de hat, and I don't know him do it, and den——"

"You sed anuf," interrupted Jack, with dignity. "Crikey, you am in the course of nature, my brodder, de same modder gib us oatcakes, and wop us when we sarcy. We grow up togedder, and git sold same time, my hunks fetch tree hundred dollar. Your cussed hunks fetch on'y two. Well, we are brodders no longer. I carse you orf; if de cap'en say 'Am Crikey your brodder, Jack?' I say, 'nebber knowed him afore, massa cap'en, 'strue as pigs got curly tails,' de capen den say, 'chuck dat dam lump of rhineoteros flesh oberboard, and ober you will go while I cuts lots ob capers on de main deck, Crikey. Git out, quick sar, and nebber come near me agen.'

Crikey, thus solemnly adjured, went out with his head bent upon his breast; once he turned a look of repentance and entreaty upon his brother, but Jack waved him off, and he disappeared up the companion-way, broken-hearted.

And Jack, agitated and distressed, also

doffed his clothes, and retired to his hammock, thoroughly vexed with the loss he had sustained, for he was a true nigger in his heart, and had he been king of the Mumbo Jumbo islands, would have sat upon his throne with an old white hat for a crown, with as much dignity as the kings of great nations wear their gold and jewels.

Poor Monkey Jack, he was brave and strong, but simple-hearted, and no child of tender years ever grieved more over the loss of a doll or a dead rabbit than he did for that missing piece of cloth, edged with gold lace and known as a cocked hat.

CHAPTER XXXVI.

REFITTING.—LIFE IN THE BAY.

HONOUR BAY was all alive; its masked owner had returned, and the herd of negroes being thereby stimulated to great exertions, buzzed about like a hive of bees on the flight all day.

Men of adventurous turn do not profess to grieve much, they do not go into the conventual mourning for a twelvemonth, and fix their faces into a sad and gloomy expression upon all and every occasion; and, therefore, although Harold sorrowed in his heart, he did not forbid the banquet usually given in the tent within the stockade to celebrate his return.

The men were merry, and to all appearance the feast was as joyous as ever; but two vacant chairs turned Harold's thoughts perpetually towards the lost lads, and he early left the table.

Jacky was there, wearing a yellow silk handkerchief tastefully tied about his head, in lieu of the lost chapeau, and when the captain retired he quickly followed his example, and sought a retired part of the wood outside the stockade, where he lay among the ever-shifting shadows of the leaves and clouds, and thought of Crikey's dream.

He thought of it so long that all idea of the place he was in faded from his mind, and he travelled in a visionary far away with Tom and in the power of the pirates, and with the vision arose the thought of the cap that was discovered, and the conviction that the boys lived, and Crikey's dream was true.

He arose with this faith strong upon him, and being now restored almost to his original strength and vigour, busied himself with looking after the refitting of the "Crucible."

Great things were to be done this time.

She was to have more men than heretofore, with ammunition and provision for twelve months.

Two of the heaviest guns from one of their prizes were to be placed amidships, and the men picked for the services subjected to a vigorous training.

Harold spent most of his time ashore: if he went on board, it was at night, and Mr. Stanchion superintended the fitting of the craft.

It was at this time that one means of Harold's for communicating with the outer world became apparent.

Outside the stockade was a small wooden house, constructed among the branches of a tree, and here resided several carrier pigeons.

These were old messengers at rest; but more came in shortly after the return of the "Crucible," and each of them bore a message from friends of our hero far away.

Mr. Stanchion was, as we have said, ignorant of the history of our hero; but one night Harold invited him ashore, and placed full confidence in him. He told the story of his disgrace, and the means he had taken to remove the stain of coward from his name—all in fact our readers know.

"If I fall during our next voyage," he concluded, "I rely on you, Stanchion, to complete my work, and at least give the true story to the world."

"I will faithfully fulfil my mission," replied the lieutenant.

"This morning," continued Harold, producing a small piece of paper, "I received this from my agent at Havannah. You must use a magnifying glass, Stanchion, for the writing is a microscopical production of a very clever creole upon his estate."

"It is, indeed, wondrously written," exclaimed Mr. Stanchion, admiringly.

"My messengers are willing, but their powers limited," said Harold; "even this was a burden to Mercury, one of the best pigeons; a little wonder this fellow is. Well, in this communication you will perceive that my case has been the subject of much discussion of late; that Wantlake's villanies go far to disprove much that was laid to my charge; in fact, were I to return I could easily clear myself; but that is not enough. I have not only myself to serve, but others."

"The two lads and Foote."

"Just so, Stanchion; it may prove a wild errand we go upon, but I have a little faith left that we shall find them alive; and while I seek them I seek Wantlake, and he must be found."

"We'll do our best, sir," cheerily responded the lieutenant; "what strong arms and faithful hearts can do shall be done."

"I am assured of it, Stanchion," returned our hero, warmly; "and now let us have a look round."

They went out, and quietly walked across the enclosure, unperceived by a number of the men who lay around a small wood fire, lit as much for look as for necessity, for the sun had not yet set.

The sailors were, as sailors always are, in a merry mood, laughing, and chatting, and smoking, as if they had known no perils past, and anticipating none to come, or that no messmates had gone from them within a few short days, never to return. Dull care never sits in the company of tars.

Mr. Stanchion made some remarks to the foregoing effect, to which our hero responded, "That it was better so."

"What's the name of that fellow?" he added, pointing to a tar who was about to favour the rest with a yarn, silence having been called for and accorded

"Sam Slideaway, he calls himself," replied the lieutenant.

"Not his name," said Harold, with a smile; "there's a good look about the fellow."

"He's the life and soul of his mess."

"He is about to oblige them with a yarn."

"Nothing new to him, sir."

"Come quietly behind this clump of cactus, Stanchion; we are not perceived, and let us listen to him. I like the look of the fellow."

The captain and the lieutenant complied, and Sam Slideaway, after a prefatory ahem, and a second demand for silence, began,—

"What I'm about to speak of," said Slideaway "happened on one of my return journeys from China, in the 'Lively Jenny,' as trim a little craft as any seaman set eyes on.

"I had a very good berth, but did not relish these voyages, for what with the Chinese, Malay, and Dyak pirates, we were always in a state of uncertainty, expecting each day to be hauled over by some of these vermin.

"But this time, all was going as merry as a marriage bell; it was summer time, lovely weather, and the winds being fair, the 'Lively Jenny' moved through the water like a thing of life.

"The 'Lively Jenny' was commanded by Captain Stanfield, and manned by about thirty men. On board there was also a lady (a widow), and her little boy about six years of age, and I can tell you that both mother and child were great favourites with the men.

"It was one morning, about the middle of July, that Mrs. Harper, our lady passenger, was leaning over the bulwarks, looking pensively across the sea.

"'Sighing for home?' asked the captain, smiling. 'Well, Mrs. Harper, with such fair winds as these, and such lovely weather, we shall soon see the white walls of dear old England.'

"'Well, to tell the truth,' said Mrs. Harper, 'I must confess that I am rather tired of my life on the ocean.'

"'Ah!' replied Captain Stanfield, 'like the rest of the fair sex, you desire change and excitement. What would you say now to a skirmish with pirates?'

"'Don't, captain,' exclaimed Mrs. Harper, shuddering, 'I cannot bear to think of them.'

"'Then we will change the topic,' said the captain. 'Hallo! here's that rogue of a boy of yours.'

"The child, or as he was called, Bertie, at this moment appeared on deck, and rushed towards his mother, and having saluted her, tore off towards the captain, and welcomed him by hugging his legs.

"'Don't come here, you scamp,' said the captain, lifting him from the deck, and holding him out at arm's length, 'or I will throw you to the sharks.'

"The child laughed merrily, as that threat was held out to him every morning and evening.

"'But come,' the captain went on, 'breakfast is ready, and we are keeping mamma waiting, so come along.'

"About noon the same day, the man on the look-out reported a strange sail, and all eyes and glasses were directed towards the stranger.

"'That's a queer-looking craft, Slideaway,' said the first mate to me, 'and I don't like the look of her.'

"'What colours do she carry?' I asked.

"'American,' was the reply; 'but if she's a Yankee, I'll eat my telescope.'

"The captain here joined us, and directed his glass towards the stranger, and as he lowered it an anxious expression had settled on his face.

"'I fear the worst, said he, in almost a whisper, for the lady was standing by. 'I believe that yonder craft bears a horde of pirates, but God grant it may not be so. Heaven knows,' he went on, 'I am not a coward, but——' here he glanced at Mrs. Harper and her boy, and his voice trembled.

"'If she is a pirate, said the first mate, I think we can show her a clean pair of heels.'

"'I fear not,' was the captain's reply. 'She is over-hauling us fast, and is crowding more canvas.'

"'Yes,' exclaimed the mate, 'and hauling down her colours.'

"The captain again raised his glass, and directed it towards the strange-looking craft.

"'Great God!' he suddenly exclaimed, my worst fears are confirmed. See, there goes that cursed emblem of bloodshed and pillage.'

"Sure enough, as the words left Captain Stanfield's lips, that cursed piece of bunting, bearing the skull and cross-bones, flew aloft.

"'No time is to be lost,' exclaimed the captain. 'Serve out cutlasses and muskets to the men. We must escape if possible, but I fear it is not so.'

"Mrs. Harper was unconscious of the approaching danger, but when asked by the captain to retire to the cabin, her face blanched, and drawing her boy towards her, said—

"'Captain, I see by your looks that we are in danger. What is it?'

"'I trust no danger,' replied the captain, 'but a strange vessel is coming towards us, and should she turn out a—a—troublesome, you would not be safe on deck.'

"Taking her boy in her arms, she went below, and no sooner had she done so than a cutlass, pistols, and muskets were served out to each man.

"Calling the men together, the captain said—

"'It must be plain to you, my men, that it is next to impossible for us to escape from yonder pirate, and that nothing is left but to fight. Undoubtedly they are four to one, but to surrender would be madness, as we should all be murdered. God grant that we may be able to resist the murderous villains, but if not let us die as Britons should, but no surrender.'

"Three cheers were given after this, and each man prepared for the almost hopeless conflict.

"All sail was crowded, but to no purpose, the pirate was slowly, but surely, overhauling, and I felt that it was a case of the spider and the fly.

"And so it turned out, the pirate fired several round shots, maiming our rigging and disabling one mast.

"Then we knew that but little hope could be entertained.

"Three boats were lowered from the pirate, each manned by about thirty cutthroats, and commanded by a black-muzzled villain, who addressed his men in the Spanish language.

"'Strike down that villain,' cried Captain Stanfield, as the pirates swarmed over the deck.

"I rushed forward, and, clubbing my musket, struck the pirate a heavy blow on the head, and saw him reel back and fall into the arms of one of his men.

"'Capture that man at any risk,' gasped the pirate, 'but do not kill him. Leave that to me.'

"Still our gallant handful of men fought on, headed by the captain; the decks were slippery with blood, and the air resounded with the groans and curses of dying and fighting men.

"I saw the captain fall, distinguished his murderer, and rushed to avenge his death, when I felt myself seized from behind, and was thrown upon my face on the reeking deck.

"The sound of the clashing of steel grew fainter and fainter, and the cries of the pirates louder in proportion, and I knew that the butchery of my comrades was near its completion.

"Suddenly the fighting ceased, and I was dragged to my feet to gaze upon one of the most horrible and sickening sights.

"The bodies of my comrades lay mingled with those of the pirates, and bloodstained cutlasses strewed the deck.

"The captain lay upon his face, with

his broken sword by his side, his hand still clasping the hilt.

"The pirates now prepared to plunder and scuttle the ship, and a number of them went below for that purpose.

"A fearful scream followed, and two villains, stained with blood, appeared, dragging the unfortunate Mrs. Harper after them, while a third followed with her boy.

"'What shall we do with her?' asked one of the villains, of the captain, who had partially recovered from the blow I had given him.

"'Take her on board,' said he; 'and take care that fellow'—pointing to me—'does not escape.'

"We were pushed into a boat, and rowed swiftly to the pirates' ship, and, in a short time the captain and the rest followed.

"'Bring the prisoners forward!' cried the captain.

"We were dragged before the villain, who stood, sword in hand, grinning like a fiend.

"'You fought nobly,' he said to me, showing a set of teeth that would have done credit to a tiger, and I will reward you. Stand aside. I will deal with the woman and cub first.'

"Mrs. Harper fell on her knees.

"'Spare my child!' the wretched woman cried.

"The blood-thirsty villain burst into a laugh.

"'Madam,' he said mockingly, 'I am always glad to oblige a lady, especially an English lady; but, under the circumstances, I must refuse. That lovely child of yours shall feed a shark, and you shall follow him.'

"'Villain! blood-thirsty hound!' I cried, and, before I could be prevented, I rushed towards him, and struck him between the eyes, felling him to the deck.

"'Thanks, signor!' he exclaimed, rising; 'your turn will come next. We will see how you can stand fire. Doutless this lady will be pleased to witness your courage.'

"The unfortunate woman buried her face in her hands.

"I now understood the villain's meaning. I was to die the most horrible death of all—that of torture by fire

"A mist gathered before my eyes, and all my past life flashed through my brain in an instant, and faces of whom for years I had scarcely given a thought rose up before me.

"'See, madam,' said the blood-thirsty hound, 'the noble British sailor lacks courage.'

"'Villain,' I cried, 'give me a cutlass, and let me stand face to face with you. It shall then be seen if I lack courage.'

"'You are generous,' said he—'kind! but—

"'A sail! a sail!' cried the man on the look-out.

"The pirate turned, and seizing a telescope, directed it towards the stranger.

"To my surprise he dropped it, and uttering a terrible curse, ordered all sail to be crowded.

"'What shall we do with these?' asked one, pointing to us.

"'Throw them overboard,' he replied; "but no, that might be dangerous, Iron them, and take them below.'

"I now guessed the truth. The stranger was a line-of-battle ship, and steering steadily towards us, determined upon seeing who we were.

I was dragged below, expecting every minute to have my brains blown out; but it was evident that the pirate expected to escape, and revenge himself on me afterwards.

I could hear the tramping of feet overhead, the orders and curses of the captain, then a crashing sound as the first shot struck, and yells and defiance and fury from the pirates.

Shot after shot told upon the pirate, and suddenly I heard a confused Babel of voices and the clashing of steel.

The pirate was being boarded, but with what success I could not tell.

The fight was soon over, and all was again silent save the tramping of feet above. I heard voices—English voices—near me, and the next instant was drawn from my place of confinement by the hands of English seamen, and carried in triumph to the deck.

"The captain of the pirates was alone alive, and he closely guarded and bound.

"As I appeared on deck he gave vent to a yell of rage, but which finished with a howl of despair, as two men advanced towards him, one bearing a rope, at the end of which was a very significant noose.

"'Mercy,' he cried, 'mercy; I'm not fit to die.'

"The officer in command replied not.

but holding up his hand, a gun boomed out, and the wretched being was hauled aloft struggling violently in his death agonies.

"Ten minutes later I was on board His Majesty's corvette, the 'Invincible,' where I found, to my delight, Mrs. Harper and her boy safe.

"Thirty days after we arrived in England in safety, and although I have passed through many dangers since that time, I always look back at it as being my narrowest escape, and am grateful to those men who so nobly did their duty in rescuing me."

CHAPTER XXXVII.

HOW CAPTAIN HARLOCH AND HIS MEN WERE SAVED.

Now to return to the time when the "Bruiser" sighted the mysterious vessel.

The shots from the "Bruiser" had apparently no effect upon the strange craft sailing by their side, and again the captain hailed her through his speaking trumpet. "Heave to, will you?"

No answer, and not a soul on board visible, in the lurid light of the electric fire.

The men clustered forward, and ever ready, as sailors are, to put a supernatural construction upon anything strange, drew closer together, and muttered "that it was the Phantom Ship."

"Vanderdecken likes such a night as this," said one; "he and his ship are never seen in a calm."

"But he's always found at the Cape," urged another.

"Bosh!" returned the previous speaker, "he's at the Cape when it's extra rough, but when it's fine, he has a look about him elsewhere. I'm sartain on it; look at her now; she doesn't ride the waves, she cuts through 'em."

"We've done wrong to fire across her bows; it'll do us no good."

"And there's the captain orderin' a shot to be pitched into her hull; it's sartain death."

"It'll be wreck anyhow," muttered one of the men, cunningly, "but if we aim over her we may be saved."

This idea was received with immense favour, and the consequence was that the shot was sent wide, and the strange craft kept on her way by the "Bruiser's" side.

"They've missed her," said Captain Harloch.

"Impossible," returned his brother captain; "I've some of the best gunners in the navy."

"Try another shot."

It was tried, with the same result; and as the weapon sent forth its flash of flame, the sky was rent in a dozen of places by lightning, the thunder crashed as if the earth had received its final blow, and the sea rose higher.

"I told you," muttered the man who had aimed the gun, "it is the Dutchman, and we may thank our stars that we haven't tried to hit him."

"Hallo there! you lubbers," sung out their captain; "can't you hit that fellow?"

"It ain't possebul to hit him, sir," said one of the gunners, called Hairy Mat, pulling his forelock.

"What d— nonsense is this?" growled the captain. In those days, captains were a little rougher than they are now. "Not hit him?"

"No, sir."

"Why not? confound you."

"It's the Dutchman, Vanderdecken."

The reply of the captain cannot be printed here; no respectable compositor would set up the language that fell from the angry captain's lips, but he concluded by calling to a middy of the watch,—

"Mr. Weston, set one of these guns, and riddle that fellow."

The middy touched his cap, and replied, "Ay, ay, sir"; but the words were drowned in a gust of wind that tore through the shrouds, shrieking like a lost spirit in torment.

The stranger still kept near them, but she had sheered off about fifty yards.

The men of the "Bruiser" sullenly loaded the gun as desired, and the middy proceeded to point it.

"It's sartin death, sir," muttered Hairy Mat.

"Don't talk nonsense," replied the mid; "she's not a phantom, but as substantial a vessel as the "Bruiser"; and what's more, I think I know her. There's pirates aboard there. Ready."

Just as they were about to fire, a mass of mist rolled between the two vessels, and hid the stranger from view.

The men interpreted that as a warning sign, and murmured louder than ever.

"The Dutchman don't want to run us into trouble," said Mat, "and he gives u lots of warnin'. Surely you won't fire, sir?"

"Won't I," laughed Weston, "just you wait until this mist is off; it's only a passing affair. I can see her. Steady."

The roar of the gun, mingled with a fearful clap of thunder, and a perfect squall of wind, nearly laid the "Bruiser" on her beam ends, and half a dozen broken fragments of spars came rattling down upon the deck.

The next moment there was a lull, and the stranger was perceived sailing as steadily as before, with her taper spars and canvas untouched.

At this sight, even the officers felt a thrill of superstition, and for a moment forgot the education that taught them better things.

But ere they had time to analyze their dread, the character of the stranger was put beyond doubt. Her deck suddenly swarmed with men, half a dozen guns sent their shot crashing through the timber of the "Bruiser," her yards swung round, and she went away before the wind, showing nought but her stern to the angry and discomfited seamen.

As soon as possible, the "Bruiser" was put upon the same course, but she was a large and heavier vessel, and by the time they were ready, the impudent stranger was dim and misty in the darkness of night.

How the men of the "Bruiser" cursed their stupidity then, and vowed unto them a feast of vengeance, it boots us not to tell, so we will leave them vainly following a vain-chase and go on board this mysterious midnight visitant.

Its captain stands on the aft deck, near the wheel, watching the "Bruiser" as she, in a comparatively clumsy manner, swings round before the wind, and turning to a man by his side, he laughs and says,—

"A good bit of fun, Hatchett."

"Which might have ended in a tragedy," returned Hatchett, with a shrug.

Mason Wantlake, the pirate captain, shrugs his shoulders too, and laughs again.

"I know the British tar well," he said; "seeing us sailing so close to them, apparently without a man on board, they took us for a phantom. I know them, Hatchet," and Wantlake roared again.

He was a big burly young fellow, and the rough life he followed had set his muscular frame. As he stood with his legs apart, with a hand upon each hip, he looked a model of manly strength.

"Their first shots were aimed wide," he continued, "purposely, I've no doubt; the last was the work of an officer, I'll warrant. Well, it was well meant, but it only took off the head of Dubois, who had no business to be peeping over the side."

He pointed to the headless trunk of a man lying on a coil of rope, and smiled cruelly. Mason had a cruel, remorseless face, which went far to keep his power over the wretches around him. There was an expression in it at times before which the strongest and most brutal of the pirates shrank.

"Wonder if Dubois felt the blow," he continued, musingly; "it was whirr! and the trunk there fell without a convulsion, but wise men tell us that a lifetime can be felt in a moment, and perhaps Dubois, when he endured that fraction of a second's pain, found in it hours of agony."

Hatchett listened to this impatiently; he was not a sentimental man, and being profoundly ignorant of everything but the art of rapine and murder, had naturally a profound contempt for learning in every form.

"It don't matter to us, captain," he said, roughly; "what Dubois felt—that's his business; our turn 'll come some day, p'raps a turn off at the yard arm, and then we'll think about it. Just now we've to get clear o' that cursed cruiser. Let the men have an extra supply of grog; it will give them courage to fight if we are pursued."

This was hailed with a shout of welcome, and the purser served out to each of the men a large goblet of pure rum. With a loud huzza of defiance the pirates raised the goblets above their heads, when a shot from the "Bruiser" shattered the goblet in Mason's hand and killed two men who stood behind him.

For a few moments all was confusion and wild excitement, but the captain ordering the course of the ship to be altered restored order again, and all was as quiet as if nothing had occurred.

"We are leaving her fast," returned Mason, "and the wind grows steadier. In half-an-hour we shall be able to set our topsails, and then the 'Bruiser,' my old familiar friend, will lumber after us in vain."

"It's a fortunate thing," said Hatchett,

"that she turned up in time for Captain Harloch. In ten days we should ha' had 'em to rights, They'd come down to their boots as it was."

"Yes! we laid the siege well, and it was a splendid idea of yours to burn the cocoa-nut grove, their last resource for food; but a blight upon the 'Bruiser' and its crew, but for them the lovely Clara would now be mine."

The foregoing conversation will explain to our readers how Captain Harloch and daughter came on board the "Bruiser." The men of the "Curlew" and their gallant captain held out in the stockade against long odds brought against them by Mason Wantlake.

That traitor to his country, and master spirit of the hordes of ruffians infesting the coast, had, after the capture of the merchantman, looked in upon various stations where choice pirate-spirits were wont to assemble, and, having reinforced his villanous crew, set sail for Cape Blanco, with the intention of capturing Captain Harloch and the lovely Clara.

He found the unfortunate party much reduced by want, and preferring strategy to fighting, he destroyed everything available for food round the stockade.

But the gallant men held out, and, although the whole party dared not leave the stockade, surrounded as it was by a host of enemies, parties of two or three stole through the cordon of foes, and went down to the seaside, where they gathered a few shell-fish, and, despite the watchfulness of the pirates, kept up a series of fires at night, to guide the "Bruiser" to their rescue.

These were lit in various places, and kept the foe continually on the alert, but they made not a single prisoner, or had a single encounter with these daring scouts of the imprisoned party.

But the shell-fish, scanty in quantity, was but a poor substitute for their ordinary food, and signs of weakness came among them. Two of the sailors died of the scurvy, and were buried inside the stockade, Captain Harloch reading the burial service over them, while the tears of Clara found a response in every eye.

The various fires brought no friend; the cocoa-nut trees had been destroyed; those who went down for the shell-fish could scarcely crawl upon their way, and one day, when they found a turtle upon

the shore, they killed it there, and cut out jagged masses of its flesh, for none of them had strength to bear it to the camp.

All this time the pirates made no attack. "We are in no hurry," said Wantlake, "and I can bide my time. That hound, Greystone, has cost me enough men. I must husband them now," to which Hatchett, his lieutenant, agreed, and said that of late they (the pirates) had had but precious little glory and no profit.

So the strategical process of starving out was carried on, as it has been, within the memory of all our readers, by a great power, calling itself the most civilized of nations.

Wantlake sought to starve some forty men and one woman; Germany experimented upon two millions, of all ages and grades of society.

Wantlake is a pirate, and Germany is ——what we will not say.

One morn—a bright sunny morn—when it seemed as if the sun had scattered every cloud to have an uninterrupted view of the scene below, the captain of the lost "Curlew" heard the sound of a gun.

He knew the ring of it, and said it was British metal.

Again the solemn boom came coursing through the woods, reaching the ears of the anxious listeners, and they cried, as with one voice,—

"The 'Bruiser!'"

Then, forgetting their sorrow and trouble, their want of food and consequent weakness, the men girded on their cutlasses and went forth, with the captain and his daughter in their midst.

Not a man barred their way, for the scoundrels under Wantlake's command had already fled and sought refuge in their rocky home and in the caves along the shore; and so the forty wan men went down to the beach and hailed the "Bruiser," lying at anchor not a mile from the shore.

The scene which followed was of a touching description.

Strong men, who could have faced death in the battle-field, wept as they gazed upon the haggard forms of the unhappy captain, his daughter, and the men.

They were taken on board, and the captain of the "Bruiser" would fain have stopped and had a brush with the scoundrels on shore, but his orders were imperative. Having rescued the remnant of the men of the "Curlew." he was to proceed without delay for Havannah.

He set sail, and within six hours, Wantlake brought out his craft from its hiding-place in one of the innumerable bays, and in a spirit of wanton frolic, acted the mad part we have already recorded.

With him on board he had four prisoners—Will Steadfast, Tom Furnace, Grim Foote, and the load captured on board the "Seagull." The other prisoners he had left behind.

The mysterious appearance of the middies and the old tar shall be told in due time by their own lips, in the meantime we will see how they fare in their imprisonment.

They were kept below during the day, but allowed to walk the deck for two hours at dusk, with half-a-dozen attendants to watch their movements—"a guard of honour" Will called it—for which, upon one occasion, he gravely thanked the pirate captain.

One thing disturbed the lad very much, and that was the reason why their lives had been spared.

"It's not because he is merciful, you know," said Will; "for Mason is nothing of the sort, and he hate me like poison."

"Perhaps he intends us for pages of some vile court he holds somewhere," suggested Tom Furnace, yawning; "pirate chaps have that sort of thing, I've heard."

"No, no," returned Will, shaking his head, "he knows that we couldn't be trusted; and when I was Harry Carlton on board the—never mind the ship—I used to rile him to that extent that I've seen the very hair of his head lift up, and sparks of fire spring from his eyes."

Tom laughed. "He must have been in an awful state of passion," he rejoined.

"That he was," said Will; "and besides, he never forgives; he's a thorough animal, that's what he is. You've seen him when one of his men turn sulky, as they do sometimes. It goes bad with a man that crosses him, I know, and mark me, Tom, it will go bad with us."

"Ask him what he is going to do."

"By Jove! I will," replied Will, "if he is on deck to-night. It won't make matters better nor worse, and it will relieve our minds."

That night—three days had elapsed since meeting with the "Bruiser"—when the lads were taken up for fresh air, Mason Wantlake was on deck, and Will, sauntering up, begged the favour of a few words with him.

"Very few, then," growled Wantlake; "I'm not so much in love with your society."

"No," returned Will, "we never got on well together; I was too much for you on board the 'Curlew,' you are too much for me here."

"You think so?" said Wantlake, with a short laugh.

"I know it," replied Will; "and I also know that although you discovered us afloat under uncommon circumstances, and that you for the present have spared our lives, it is not done from any motive of mercy."

"You think so?" again said the pirate.

"Yes," said Will; "I look upon my rescue as a sort of out of the frying-pan into the fire. What are you going to do with us?"

The question was abrupt, but Wantlake was prepared for it, and smiled sardonically.

"You would like to know?"

"I should, it would put my mind at rest."

"It will certainly give you food for reflection," replied Wantlake, slowly; "you see my lieutenant there, Halkett, or Hatchett, as he is as often called?"

"Yes! I see him."

"Hatchett, or Halkett, my dear Carlton," (Wantlake was as smooth and playful as a cat with a mouse) "has travelled a great deal, has seen strange lands, and mixed with strange people. He was once a slave."

"A slave!" exclaimed his listener, startled; "in the Moroccos?"

"No, my dear fellow, but among white men; he was a slave, was harnessed to vehicles and whipped like a cur, washed and housed after the manner of swine, passed a solitary life and only saw the face of a man when it came to frown upon him, never heard a voice but it cursed him; he sank so low that he neither washed or changed his clothes, and when his attire rotted away he went naked without thought or sense of his degraded condition. He lost all knowledge of time; in fact he had fallen to the level of the pigs he guarded. Harry Carlton, alias Will Steadfast, I'm going to take you to that happy land and sell you for a slave."

CHAPTER XXXVIII.

THE LAND OF CAPTIVITY.

As these terrible words escaped the lips of the pirate, he turned upon his heel and walked to the poop, leaving Will Steadfast in a state of agony impossible to describe.

To be sold for a slave.

Now that Wantlake named it, he remembered having heard of that horrible place, but the accounts had always been the vague utterings of men who had heard of such a place but never seen it; but there before him was a man who had endured the horrible fate, one who had been sent out to that line of life and lived as the swine.

But even while he thought of it, a ray of hope came.

Halkett had escaped; he had returned from the awful land, and what one had done another might do.

"I'll ask him a little about it," thought Will, "he doesn't look very amiable, but he can only refuse me."

So Will went up to the pirate lieutenant, and politely bowing, asked him if he was at liberty.

Tom Furnace was standing by, but receiving a warning gesture from his friend, he retired a few paces away.

"What do you want, reefer?" growled Halkett.

"Your captain has been talking about the time you were sold for a slave," returned Will, "and I should like to know a little about it."

"'Taint a pleasant subject," replied the pirate; "but what makes you interested in it?"

"Because I am to be sold myself."

"Whew!" whistled Halkett, "that's his game, is it? He must have some cause for being so d—— spiteful."

"He hates me," said Will; "what I want to know is, what chance shall I have of escape? You got away you know."

"Look here, my lad," said Halkett, in a kinder voice than he had hitherto used, "don't you think of escape; it aint to be done. I was brought back by my master. I'd saved his life more than once, and he turned soft in his old days; but he was the only kind-hearted man in the place, and now he's dead."

"What part is it? where is this horrible place?"

"It lies fourteen hundred miles south of Guiana," replied Halkett; "we shall drop you at Cayenne, and you'll be taken off with a batch of convicts, men so bad that they won't have them in the worst colony in the world. I remember, when I lay there, never mind what for, if I had the same chance I'd do it again—well, I was lyin' there for some time—at Cayenne I mean—and I'd a chance of seein' many things that took place there The very Injuns were worse than Injuns are anywhere else, which may not seem possible to you, but it's a fact."

He paused and looked at the sky, as if he saw there the land he spoke of, and went on speaking softly, and, withal, in a somewhat musical tone.

"There was a young middy fellow there, just like yourself, wrecked and made a prisoner of; an old skunk bought him, and although the lad was allowed to roam a bit about the woods, he had a pretty sharp eye kept on him, specially by several Injuns hanging about the place. One day he found these angels quarrelling, and having by some means got hold of a weapon, he stepped between them. This we learned afterwards, and it seemed that the quarrelling parties both turned on him, and—it's as true as you're there, my lad —flayed him alive."

"Good Heavens!" exclaimed the lad.

"It's true," said Halkett; "they did it, and all the notice taken of it was by the proprietor, who swore at the Injuns for spoiling his property. A bad lot, my lad, and although I ai'nt much given to feeling for other people, I'm sorry for you."

"But surely there must be some kind masters?" urged Will.

"They've ris' up lately, then," coolly returned Halkett; "but I can't talk no more to you; there's the captain looking as black as thunder at me for jawin' so long, and next to a para master I think he's the man for a downright bit of ferocity if he's riled."

Throughout the night the two lads talked of horrible life in store; fain would they have communicated with Grim Foote, but that worthy old tar was now kept strictly apart from them, and when, at last, they were ordered below, they received an intimation that in future they would be kept below.

"It's plain to me," said Will, "that this horrible fate is reserved for us. Poor old Grim will be compelled to join this horrible crew."

"He'll die first," rejoined Tom.

IN A GIANT'S GRIP.

"Men cling to life," said Will, shaking his head, gravely, "as you and I do now. Are you prepared? Am I prepared to cut short the breath of life? No: remember the greatest piece of philosophy ever framed by the greatest of writers:—

For in this sleep of death what dreams may come,
When we have shuffled off this mortal coil,
Must give us pause. There's the respect
That makes calamity of such long life.

"And, if ours is long, let us bear it, Will."

"Like men," rejoined the boy, with the dawn of a smile upon his face. "Tom, we've had a long night of it, and I am sleepy."

And then, with the awful shadow of slavery, and the worst form of slavery the world ever saw, hanging over them, the two brave boys lay down and slept.

In a narrow cabin, guarded night and day, they passed six long weeks, forty-two days, of drawn-out misery.

What resources they had to wile away the time, the old stories they had heard or read were told again and again,

especially those relating to escape from captivity and peril; sometimes they sang, affecting to keep up their spirits, but the imprisonment had weakened their voices, and the song was, at the best, a sad one.

The swans die singing, but they could not tune more fitting melody for the hour of death than the notes which came from the lips of the captive boys.

Their food was bad, the water was scant, the air of their dungeon, for such it really was, foul; but they lived through it all.

Wantlake never came near them, and the sentries never spoke; if questioned they made a sign that they were forbidden to communicate with the prisoners, but never uttered a word.

Thrice a commotion on deck raised their hopes that a friend was at hand; but nothing came of it, but a few shots fired, and the after drunken revelry of the pirates as they celebrated another deed of lust and rapine.

"Another victim to their murderous

11

ferocity," Will said, with a sigh, upon the last of these occasions; "another gallant vessel scuttled and sent below to be recorded in the books at home, sailed from such and such a port, on such a day, and not since heard of."

"There is a long list of them, Will?"

"A long list, Tom; and a weary time it is for friends watching and waiting for tidings concerning the hapless men and women on board."

"As some may wait for you and me, Will."

"As some may wait for us, Tom."

After this time, they ceased to count the days; but waking one morn, the stillness of the vessel, it scarcely rocked upon the quiet waters, and the bustle on deck warned them that they were in a harbour of some description, and for the first time their sentry, a grizzly old man, replied to their queries,—

"Yes! they were in harbour—came in last night."

"What harbour?"

"That I cannot say! The captain bade me tell you to prepare for shore."

"Shall I see Foote?" asked Will.

"The old sailor? no! nor the great lord we have had prisoner with you. They will remain on board for the present; but I must say no more—I have already said too much."

And nothing more could they get out of him.

An hour or so later two men came down, and throwing open the door, bade the lads follow them. For many weeks they had existed in a semi-darkness, and a broad band of light falling through the hatchway completely dazzled them, and they blundered in their footsteps.

"Steady it is," said one of the men, not unkindly; "you'll be used to it shortly—put this handkerchief over your eyes."

In a few minutes they could bear the light, and told the men they were able to proceed. Their destination was the chief cabin, and there they found Mason Wantlake and a tall Spaniard of powerful build, smoking a cigarette.

"These are the cattle," said the pirate, coolly, "mere colts, but with proper care will make useful animals."

"Caramba!" muttered the Spaniard, "they are thin."

"They've been too long in the stable," laughed Wantlake; "give them some fresh air and a week at grass, and you'll have no cause to complain."

He spoke brutally, and the blood of the boys boiled, but they felt that any resistance they could make would only add to their sorrow, and wisely refrained.

"They are dirty—Malediction," said the Spaniard.

"There is water and soap on board, they shall be scrubbed," replied Wantlake.

"Well! I will try them—and the price?"

A deal of whispered haggling thereupon ensued, but it ended in the production of a bag of dollars, and a considerable portion thereof passing into the pirate's hands.

"I will send them ashore," he said, pocketing the last coin, and took a ceremonious leave of the dealer.

When they were alone, Will, checking a rising sob, turned to Wantlake, and said,—

"Mason, have you no mercy?"

"None," was the calm reply.

"What have I done to deserve such a fate?" urged the boy, "tell me that."

"I hate you," returned the pirate, "for your monkeyish tricks when we were in the 'Curlew' together; but I hate you more for the love you have shown the dastard Harold Greystone."

"He is no dastard," said Will, "and you know it. We had but one on board the 'Curlew,' and he fled, turned traitor to his country and herded with murderers and robbers."

Wantlake uttered an oath, and half drew out a dagger, but thrusting it back impatiently, he replied.

"Harry Carlton, we both fled the service, and are therefore equals in the eyes of our countrymen. So you needn't sing the song of virtue. You are an impertinent young whelp, and I would have spitted you for the words you have uttered, but that it would be an act of mercy. Such a thing I have sworn never to show, and least of all to Harold Greystone and you."

CHAPTER XXXIX.

THE STRANGE MESSAGE.—JACK RECOVERS HIS TREASURE.

AT this time, while Mason Wantlake was carrying matters with a very high hand after the desires of his heart, events were happening, many miles away, of a natu ikely to interfere with his unlawful and villanous acts.

Harold Greystone and the "Crucible" were ready for sea.

He had not hurried about it. All that could be done in fitting out the vessel was done.

All that ingenuity and great resources could accomplish was accomplished, and, one fine morning in the autumn of the year, the gallant "Crucible" spread her canvas before the wind, and sped away as useful as a bird.

"This time," said Harold to his lieutenant, "I am resolved to capture or kill that scoundrel, Wantlake. Once upon his track again, I will follow him to the North Pole. It shall go hard with me if he escapes me again."

The feeling which prompted him to speak thus was not one of absolute revenge.

His wrongs certainly created in him a desire to avenge his sufferings, but his main motive was to take back Wantlake to the seat of justice, and force from him a confession of the events on board the "Curlew."

Could he but have known one thing, he would have pursued the ruffian with a different feeling, but he would have pursued him still; and that one thing was—Captain Harloch and even higher authorities had put their heads together, had weighed the different events in connection with the lives of our hero and Wantlake, and arrived at the conclusion that the former had been foully outraged and wronged.

They were prepared to receive him kindly, and investigate his case thoroughly, should he return; but there was a deep mystery attached to his fate, although they rather suspected that he and the mysterious captain of a wondrous privateer were one and the same.

Rumours innumerable reached the ports in the south and extended to England. Stories of English vessels stopped and courteously dismissed by a masked captain, who bade them go unharmed upon their way. Sometimes he had prizes in his wake, so ran the stories, but they were always of foreign build, French or Spanish as the case might be, and this, added to the banner he bore, with its motto "For Honour we fight," all pointed to Harold as the mysterious hero.

Harry Carlton, alias Will Steadfast, had been partly recognised, too, by an old salt who knew him when he first went to sea, but as the weather-beaten tar said, "He were growed that tall and handsome, and not pale and delicate, like a girl, as he was when he first boarded, but strong as a young tiger, and it was difficult to swear to h·m."

As for Clara Harloch—pretty gentle Clara—she knew that this hero was her also, for had he not said on the night he left the "Curlew" that he was going forth to fight for his good name, and did not this wondrous little craft announce to all that those on board fought for "Honour!" not for glory or gain; but for honour alone.

But as two years had passed away and still no sign of Harold, her heart grew weary with deferred hope, and oft she sighed—"Will he ever return?"

He will come back, Clara, ere long, a fitting type of the naval heroes of England, with such a train of prizes in his wake, that no man shall call him coward, and not lie, and his native land shall ring with the story of his deeds.

But in the meantime his task is not completed, and we, as in duty bound, return to the "Crucible."

She was sailing in a north-westerly direction, back towards Cape Blanco, the very opposite to the course taken by the pirate, our hero's foe. In fact, one night the two enemies crossed each other, and neither knew nor suspected the proximity of the man he hated; so each kept on their way, the sea between them growing wider and wider.

On the following morning the man on the look-out gave warning of something ahead.

"What is it?" sung out Harold.

"Can't tell 'zackly, sir," replied the man, shading his eyes with his hand; "it looks like a man's head bobbing about."

"Where away?"

"About half-a-mile to the south."

"A bottle, I suppose," said Harold to Mr. Stanchion; "a message from some poor, shipwrecked wretches. Bring-to and send a boat after it."

The cutter was manned, and went in search of the object. It proved to be a bladder, with the open end tightly and scientifically bound.

"That's a sailor's work," said Harold, as he received it, "and bears, I fear, news of crime and of sad disaster."

He ripped it open as he spoke, and a small piece of folded paper fell out. As he raised and opened it, the blood rushed to his face—the hurried scrawl was in a hand he knew too well.

"Britishers, to the rescue!

"Several English prisoners are on board a pirate craft, commanded by Mason Wantlake, bound south for some slave market. By our brotherly love as a nation, come to the rescue, or warn any cruisers you may meet.

"WILL STEADFAST.
"TOM FURNACE."

There was nothing more, but it was a clue. Going south, and the "Crucible" on the opposite tack! Harold thanked Heaven for wafting the message towards him, and with feverish energy wore the ship, and crowded on all sail.

"Five days lost!" he muttered; "five days, fatal, perhaps, to the poor lads!—slaves too!—but they are white, and there is no market for them in the south, that is in the east.

He had several men among his crew who had spent a life of hardy adventure wandering hither and thither as the whim took them, and of these he made inquiries. One only knew anything about it, and he indicated the spot spoken of by Hatchett to Will Steadfast.

"It's the only place down south, sir," he said, in conclusion, "and if they are reely gone there that's where we shall find 'em."

And Harold bore down towards the coast of Guinea to look for his lost friends.

The word "friends" reminds us of two we have neglected of late—Monkey Jack and his amiable brother Crikey. Jack had thoroughly recovered from his indisposition, but not from his loss. That could never be replaced.

He wore a yellow silk handkerchief now tightly, and with a certain amount of picturesqueness, bound about his head, but it was but a poor compensation for that glorious and impressive hat, apparently lost for ever.

The coolness between him and Crikey was sustained; indeed they never met, the wretched cause of the misfortune kept carefully out of his brother's way, appearing on deck but seldom, and then only when he was certain that Jack was in his hammock or fully engaged below.

There was another man on board on whom the loss created an impression, but of a different nature, and that was Duncan, the avowed foe of Monkey Jack, and h went about with an unwonted elasticity and with a smile upon his face, long stranger there.

And Jack had no longer the heart t enter upon an encounter with his ol enemy; he felt that Duncan had, to use somewhat slangy, but expressive phrase "got the pull of him;" and that he (Jack without his hat was a king without crown; the symbol of his power was removed, and he was reduced to the level of ordinary mortals.

But one night when the "Crucible" had been two days on her southern course, Crikey came unto his brother, as he sat moody and disconsolate in the purser's cabin.

"Jacky," he said, "I not keep you one moment."

"Go 'way; git out ob dis," returned Jack, waving his hand; "I neber know you more."

"But, Jacky——"

"Crikey, once I lub you fondly. I t'ink kindly ob you, if I sw'ar at your po'try, but you coms like a ti'ef in de night, an you steal my hat."

"Jacky," said Crikey, with tears in his eyes, "I no steal it, I borrow it, t'inkin' I get some spinspiration from it, and fight somet'ing like my brodder (Jack smiled complacently at the compliment, and listened with a more kindly air), and I get dat spinspiration, and bowl ober dem slaber chaps like peelin' onions, but I lose dat hat; nebber mind, Jacky, I t'ink I find it."

"What?" cried Jack, springing to his feet.

"I t'ink I find it," repeated Crikey, slowly; "now, Jacky, you see how jolly ole Duncan am lately?"

"I see dat, Crikey."

"And him allers smilin' all ober him face."

"I bile ober when I look at him, Crikey."

"Ah! dat de secret," said Crikey; "de next time he pass you grinning, you take him by de throttle, and ax him for your hat."

Jack looked earnestly at his brother, a he would have looked at a rare jewel or very warm friend, suddenly and unexpectedly discovered; the stern expression of his countenace relaxed, his eyes beamed with joy, as he extended his arms.

"Crikey," he cried, "come to you

brudder's buzzum; dis am de happiest moment ob my life."

Crikey gladly obeyed, and the two brothers embraced in a very impressive manner, and then the happiest of the two retired, singing the refrain of his favourite song,—

> Ob all de Cuban bumboat men,
> Dat up to ebery game,
> Dere's one dat lick de bilin' lot,
> An Crikey am him name.

Anxious not to lose any time, Jack went at once upon deck, prepared to confound the smiling Duncan.

That individual was there, leaning against the capstan; he surveyed the negro with a supercilious smile, directed especially at the silk handkerchief which garnished his head.

"You smile, sar?"

The voice of Jack was firm with a stand-no-nonsense sort of ring in it. Duncan had not heard it of late, and his countenance fell a bit.

"You smiled, sar?"

Jack altered the sentence to the past tense as Duncan's countenance changed, and his tone increased in fierceness.

"I believe I did," returned Duncan, after a pause; "no harm in that,"

"But you smile at me," said Jack.

"O, no, nothing of the sort," hurriedly replied Duncan, preparing for a retreat, "never thought of such a thing."

"Don't move an inch," said Jack, with a warning motion of his fist, a very respect-able rival to a leg of mutton, "'cause I hab more questions to ax you. Where am my hat?"

The colour of Duncan's face faded out, and the knees of that worthy plugger knocked together.

"Your—your hat?" he gasped.

"My hat," returned Jack, firmly, "dat Crikey lose, an' you pick up somewhar; out wid it, or—" and Jack concluded with a pantomimic performance, expressive of mortal combat.

"I certainly picked up a hat," said Duncan, with a slight cough, "and if it is yours, you are welcome to it, but I have my doubts——"

"Prejuice dat hat," interrupted Jack.

"I don't think I know exactly where I put it," said Duncan, meditatively. "Let me see—let me see——"

Monkey Jack eyed him for a moment with no friendly eyes, and suddenly acting upon the thought running through his brain, he seized the meditative carpenter by the throat, and shook him to and fro.

"I squash de life out ob you," he said, "I turn you inside out. Where dat hat? you nail-dribing, hole-stopping nigger."

"O, lor'," gasped Duncan, "I'll—I'll give it up. O, lor', I'm strangle—ugh! O, lor'."

In the end, Duncan produced the ori-ginal article from a locker, surrounded by many laughing comrades, as he declared, with tears in his eyes, that had he known it was Jack's hat, he would have rushed over the world to restore it. To all of which Jack smiled with immense significance, looking as wise as a black Solomon.

"De next time," he said, emphatically, "you put one finger on dis hat, de 'Cru-cible' will want a carpenter."

Leaving Duncan without a doubt as to the meaning of his words, Jack went on deck, another being to that he had been for several weeks past; in fact, with all the insignia of his power once again in his possession.

"The darkey was himself again," and Crikey, the proudest and noblest of bum-boat men, was once again, in a metaphorical sense, lying "in his brother's bosom."

CHAPTER XL.

UNCLE AND NEPHEW.—A DARK DEED.

LORD SANCROFT was a prisoner on board the craft commanded by Wantlake, and as we have seen, was treated with very re-markable courtesy—the why and where-fore of this we will now explain.

His lordship was uncle to the pirate, and Mason had spared his life from the first, not from any strict merciful motives, but for an object of a more selfish nature, and that a short conversation between him and Lord Sancroft will explain.

"You may rely upon me, bad as you are, not to betray you—if my life is spared and I am allowed to land at any port."

It was Lord Sancroft who spoke, and as he uttered them in a quick impassioned tone, he leaned forward, eagerly scanning the face of his nephew, who sat on the op-posite side of the table.

"My lord," returned Wantlake, "I can-not trust you—yet! Not that I doubt your honour, for the word of Lord Sancroft is his bond; but I cannot touch at any port where I could land you with safety to us both—and now respecting your son?"

"I have lost him, I tell you once again!"

replied his lordship. "He disappeared in a most suspicious manner—kidnapped or murdered, I fear, for all efforts to discover him have been in vain."

"What would be his age?"

"About sixteen."

"And with him the title dies out?"

"Unless you had been in a position to assume it—which admits of no discussion," said Lord Sancroft, coolly.

"But is there no chance of my peccadilloes being overlooked?" eagerly asked Wantlake. "Money can do much, especially in England. Influence can do more; witnesses can be purchased to swear anything ——"

"My dear nephew," interposed his lordship, mockingly, "were you to show your interesting countenance in Great Britain, you would become practically acquainted with the criminal laws, ending with a brief experience of the pangs of death, by the hands of the common hangman; as you value that life of yours, don't think of it."

But Mason did think of it, and the more he thought of it the more feasible did the working of a certain scheme appear.

Lord Sancroft out of the way, and his cousin not to be found, he was the proper owner of the title, and, if possible, he would claim it—but how?

After much thought and deliberation he worked it out thus.

He would boldly return to England, and lay claim to the title—after disposing of his lordship in a manner which shall hereafter appear—and, trusting to the law's delay, and the confusion to be created by conflicting evidence, boldly deny the evidence of Captain Harloch.

"What they can prove against me, I will swear was compulsory," he thought; "but who are the witnesses against me?—Harloch, and a few of the men. The men can be bought and kept out of the way. All other witnesses to my crimes are either aboard here or down at the bottom of the sea, except my dear and beloved friend, Harold Greystone—and he is an outlaw. But it's a risky game, a very risky game, and yet others as bad have been played; and now I'll venture. But first his lordship."

He summoned to his presence two of his most trusty men—one a negro, the other a mate of the vessel—both unscrupulous, and utterly without conscience.

"Samson, I want a little affair done to-night."

"Yes, sar," grinned the negro.

"And you, Withers, had better give him a hand."

Withers touched his forelock. He was a man of many (dark) deeds, but few words.

"You know his lordship, both of you?"

They signified their assent.

"He will take the air to-night," pursued Wantlake, "about his usual time. Most of the men will be ashore, but I presume you will be on deck. His lordship is very careless; keep an eye upon him and should he fall overboard to seaward let me know."

The scoundrels grinned, the negro showing the whole of his glistening teeth.

"You will be careful," added the young pirate, in a whisper, "I suspect his lordship of having obtained possession of arms. Now go, and when you have anything to say, return. In the meantime, you had better have something to while away the time; open that locker, and take one of the bottles you will find there."

The negro took one of the bottles of French brandy, and retired with his mate to drink themselves into a fitting state for the foul deed.

They knew their leader well, and a hint from him sufficed; besides he was a liberal paymaster, and they felt certain of receiving a substantial reward when they reported the accident.

Why Wantlake thought it necessary to act this subterfuge was best known to himself; in the place they were in, it was scarcely necessary to hide any crime, even murder, for such events were of daily occurrence, and passed unheeded as matters of no moment.

When Lord Sancroft came on deck that evening, the moon had risen, shedding its light upon the rambling town, upon the shore, and the scanty shipping in the port.

His lordship was treated with this lenity, as he had given his word that he would not attempt to escape, until he had given notice of his intention to do so or violence had been shown him.

"In that case," he said, significantly, "I shall not fall alone."

These words were uttered on the day previously, and were the means of inducing Wantlake to think that his uncle had by some means obtained possession of arms.

It would have been a very easy affair to

CRIKEY WAS THE FIRST TO RECOGNISE THE CHILD

have him seized and searched, but Mason shrank from that course as he shrank from openly expressing his desire to have him barbarously murdered.

He tried to cheat his conscience, and, if the truth must be told, partly succeeded, as most of us can do every day in smaller matters.

Lord Sancroft found the deck deserted, and for a while paced pensively to and fro, but growing weary, he leant upon the bulwarks, and looked towards the town.

It was a scant, low-looking place, with a vast tract of barren land on either side, and hills beyond, lying like clouds in the moonlight.

A few people were moving about, and one boat was crossing the harbour, but the greatest signs of activity came from several large houses near the shore, where every window was lighted up, and from whence the voices of men came floating over the water.

These were the gambling hells—the only places of public resort in the town.

"No escape here," thought Lord Sancroft, "even if I had not given my parole. Starvation on either side, a wild country beyond, and no refuge in the town, for they are all knaves and rogues to a man. Ha! who's that?"

He turned sharply, Samson and Withers within a few paces of him, affecting to coil a rope.

"What do you fellows want?" His lordship's hands were in the pockets of his coat, a fact which did not escape the notice of the negro and his companion.

"Nothin', your honour," replied Withers, touching his forelock.

"Then retire to another part of the vessel."

"I don't see no reason for doin' that," replied Withers, "do you, Samson?"

Samson grinned, and uttered a guttural sound of approval. He did not see any reason, and he didn't mean to go.

"As I suspected," replied Lord Sancroft, coolly. "My time has come. I have been left to the tender mercies of you men, but, as I warned the young scoundrel, my relation and your master, that it would be dangerous to interfere with me, I think it right that you, too, should know that I am in possession of these toys."

Lord Sancroft produced a brace of pocket pistols, and was about to present them when Samson sprang upon him,

dashed one from his hand while Withers seized him by the wrist.

Two fearful blows upon the forehead from the powerful hand of the negro stunned and dazed the struggling nobleman, and raising him in his arms, Samson bore his insensible burden to the ship's side.

"Better make sure," whispered Withers, producing a long keen knife.

"He sure enuf," returned the negro, and without any apparent effort he hurled the inanimate form into the sea.

The night was calm, not a breath of wind stirring, and the splash of the falling body sounded loud and startling in the stillness. The two men leaned over the ship's side watching the disturbed water subside and the bubbles rising slowly to the surface.

"Gone!" said Withers.

"Him berry much gone," grinned the negro, "dis his last accident."

Withers smiled harshly, and was about to dive below, when a shrill cry fell upon his ears, and one word rung out bold and clear.

"Father!"

He paused and looked at his companion in a state of the utmost astonishment. The negro returned the stare, and then acting upon a mutual impulse they rushed to the side of the vessel.

The ocean lay smoothly reflecting the silver rays of the moon, not a ripple ruffled its surface, all was still as the grave.

"I must have been mistaken," muttered Withers; "what did you hear, Samson?"

"Somebody cry out."

"What did he say?"

"'Fader!' dat de word."

"We can't be both mistaken," rejoined Withers, looking round with a half-alarmed expression, "it came out bold enough. By George, it's a startler. Who can it be? we ain't got no fader on board, at least we ain't got 'em and their children too. Samson, it's them cubs havin' a game with us, give 'em a look up."

Samson went down to the prisoners, Will and Tom, who were now confined in a more airy prison-house, and found them both asleep. This fact reported to Withers appeared to solve the mystery.

"One of 'em hollowed out in his sleep," he said, "and it bein' so precious still it sounded jolly loud. Samson, make some grog."

The grog was made and drunk, but the cry still haunted him, and when Mason Wantlake came on deck, flushed with drink, and angry with losses at the gaming table, he at once proceeded to impart the events of the evening.

"His lordship have disappeared,——" he began.

"Not now—not now," returned Wantlake, savagely; "another time."

"Werry good, sir," muttered Withers; "but there's somethin' odd about it, sir, as wants an explanation."

"Odd?—about what?—speak out, man, and don't stand there like a petrified specimen of ruffianism," cried his leader.

Thus mildly adjured, Withers told his story, with certain decorations, but putting due emphasis upon the cry he had heard. The account interested Wantlake, more so than the narrator anticipated.

"The cry was—Father?"

"Yes, sir."

"And the voice seemed to be young?"

"Quite boyish, sir!"

"Ha! bring the two prisoners to me—the lads I mean."

"I don't think it's them, sir! Samson found them asleep."

"Bring them at once."

In ten minutes the boys were closeted with their captor, who abruptly addressed Tom Furnace, as he wished to take him unawares—

"Who are you?" he asked.

"Tom Furnace, mid of the 'Crucible.'"

"We all know that," rejoined Wantlake; "but who is your father? and when did you see him last?"

The colour left the boy's cheek, and Will, too, turned pale, while they both lost their powers of utterance.

"You saw him as he plunged from the side of this good ship—when he committed suicide in fact," said Wantlake.

Tom's face cleared a little; but he made no reply.

"It is a strange fact," pursued the pirate, "that you and I should be so near and not know each other. We are cousins."

"A relationship I ought to be proud of," returned Tom, bowing sarcastically.

"Proud of it or not, the fact remains the same. When your father, Lord Sancroft, committed that rash act ——"

"When he was murdered, you mean!"

"Committed that rash act," repeated Wantlake, "you observed him fall into the water from the small light in your cabin. Is it not so?"

"You are near the mark."

"And you recognised him?"

"It was difficult to do so after the cruel blows he had received."

"He struck the ship's side, doubtless," returned Wantlake, coolly; "but as you now recognized him, and I am fully assured of the relationship between us—you may rely upon my taking the utmost care of you."

He touched a bell, and Withers appeared.

"Take these cubs to their den again, and come to me."

The cubs, without a word, followed Withers to their place of confinement, and were shut in once more. Withers returned to his leader's cabin.

"I've fathomed the whole of the mystery," said the pirate, "therefore you may as well drop the subject. It's not worth talking about. He saw the face of Lord Sancroft, and detecting some likeness in it to his father, he called out."

"He worn't in no great hurry about it, then," returned Withers, "for it was nearly a minute arter his lordship was—tumbled in, that he hollered out."

This reply gave Mason Wantlake food for reflection. Nearly a minute?—then it was plain Lord Sancroft had risen to the surface, but Withers stoutly denied it.

"We kept a sharp look out on the water, and he never rose," he said, "never showed above the water; if he had, we should have been down on him—neither Samson nor me ain't of the merciful sort."

A knock at the door interrupted the conversation, and the new arrival being bidden to enter, Hatchett appeared. His eyes were bloodshot, his dress disordered, and his whole appearance that of one freshly awakened from a sleep of debauch.

"Now, Hatchett, what do you want?" asked the captain, impatiently.

"A few words; but as you are engaged ——"

"Never mind—Withers, you may go. Now, Hatchett."

"You and I," began Hatchett, "know each other pretty well."

"Thoroughly, I should say," rejoined Wantlake.

"And you wouldn't take me for a soft-hearted fool?"

"I give you credit for being a thorough cold-blooded scoundrel," replied Wantlake, "and therefore in every way suited to the post you hold."

"Then you're wrong," said Hatchett, doggedly; "I've turned soft-hearted, and I'm goin' away."

"What's this?" exclaimed the other; "are you going to blab?"

"No, I'm not; but I've turned soft-hearted, and it's over them two boys; you are not going to sell them?"

"They are sold."

"But are you aware," urged Hatchett, "what sort of life they are going to?"

"Judging by the graphic accounts I have received from you," coolly replied Wantlake, "I should say it is veritably and truly a hell upon earth."

"It is, sir," returned Hatchett, warmly; "no man can tell what it's like unless he's gone through it, and then if he have the heart, or a bit of the heart, of a man in him, he'd not wish even a dog to go into it. Spare the youngsters, blow their brains out, it will be a merciful act in comparison; but don't send them there."

"Hatchett," said Wantlake, "you've been drinking yourself into a maudlin state. Have another nap, and then come to me again. You'll have slept it off by that time."

"Not a bit of it," replied Hatchett, "not if I slept for a thousand years. Don't sell the lads to such a life."

"Go to sleep again," was all the reply vouchsafed by Wantlake, and Hatchett left the cabin.

CHAPTER XLI.
THE "CRUCIBLE" REFUSES TO FIGHT.—A SLIGHT MISTAKE.

FAST before the wind, as if it knew the errand it was on, sped the "Crucible." All on board eager for the time when the pirate they sought should be again within reach of her guns. More than once a sail hove in sight, tempting Harold to diverge from his course, and add another leaf to his wreath of victory, but he resisted it, and kept straight on his way.

"The wealth of a nation should not turn me, Stanchion," he said to his lieutenant, "now that I can guess the whereabouts of the poor lads. Heaven send we may be in time to save them."

"Amen!" rejoined Mr. Stanchion, "and at the same time send perdition to the pirate scoundrel."

"Not at fust, sar," broke in Monkey Jack, who was standing near. "I hope to hab one leetle turn up wid him, and when I hab done wid him," he added significantly, "he want berry little more."

"No, no, Jack," said Harold, "he must be left to me, unless you can bring him here alive, in that case, I shall be ever indebted to you."

"You nebber 'debted to Jack, sar," returned the faithful negro; "he owe you much, sar, too much for one nigger to count, sar, and derefore he nebber able to pay it."

"Jack," said the masked captain, "where is your brother?"

"My brodder, sar?"

"Yes, he who is called Crikey."

"Ah! I 'member now you mention him, sar," replied Jack, as if he were suddenly enlightened. "I believe him somewhar 'bout de ship, sar."

"But I never see him."

"No, sar, he nebber come on deck when it daytime, Crikey too modest—him blush all ober, sar, when him show him hunks to de cap'en, sar."

"I should like to see a nigger blush," said Harold, aside, to the lieutenant. Then aloud, "Jack, what are your brother's duties?"

"Him help de cook, and out ob de cap'en's way."

"But I have heard better than that of him, Mr. Stanchion says he followed me throughout our last affair, and fought well."

"Like a lion," confirmed the lieutenant.

"Crikey fight berry well when him monkey up," said Jack.

"Well, as that is the case," rejoined our hero, "let him leave the cook, and learn to work the guns. We shall have rough work shortly, and all the good hands we can obtain will be wanted."

And thus it was that Crikey was emancipated from his life below, and came on deck, where his endless fun and good humour helped to while away the monotony of the voyage.

The innumerable songs he sang of the real and imaginary glories of the "Crucible" would have filled a volume, and he had a verse for everybody on board expressive of their various qualifications, which he sometimes sang throughout round the galley fire.

The days passed swiftly by, a fair wind kept them bowling along until some evil star threw the "Crucible" in the way of a powerful French cruiser.

"I shall keep my word," said Harold; "we have no time to fight, keep off another point, and we shall be able to run by clear of her guns."

But the Frenchman was well manned, and a good vessel to boot, and she drove the "Crucible" further out of her course, until Harold despaired of escaping without a brush.

"She carries eighteen guns," said Mr. Stanchion, "and has nearly double the quantity of men we have—a meeting would be no child's play."

"I care but little for the fight itself," said Harold; "but we have no men to spare, and no time to lose; but prepare for action. If the night does not allow us to escape, we must fight it out in the morning."

The night at first did not favour them, and the Frenchman, elated by the supposed cowardice of the little craft, showed up boldly in the moonlight, the "Crucible," of course, being also plainly visible to the foe.

Harold ordered every light to be extinguished, and kept upon the deck all night.

And the men clustered forward, with their eyes upon the heavy craft in pursuit.

About midnight, Harold, who had been keenly watching the sky, pointed out a few small clouds rising in the west, separate specks of mist fantastically shaped, scattering across the heavens as they came.

"We shall escape her yet, said Mr. Stanchion.

"No," returned Harold; "she is too well upon our course, and, with the morning's light she would be upon us; but I have a plan which I think will spare us a fight. Let the men prepare to furl every sail."

"Every sail, sir?"

"All."

Accustomed to obey, and having perfect faith in his young leader, the lieutenant gave the necessary orders, and the men crowded on the yards.

Harold remained watching the rising clouds.

They soon increased in number and size, some passing across the moon, obscuring it for a moment; and, at length, several united, and, forming a huge mass, came straight across the sky.

"Stand by, men!"

The men stood ready, and, as the cloud touched the silver orb, the voice of Harold rung out clearly,—

"Furl all sails!"

And, long ere the moon reappeared, every stitch of canvas was furled, and the masts of the "Crucible" stood out almost naked against the sky,

The effect upon the Frenchman was what our hero anticipated.

The little craft, hitherto so plainly discernible, disappeared, her black hull rocking idly upon the sea.

Still the object of the captain did not appear clear, and something like murmuring arose among the men.

Was the captain going to strike his flag?

"Silence fore and aft," sung out Harold. "Mr. Stanchion!"

"Sir."

"Let every man be ready, and when I give the order let them smartly set every sail."

"Ay, ay, sir."

"What can he be up to?" thought the lieutenant—"some new tack. Well, he's a ready fellow, and will pull us through."

Harold could see that the captain of the French craft was puzzled.

He had lost sight of the "Crucible," and while he was visible to our hero sailing clear across his bows, the sea was tenantless to him.

Our hero, waiting several minutes, the foe getting nearer and nearer, until another huge cloud obscured the moon.

Then the word was passed, and swiftly the canvas bellied out before the wind, the helm was put up, and the "Crucible" rushed down upon the foe.

Those on board the Frenchman were looking ahead, endeavouring to pierce the gloom, but little anticipating the danger on their weather quarter, but when once again the moon shone forth, the white canvas of the "Crucible" was seen by a score close under their side.

With a yell of rage and affright the men ran to their guns, but it was too late, two guns sent the same number of shot idly over the sea, and then followed a crash.

The noble vessel, as indeed it was, although owned by a foe, heeled over as the privateer struck her; the water rushed into the portholes on her lee; yells, oaths, and screams startled the stillness of the night, and the "Crucible" glided over the spot where a gallant ship and all on board had sunk beneath the blue waves.

"I would have spared them if I could," said Harold, with a sigh, "but it was impossible."

He shortened sail, and hovered about for awhile, bent upon picking up any of the survivors, but nothing more than bubbles arose to the surface—the unknown craft and all its teeming life on board had sunk for ever.

"Crikey," said Jack, "dem all gone."

"Eberyone, Jacky."

"De Frenchman hab good vessel an' good men, but he lose 'em troo one t'ing."

"What dat, Jacky?"

"He make one little mistake; he run arter de 'Crucible,' he should hab run away from it; no man can run arter our cap'en wid compunity."

CHAPTER XLII.

OUTSIDE THE PORT.—JACK GOES ON A MISSION.

THE information Harold Greystone had obtained was of the right sort, and he was bound to the very spot where Mason Wantlake had taken refuge with his crew.

The coast near Cayenne was sighted ten days after the encounter with the French cruiser; and the spot being of a very dangerous character, Harold did not venture near until night had fallen, then he dropped quietly down, and anchored at the harbour's mouth, unperceived by any of the Spanish or French authorities on shore.

"What we have to do must be done swiftly," he thought; "in six hours it will be daylight again, and I away. A moment's thought, and then to work."

He had dropped down without any very definite project; in fact it was impossible to make any settled plan, for he neither knew the country nor the people, and he was far from certain if his enemy and the captive lads were there.

But he had, just at sunset, advanced far enough to perceive that several vessels were in harbour, apparently vessels of war, and he determined at once to ascertain their character, and whether any of them were commanded by the man he sought.

But how?

That was the poser; but after much cogitation, he hit upon an idea which promised to lead him out of the difficulty.

He sent for Jack, and that worthy responded immediately to the call, with the famous hat under his arm, and a stat collar, newly starched, that would hav done credit to the Original Christy Min strels.

"Jack," said our hero, "you are a goo swimmer."

Jack rolled his eyes, a sure sign that h had a favourable reply to give, and decla red "that he would swim round de worl if somebody would only go wid him to gi him meat and drink."

"I shall not tax you to that extent," returned Harold, "but you and Crike start in the cutter with muffled oars, pul into the harbour, and get sufficiently near without running the risk of being seen then swim to the vessels, and get me al the information you can."

"I bring all I can, sir," said Jack, confidently, "and dat no little. If Massa Will or Tom dere, Jack find 'em."

Proud of the confidence placed in him, Jack took a respectful leave of his captain, and sought Crikey, whom he thus solemnly addressed,—

"Crikey, de time hab come when you are to show de cap'en if you am worthy of bein' my brodder. You am not to ax any questions, but do jest as I tell you, or you'd better drown your hunks dan eber show your nigger's head on board ag'in."

Crikey promised to obey, and in a few minutes the cutter was prepared, and stealing quietly into the harbour.

In the stern sat Jack, keen and earnest now that real business was on hand, looking out with eager eyes towards the lights on board the vessels, and from a few windows in the small town.

Suddenly he held up his hand, and Crikey ceased rowing,

Jack divested himself of his hat, coat, and boots.

"Wait for me here," he whispered, and slipping quietly into the water, disappeared.

His brother lay over the boat's side, watching the light, rippling track he left behind, until that, too, disappeared, and then he sat motionless, with eyes and ears ready for anything around him.

In a few minutes he distinguished Jack returning, his round, black head showing like a bladder on the surface of the water, but to make sure he poised an oar ready to strike.

"Dat you, Jacky?"

OUR HERO BROUGHT BEFORE THE PIRATES.

"Yes, Crikey, pull lower down to next ship, dat big ship ober dere."

While Jack swam by the side of the boat, Crikey sculled slowly in the direction alluded to.

When within safe distance he rested, and Jack, with a warning to him to be watchful, once more disappeared.

The vessels, dimly visible around, were all very quiet, apparently deserted; but from the shore came sounds of revelry, which Crikey, with his knowledge of harbour life, correctly assumed to account for the quietude on board.

The majority of the sailors were on shore, keeping the birthday of some patron saint in a way worthy of their occupation at sea.

The riot and noise increased on shore, and Crikey watched long and anxiously, but Monkey Jack did not reappear.

A disturbance on shore, the cries of men in passion, the shrieks of a wounded or slain man, and all still again; but no Jacky, and the heart of Crikey grew heavy.

More than two hours elapsed, and far away in the east the sky was losing its inky blackness; in another hour it would be dawn.

In a moment, like a flash of light, a thought came across Crikey, and he felt as if he had been heavily smitten by a blow.

"De shark," he moaned, while tears ran down his sable cheeks; "de shark hab eaten up my Jacky, and I shall nebber see him more."

CHAPTER XLIII.

FATHER AND SON.—A WELCOME VISITOR.

WILL STEADFAST and his friend Tom sat side by side in their prison house on board the pirate craft.

It was a small cabin, with only a bull's-eye porthole to admit air and give light; escape by that means was, therefore, hopeless; and outside the door a burly ruffian, armed to the teeth, stood day and night.

He was faithful to his post—the escape of the prisoners, whether by his connivance or not, entailed upon him the extreme penalty of death—he was, therefore, as vigilant as the spider with its prey fast bound in its web.

The unhappy lads made much of the bull's-eye, as all prisoners make of trifles, and one or the other was perpetually by it, watching with wistful eyes the ever-changing sea.

Fortunately for them, this only communication with the open air would open, and by keeping it always thrown back, they could sniff the sweet breeze as it whistled past—a boon, indeed, to the boys, for the general air of their den was poisonous.

It was while watching thus one eve that Tom Furnace witnessed the foul deed by the negro and his accomplice upon Lord Sancroft, and while he was yet staring at the spot where his lordship had disappeared, an arm was thrust through the port-hole, and the face of the outraged nobleman appeared.

The moon shone full upon it, and Tom recognised his father. Despite the startling nature of the position, Lord Sancroft, a man whose presence of mind seldom deserted him, put a finger of his free hand upon his lip as a signal to be silent.

Thus, with Tom dazed, and Will wondering without, until the retreating steps of the ruffians left them at liberty to speak, then Lord Sancroft, in a low trilling whisper, murmured—

"Is that form a reality or a mocking vision—do I behold my son, Percy?"

"Father!" returned the lad, "it is, indeed, your son—a miserable prisoner."

Lord Sancroft extended his disengaged hand—Tom raised it to his lips.

"I cannot stay now," said his lordship, to learn how the wondrous ways of Providence have brought us together. My life has been attempted here this night, but I will outmatch the ruffians. I shall be near you, Percy. Who is that with you?"

"My friend and companion in misfortune—Will Steadfast."

"And happy am I to share the sorrow of such a friend," said Will.

"I cannot see your face," replied Lord Sancroft, "but I hear your voice, and it has an honest ring with it. Farewell, my dear children, we shall, I trust, meet again under more favourable circumstances."

He touched a hand of each and disappeared, climbing upwards towards the deck.

There all was clear, and there we will leave him for the present, and return to the imprisoned boys below.

Tom was naturally overwhelmed with astonishment at the appearance of his father, whom he thought was many hundred miles away, at such a time and place; but half-an-hour's whispered conference put matters tolerably clear before him.

"He was a passenger in some merchant-man," said Will, "and captured by that scoundrel, Wantlake, who you say is your cousin. He resolves, after keeping his captive for a time, to get rid of him, and either with his own hand or that of his able and in every way worthy assistants, he is thrown overboard."

"And being a really marvellous swimmer," concluded Tom, "dives deeply and comes up by the ship's side. He climbs to this port-hole to rest for a moment before making for the shore, finds us here, and resolves to hide on board and try to work out some means of escape."

Later in the evening they had the interview with Wantlake already recorded, and although it was evident that Lord Sancroft had eluded the vigilance of the pirates, who knew not whether he was dead or alive, they were nevertheless anxious and nervous throughout the night lest he should be discovered.

The night, however, passed away, and the almost deserted ship remained quiet, for, as we have intimated, all the pirates ith two or three exceptions, were on ore, holding high carnival in the drinkg dens and gambling places, and those board were there solely to guard against he escape of the young middies.

In the afternoon, prior to his departure or the shore, Wantlake sent again for the risoners, who were marshalled into his resence by a huge ruffian, nearer seven han six feet in height, the sentinel over hem for the day.

"Bring the young whelp forward," said Wantlake, pointing to our hero.

Before the men could move, the young privateer sprang in their midst, and threw pen his cloak.

"I am here!" he said, proudly; "what want you?"

The pirate's lips curled with scorn, as he surveyed the handsome youth.

"As I shall be on shore to-night," said Wantlake, bantering, "and you depart to-morrow with my Spanish friend, I have sent for you to bid you adieu."

"That is," said Will, "to gloat over our misery, and to add what insult your petty nature can conceive to the injuries you have inflicted upon us."

"That's about it," returned Wantlake, coolly, "by the way, you fetched a handsome price, and it came in handy at the present moment, for the demon of ill-luck has followed every throw of the dice, and every shuffle of the cards."

"To be followed in the end with a Spanish knife planted in your false heart," said Harry. "But have you done with us?"

"You may go," rejoined the pirate, with a diabolical sneer; "and a pleasant journey to you. Don't thwart my Spanish friend, for he has an ugly habit of spurring the laggards on their way. Whips, my dear boys, with wire lashes that cut and sting. Farewell, and once more a pleasant journey to you."

They returned his sneer with undaunted looks, and went back to their place of confinement.

The burly pirate turned the key, and, left alone, they threw themselves down in utter despair.

"Is there no hope?" moaned Tom.

"None that I can see," said Will, brushing away a tear from his eyes; "but, once clear of this rat's hole, I will make one bold rush for life; they can but kill us, and death is better than slavery."

"What monsters there are in this world!" rejoined Tom, after a pause.

"I used to think old Benson a cruel brute," said Will; "he used to let into us very stiffly; and Wantlake was bad enough on board the 'Curlew'—he was a beast then, now he is a devil."

As the hours passed away, and the strange captivity in store for them drew nearer, they grew more hopeful.

The prospect of being once more in the open light of day was cheering, after their long confinement, and a hundred ways of escape might offer.

"It wouldn't be so bad if we could get away, Will," said Tom, "we could build a hut."

"With what?"

"Well, we haven't any tools," returned Tom, positively laughing. "I forgot that, but we could live in a cave for a time, and gradually work our way to a more civilised place."

"Well, so we might. It's dark soon to-night."

"Rather cloudy," returned Tom, looking out of the bull's eye.

"Anything moving?"

"Not that I can see."

Two hours later Will asked the same question, and Tom, who was again by the little opening, returned the same answer.

"I thought I heard something," said Will, "like a fellow swimming."

"I heard nothing, but you have a good ear, Will. It may be my father."

They listened intently for some time, but all was still as the grave.

Half an hour might have elapsed, when Will spoke again.

"Our sentry outside is grunting in a queer way."

"I hope he's in a fit," rejoined Tom.

"If we were certain of it, I'd make a bold rush at the door. Hush! don't you hear him?"

"He certainly is making a strange noise; a gurgling sort of sound. Drinking, perhaps."

"No; he's all right; he's unlocking the door."

They stepped back, and, reclining upon the ground, affected to be asleep, being in no humour for a conversation with the fellow.

Whoever entered came in very softly and halted a few paces from the door.

His breathing was heard distinctly in the stillness of the place.

This conduct was unaccountable, as their jailers usually swaggered in, either to summon them gruffly, or to cast down their food as they would have given it to a dog.

Will thought that his time was come, that murder was intended, but a different thought entered Tom's head; and rising, he whispered in an eager tone—

"Father."

There was no reply for a moment, and then, in a dear familiar tone, four words fell upon their ears—

"Dat you, Massa Will?"

They could not repress a cry of joy, and leaping up seized the faithful negro and hugged him in an ecstacy of joy.

"O! Jack, faithful and true, how came you here?"

"Tell you, sar, by-em-bye; we get away now."

"But the sentry, Jack?"

"Him outside, sar."

"Is he a friend?"

"He nothin' 'tickler now," returned Jack; "he no frien' nor foe to any man. I jest gib him one nip on him throttle, and him lay down quiet."

The gurgling sound was accounted for now, and both the lads shuddered as they thought of that quiet struggle in the dark, with Jack crushing out the pirate's life.

"You're very wet, Jack?"

"Yes, sar. I swim har, and you must swim back. Crikey lying off wid de boat. Come, genelmen, no time to lose."

But Tom whispered in the ear of his friend, "My father; I cannot go without him."

Will could not but reverence the feeling of his friend, and accordingly, in a few words, Jack was in possession of the facts connected with his lordship.

"He is hiding somewhere about the ship, I am sure," said Tom.

"And I find him, genlemen," replied the negro; "you keep quiet har. De genelman outside berry sound asleep, but de oders are awake."

Jack went out stealthily, leaving the door open, with a final injunction, if any of the crew approached, to make a rush for the deck, and swim out due west to where Crikey was waiting.

"Dis light I blow out before I snuff him," said Jack, kneeling down outside and re-lighting his lantern; "dere he is; he nebber do harm any more."

The herculean pirate lay upon his back, his ghastly, distorted face turned upward to the beams overhead, with "no speculation in those staring eyes of his"

"A ghastly sight," said Tom.

"It's not pretty," said Jack, laying a piece of canvas over the awful face, "and Jack not lub to make him so; but I do it for Massa Tom and Will."

"As you have done a thousand other deeds," said Will, extending his hand. "But away, Jack, and find Lord Sancroft.

Jack crept away then, and the boys dragged the body of the slain pirate into the cabin, locked the door, and sat down quietly outside to wait for the return of their faithful friend.

The lantern they hung up in such a way, that while it lit up the passage it left them in the shadow of the main mast and a pile of old sails. It was fortunate they did so, for within a few minutes of Jack's departure, a sailor, much the worse for liquor, came rolling down the ladder from the deck, and advanced towards their late abode.

"Griffin," he said, "I have come to have a friendly glass—hallo—not here, this won't do, Griffin. In with the reefers, p'raps."

He tried the door, and found it fast, Will having taken the precaution to remove the key.

"Werry bad, Griffin," muttered the sailor, as he retraced his steps, "and bad for you if the captain knew it. Ah!—but I'm not the man to inform on you."

When he was gone, the boys exchanged congratulations; everything seemed favourable to them, and escape seemed certain.

But Jack's absence was so long that more than once they believed he had fallen into the hands of the enemy; the silence around them, however, reassured them.

"Jack wouldn't give in without a fight," urged Will, "and we should be sure to hear it."

At last, after nearly an hour's absence, he came, followed by Lord Sancroft, pale and wan. We must pass over the meeting, brief but passionate, which ensued between father and son, and accept the hint from Jack, that "It is time to go along."

"I found him in de hold," whispered Jack to Will as they moved forward "hid in de tub, and fust he took me to anoder nigger, and show fight, but I hold him tight, and say I am a fr'en.' Yah! golly, him berry pleased den."

Jack reconnoitered the deck and announced it clear, also that the daylight would soon be there, for the eastern sky was growing light.

"Now," said Jack, "if dere is any genelman here dat can swim, or not swim berry well, dis chile take him on him back."

But all could swim, and swim well, and the offer was declined.

"Den dere nuffin more to do dan slip in quietly and swim to Crikey."

Throwing a rope over the vessel's side, he slipped down, Lord Sancroft followed, Tom and Will glided like shadows into the cool sea, and swam in the wake of Monkey Jack.

The morn was coming truly, but the sky was yet dark, and the objects as colourless as ink; objects a few yards away were invisible or dimly seen in the gloom of the "darkest hour of the night," that just before the sun appears.

Stemming the water powerfully but silently, Jack led the van, turning his head every few minutes to see that his charges followed and received assurance from them in a low tone.

"All right, Jacky."

Lord Sancroft kept by his son, occasionally whispering to him words of encouragement and mentally congratulating himself upon the wisdom which had prompted him to make swimming a part of the boy's education.

"Jacky!"

"Yes, massa Will."

"Is the 'Crucible' here?"

"Yas, jes' outside de harbour. We see him presently."

"How much further have we to go?"

"Gettin' tired, massa Will?"

"No, but the water is precious cold, and there might be sharks about."

"If dere is dem," said Jack, coolly, "I go fust. Shark like white man berry well, but he lub de nigger. Him stronger flavour dan white man. Keep your wind, massa Will, we some way to go yet."

They swam another yard silently, and then Jack wavered a little in his course and looked anxiously about him.

"Where de debil is him?" he muttered, "I gib him somefin' if him don't show up."

"What's the matter?" asked Lord Sancroft.

"We not reach the boat yet," replied Jack evasively.

"Then keep straight on, there's nobody winded yet."

"No use to keep straight on," replied Jack, slowly, "dis am de place where Crikey ought to be."

"In plain terms, you have missed the boat, or the boat has missed you."

"Dat true enuf, sar, but I give it to dat dam Crikey, when I get him."

"Ah!" said Lord Sancroft, significantly, "with the proviso that we get out of this. I see something floating there."

"It's a harbour buoy, sar, not'ing more."

"Let us rest there. I am not so young as I was."

They all swam to the welcome relief, Tom and Will climbing up and seating themselves on its flat surface.

Lord Sancroft and Jack simply clung to the side, the latter endeavouring to pierce the surrounding gloom with his eagle eye.

"No boat, no Crikey," he muttered; "where him get to?—cus him thick hide! Yah! and de sky soon be white and de sea green.

"Shall we shout for him?" suggested Will.

"No, Massa Will, we might bring pirate and not Crikey, but I t'nk I make him hear."

He uttered a strange sound like that of the string of a harp hastily touched, and listened.

No response, and he repeated it Not a sound in reply.

"Him gone away, or taken by some t'ief," wailed Jack.

"Cannot we reach the 'Crucible'?" said Lord Sancroft; "we are all refreshed."

"Too far away, sar, and daylight come long afore we reach it."

"It is coming now."

A ray of light shot half across the sky, flickered and faded out.

The dawn was at hand.

CHAPTER XLIV.

THE PIRATES ASHORE.—THE RESCUE.

"CANNOT we swim to the shore and hide?" asked Will.

"Might do dat, sar," returned Jack.

"Then, as a last resource, we will try

it," said Lord Sancroft; "in another minute the sun will be up."

A cry from Jack startled them all; he was looking towards the land, now growing visible out of the darkness of the night.

"One, two boat," he cried, "and now it too late to get away. O! Crikey, where am you?"

He glanced swiftly round the harbour, and at the same moment a loud shout from the shore told the four men and lads clinging to the buoy that they were perceived.

. . . .

During this eventful night Harold had kept watch upon the deck, listening to every sound with the hope of hearing the welcome voice of his messenger returning with good or evil tidings; but as the hours passed away, and he came not, he grew restless and excited, pacing the deck with quick steps, and bewailing the apparent unsuccessful issue of his faithful negro's mission.

"Better have gone myself," he thought; "I might have accomplished the feat, or spared him from running into danger."

"Dawn at hand, sir," said Mr. Stanchion.

"Have all ready to run out as soon as the sun appears. I shall wait till the last moment, or stay at any risk; I will not budge, come one, come many, and I will fight them all."

. . . .

In a long room, gaudily furnished, about a hundred men—French, English, and Spanish—were assembled.

It was easy to see that each and all were outcasts of their several nations, for their faces bore that deep, merciless, relentless expression which stamps the man society has cast off.

Knaves and gamesters all, but none so much of a knave and gamester as Mason Wantlake, the young pirate.

He sat in the midst of a party numbering, perhaps, a score, while the rest of the company crowded around, every eye upon the rolling ball, as it wound its way around the magic circle of roulette, so fraught with fortune—bad and good.

A feverish gnawing of the lips told of Wantlake's excitement.

By his side lay a small, very small pile of gold, and, as each coin was staked, ill fortune followed it, and the merciless croupier swept it into the yawning bank.

He had played upon the red, and black obstinately came.

He tried the black, and the fatal rouge turned up treacherously.

He staked small and large, and each successive stake followed the same path which led to ruin.

"What curse is upon me?" he muttered

And then came a still small voice in his ear—the voice of conscience,—

"It is the price of blood—the price of human flesh."

But he refused to listen, and pursued the game feverishly and desperately.

The fortunes of the other players had varied, and the persistent ill-luck of Mason Wantlake, so marvellous and strange, absorbed all the attention of the spectators

"Give it up," said one, in a friendly tone; "the black shadow is upon you tonight."

Wantlake turned his bloodshot eyes upon the speaker and scowled,—

"What care I for your shadows?" he said, "I am not a superstitious fool."

"May be, or not," returned the man "the shadow is on you. Just as it was on Dark Luke last year. He lost everything—money, ship, down to his very clothes. He sat where you are sitting and when he rose up with every rap gone he cursed the black shadow. Madness it was, for he left this room and was never seen again until he was found in the Red Gully half eaten by the vultures."

"Bah!" exclaimed Wantlake, as he pursued the game, "idle stuff. D— the black shadow."

Several of the listeners, half-cast Spaniards, shuddered and withdrew from the vicinity of the speaker. Wantlake, with forced composure, went on with the game.

At length he rose from the table without a coin, the last was gone, and he was about to depart, when the croupier, a Frenchman, bowed politely, and inquired—

"Has monsieur finished? the night is yet young."

"I have nothing more," muttered Wantlake, "my last rap is lost."

"Monsieur has some property, perhaps. The bank will advance."

"Half of a craft lying in the harbour's mine," said Wantlake.

"A trader, Monsieur?"

"Yes! she trades—upon the sea."

"Ah!" said the croupier, with a shrug

CRIKEY'S RETURN TO THE BOSOM OF HIS FAMILY.

is worth but little, but the bank will advance two hundred on it."

"Give me the money," said Wantlake, desperately, "my luck must turn. Quick, you scurvy Frenchman. Down with the gold."

Heedless of the insult, the imperturbable Frenchman counted out the money, a second man in the meantime drawing up a brief rough draught, which Wantlake signed. Then the game was renewed.

Renewed, indeed, and carried on as it had begun; the "black shadow," was upon the unfortunate wretch, and lower and lower sank the pile.

Thrice he rose up and went to a side table for drink, pouring down his throat the fiery liquid like water. The spectators watched his growing fever, and whispered that he would share the fate of Luke in the Red Gully.

"Gone!" he shrieked, as the croupier swept away the last stake. "Ruined, penniless, and in such a place as this."

"You are one of many," said a man at his elbow; "think you we would stand idly by the table but for empty pouches?"

The young pirate turned away, left the room, and walked hurriedly towards the shore.

"I will defeat them yet," he thought, "I can get to sea in an hour, and catch me who can."

It was early dawn, and the water reflected the streaks of light in the sky. He scanned the harbour, and the buoy caught his eye—clinging to it were four persons, three of whom he knew.

"Curses," he shouted, "but they shall not escape me. "Ho! there, boat ahoy!"

The men sleeping in his cutter sprang up, and he was about to enter, when a hand was laid upon his shoulder. Turning, he beheld the croupier, supported by a dozen of the most villanous fellows from the gambling saloon.

"Monsieur, you cannot go on board."

"Why not?" demanded Mason, with a scowl.

"You are no longer captain; the ship is ours, and we appoint another."

Wantlake carefully considered his position. The men in the cutter were but six in number, and but lightly armed. His opponents numbered a dozen, and every man bore a rifle; resistance was useless.

"Well!" he said, affecting to laugh, "law is law, and I must yield. But see there, by the buoy?"

"I see four men," rejoined the croupier, composedly.

"Four prisoners of mine, and worth a fortune. Will you let them escape?"

"But we are too late, there is a boat, monsieur, and a cursed nigger—who is he?"

"He belongs not to this place, monsieur; and see, there is a strange vessel by the harbour's mouth."

"The 'Crucible,' by the light of day!" screamed the young pirate; "summon the men—we will fight her—do you hear me, men? On board at once."

"Monsieur forgets that we have no quarrel with yon vessel," said the croupier, with the same composure; "she is well armed, and her guns appear to be ready, We should risk too much by attacking her."

"What of that? Get ready, my men."

"Monsieur persists in forgetting that he no longer holds the command."

"A blight upon you!" yelled Wantlake; "will you detain me now? I will come back with the craft or forfeit my life."

"Monsieur's life is only valuable to himself."

"O! what a fate is mine," groaned the miserable wretch, "foiled by all, thwarted in every way. In five minutes they will be on board, and already the "Crucible" spreads her sails, and see there, they mount her side, look at the masked hypocrite, Harold Greystone, how he rushes to embrace the cubs. Stop, you coward, I will meet you alone, hand to hand. The sails spread, the very wind conspires against me. Too late—too late!"

And frothing at the mouth in impotent rage he grovelled on the beach like a trodden worm.

The croupier stepped into the cutter, showed his authority to the men, and bade them pull to the vessel.

"Monsieur, the ex-captain," he said, "will find the morning air upon the beach refreshing; he will soon recover."

The men, who had but little love for anything beyond themselves, left their late leader without the least compunction, and conveyed the croupier and his comrades to the pirate craft.

In a few minutes Mason Wantlake recovered from his paroxysm of rage, and staggering to his feet passed his hand across his brow. The night's debauch, the excitement he had undergone, had done their work full well, he looked ten years older; the conditions attendant upon a life of dissipation and forced excitement, premature old age and decay, would soon be fulfilled.

"O! what a fate is mine," he moaned again. "How long have I lived? I know not; but yesterday I thought my manhood scarce reached, and now I seem to have crawled through a century of misery. O! come back my youth, my boyhood, the happy hours on board the "Curlew." Welcome a thousand humiliations. I will even ask pardon of him I most hate, Harold Greystone; but, oh, Heaven, spare me from a life in such an earthly hell as this!"

"Signor Wantlake."

Another voice by his side; was there more trouble in store? He looked around, and within a few feet stood the Spaniard who had bought for slaves Will Steadfast and Tom Furnace.

"The Signor is unwell this morning," said the Spaniard, gravely.

"I am ill at ease," returned the pirate. "Signor Tralu knows that a night's drinking has its punishment in the morning."

"But science has provided a remedy," smiled Signor Tralu. "I am but a student in medicine, but I can relieve the throbbing head and fevered pulse."

"But not the aching heart," thought Wantlake. "I thank you, Signor, for your kindness, and accept your offer."

The Spaniard piloted his companion through the meagre town to a strong house, built on the verge of a hill, and surrounded by dense foliage, hiding it from the prying eye of man.

"You have an excellent place here, Signor," said Mason Wantlake.

"For the purpose it was built for," returned the Spaniard, drily.

"It is almost a fortress."

"To the means that could be brought against it here it is impregnable."

They said no more until they had crossed the portal; a stout, iron-studded door closed upon them, and Mason Wantlake found himself in the grasp of several men.

In a twinkling every weapon was removed from his person, a rope was passed around him and he was a prisoner.

Signor Tralu stood by, looking calmly on, while Mason, startled, and almost paralysed by the sudden attack, recovered his scattered thoughts.

"This is sorry hospitality," he said, at length.

"It is the best my poor house affords," returned the Spaniard, mockingly.

"What means it, Signor?"

"This; you have received the money for the lads I bought."

"I have."

"And lost it."

"For the present, but with good luck I may regain it."

"Good luck attends not upon the gaming-table, Signor Wantlake. You also lost your share in the vessel."

"Such, indeed, is the case, Signor."

"And last, but not least," said the Spaniard, sternly, "your prisoners have escaped."

A shudder ran through the broken form of the young fellow; he began to suspect something now.

"Escaped," continued Signor Tralu; "the ship is lost, my money gone—what then remains for me?"

A wild despairing glance from Wantlake was the sole reply.

"Can you not guess?"

That heaving breast, those painfully knitted brows, told that he knew his fate. The Spaniard smiled.

"All that remains for me," he said, "is you—as a substitute. You are of less value than the boys, but you are better than none. Remove him."

And it had come to this!

The fate he heartlessly designed for his young prisoners had fallen upon himself.

He was a slave.

Humbled, broken down, he meekly shuffled after his captors, was thrust into a rude cell, and throwing himself upon the straw, wept as a broken-hearted man alone could weep.

CHAPTER XLV.

CRIKEY'S EXCUSES.—A FEW NECESSARY EXPLANATIONS.

"DE tide carry me away at first, Jack; and den, not knowin' the j'ography ob dat place, I git run down behind dat ship."

"Dere's no obscuse, Crikey," returned Jack, loftily; "a proper bumboat man ought to know ebery inch ob de ocean!"

"But de harbour not de ocean," urged Crikey, cunningly.

"What am it, den?" demanded Jack.

"De harbour am a sort ob—kind ob hole and corner place, dat nobody nebber understan'," returned Crikey, with more vagueness than consistency.

"Dat obscuse not wordy ob my brodder," said Jack; "you lib all your life in harbour."

"Ah! but dat a real harbour, dis one a dam imposter."

Jack leaned against a gun, and surveyed his brother with a look of profound admiration.

Crikey repeated his remark respecting the harbour being an imposter.

"Crikey," said Jack, after a pause; "a nigger no use unless him be a confounded fool! den he make people laugh, and him berry much respected. But de nigger dat try to make himself senstible git all de kicks an' none ob de coppers; dat not your case; you de biggest fool dat ebber hab wool. Yah! golly; you am all dat."

The adulated Crikey smiled meekly, as if he felt himself undeserving of such an unequivocal compliment, and replied—

"Dere must be trufe in dat—for everybody says so in ole Havannah. When I bring home Cap'en Spiker two more shirts dan he send to de wash, he call me fool —next week I bring him home two short, and he call me fool again—and he 'peat dat complimen' ebery time he see me, and shake him fist just like a brudder."

"Him great fren'd ob yours, Crikey?"

"Two buzzums, Jacky, we was! Den, when he 'spect his child 'ome from England, where him been stayin', and de ship don't come, he clutch him wool like mad; an' Mrs. Spiker—nice lubly creetur— allus down on de beach lookin' for dat ship. So I say one mornin' to her— 'Missus,' I ses, 'I find dat boy—him sure to be alive, for last night I see two gen'lemen seagulls hab a desp'rat' fight, and neider of dem lick, but bof run away.' Just dat moment, ole Spiker come up, and gib me a lob wid him foot. 'You fool,' he ses, and I go away wid a t'ankful heart."

"An' you find dat chile, Crikey?"

"I did, Jacky! One mornin' I go with my boat to meet a frigate dat is 'spected, but it don't come cause idiot-officer run him on a rock; but I seed a ship a-rollin' about jes' as if him habin' a lark to hisself. I go near and read de name—it is de 'Rosemary'—what Cap'en Spiker 'spected. I row back like mad and run up

to him house. Missus Spiker just running out de coffee from de pot, and when I yell yell out 'De 'Rosemary' come!' she shriek, and tossin' up de pot, put de coffee all down the cap'en back. He call me fool agen, den I bow bery t'ankful—den he rushed out with Missus Spiker, and I show dem de ship— dey jump into my boat, and seberal sailors jump in too. Away we go, and when 'arf way, one ob de sailors cry out—'She's desarted!' Den de cap'en full in a fluster, shake him fist at me fur'us as a bantam cock when him licked. But we reach de ship and climb up de side. I carry up Mrs. Spiker, and sure enuf, dere not a soul on board, and she was water-logged. Missus Spiker scream; but it answered from de cabin, and up came a boy followed by a dog. It was lilly master Spiker, and I know dat chile."

"How you know him?" asked Jack, "you neber see him afore."

"I know him, Jacky, easy," returned Crikey, "'cause him not a bit like him fader. Lor! it was golly. Missus Spiker hug him fur'us, and ole Spiker forget him dignity, and cut a nornpipe, den the sailors cry dat she is goin' down, and we all make for de boat and pull ashore. De 'Rosemary' went down, and two day a'ter de 'Rosemary' crew turn up, and all de 'scuse de hab is dat de boy couldn't be found when dey left. Old Spiker call dem eberyt'ing, and to me behabe berry generous."

"What did him do?"

"He promised to get me de washin' ob de frigate when she come, but she nebber come, and I don't git it. De Missus, howeber, do berrer, gib me de run of de kitchen, and den I hab much fun and feed like de pig."

While Crikey was revealing this remarkable memoir of his life, Will Steadfast was below with his friends, relating the story of the escape from the burning French vessel.

Our readers will remember that when this capture was destroyed by fire no apparent remnants of her remained; she blew up, scattering fragments of timber far and wide; and all that appertained to life seemed to be destroyed.

"By some means," Will began, "the prisoners on board managed to get free, at least part of them did, but I, happening to be on watch, detected it. Calling to Grim Foote, we battened the hatches down, keeping all below but Tom, Grim, and myself. We at once resolved to communicate with the 'Crucible, and as she was not far away, Tom and I jumped into a boat which was towing astern, intending to pull over to avoid delay, Grim remaining on board. Poor Grim! I wonder where he is."

"An old weather-beaten sailor, who fell into the clutches of the pirates with you?" asked Lord Sancroft.

"The same."

"Ah! there is a story connected with him which I will tell you by-and-by. Proceed."

"There were no oars in the boat," continued Will, "and we called out to Grim to fetch a pair. He came to us in a few minutes, saying he could find none, and that everything of that sort appeared to be stowed away. We urged him to look again, as the position was dangerous, but at that moment a lurid light came through the crevices of the hatches, and showed the vessel to be on fire.

"Our first impulse was to release the imprisoned wretches, but we were unable to do so, for the fire had gained such strong hold that it was working its way through the deck in many places, the rest being too hot for our feet.

"It spread so rapidly that I was certain the ship had been prepared for destruction, if it fell into the hands of an enemy, although the conflagration, when it did take place, was no doubt accidental, some of the men smoking, or a light falling from a lantern.

"The fire comes from the hold," said Grim Foote, "and it won't be long before it reaches the magazine. Push off, my lads."

"We urged him to come, but he would not consent until we positively refused to leave without him. Oars, I say, we had not, but we had several pieces of planking, with which we hoped to reach the 'Crucible.'

"I need not describe the fire now, but in the end the vessel blew up, before we had paddled a clear hundred yards away, and a huge mass of timber, falling across the thwarts of our boat, upset her.

"For a moment I was stunned, but the noise of rushing water restored me, close by me was the boat, with Tom and Grim endeavouring to right her, I swam to them and gave my aid, and at last we succeeded,

but alas! we were now entirely at the mercy of the elements, for everything that could be of service to us had been washed overboard, and a strong current carried us away.

"We shouted until we were hoarse, but further and further we floated away, until the lights of the dear old 'Crucible' faded out in the distance, and we could see nought but the stars and the dimly flashing waves.

"Never shall I forget the horror of the morning when the sun rose up, and showed us a clear sea.

"The 'Crucible' was gone, and we were floating further and further away, without an oar or rudder, and the boat entirely bare of food or drink.

"Throughout that day we floated until the tide changed, and, when the stars came out they found us riding back towards the scene of our disaster. Hungry, thirsty, and hopeless, what hope could we have upon the boundless sea?

"Two days passed, and we were still idly tacking to and fro, driven at times from our course by the changing wind; and then I lost count of time, and power to reason upon the awful nature of our position; but I have a dim remembrance of Tom's falling helpless by my side, and old Grim standing up in the steering, watching for our only hope—a sail, until he, too, sank down, and then, in a listless, dreamy state, lost to all sense of suffering, we floated o'er the waves.

"Days or hours only—I don't know—may have passed when a hoarse cry from Grim arouses us; we staggered to our feet, and there, close by us, loomed a vessel—the craft governed by that demon in human form, Mason Wantlake.'"

The rest of Will's story is known, but the fate of poor Grim Foote has yet to be told, and Lord Sancroft shall reveal it.

"The sailor you name," he said, when Will had concluded his story, "died on board the pirate craft. He refused to reveal the nature of our friend's resources (indicating Harold with a graceful motion of his hand), his place of abode, and how he became possessed of certain knowledge, and, being given the choice of turning traitor or dying at once, died like the man he was. Hatchett, the lieutenant, obeyed the orders of his superior, and blew out his brains."

"Poor Grim!" the words passed round,

and the eyes of three were dimmed with tears.

"He was a good sailor," said Harold, breaking silence for the first time, "and faithful to me, as indeed are all the noble fellows around me. My lord, I owe you apology."

"May I ask on what account?" said rd Sancroft."

"For wearing this mask, and concealing my name."

"You owe me nothing, sir, but an opportunity for showing you how grateful I am for the saving of these two lives," said his lordship, laying his hand upon his son's shoulder.

"But a few words are necessary," rejoined Harold. "My lord, I have been bitterly wronged, so bitterly that my honour and courage, dearer to me than life, were successfully impugned. I swore that no man, but one—Will Steadfast here—should, with my consent, see my face, or call me by name, until I could give such evidence as would restore me to the world as I was and as I am. The time is coming." Harold's face was flushed down to the chin beneath the mask. "I have such proofs, such records of courage to attest my innocence of the foul charge as shall convince and bring to the blush all who believe my accuser—Mason Wantlake, pirate on the high seas."

"He your accuser?"

"Lord Sancroft, we were brother mids on board the 'Curlew;' we loved the same object, he was nought and I was all to her; he could not enjoy, but he could spoil her love. When the accusation was made I fled—as matters stood, a trial would have been fatal to me and our love. Will Steadfast, faithful and true, came with me, the only one out of all on board who who had real faith in me."

"And what do propose doing?" asked rd Sancroft.

"To sail with my prizes into some port where an English admiral can be found, and by the evidence of my prowess give the charge a lie."

"Is there not a shorter and safer way?" hinted Lord Sancroft. "I have interest at court; make sail at once for England, and I promise all shall be well."

"No, my lord," returned Harold, firmly, "I will not creep into favour; I will convince. When I disclose my name there must be no suspicion of my courage left,

even prompted as I am by the happy issu of this day's work, to leave these scenes danger for ever."

"Whatever dangers lie ahead," sai his lordship, "my son and I will share."

"For the present, then," said Harold "I shall lie off yon harbour until th pirate comes forth; once he is captured I will but seek my home in Honour Ba for a few short days, and then sail fo Barbadoes, where I hope to find the me who will restore my name."

Bowing with infinite grace, he left th trio, Lord Sancroft and the lads, to them selves.

"It seems to me," said his lordship suddenly addressing his son, "that you are marvellously acquainted with thi craft."

Tom blushed, and looked at Will, with out replying.

"I never inquired," continued Lord Sancroft, "how you came together; but now the whole is clear. How could you sacrifice a career for such a life?"

"There is no career, sir, more worthy of your son. We seek to restore the honour of a noble fellow, to rid the high seas of its horde of murderers; and, when an opportunity offers, fight for the glory of our country. There is no stain upon the 'Crucible' which any of His Majesty's crafts would not be proud to own."

"Right, my son," replied his lordship, "your instincts are worthy of our name. Honour and love of country before everything."

Unconscious of the fate of his once remorseless foe, Harold kept the 'Crucible' within sight of land throughout the day, and at night ran in closer, and cruised about, keeping a jealous eye upon the entrance to the harbour where the pirate vessel lay.

The next morning she was still there, and by using the glass, our hero made out that a great bustle was going forward on board; in fact, there was convincing proof of her being actively preparing for sea.

Orders were at once given on board the 'Crucible' to prepare for action, and with just sufficient sail to keep her before the wind, she hovered like a falcon above its prey.

About noon he stepped below, but had barely reached his cabin when Mr. Stan-

THE LONG WHIP CURLED IN THE AIR.

chion hurried in with the news that the pirate was coming out.

The eyes of Harold glittered beneath his mask. Was the hour he had so long sighed for at last approaching, the last link of the chain of proof about to be forged? "Once in my power," he thought, "I will tear a confession from his heart. He shall speak the truth, and then when all is known ———. Ah!" and visions of the lovely Clara, and a home in dear old England, uprose before his mental vision.

"She comes on boldly," said our hero.

"She does," replied the lieutenant, who stood by his captain's side, Monkey Jack, in full fig, in the rear.

"Golly! de snake am runnin' bang into de lion's jaws," muttered Jack.

"There's something suspicious in this bold approach," said Harold, taking his glass from the binnacle. "She must be heavily manned to risk so much. No; her decks are almost clear, and the ports are closed."

"Trust not too much to appearances, sir," smiled Mr. Stanchion, "remember the ruses we have played."

"But there is no ruse here. Stanchion;

can we have mistaken the vessel? She carries no colours. Ah! there goes the ball of bunting; it unrolls. Good Heavens! it is white."

The pirate had run aloft a flag of truce.

The deck of the "Crucible" was, by this time, alive with curious observers, among them the mids and Lord Sancroft, who said,—

"I should not trust that fellow. He would smile in your face, extend the hand of friendship, and then stab you to the heart."

"All is prepared for treachery," returned Harold. "Mr. Stanchion, look to the guns, and have the men ready to repel boarders. Ha! another move."

The pirate suddenly shortened sail, and hove-to. A boat was lowered, and six men, with another on the stern-sheets, came towards the "Crucible."

Wondering more and more, Harold and his followers awaited their coming. The man in the stern-sheets was not Mason Wantlake, that he could see, but Lord Sancroft revealed his name.

"It is that fellow Hatchett, the murderer of Grim Foote."

Harold frowned, and a nervous twitching of the fingers betokened but little mercy for the pirate.

CHAPTER XLVI.

HATCHETT'S FATE.

THE boat, however, touched the vessel's side, and Hatchett stepped boldly and lightly upon the deck.

Touching his cap to our hero, he glanced coolly over the other persons around, and began—

"You know that vessel, sir?"

"I do!" was the cool reply.

"And who commands it?"

"Mason Wantlake."

"Then you're wrong, sir," chuckled Hatchett, "he'll never command a craft any more."

"Is he dead?" cried our hero.

"Not yet," coolly replied Hatchett; "but I reckon he'll have a short life and a merry one of it now; those two young gentlemen at your elbow were sold by him."

"The dastard did sell them, I believe."

"And lost the money at the gaming-table, also his share of the craft, and as the youngsters got away Signor Tralu keeps Wantlake in their place, so I am appointed to the vacant captaincy of the vessel."

"Of the pirate schooner?"

"No longer a pirate, sir, but a peace[ful] trader."

"Where to?"

"Now don't you be particular," sa[id] Hatchett, in a confidential tone; "[we] haven't a quarrel between us, and tha[t's] why I ran up the flag o' truce. You c[an] let me pass."

"Not a pirate shall escape me by m[y] will," returned Harold, firmly. "You a[re] no trader. As for your master, the sto[ry] you tell may be true or not. You may ha[ve] run away with the schooner for aught [I] know; but be it as it may she does n[ot] pass."

"But come, this isn't fair," began Hat chett.

"Pirate dog," cried Harold, with flash ing eyes, "get back to your ship, and pro vided you hoist no sail, I will respect you[r] flag of truce for half an hour, then pre pare for a fight for life and liberty."

"If that's your meaning," returned Hat chett, "I'm your man; but look y[ou] youngster, if I get you now, it'll be [a] short shrift and a long plank, I tell you."

He swung himself over the side, an[d] ordering his men to pull like fifty, re turned to the schooner. The "Crucible[" drew slowly nearer, and preparations fo[r] the ocean duel were carried rapidly forward

As soon as Hatchett put his foot upo[n] the deck of his craft, one of the men calle[d] his attention to a signal flying at th[e] harbour.

"Signalling me to return," he muttered; "not if I know it. I'll have a fight with this youngster, invincible as he is, and either make good work of it or end this life for ever."

His ship was ready for action, and after a few words, he ordered the colours of the pirates—the skull and crossbones—to be run to the mast-head. To this signal of defiance, the "Crucible" replied with a shot clean through his hull, and the half-spent ball went skipping over the seas beyond.

"He carries good metal," muttered Hatchett, and baring his arms he took up his post on the after-deck.

"Port your helm," he cried, "and run down upon her lee quarters—reserve your fire, until within a hundred yards, then blaze away."

Harold was too good a seaman to give his opponent the advantage in manœuvr[ing]

ing, and porting his helm he brought the vessels broadside to broadside.

Guns of good calibre, and well served, played havoc with the pirate schooner, cutting away her bowsprit and unmanning her guns. The rest, badly worked by the unnerved men, fired wildly, and with but little effect.

"Confound you there!" roared Hatchett, "he'll honeycomb us—smart there, you lubbers, and stand to your guns—the first man who flinches I'll blow out his brains, by Heaven."

The men muttered something in reply, about it being little odds who shot them, if it must come to that, continued doggedly at their work, without the spirit that almost insures victory, no matter what the odds, and when a comrade fell left him lying to groan and curse away the remnant of his brief existence.

"I'm getting the worst of this," muttered Hatchett, as he looked at his blood-stained deck, "but what matters?—I've little left to live for. Fire away, you hounds."

Another broadside from the "Crucible" completed the confusion of the men, and one ran to the mast to haul down the colours.

"What are you doing there?" roared the pirate chief.

"We can't fight him," muttered the man; "he's too strong."

"How do you know," yelled Hatchett; "we've only just begun. Stick to your gun, and leave that rope alone."

Most of the men had turned from their posts to listen to the altercation, their faces giving unmistakeable signs of agreement with the course proposed by their comrade.

As they stood thus, a chain shot tore through their midst, leaving behind it the mutilated remains of half a dozen men.

Then uprose a clamour of voices urging he who held the rope to strike the colours, but Hatchett strode to his side and bade him leave them alone.

"I prefer obeying a dozen masters to he voice of one," was the dogged reply.

And, the next moment, he lay upon the deck, with his head shattered; and Hatchett stood over him with a smoking pistol in his hand.

"To your guns!" he yelled, hoarsely. "The first man who refuses shall follow his fool."

He stood dauntless in their midst, pointing to his unmanned guns.

But not a soul stirred.

"We can't fight the masked captain!" shouted one of the men in the rear; "he carries a charm."

"He carries pluck!" said Hatchett, bitterly; "and that you all lack, you curs. To your guns!"

"We won't! Down with the colours!"

"The first men who touches them dies."

They rushed upon him in a body, and the first two fell, one with a bullet through his heart, the other with a fearful cutlass gash from eye to chin.

Hatchett fought bravely; cut and slashed his way through them, and stood by the hatchway, while the shot of his wondering foe tore up the decks, and scattered death and destruction around.

The men stood facing him like a pack of wolves at bay, their bloodshot eyes ablaze with baffled rage.

"Cowards," he cried, "will you strike your colours or fight?"

"Strike them," they yelled; "how can we fight the masked hero of the seas?"

"Do then," he yelled, "and I will hoist them higher than before."

The spreading bunting came running down, and Hatchett, shaking his fist at the men, rushed down below.

In a moment, as if by inspiration, they divined his object.

"The magazine!" they yelled, and some rushed to the boats, while a few of the more daring followed in the wake of their leader.

All were too late, the decks opened with an awful roar, the white smoke and glaring flame shot up into the air, burdened with a million fragments of the doomed vessel, and the mangled fragments of the wretched men.

Far and wide were the fragments carried, falling upon the restless waves, and raining down upon the deck and rigging of the gallant 'Crucible.'

By what means the explosion had occurred neither Harold nor his men could tell; they had, it is true, marked the confusion on board the enemy, but were too far away to interpret it.

As the blackened corpses came down with a mighty splash, two falling within a few feet of the little cruiser, Harold awoke from his astonishment in a sense of what he owed to his fellow-countrymen.

"Out with the boats!" he cried, "one life spared may give to the world a repentant man."

The boats swung out and dropped into the sea, still seething with the force of the explosion, and pulled hither and thither amongst the floating fragments of the wreck.

For some minutes nothing rewarded their search, the powder - bescorched corpses sank beneath the blue waves, and were seen no more, and the timbers of the vessel were rent to matchwood; but at last they descried the resemblance of a man floating, and feebly swimming on the surface of the ocean.

They drew him on board and pulled with him to the 'Crucible,' a disfigured piece of humanity with every vestige of hair gone, his flesh rent and torn, and nought but burnt and saturated rags to show that he had worn clothing.

They laid him tenderly down in the last convulsive agonies of death. Lord Sancroft, Harold, and the middies knelt down by his side to see if they could catch his words, for his lips were moving.

"You—don't—know me?" he said, but his voice was so low and feeble, that none but Harold caught his meaning.

"No," he replied, "no—it is no—not Mason——"

"Bah!" impatiently returned the wounded man, with an impatient twitching of his face. "I am—Hatchett—Hatchett, the pirate—but I can give you —news of—your friend.—He is a slave."

And even then the torn and blackened face looked triumphant, as if he rejoiced in the fate of his late leader.

"You could—not wish—him a worse fate," he went on; "this end—of mine— is joy—compared to it."

And with another triumphant glance he closed his eyes and died.

They covered him for the time, but in another hour his body was committed to the deep, and thus ended the career of Hatchett, the pirate. No other man of the crew was discovered, all had perished by the rash, mad act of their determined leader.

He had kept his word, and when they hauled the colours down he hoisted them higher than before and scattered their blackened ashes to the four winds.

So perish all who carry such colours and every flag they flaunt in the sight of Heaven.

The news imparted by Hatchett caused Harold a deal of deep anxiety, for here was another stumbling-block to the full and perfect restitution of his honour he so ardently desired.

Wantlake, a white slave, and carried far away to the interior of South America, was a great and important witness lost; for it was, as Harold knew, folly to hope even for his return—as well look for the restitution of Hatchett from his grave beneath the sea.

For three days, he hovered about the coast, hoping to gather further tidings, and here he nearly lost his chance of righting himself with the world.

He had anchored close to the shore, where the coast seemed to be entirely uninhabited, and Monkey Jack was despatched with a dozen of men for fresh water.

The faithful negro returned with his men, and announced that he could see no signs of living beings; but here, for once, his intelligence was outwitted by a tribe of Indians living along the coast.

They had marked the arrival of the "Crucible," and lay hidden inland until night; then, from a creek they hauled out their canoes, numbering about twenty, each capable of carrying ten men.

Stealthily they paddled towards the little cruiser, when, unsuspecting of the coming danger, Will Steadfast kept his watch, with the usual complement of men.

He was thinking of home and friends, and conjuring up joyous visions of a happy return, when a slight grating sound fell upon his ear.

In a moment he was on the alert, and rushing to the side, saw, and understood the whole danger in a moment.

Two of the canoes had reached the "Crucible;" the rest were but a few yards away.

He had no arms; his cutlass and pistols were below, but quick as thought he ran down the companion, aroused Tom and Jack, and returned to the deck.

The Indians had not yet mounted the sides of the vessel; it was a work they were not accustomed to, and, with their usual caution, they waited for the whole of their body to arrive ere beginning the attack.

Will whispered the nature of the danger

to the men of the watch, and bade them be ready to defend the "Crucible," until their comrades was aroused by Jack, whom he had commissioned to that duty.

"Is that a powder-box, Harris?" he asked one of the men.

"Yes, sir."

"Quick with it here; they are coming. I will give them a warm reception."

Rapidly he emptied the contents close to the bulwarks, and laid a train to the binnacle.

Bidding the man stand aside, and awaited the foe.

All this transpired in a few moments, and just as the Indians came over the side with the silence of shadows, Harold, Jack, and the crew tumbled on deck, and a bright flash dazed and blinded them.

"All right," shouted Will, "I've only scorched a few of the beggars; they're to landward."

Twenty pistols were fired into the darkness, and the involuntary screams of the wounded men told that they had taken effect; then a dozen of the crew stepped forward with torches they had ignited, and boldly sprang into the rigging.

Fortunately for them, the savages were but poorly armed, and were too much disordered to use their spears and puff darts effectually, the rocking movements of the canoes further unsteadying their aim.

The Indians who reached the deck were cut down at once; and as there were no enemies to fight hand to hand, the tars proceeded to deal with those iu the canoes below, and plentifully peppered them with pistol bullets, and their canoes with cold shot.

The light fragile structures could not resist the iron missiles, which crashed through their sides, and the water flowing in, the now yelling, furious savages had to swim for their lives.

Five of the canoes were destroyed thus, and then the rest sheered off, but a small deck gun opened its fire upon them, and, judging by the screams and sounds of confusion, added further to their list of destruction.

They came no more, and in the morning the coast looked as quiet as before.

The men, from the captain downwards, had not received a scratch, and looked upon the affair as a bit of fun; but there was one on board who took it much to heart, and that was Monkey Jack.

"To t'ink," he said to Crikey, "dat I come an' tell cap'en dat dere no libin' soul on shore, and den a swarm ob dem turn up in the middle ob de night. I not comprefend dat; do you, Crikey?"

"Yes, Jacky, I complefen' it, easy," replied Crikey, "dem not mortal, dem brown sabages. It all a mistake to say de debil black, him brown, and dem cursed niggers am his children."

CHAPTER XLVII.

CRIKEY PAYS A VISIT TO THE WIFE OF HIS BOSOM.

HAROLD held many consultations with Lord Sancroft, who proved himself to be a keen man of the world, and his advice was as follows:—

That he (Lord Sancroft) should, as soon as possible, be landed in Cuba, where he would put himself in communication with the authorities, with a view to a full and impartial trial of our hero and his friend Will, and this trial Harold insisted upon, resisting the kind offers of his lordship to use his influence and get it settled in a quiet way.

"I applaud your courage and principles," said Lord Sancroft; "but you know the prejudices of the naval authorities, and how strong the evidence needed to clear you from all the stigma of desertion. Let me use my personal influence."

"To obtain me an impartial court, yes. To give me back my position without such a trial as shall convince all that I have been foully wronged, no!" said Harold. "Much as I should rejoice to receive a favour from your lordship, I must in this case decline. My path back to honour must be straight and true."

"An obstinate dog," returned Lord Sancroft, with a smile, which showed how much he applauded our hero's resolution. "Well, put me ashore, and, to show what faith I have in you and your ultimate restoration, I shall leave my son with you."

A cordial shake of the hand ended the conversation, and the "Crucible" was steered for Cuba.

It was a risk to run, for many of the English cruisers and men-of-war might be expected to be met with there.

But Harold did not shun it, and the course he had resolved to act upon was to run in at night, land his lordship, and put out again, returning on the following night for the boat.

The next question was, whom should he send?

And then he remembered that this had been the home of Crikey, and it was more than probable that that gentleman knew every inch of the ground.

He therefore despatched Jack for his brother, and presently Crikey in person, in a trembling state, and anticipating a severe reprimand for some forgotten evil-doing, stood before him.

But when the darkey understood the object for which he had been summoned, his countenance beamed with joy, and he declared that he would land his "royal highness" safe and sound.

"I get into de harbour, sar," he said, "at any time. I know jest de place whar oder niggers used to smuggle t'ings, and I land him dere, and hide de boat; den if de 'Crucible' lay off de forelight I come on board agen."

"Very good," said Harold; "we shall be there. Do your duty well, and this service will not be forgotten."

Crikey and Jack returned together, the former in a state of excitement, for which Jack was not entirely able to account, but he was soon made fully acquainted with the cause.

"Jacky, I go to Cuba."

"I know dat, Crikey."

"And who you t'ink I see dere?"

"P'raps," said Jack, with dignity, "dat you jes' shut up dat grinnin', and let me know."

"Jacky," replied Crikey, in a thrilling whisper, "I go an' see my ole missus."

"What missus?"

"Chloe, my wife; dat de missus."

"Oh!" said Jack, a little drily, "what sort o' ception will she gib you?"

"It sure to be warm," replied Crikey, after a little reflection, "but what sort o' warm I not able to say."

"I t'ink," grinned Jack, "dat it will be a crockery warm."

"Chloe is good girl," returned Crikey, looking rather offended, "and berry 'fecti'-nate —— sometimes; oder times she beat all Cuba for bobbery. I once see her lift a nigger by his ha'r, and knock him ag'in de door until de panel fly out."

"And de name ob dat nigger?" asked Jack, with a sly look.

"I not know him name," returned Crikey, evasively, "but him modder wash for de Lord Admiral, until she sell him frill shirt, and den she cut clean away, and nebber come back no more."

Jack made no comment upon the brief history of this extraordinary nigger, whose mother had proved such a disgrace to her sex, but he rolled his eyes, and glanced to seaward in a very knowing manner; then as the voice of his captain was heard calling him by name, he nodded to Crikey and retired.

The next evening, just before sunset, they sighted Cuba, and hovered about until darkness had settled upon the sea.

Then the "Crucible" ran in, until the lights of the town could be fairly distinguished, and the boat was hoisted out.

Lord Sancroft was ready, and bade his friends adieu, adding a few words of especial tenderness to his son in an undertone; then he stepped into the boat, and Crikey, plying the oars briskly, they quickly disappeared.

The last words of the captain to Crikey were—"To-morrow night, north of the beacon light."

To which Crikey replied—"I come, sar, sure as Chloe, my wife, am a lubly woman."

The parting between Jack and his brother had been wondrously affectionate; and upon being asked if he really intended to call upon his wife, Crikey rejoined,—"She am de wife ob my buzzum, an' de joy ob my heart. I too much ob a man to let her pine away altogedder."

Throughout the next day the "Crucible" kept just without sight of land, undisturbed by any of the cruisers then lying in port. A few fishing boats passed her outward bound, but they went their way unheeding and unheeded.

At night they ran in again, and hovered around the place appointed; nor had they long to wait, for a boat drew nigh, was hailed, and the voice of Crikey replied.

The next minute Crikey was on board, standing before his captain.

"You landed his lordship?"

"Yes, sar."

"Unobserved."

"Dere not a soul about, sir. Naval officers gib a ball, and eberybody berry drunk; de wharf full ob helpless niggers, sar."

"Sorry to hear it, Crikey. You may go below."

Then Jack, burning with curiosity, took him in tow, and smuggled him into his own little cabin, where the black bottle and glasses were ready for instant use.

Pushing his brother upon a locker, Jack inquired—

"You see your wife, Crikey?"

Crikey rolled his eyes round the cabin, until they fell upon the bottle of rum.

Pouring out some of the spirit, he drank, and slowly rejoined—

"Yes, Jacky, I see ole Chloe."

"Dat right, Crikey, and you met frien'ly."

"Trufe is trufe, Jacky," replied Crikey; "and it must come out like cotton pod at de proper time. I not sw'ar I meet Chloe quite frien'ly."

"Tell me de story, Crikey, and I judge if it frien'ly or not."

Settling himself into a comfortable attitude, Jack prepared to listen, and Crikey, after another little refresher, began—

"Arter I land him lordship, I t'ink it berry late, so I make up my mind to wait till de mornin' afore I show my nose at de lodge ob de farm where she live, so I jes' pick up wid two niggers dat got a bottle ob rum, found dat mornin' in a cap'en's cutter, and we pass a happy night in a big lot of sugar casks, and in de mornin' I wake up wedged tight 'tween two, wid my feet de wrong way in de air.

"But I jes' turn myself about an' t'ink ob Chloe, so I hab a wash, and walk down town to buy some clothes dat do credit to me and de wife ob my bosom. I get a lubly weskut, spankin' leg-cubbers, an' a coat dat de parson might be proud on; den I walk out to de lodge whar' Chloe live, and dere I see her lubly face a-looking up an' down de street.

"I go up to de door, Jacky, tippy-toey, tippy-toey, den I put my head in an' say, 'Dat you, Chloe?' jes as I say, 'Dat you, Jacky?' when we meet; she turn round, catch sight ob me, and nebber while I hab a spike of wood in my head shall I forget de bosforus 'spression ob her eye."

"De what?" interrupted Jack.

"De bosforus 'spression ob her eye."

"You mean the fossyfus 'spression, stuff dat they make matches ob."

"Dat de stuff, Jacky; de fossyfuss lumerous 'epression ob her eye, made somet'ing like cold water run all down de back ob dis chile into my boots, for I hab seen dat 'spression afore.

"'So you bring your lazy hanks har' again,' she ses.

"I work up a smile, Jacky, and say, 'Yes, Chloe, dear, I jes' look in to see you, no wus dan when I lef' you.'

"No sooner I speak dem words, Jacky, dan wid a bamboo she gib me one across dis chile's head dat made forty million stars in de daytime.

"Down I go wid a howl dat brought a lot ob pigs and niggers to de place, an' sech a bobbery was dere dat de whole place was in a fluproar.

"'Hab him wool,' screamed de niggers, and Chloe hab it so stiff dat dis chile's wool fly about de air like fedders arter a big cock fight. Jes' look at dis head, Jacky, an' see de work ob Chloe."

"She hab made some cl'arings," said Jack, after inspecting the assaulted cranium, "but p'raps de wool come ag'in. Go on, Crikey."

"De weskut, leg-cubbers, an' coat dat de parson might be proud ob, got ruinated, and when she tired I get up an' stagger into de roadway, an' dere I stand an' make up farewell poetry—

"Good-bye, Chloe, dear,
T'ink no more ob me,
I no more comin' har',
But goin' out to sea.

And what do you t'ink she say, Jacky?"

"Told you nebber to bring your hunks anigh her ag'in, p'r'aps," suggested Jack.

"No, Jacky," replied Crikey; "she invite me to come anoder time. 'You come here agen,' she said, 'and see what you get.' But I don't t'ink I shall go, Jacky, 'cause you see de meetin' was not 'zackly fren'ly."

"How did you get on togedder afore?" asked Jack, meditatively.

"Like oder niggers," replied Crikey; "one lilly fight ebery day in de week, an' big one on Sunday, nuffin more."

"Dat 'bout the aberage," said Jack, "and dere nuffin else 'twixt you?"

"Nuffin, Jacky."

"Den I know de reason, Crikey, ob de 'strordinary 'ception ob Chloe."

"What am it, Jacky?"

"Bend down your head, Crikey," and Jack, in the most sepulchral tone, whispered in his ear—

"She got anoder ole man."

The electrical effect of this communication upon Crikey was astounding.

He sprang to his feet with glaring eyes, and the remnant of his "wool" deliberately uncurled and stood erect before his brother's eyes.

"Don't say dat, Jacky," he cried, "for if dat cole-blooded hunks an' dis chile eber meet dere will be only one left."

"Crikey, make no slolum wows," cried Jack, in a warning voice.

"Why not, Jacky?"

"'Cause while I look upon you, my brodder, Crikey, I hab a presentimental come ober me, and dat same presentimental tell dis chile dat one day you and Chloe's oder ole man will meet."

Pens, ink, and paper fail to do justice to the solemnity of the above warning, and we will only state that Crikey was duly and earnestly impressed, even as Macbeth was by the warning of the witches on the heath. It was possible that he and the other "ole man" would meet, and if they did what then? Would Crikey or the old man fall? Ha! there was the mystery, and at this point we leave it for a time. Perhaps in some future chapter of this story the meeting will be recorded, and all doubts upon the question be solved.

. . . .

Away now to a more solemn scene, where, across a burning plain, without shelter from the all-powerful sun, a file of weary men are travelling; not pilgrims these, for they are bound and carry burdens, and by their side ride mounted men in the gaudy attire and sombrero of the south, who twirled their long whips and urged forward their wretched captives with oath and thong.

"Diabolo! you dogs lag," cried one; "forward, or the Don will arrive before."

"It is the fault of yon heathen hound," rejoined a second horseman, pointing to the figure of a tall young fellow in naval attire, who carried a huge portmanteau strapped to his back.

A twirl of the whip, and the sharp thong of the lash sent forward with a spurt the young fellow indicated, who turned a look upon the man as if he wished to print his face upon his memory for future vengeance.

"Scowl not at me," grunted the horseman; "by the light of my fathers, I'll cut the frown from your face with my whip. Malediction! Shall a true son of the church be scowled at by a heathen dog?"

"He has high blood in him, Pedro," laughed the other, "and the lash tickles his hide hugely. Give him another taste."

Pedro complied, and as the prisoner leaped forward with a bitter cry, laughed aloud, the other horsemen joined in the merriment, and they too emulated the joke by lashing some miserable objects near them.

Wretched Mason Wantlake, miserable betrayer of a comrade's honour, has all your plotting, scheming, and outrages innumerable, come to this? Look at him now, as he rolls his wild eye over the plain, and turns his parched and blackened tongue in his mouth, and guess what thoughts are roving through his brain.

Thoughts of repentance? No! The slight turn in the disposition of his heart had given way under the lash, and he lived again, but for vengeance, every blow and taunting word he hugged to his heart, and swore to avenge.

He would be sure and secret, but, first of all, the Don who had decoyed him to this should suffer. Mason had intended to fall foul of him upon the road, but the wily Spaniard sent his train of captives on ahead while he followed by easy stages.

But for this hope of vengeance the young sailor would have dashed out his brains against a stone. For that he bore contumely and the lash, for that he still carried burdens like a beast, and toiled on his weary way beneath the burning sun.

The rest of the train of slaves were, with one exception, negroes; the dark-skinned thoughtless sons of Africa, born and reared to slavery, accepting their lot, if not with cheerfulnesss, at least with resignation.

There were men, and women, and a few children, but the children carried not burdens, not that they were spared from motives of mercy, but because it was not policy to overtask the sapling while it was young. Tender masters that these slave-owners are!

The exception alluded to was a young sailor with a handsome open face, who trod lightly and walked erect, as if no misfortune could bow him down, and that a life of joy and freedom lay at the end of the journey in lieu of an awful captivity.

When first they started, he and Mason had been far apart; but by degrees, after their various halts, the young sailor worked his way nearer to the only other white man of the gang, for whom he felt a natural sympathy and desire for his companionship.

It is probable that the Spanish drivers

would have checked this movement but for the young sailor, by his unflagging pluck and ever-smiling face, having won their admiration, and they let him gradually advance until he was side by side with the gloomy pirate whose light of life was lost in the darkness of his soul.

He glanced for a moment at the new arrival, and then sulkily looked in another direction; but the young sailor was not to be put off thus.

"Cheer up, comrade," he cried, "for comrades we are—in misfortune. Don't make things look blacker than they are—Heaven knows they are black enough, without our frowning upon them!"

"If I could blacken yon sun with my frowns—I would," muttered Wantlake.

CHAPTER XLVIII.

THE LAND OF CAPTIVITY.—WANTLAKE'S VOW.

"AN impious wish," returned the sailor, "and one that is not natural to you, I'm sure. Come, mate, let us jog along pleasantly together, and half our trouble will be gone. We can't shake hands, for these gentlemen of the sombrero have packed them away, but let us touch elbows."

With a wondrously merry smile upon his face, he performed this ceremony, and Mason, surly brute that he had become, was touched by his geniality.

"You are a good fellow, whoever you are," he said; "but let me be. I'm a lost man—body and soul—here and hereafter."

"Again wrong," said the other, grave in a moment; "no man should say that if he has the heart of a man in him. Lost! yes we'll be lost," he added, in a low tone, "and some of these Spanish mongrels will have a devil of a job to find us."

The dawn of hope which flashed for a moment into the face of the young pirate quickly faded out, and he gloomily rejoined—

"Don't think of escape—it's impossible in such a country, and surrounded by a race of fiends, who have tortures for pastimes, and love cruelty for cruelty's sake."

"As many others do."

"True! but none torture as they do, have you felt it?"

"No!" returned the young sailor.

"I have," said Mason Wantlake, with a gesture of despair. "My flesh is cut and scored and maimed, until I was reduced to a proper state of subjection; but

I bide my time," he hissed, "that's all, I bide my time."

"And I also," rejoined the sailor; "but until that time comes, let us while away our time as pleasantly as we can. My name is—perhaps you don't care to hear my name."

"Yes, tell me," replied Mason, gloomily, "it's a better loved and more honoured one than mine."

"It's loved pretty well, in one quarter particularly," laughed the sailor, "but as for being honoured I don't know. I never did anything to distinguish myself, and I never shall. Well, my name is Cecil Warren, awfully high sounding, but I came of a family as poor as church mice—and poorer."

"But the family is good," said Mason, who was rather a stickler for blood and birth.

"The family is good, as you say," replied Cecil; "but let a curate with forty pounds a year be of ever so good a family, he'll find it hard to live; and my father is a curate, with nine olive branches."

"Why did he marry?" mechanically asked Mason.

"Because he fell in love," merrily replied Cecil, "and believed in a cottage and a crust; but as we came one by one into the world, the crust got smaller and smaller, and by the time I was fourteen—I'm the third child—I began to perceive that there were too many mouths to feed, so I ran away to the nearest port and shipped for sea. But there's the signal for the noonday halt, and we shall have one hand released to feed with—if you are willing, I shall be happy to shake hands with you."

"By all means," returned Wantlake; "but you would not be so anxious to do it if you knew how stained with crime is this foul hand of mine."

The latter part of his speech was spoken in an undertone, and was not remarked by his companion, who, in obedience to the sound of a horn, blown by one of the Spaniards, had already settled down upon the ground for the noonday rest.

For three weeks the train of captives pursued their weary course, now across plains, where the hot rays of the sun scorched their heads and blistered their feet; now through the forest wild, where the vast trees spread forth their branches, and made the air in its coolness like the breath of Heaven to the wretched men.

Onward. for three long weeks, they went further and further away from the haunts of civilised men.

There were times when Mason Wantlake felt tempted to throw aside his burden, and bid his captors do their worst, and indeed he would have done it but for Cecil Warren, who warned him of the folly and madness of such an act.

"They will but lash and bind you," he would say, "not kill you outright, for you cost money ; and if your life is unbearable now, what would it be then ? Courage and hope, my comrade ! courage and hope !"

"But I am too far gone," murmured the pirate. "You with your pure young soul can brave them and fight manfully against a gloomy fate ; but I—I—what hope is there for such a wretch as I am ?"

"There is hope for all," would Cecil say, and then turn the subject to one of a lighter nature ; tell stories of his life at sea, of his adventures on land ; even of his school days, where many a prank was played, and in the end he wiped out some of the dark shadow lying on Wantlake's soul.

"What beautiful trees !" said Cecil, as they passed through a grove of banana trees ; let them treat us as they may, they cannot rob us of our love of nature ; they cannot shut from us the glorious light of Heaven, at least for awhile."

"Ay, ay," rejoined Mason ; "but I have no thought for such things ; it is the coarse, rough food, and the being treated like a dog that grates upon me."

"As for the food," laughed Cecil, "it's quite equal to the stale biscuit and salt pork I had on board the 'Merlin,' when we lay for five weeks in a calm, as the poet says,—

'Without a breath or motion,
As idle as a painted ship
Upon a painted ocean.'

Ah ! what a time that was ; we fiddled and danced, told yarns, fished, until not one could fish, spin yarns, fiddle, or dance any more ; and every morn every man jack on board was up looking for the breeze that would not come, and our prog and water got lower and lower. Gad ! until we began seriously to think that cannibalism might in the end be practically introduced among us. But we kept up our hearts, and one night a cloud wiped out the stars, the wind came, and the rain fell, and we spread all canvas, reaching port just as the cook was making arrangements for a hash of sawdust and old boots."

"Silence there !" roared one of the drivers, smacking his long whip.

"Certainly," replied Cecil, under his breath, "anything to oblige a gentleman of your rank and standing, especially when you put the request so forcibly."

The man rode up at that moment, and stared at the two with a scowl on his dark, handsome face.

"You talk too much," he said.

"By the gracious permission of Signor," replied Cecil, bowing and smiling, "it lightens our load, and reserves our strength for the labour of the land we are going to."

"Carambo ! you will need it," said the man, grimly ; "the Don allows no shirking or smiling when he can stop it."

"If he cages a bird does he stop its singing," asked Cecil.

"You will find him a strange man," was the reply, "and your only hope is to do his bidding."

"I am all obedience," returned Cecil, and the man, with a mixed frown and smile upon his face, rode forward.

At night, when they halted, the prisoners were all tethered together, much after the fashion of cattle, by a strong but light chain, carried by one of the slaves during the day, and any attempt to escape was, therefore, hopeless ; and during the day the thought of it was madness, for the guards were mounted, well armed, and each carried at his saddle-bow the fatal lasso.

So the captives went forward, without a loss from their ranks, except one Indian, who died from sheer fatigue, and at length arrived at their destination—a valley lying in the centre of a circle of rugged hills.

Here nature had been prodigal indeed ; fruits and vegetables of the most choice description, grew in luxuriant wild abundance, vines trailed on the ground, or climbing the trees, hung in graceful festoons from the branches ; the pomegranate and the melon lay in heaps, neglected, rotting in the midday sun, and the ground was literally carpeted with myriads of flowers of every varying hue.

In the midst of this scene, a little land of enchantment, rose up a huge building entirely constructed of wood, but erected withal with so much taste, that it looked like a palace wrought by the spell of fairies, so light and graceful was it in every way.

Gossamer creeper-plants hung heavy with blossom round the doors, verandahs, and gables; gorgeous birds perched upon the roof, or strutted with the freedom of pets upon the lawn and terrace; and in the centre of a crystal pool a fountain sent forth a hundred jets, cool and grateful to the eye.

And music, too, comes from the interior, such wild melody as once rang through the halls of the Alhambra, the prelude of a song apparently, for shortly a voice joined in, the sweet voice of a woman—

"Hark, why that sadly, solemn passing bell,
And why, my heart, why this unusual gloom?
Alcasto's dead, the mournful murmurs tell,
E'en now they lodge him in the dreary tomb.

"Alcasto dead! then welcome darkest night,
Fast flow the grateful tear, there's cause to mourn:
Dear, best of friends! what now can yield delight?
For thou canst never, never more return."

The wild melody ran sweetly o'er the valley, reaching the ears of the miserable captives, who stood in silence until the verse was done.

Then came the harsh command to move forward, and Cecil, who was himself strangely touched, looked at Mason Wantlake, and saw a tear glistening in the pirate's eye.

"All is not lost, then, yet," he thought; "the blackest nature has an oasis in its desert of crime."

The captives were not led to the houses, but, turning aside, the Spaniards piloted their charges to a range of low-built huts, lying in the midst of a dense cluster of acacia trees, and there the burdens were deposited on the ground, and every man set free.

One of the Spaniards then came forward, and told Cecil and Mason that they were free to roam at will for a mile around, but no further.

"Wherever you come to a red flag planted in the ground," he said, "you will do well to halt, for it is death to go beyond. Any attempt to escape will be futile, for every outlet from the valley through the hills is guarded. We have men in plenty, and bloodhounds too. I speak to you because you are Englishmen, and I know your nature. These worms," he added, with a contemptuous wave of the hand towards the Indians, "will not attempt to escape."

"What are our duties, signor?" asked Cecil.

"Nothing as yet but to obey," was the reply. "When Don Tralu arrives he will dispose of you."

"And when will the Don arrive?"

"At his convenience; but you will hear of it as soon as he considers needful."

The cool contempt of the Spaniard galled the prisoners excessively, and Wantlake made a slight movement, as if he would have struck him, but Warren quickly stepped between, and, with a slight bow to the Spaniard, led his comrade away.

"No use—no use," he said; "let prudence for the present be the better part of our valour; let us mature our plans, and, when there is a fair chance of a fair fight, show these sombrero-wearing gentry the stuff we are made of."

"O, for a good cutlass and a brace of pistols," groaned Wantlake.

"And a pair of Spaniards in a nice bit of open ground," said Cecil Warren. "But come for a stroll, and keep your eyes open for the red flags, for bad as our life is, I don't care to part with it yet."

Don Tralu was not very far behind them, for he arrived the next day with a train of followers, and a circle of friends, who came with him to enjoy a few months' seclusion in what was known as "Tralu's Paradise."

In two days the house with the flower-covered gables was a scene of riotous gaiety, and the captives, lying in their rude sleeping hut, heard at night the songs and merry laughter of the revellers wafted in the air—and groaned in their misery.

"A heaven to them, a hell to us," said Cecil, on the second evening, as he lay upon the moss-covered ground, looking up at the refulgent stars; "and he might make it a heaven to all."

"But little thinks of us," muttered Wantlake; "hark there—a song again."

"And every word of joy should be a shriek of agony," said Cecil; "look at our fellow captives, so silent and dispirited, remnants of a broken and oppressed race."

"But they are accustomed to their lot," said Wantlake, "they have never known the blessings of a civilized life. What to them is freedom—a thing untalked of and unknown among their tribes. As the stream flows so goes on their lives—following the course laid out, and never turning aside until it goes out into the broad ocean of death and becomes lost in the vastness of eternity."

"I am glad to hear you speak thus," rejoined the sailor, "it is the first time since we met that you have spoken so long and earnestly."

"I am changed," replied Wantlake, "and by you, Part of my rugged nature is already gone for ever. I hope to live—not for myself alone—but for a reparation that is due to one whom I long hated. The confession is humiliating, but I make it."

"The spirit of a true man prompts you."

"Can you hear it and not despise?"

"I could hear more, and regarding you with the affection of a brother, look forward to a brighter and better future in store for you."

"Cecil," said Wantlake, for the first time calling his companion by his Christian name, "I will make to you a full and free confession—then think of me as you may—I deserve the worst construction you can put upon my acts, and ten times more."

Cecil listened to his story, plainly and truthfully told without flinching, without any attempt to excuse, or by explanation put a better face upon the main facts, that he, Mason Wantlake, had been a ruthless scoundrel, and his actions had been in every way worthy of the name.

"I must confess," said Warren, when the story was told, "that many and dark have been your deeds; but I am not your judge. I pity you, for all your deeds have most surely recoiled upon yourself—you are also my companion in misfortune, and that is always a strong bond between men, and I will remain your firm and faithful friend, and help you back on the path that leads not only to life and liberty, but to atonement."

Overcome, Mason could only press his hand, and signing to Cecil that he wished to be alone, he strode away among the trees, and did not return until the night was far advanced.

What he did there it is no purpose of ours to inquire into; but Cecil noticed that many of the hard lines, indicative of bad passion, were gone from his face, and that he spoke as soft and gentle as a woman. The stern unyielding heart had broken at last.

The next morning Don Tralu sent for them, and they were brought into his presence strongly guarded. The Don expected a string of vehement reproaches from Wantlake; but to his astonishment the young pirate was meek, and bowed down as if he was resolved to submit passively to his fate.

"This is well," said the Spaniard; "I am glad to find that my servants train so well. You have thought better of your ravings."

"I have thought better of all things," rejoined Wantlake, quietly.

"Even of me?" sneered the Spaniard.

"Even of you," repeated the other; "it matters not how or why, but I do so with my whole heart."

"And you, signor," said the Don, turning to Cecil, "are you, too, reconciled to your lot?"

"I have seen and endured too many changes to be otherwise," cheerfully replied the young fellow; "all I ask is fair treatment at the hands of yourself and men."

"And a reasonable chance for escape?" asked the Don, with another sneer.

"Decidedly," said Cecil; "you can barely expect us to endure this captivity without some hope of freedom."

"Then put it aside here," cried the Don, imperiously, "for there is none, every pass around here is, as you have doubtless been told, strictly guarded, moreover, you will be sent a few miles from here, and placed where what little hope you have now will fade away. See yonder hill?"

The two captives turned, and following the direction of his finger observed a bare rugged hill, the only one of the chain without verdure.

"Years ago," pursued the Spaniard, "my ancestors found out its value, and established a mine there; wars with the natives compelled its abandonment, and half the works are flooded, but I have begun to restore it, and you shall help in the great work."

"That is, we are to be sent to the mine," said Cecil, coolly.

"It is so."

"And how often shall we be permitted to return to the light of day?"

"As often as your conduct deserves it I make no promise."

"Well! so be it," rejoined Cecil, with affected resignation; "give us fair food and treatment, let us work together, and you will have no cause to complain."

THE WRECK OF THE "CRUCIBLE."

The eyes of the Spaniard twinkled with delight; he had not anticipated so much submission from his prisoners, and charging it all to the discipline of his faithful followers, he bade them remove the captives to their destination, thoroughly satisfied with the interview.

"Patience and hope," whispered Cecil; "I see a way out of this."

"If you can see a way out of the bowels of the earth," returned Wantlake, with a faint smile, "you can see anything."

"I can see further," rejoined Cecil, "I can see the road back to dear old England, straight across the blue sea which laps the shore of this unhappy land."

CHAPTER XLIX.

HUNTING A SHADOW, CRIKEY MAKES HIS WILL.

SHORTLY after the landing of Lord Sancroft at Cuba, the true story of Harold's exile was rumoured about, and he became identified with the strange vessel which had done so much in such a little time.

Our readers know that the "Crucible" had encountered many British merchantmen upon her way, and bade them go unharmed—indeed, in many cases, when contrary winds had kept them long upon their course she had relieved them from her store—and many and strange were the stories told of this strange rover upon the high seas.

But now all was known, and in every mouth were the gallant deeds done by the young captain; who had fought for his honour and sworn to hide his face until that honour was restored, and every speaker praised the gallant hero's name.

Captain Harloch heard it with unfeigned delight, for he had loved Harold years ago, and regretted his downfall as he would that of his own son, but it remained for him yet to learn how dear the young adventurer was to the heart of his daughter Clara.

She came to him when the story was in every mouth, as he returned from a meeting with some of his brother officers, where the question of our hero had been discussed, and laying her head upon his bosom, simply said—

"Father, find my Harold, or I shall die."

She had no need to say more; all was told in her face, and the strong old sailor swore to her that the lad should be found "if he was above land or sea."

"Already, lass," he said, "is his pardon, and that for Harry Carlton, written out, and to-morrow the 'Bruiser' sails in search of 'em with a white flag running at the fore. Sancroft says he'll not come until he's found that scoundrel Wantlake, but we will try him."

"Take this message from me," said Clara, "and he will come."

The "message" was a ring from her finger, one that he had given her during the happy days spent on board the "Curlew," and this, with a few loving words, was enclosed to Captain Harold Graystone, of the "Crucible."

Charged with this precious burden, the "Bruiser" went forth in a direction indicated by Lord Sancroft, whose last words were, "he will not come until his evidence is complete," and the captain of the "Bruiser" replied, "If he doesn't he's a donkey, that all I can say," accompanying the remark with a roguish look at the charming Clara, who hung upon her father's arm close by.

So the 'Bruiser' sailed for the first time since her fitting out on a peaceful mission; but along she sailed, with her officers and men ever on the lookout; many a time the watchers cried, "That's the 'Crucible,'" as some vessel hove in sight; but it either proved to be another craft, or the chase was lost in the darkness of night.

Once, indeed, they saw her, and Harold saw the "Bruiser," but ignoring the white bunting he crowded on all sail, and was quickly lost to view.

"I'll not return," he said, "and let those catch me who can."

"An' who do dat, sar?" rejoined Jack, at his usual post; "dey jes' as soon catch little pig wid a greasy tail."

"Are they so difficult to catch, Jack?"

"Dere noffin' like greasy pig anywhar, sar. Once in Cuba, sar, Massa Sunfly, a genelman dat own large 'state, an' plenty ob nigger, hab one ob him pig get loose, an' he shout out, 'Now, you cussed niggers, catch dat pig, or I peel orf your hides wid dis whip.' Well, sar, ten niggers stand near, an' dey all say, 'No use, sar; him got a greasy tail, somehow.' Massa Sunfly berry passionate man, an' him look round wid a black face, an' say, 'Cut, you cussed debils, an' catch him, or I grease you.' Away dey all go, all togedder, an' de pig him bolt through hole in de fence, an' go straight away, wid all dem black children arter him, full pelt. De pig cross de road, dey cross de road, dey all go into de wood, but no pig nor nigger, sar, eber come back."

"That's a very good story, Jack," said Harold, "but I suspect that the niggers did not care to return."

"Dat about, sar, in doubt de pig, and as dey couldn't catch de pig dey berry quietly got into a boat dat happen' to be on de shore, an' make clean cut away ob it."

"And the pig, Jack?"

"Him still wag him greasy tail, and walk about somewhar like a genelman."

Harold walked away smiling, and Jack, conscious of having distinguished himself, strutted up to Will and Tom, who were in the bows watching a troop of porpoises at play.

"Good ebening, genelmen."

"Ha! Jack," said Tom, "I saw you with the captain, but we did not like to intrude."

"No intrushing," rejoined Jack, graciously. "I jes' tell de cap'en a lilly story, an' it make him smile."

"If it did that," said Will, "it will make us laugh; let us hear it."

Jack repeated the story, word for word, and the boys laughed, but Will had something to say upon it.

"I can understand the niggers running

"away," he said, "but why did the pig do it?"

"Dat a posler," said Jack, planting five fingers in his wool.

"You see, Jack," continued Will, "that pigs don't run straight off as a rule; they go round and round, but never go far from their grub."

"You right, Massa Will, an dat story a lie. Crikey tell me dat last night, but him a true nigger an' uncommon liar."

The object of this eulogy at this moment put his head above the fore hatchway, and beckoned to his brother in a very solemn manner.

Partly curious, and partly acting upon a resolve to reprove him for his falsehood, Jack obeyed, and followed his brother to the cabin below.

It was empty of all but themselves, and upon the little table in the centre was spread pen, ink, and paper.

"What am you conceibing of now, Crikey?" asked the astonished Jack.

"Jacky, I conceibe it time to make my will."

Crikey uttered these words with impressive solemnity, and looked as if he was fully conscious of life being a vale of tears.

"Make your will, Crikey; how you do dat? who teach you to write?"

"I nebber taught, Jack; and derefore can't do it, Jackey."

"De same 'stounding igmaflance is dis chile in," replied Jack, "an' he not able to help you."

"But you get somebody," said Crikey, with a cunning leer. "You get de cap'en, p'raps?"

"Him!" exclaimed Jack, horrified. "What next you t'ink ob; p'raps you like him black your botts?"

"P'raps Massa Steadfas' do it den?"

"I'll ax him," replied Jack, "'acause he good-natured piccanniny. I bring him, Crikey, in a twinkering."

Jack kept his word, and quickly returned with the middies, both of them much amused with the novelty of a nigger making his will, and inclined to make fun of it, but they kept their countenances marvellously, and Will took his seat with becoming dignity, Tom stationing himself on his right.

"Do I understand you rightly, Crikey," asked Will, "that you wish to dispose of your personal property; in fact, make your last will and testament?"

"Dat my 'tention, sar, wid your leave," replied Crikey.

"And that I am to write it down?"

"Yes, sar."

"Then begin."

"All ready, sar. I, Crikey, ob ole Cuba, do leab all my property to ole Chloe, de woman dat I lub with my ole heart, but who take up with anoder ole man, and gib me such a cockshy in my bozum, dat if I eber recober, it will be next door to a miricle."

"Shall I put that down, Crikey?"

"Ebery word, sar, if you please—dem most important to de document."

"All down, Crikey—fire away."

"I now purceed," continued Crikey, "to name my property which I leave to ole Chloe, dat take up wid anoder old man."

"You said that before, Crikey."

"Dat true, sar—and now I come to de property—fust I gib to ole Chloe dat—ole Chloe, my boots wid de gold spurs, and de blue jacket wid de gold braid."

Jack opened his eyes very wide, and stared. Will coolly penned the words, and Crikey proceeded.

"I also gib her my pistols dat hab de two di'monds in de handle, and de cutlas wid de emerals all down de blade."

The eyes of Jack opened wider, and rolled spasmodically. Will, unmoved, proceeded.

"Emeralds all down the blade—right Crikey, go on."

"And I gib to the same Chloe dat take up wid anoder ole man—de two bags of gold doubloons, and de silver bar, also, de two brown horses dat I bought for seven hundred dollars—got dem down, sar?"

"All right, Crikey—let us have it."

"And to de same ole Chloe, I gib de house and garden, where the banana grow, and de little pigs squeak all de day long."

"Any of them with a greasy tail?" Tom asked, quietly.

"Him not dere, sar," replied Crikey, rolling his eyes at Jack—"him in de next estate."

"Is that all, Crikey?" asked Will, looking up.

"No, sar! dere a little more."

When this announcement was made, Jack leaned forward in a state of breathless interest—Crikey to be the possessor of so much property and he not know it—it was astonishing.

"De nex' w'ile," pursued Crikey, "is de small shay that I did drive de brown pony in—dat I leave to Jacky, and my gold watch an' ring."

More wonders—Crikey with a gold watch and ring—what next?

"All the rest ob my property go to Jacky too—de two lilly cocks dat crow ebery morn, and de peacock dat sp'ead him tail when him out courtin'—dat all, Massa Will, and tank you kindly."

"Nothin' else?"

"Nothin' more, sar."

"Then sign your name here."

"Me not able to write, sar."

"Then make a cross—like this."

Crikey, with much deliberation and exhibition of tongue, made a cross about three inches long, and laid down his pen with a glow of satisfaction on his dark countenance.

"Now for the witnesses," said Will. "Tom, you will do for one, and Jack for the ot'er."

"Afore I put down dat mark," interposed Jack, waking up as one does from a dream, "I like jes' to ax my brudder Crikey a few questions."

"Quite right and proper," said Will.

"Now Crikey, sar, you listen to me."

Crikey turned his large dark eyes upon his brother, the tip of his tongue peeped from his mouth, and his strong muscular hands were tightened together.

"Whar you get all dat property, sar?"

The stern voice of Jack rang through the little cabin.

Will and Tom fixed their eyes upon the willmaker, who, with the utmost deliberation, replied as follows:—

"I not got it yet, Jacky, but I make de will in case I ever hab it."

This astounding reply fairly staggered his listeners, Jack remaining in a fixed attitude, with vengeful eyes fixed upon his brother.

Will was the first to speak, suppressing a violent inclination to roar.

"But, surely, Crikey, you have some of it," he said.

"No, sar."

"No gold-laced coat or boots with gold spurs?"

"Neber hab 'em, sar."

"And the shay and brown pony?"

"Neber see 'em, sar."

"The gold watch, the little farm the peacock?"

"I hab not nuffin, sar; de ole bilin' lot hab to come."

Will, unable to question him more, rose from the table, and, followed by Tom, rushed upon the deck, where they roared in concert until their sides ached again.

Jack meanwhile remained with his eyes fixed sternly on his brother, who quivered beneath his basilisk gaze, awake at last to the enormity of his crime.

He stood on one leg, shifted to the other, folded his arms, unfolded them, scratched his woolly head, and still those eyes of Jacky never left him.

"Crikey," said the sable hero, at length, "you put me down in your will for shay an' pony, gold watch an' ring, an' two lilly cocks dat crow ebery morn, an' de peacock dat spread him tall when him courting—dem are de t'ings to leab to me."

"Dat's true as Chloe lubly woman, Jacky."

"And den you say you habn't 'em."

"Not yet," said Crikey, mildly; "but p'raps I do, some day."

"You hab better get dem afore you die!" rejoined Jack, shaking his huge fist as he left the cabin, "or it will be berry much de worse for you."

CHAPTER L.

THE "CRUCIBLE" ASHORE.

HAVING made his will, Crikey to a certain extent retired into private life, and for several days was not seen upon the deck, although his voice was heard discoursing fragments of sweet poetry of an impromptu nature.

It was well for him, perhaps, that he did keep out of the way, for Jack did not get over his indignation, and the sun set twice upon the anger he felt for his brother, but at last he joined in the general opinion of his friends respecting the affair, and laughed with the best.

"Crikey sartainly am true nigger," he said to Will, "dere am a genus bout him dat no man on board but him hab. He true nigger."

One individual was disposed to be rather offensive, and ventured to chaff Jack; this was Duncan the carpenter, but he made a mistake as usual.

"I should be glad of a lift, Mr. Jack," he said, "if ever I meet you on a road with that pony an' shay o' yourn."

"What you say, sar?"

Duncan repeated the observation, rather

slowly it is true, but the eyes of his mess-mates were on him, and he repeated it.

Jack walked quickly up to him, seized him round the waist and flung him down the hatchway.

"Ask Crikey when him hab it ready," he said, and walked away.

After this Duncan abandoned the will question as he had abandoned others before, and Jack, conscious of having sustained his dignity, recovered his good humour, and so far relaxed as to invite the carpenter to make one in the consumption of a bottle of rum.

The "Crucible" had been bowling gallantly before an easy breeze since the landing of Lord Sancroft, but on the third day following the making of the important will, the light fleecy clouds hitherto observable in the sky changed to dark heavy patches, and the wind, instead of blowing steadily, increased in strength by fitful gusts that tested the strength of the vessel's cordage.

All but the storm sails were furled, and with these the "Crucible" still went swiftly before the wind, rising like a bird over the ever-increasing waves.

Darker grew the sky, louder roared the wind, shaving off the waves' summits as it went shrieking by, and filling the air with fragments of foam. Higher and higher rose the sea, and faster sped the little craft before the ever-increasing gale.

Hark! was that thunder? No, nought but the roaring of the wind, now at such a height that Harold by the wheel gave his orders to deafened ears, and the men on deck clung to the belaying pins and stays as the only means of keeping their feet.

The "Crucible" rolled and plunged fearfully, sometimes with her bowsprit buried in a huge wave, sometimes with it high in the air, as she topped a heavy sea, when the shrieking wind caught her again, and drove her into what may truly be termed "a vast valley of water."

One by one those below crept on deck and joined their comrades, most of them, hatchet in hand, ready to cut away in case of the masts yielding, but they were tough and true, and would not yield.

Onward, like a steed goaded to madness, she sped, while the waves rose still higher, and the wind roared and shrieked with increased intensity.

Whither are we driving to? was the thought uppermost in most of their minds, and every eye was fixed ahead, as the point of danger.

For hours they travelled thus, and night came without a lull.

Throughout the night they rushed madly o'er the sea, and with the grey dawn a fearful danger lay before them.

A long line of foam leaping high against the murky clouds, and the steady rushing sound of breakers, high above the wind, which once heard is never forgotten.

No hope, right and left, for far away the line extended, with here and there a head of rock, uprising as if to view the destruction spread by the angry waters.

No hope, for the wind is dead in shore, and already the "Crucible" is too close in to wear, if even she could carry the sail to do it, and close to the wheel stand Harold and Mr. Stanchion, ready to take advantage of any loophole for escape, while the rest silently prepare for what seems imminent death.

Nearer and nearer; the spray rains down upon them like a heavy shower, the waters rise and shriek around them, and beat the vessel's sides; then comes a feeling as if gliding in still water, and then the "Crucible" strikes heavily upon a bank of sand, and heels over.

"Steady, men," roars Harold, through his speaking trumpet, "the greatest danger is past."

It is so, for behind lays the long line of rocks, which they have somehow, as it appears, miraculously passed, and the "Crucible" lies upon the soft sandy shore of the mainland. They had yet to wade through the surf to the beach, and a difficult task it was—but by assisting each other they all got safely to land.

It seemed then as if the sea was satisfied with its work, for the wind fell almost immediately, the clouds dispersed, and the sun came out, shining upon the sides of the helpless little craft as she lay upon the shore of a land of beauty.

A land of beauty we call it, and indeed it was—golden sands upon the shore, verdure-covered cliffs uprising, feathery foliage crowning their summits, and a score of glittering cascades leaping into the sea.

The hum of insects and the cries of strange birds filled the air; seagulls flap their wings and perch upon the masts, wondering what monster from far-off worlds has invaded their domain; dolphins sport in hundreds in the subsiding sea, and the men of the "Crucible" stand looking on as if it were a dream.

The water having receded, they can land almost without the assistance of boats, and the first care is to shore up the craft and to see what injuries she has suffered.

It is found that, beyond a leak of minor importance, she has suffered little; but she lies upon the land high and dry, for the tide soon leaves her, and what power that can be brought to bear upon her shall get her off?

"The 'Crucible' has found her resting place," said Harold, as he viewed her sadly from the shore.

"She lies like an old war-horse," rejoined Mr. Stanchion; "and a glorious stable she has found."

"It is indeed a Paradise," said Harold, looking around; "but there are too many Adams without an Eve," he added, with a smile.

"Some men would think it the more like Paradise," returned the lieutenant; "but I suppose they are cynical brutes."

"Undoubtedly," said our hero. "Will you get the provisions ashore, and make what arrangements are needful for the present? When we have rested for awhile I will take the bearings of this place. Jack."

"Yes, sar."

"Rig me up a little awning on the sand here; I am tired and worn out."

Quickly done, with a couple of poles and a sail; and others, also, beneath which the whole of the weary company lay down to rest after the perils of the night, one only remaining on watch.

CHAPTER LI.

THE GOLD MINE.

"FORWARD, you hounds! we shall not reach the mine by nightfall."

It was a Spaniard who spoke, one of the men who had brought the train of slaves from the coast, and those he urged forward were Mason Wantlake and Cecil Warren.

"You lag, you dogs, you lag," he cried, and the long, cruel whip whirled menacingly through the air.

"It is so hot," returned Warren; "the sun scorches like an oven."

"It should roast such pigs as you," cried the Spaniard, who, strong in the support of half a dozen comrades, could afford to insult the prisoners with impunity.

Neither of them replied, for they knew it was useless.

What were they, without arms, against such ruthless ruffians?

"Patience and hope," muttered Cecil.

"Patience and hope," whispered Mason; "give me a chance, and I will make these Spanish curs dance yet."

As Warren had said, the sun scorched them like an oven; the air seemed full of flame, and the broad foliage of the trees drooped beneath its rays.

Presently they came to a pool of water, muddy, for it had been disturbed by some thirsty beasts, but they—prisoners and jailors—lay down together, and lapped it like dogs, until the veins of their foreheads lay up like whipcord.

"Who knows the blessing of water," said Warren, "but he who has almost died of thirst?"

"Wine pales before this muddy pool," rejoined Mason; and then came the cry of the Spaniards, urging them forward.

A little after noon they reached the base of the barren hill, and commenced an upward ascent by means of a rough roadway.

Fatiguing work, but a cool breeze swept over the mountain, and gave them great relief.

Up, up, they went, to the great astonishment of the prisoners, who soon learned that the opening of the mine was near the summit of the hill, for a few huts dotted about appeared to view, after an hour's upward toil.

"Our forefathers knew how to dig," said the Spaniard who had previously spoken. "A thousand men might be at work there, and all at the mercy of one man, as you shall see. The bowels of this mountain makes a glorious prison house."

"The Don might have spared us this," said Mason Wantlake, gloomily.

"The Don knows his men," grinned the Spaniard; "he knows that an Englishman will work to while away his time, while your Indian will dig a hole, lie in it, and starve, rather than work in the underground. Ah! the Don is a keen one."

"A scoundrel," muttered his listeners.

The huts grew larger, and as they drew nearer two or three forms appeared to be moving about. These proved to be Spaniards, attired somewhat after the fashion of the others, but the materials coarser.

They came forward and hailed their countrymen with joy, and for some minutes occupied themselves with an interchange of news, those lately from the coast giving their intelligence first.

"And how goes the mine?" asked one of the drivers; "at last does it flourish, Carlos?"

"Bad," replied Carlos, with a shrug; "they die like rotten sheep, to spite us; there are but three now."

"Why do they die?"

"They say it is dark and cold, and the last one who died call it a hell. He stole away into some of the old workings and lost himself, hoping to find an outlet from this place, but our fathers knew better; there is but one door to the mine, and we keep the key. Well, this bold fellow, he was not twenty, stole away and died. We missed him, and should never have found him, but that his body stank, and the lizards were journeying towards it by hundreds."

"And have you buried him?"

"We dragged him to the new working, and bade the others do it, and, on my word, they went speedily to work, and put him beneath three feet of crushed quartz."

Mason and Cecil listened to the narrative horrified, and exchanged glances indicative of an instantaneous mutual resolve to make one bold run down the mountain for liberty and life, but the Spaniards seemed to interpret the look, and closed around them.

"This way, senor," said Carlos, taking off his hat with mock politeness; "welcome to our humble palace."

They followed him to the edge of a large hole in the earth, with a large bucket swinging over it from apparatus something after the style of an old-fashioned well, and, obeying a sign from him, they took their seats therein.

In an instant the mountain seemed to rise, and the walls of the well-shaped opening glided rapidly upwards. They did not descend far, not more than fifty feet, perhaps, when the bucket stopped with a rude jerk, and threw them out upon the floor of a small square chamber.

A hoarse laugh from above showed the cause of the accident, and then the bucket glided back again.

"A joke of our Spanish friends," said Warren, brushing himself with his hand, "they make merry with us."

"Would you spare such wretches as these?" asked Mason gloomily.

"No," returned Warren, "averse as I am to murder in cold blood, I would willingly crush them like vermin beneath my feet."

The little circle of light in the floor darkened, and the bucket again descended, this time with four Spaniards, who bore in their hand torches ready for lighting.

Whether by accident or not, the bucket again rudely clashed with the floor, and the Spaniards were sent sprawling. It was the prisoners' turn to laugh, and they laughed heartily

"That's about the last laugh you will care to utter," said Carlos, grimly, "why dost thou growl, Guilemo?"

"I've lost my stiletto," grunted the man,

"Look for it on thy return," replied Carlos; "we must get away, or it will be dark ere we return."

Lighting a torch, Carlos pointed to an opening, and bade the prisoners descend. They could see no steps, and hesitated.

"It is an incline shaft," he explained, "and will carry you safely."

"Better a yawning gulf," they both thought, and committed themselves to the mercy of the strange road.

Seated, it bore them rapidly downward for a distance, as near as they could guess, of about two hundred feet. There, some soft substance, sand and dry leaves, mixed apparently, checked their progress, and they stood up in pitchy darkness,

"Guilemo has lost his dagger," whispered Cecil.

"I heard him say so," rejoined Mason.

"But he'll never find it again."

"Why not?"

"I've got it."

"Give me that dagger," returned Mason, with a touch of his old fierceness, "and let me have the blood of one Spaniard."

"In good time," replied Warren; "for the present we are too near the upper air."

The Spaniards now appeared in rapid succession, each bearing a torch, and Guilemo still growling about the loss of his stiletto.

"The gift of my father," he said "Diable! I would not have lost it for a million piastres."

"You shall have it again," thought Warren.

Carlos took the lead, and led them through a long gallery, cut apparently out of the solid rock, the ceiling glittering with fragments of the precious metal.

"Here," said Carlos, halting at the end and tapping the wall, "we are not many feet from the outer slope of the mountain; you English would have dug the surface, our superior race prefer to honeycomb it, although but a shell, twenty men could not work their way out in a week—our prison-house is safe."

A horrible thought came over Cecil—what if the upper part of the mountain should crush this shell, and falling in, entomb them for ever? He shuddered in spite of himself, and Carlos grinned.

"There is a working below," he said, "and ten years ago the mouth of it fell in, shutting from us twenty men of mixed races; we could not reach them, and there they perished."

"Left without food or hope of escape?" involuntarily asked Warren.

"Some had no food," was the reply; "but the others probably survived them many days, for they were cannibals."

It was the design of the Spaniard to horrify his hearers, and he did it effectually; it was also his desire to break their spirit, but that could never be done, and Cecil answered—

"Their short captivity was fearful, but better than the longer one."

"The signor will find life sweet," said Carlos; "every captive sentenced to death leaves his dungeon as he would a home."

There was so much truth in this that his listeners made no reply, and followed him through a second winding gallery, sloping gradually downwards, at the end they found another opening.

"Another gentle ride, senors," said Carlos; "but be wary of the bottom, for a few feet beyond is a rent that goes to the heart of the mountain, and no man has fathomed it."

Cecil and Mason went down, side by side, their arms linked, and arrived in safety below.

The air was rigid here, cold enough for th icy regions.

"Now's our time," whispered Cecil, hurriedly; "I would have spared these men, but it cannot be done. Carlos says says no man has ever found the depth of the invisible rent near us. He shall fathom it. Seize his torch, and I will do the rest."

The unsuspecting Carlos quickly followed, holding high his torch.

Quick as a flash of thought Mason seized it, the dagger gleamed, a quick, cruel, sharp stroke, and the cruel Spaniard was no more,

"Heaven bear me witness," said Cecil Warren, "I would have avoided this."

Close to their feet was the chasm spoken of, a huge rent in the floor of a huge cavern.

Mason held the torch above his head, but its light failed to pierce more than a few feet of its darkness.

"A grave deep enough," he said; "throw him over."

"Not yet," returned Cecil; "hush!

"Is all right below?" cried one of the men above.

"Ay, Guilemo," replied Cecil, imitating the gruffness of the voice of Carlos.

The other two men came before him, the first in his impetuosity, trusting probably to the staying hand of Carlos, plunged forward and pitched into the yawning chasm with a wild cry of despair.

The next, quickly following, was stunned by a blow from Mason's fist, and Guilemo coming last was met by Cecil.

"Guilemo," he said, "take back your dagger."

The Spaniard saw the impending blow and throwing up his arms, received it in the fleshy part, just below the elbow.

With the cry of a wild beast he seized the youth round the waist and dragged him towards the precipice.

But Mason Wantlake was at hand, and Guilemo was no match for the two.

Necessity bade them do it, and after a few brief struggles he took back his dagger to his heart.

"We must change clothes with these Spanish cattle," said Mason, "it will give us a better chance of escape."

"And this man?" pointing to the Spaniard who lay insensible.

"Must follow the others; in that lies our only chance of safety. Remember, Cecil, that we have other enemies about, and down by the house of the Don there are more."

"So be it," said Cecil, with a sigh, "but it's an awful ending for such a man."

They took off the outer garments and arms of Guilemo and his insensible comrade, and cast them over into the unfathomed depths of the mighty grave.

"There are two things to think of now," said Cecil; "our own safety and that of the other wretches here. We cannot, in all mercy, leave them, and we are armed with sufficient weapons to send a dozen men into eternity—two stilettoes and two revolvers."

These were the arms they had found upon the men, together with a small supply of ammunition, and, what was quite as good, a rough map of the country between their prison and the coast.

This Cecil carefully folded and put in the sash around his waist, lately the property of Guilemo.

"We might lose ourselves in this underground quarry," hesitated Mason. "We can do little to save them."

"We can but try. Shout."

Their voices, raised to the utmost, found a thousand echoes.

Some from behind, some before. and in the chasm they died away with a roll like distant thunder.

At first it seemed as if there was no reply, but Cecil declared he heard a voice.

"It's feeble, and not far away," he said, "but where?"

"Ay, where?" echoed Mason.

"Shout again."

"Ho, ho! prisoners, come forth! Liberty is at hand."

A faint light glimmer from the right, and the wan resemblance of a man crawled from a niche in the rocky wall.

"Who calls?" he feebly moaned, as he crept forward; "who talks of liberty, or is it one of the mad dreams I've had of late?"

"It is true," cried Cecil advancing, "and we, Englishmen and true, talk of life and liberty."

"Then our prayers are heard at last," cried the wretched man, falling on his knees and sobbing aloud.

"My poor fellow, bear up," cried Cecil, throwing his arms around the wasted figure; "you must rouse yourself, for we have one struggle yet to make for liberty."

"Say you so?" returned the poor fellow, "then this arm is not too palsied to strike; have you arms?"

"Only these," replied Cecil; "but there are more in the huts above, and, with caution we may obtain them; where are your comrades?"

Mason Wantlake, holding the torch closer to the apparent old man, was astonished to perceive that he had scarce reached manhood, and was, at the outside, no older than Cecil Warren.

"How long have you been here, poor boy?" he asked, with more kindness in his tone than he had ever shown before.

"I know not!—ages perhaps—I cannot tell," replied the wan youth.

"Where are your comrades?"

"They lie there!" he said, pointing to the niche; "but they are asleep. They fell off talking of their old homes, and the games they had at school. Come gently, for they have been ill of late and need rest."

No need, oh, Heaven, to follow the youth so gently—for his comrades have fallen into a sleep from which earth knows no awakening. In a rude chamber, cut from the rock, they lay upon a bed of dried ferns; their youthful faces—for they, like the other men, were young, with such a smile upon them that tears were brought into the eyes of even Mason Wantlake, and the last stubborn barrier of his heart was broken down.

"What a sight is this!" he cried.

"I knew not they were dead," said the youth, wiping his eyes; "poor fellows! they have suffered much—as all have here."

"Let us get out of this," said Mason; "for there is work to be done with the scoundrel who fattens on this place. I shall not rest until I see the sky redden above the flames of that nest of his."

"Can you bear the journey to the upper air?" asked Cecil, addressing the youth.

"A journey to see the sun or stars!" he cried, "dying I would crawl a hundred miles to view them; but my poor comrades here?"

"Let them remain—we will block up the entrance with the broken rocks lying outside. We could not find them a fitter resting place."

Before leaving they gathered together a few rough miners' tools—the small pickaxes, drills, and a lantern—knowing that things might prove useful.

With a last reverential glance towards the dead captives, they went out, and closed up the opening with a pile of rock, and then began their upward journey.

It was long and painful, the more so as the released youth was terribly exhausted, and frequently halted, half fainting, by the way; but it was accomplished at last, and they halted beneath the opening that led to the upper air.

It was late now, and the stars were out—one of the largest twinkling above them, as if it bade them welcome once more beneath its gem-like ray.

"What now?" asked Mason.

"Go boldly up," said Cecil, "there will not be more than two—seize them and bind them—quickly if we can—if not, Guilemo's dagger."

"Cecil, you are growing bloodthirsty."

"Mason, it is no crime to kill a hyena, nor a man-eating tiger, and what hyena or tiger ever possessed one iota of the devil lying in these men's hearts?"

"True; now how to get up? There must be some preconcerted signal, some password between these men, and we have it not."

"We must not risk it," mused Cecil, "one false step and before we could get out from here they would be upon us. We should have no chance, they could fire on us—pelt us with pieces of rock."

"Or, what is more in accordance with their cowardly nature, close up the opening and leave us to starve."

"It seems to me," said Cecil, "that yon bucket swings half way; but first put out this torch, it is useless now," he put his foot upon it and resumed, "It seems to me that I could reach it, if I can get to the ceiling of this den, the sides of the shaft are very rough, and sailors, you know, are cats; Mason, give me your shoulders."

With the agility of an acrobat Cecil climbed up the body of his friend and seized the rude projections of the orifice and proceeded upward with the skill and address of a practised climber to the huge bucket. From thence he climbed the rope, and, reaching terra-firma, gradually lowered the means of escape.

"One at a time," he whispered, and Mason, with a self-denial which he was every hour growing more worthy of, sent up first the feeble youth who had spent such a terrible time underground.

Cecil, by a great exertion of his strength, managed to bring him to the surface, and the combined powers of the pair brought up Mason Wantlake.

The trio stood for a moment to breathe the pure air of Heaven, and then stealthily commenced the descent of the mountain.

CHAPTER LII.

RETURN TO THE "CRUCIBLE."—NEGRO CITY.—STOWING AWAY FOR A LONG TIME.

WE must now hasten back to our friends the "Crucible," for concerning their doing there is yet much to tell. The noble little vessel, "hero of a hundred fights," lay high and dry upon the shore, the tide had receded almost as far as the line of rocks, nature's breakwater to the coast.

It was a sore dilemma for Harold and his crew, for the "Crucible" was helpless, and the surveys they had taken from the highest points of land near them showed that they were lying upon an apparently uninhabited place. He could see the coast for many miles on either side, fertile here and barren there, but no sign of the habitations or the presence of man.

They took the bearings of the place, but the instruments had suffered much, and were put out of order by the late gale, and were therefore not reliable, but as far as they could judge, they had been cast upon the northern part of the South American continent, about four hundred miles below the Isthmus of Panama.

Jack proved to be of great service, for he discovered certain signs that at one period of the year the tides ran high, sufficiently so to float the "Crucible," and gave it his opinion that the high waters had been gone about ten moons, and might be expected to return in two.

Harold, as we know, had great confidence in him, and preparations were made for a two months' sojourn on the land.

All the provisions and ammunition were taken out and stowed away in various caves in the cliff, and on its summit the sailors erected a small fort, which they fitted up with a few of the smaller guns, which had already done such good service.

The rest were carefully stowed away, and anchors fixed to prevent the "Crucible," when the high tides came, from either dashing against the cliff or running out to sea.

"Dis de sort ob life!" said Jacky, "I tink, massa Will, dis berry much better dan shipboard—for a change."

"It's a change, Jack, truly," replied the mid; "but for a regular thing it wouldn't do. We shall run precious short of grub in a couple of months, if she doesn't float."

"She floot right enuf, sar; you see de 'Crucible' bobbin' about like a cork afore you two munfs older."

"Ah! de 'Crucible' can bob about hen him dander up," interposed Crikey, aggering past with his private and personal luggage in an old box.

Now, since Crikey made the will so aught with good fortune for his legatees, coolness had existed between Jack and im, and Jack, looking upon this interposition of his brother's as a confounded iece of impudence, forthwith, with incredible agility, picked up the box and ent Crikey's private property into the air.

Unfortunately, too, for Crikey he had lmost scaled the cliff when thus assaulted, nd the box, rolling down with a bounce rom point to point, the lid opened, and ut flew such a miscellaneous collection of rticles as only a nigger could collect.

Odd boots, the handle of a saucepan, the ace of an old clock, two bradawl handles, n old white hat done up in paper to preserve it, and supposed to have been the crowning glory of Crikey's wedding, a handful of nails, some chickens' feet, highly preserved, and a multitudinous collection of other articles, among which brick figured conspicuously.

"What dat for, you Jacky?" he cried, ildly; "ain't your brodder to open him ouf but you must—must put your dam ly foot in? Dere more propity in that x dan de 'Crucible' worth, and yet you ck him up like old rubbish."

"Go away, sar," said Jack, loftily; you not my brodder."

"You said dat afore," returned Crikey, but you know better dan to turn orf—it ebil day for you when you do. You help e, sar, to pick up dem wallybles, or I st you orf."

"Ah! do, Jack," interposed Will; brothers should never quarrel. I'll give ou a hand, too, Crikey."

"I tank you for de honour, Massa Will; you will look for dat brick I be bery nkful."

"Is it such a precious relic, Crikey?"

"Yes, sar; it de fust piece ob crockery t Chloe trow at dis chile on our wedding y."

Jack could not refuse to help as Will eadfast had volunteered, and between e trio most of the "valuable property" s recovered—the brick last of all, for it forced its way into a crevice of the f in a most surprising manner, and was found for a long time, and when it was

found had to be dug out of the stiff clayey soil.

When all that could be found was secured Crikey crept cautiously away and bestowed his worldly wealth in a very secure hiding place.

Several subsequent days passed very busily, for every precaution had to be taken, not only against any possible enemy in the form of man, but against the various fevers known to be rife at times upon the coast.

CHAPTER LIII.

JACK GIVES THE "TOE-AND-HEEL CORKER."

EXCURSIONS were made inland, limes and other fruit preserved, and the men put upon a daily regimen, as if they were in a garrison town, for Harold knew the value of discipline, and taught his men to appreciate it.

But there was great liberty, nevertheless, and a merry party generally assembled on the cliff in the cool of the evening, when Crikey added to his other accomplishments a very fair performance on an old fiddle; and the British hornpipe (or the then known version) was danced with many private effects, according to the taste and fancy of the performer.

At such a time Harold and his officers would look on, among whom Jack considered himself, and he would stand by his chief's side, and smile benignly upon an extra effort of a heated performer.

"Keep a goin'" Crikey, too, would cry, as the perspiration rolled from his dark brow. "De niggers ob Cuba pretty good at toe an' heel, but dey jes' nothin' to me. Kick up de dust an' be happy."

But one night—never to be forgotten by the heroes of the "Crucible"—Jack came forward and volunteered to dance, and a ring was made by the men, who grinned at each other hugely, as if they expected some fun.

"Tink I fiddle for you?" asked Crikey, after a long indignant stare.

"I didn't tink, I know it," replied Jack, firmly; then, in an undertone, "why make dam extrabishum ob our feelin's, I'm a-goin' to gib de toe an' heel corker."

"All right, Jacky," returned Crikey, "dat a sight I hab not seen for long time. I know de tune. Ready am you?"

"Right it am, Crikey."

The "toe-and-heel corker," as Jack called it, proved a wondrous and overwhelming success, and any description that we might attempt to give of it would but faintly depict the extraordinary performance of that extraordinary nigger.

Jack twirled on his toes, on his heels, and upon another portion of his frame more adapted to a chair; he leaped, sprang, and swung his arms in the air, occasionally twirling a summersault in the most approved fashion.

Sometimes he subsided into what now-a-days would be called a " walk round," but at the time of our story was called " the refresher;" and then as he strutted round the circle he would defy competition in fitful gasps.

" Do dat—some—ob—you—where— ole Duncan—let him stan' ferrard—yah— golly—here we go !"

And on he went, until exhausted nature could hold out no longer, and then he sank exhausted upon the turf, amidst uproarious applause.

Harold remained during this scene apparently absorbed in it; but his thoughts soon travelled far away, first to Clara, then to the land to which he knew his enemy had been borne.

He had made many inquiries respecting it of the men, and although several had heard of it, the little information they could give was vague. " It was somewhere on the borders of Brazil," or " It laid southward," and some said it was only a bogey to frighten away people.

But the dying words of Hatchett were all-sufficient evidence. Mason Wantlake was a slave, but where ? Our hero, had he known, would have tramped a thousand miles to wring the confession he wanted from his heart.

And while the stars looked down upon the midnight mirth of the little camp upon the cliff, three figures are stealing down the hill-side from the fatal mine, leaving behind them four men stiff and stark in the huts, whom they fell upon in their sleep, and crushed out their lives, as if they were wild beasts.

Even Cecil Warren had forgotten his sentiments of mercy.

The sight he had seen in the mine had hardened his heart, and he said within himself,—

" Why should we spare these men— these monsters ?" and when his turn came, he slew them without compunction.

Mason would have fired the huts, but Cecil said,—

" Shall we give Don Tralu a warning beacon. No; rather let us steal down upon them quietly. It is our only chance of crushing the hornet's nest, and escape with our lives."

They reached the foot of the slope before dawn, and lay all day beneath the shade of a group of trees, waiting for night and vengeance.

While lying there, the young fellow they had saved told them something of his history, and the events that had brought him to the sore straight they found him in.

" My name is Richard Thorn," he said, and having a liking for the sea, I persuaded my father to get me a ship. He was not rich or influential enough to obtain a berth in the navy, but he had a friend connected with the merchant service, and I was put on board the " Bulldog," a fair sized brig, trading to Havannah. I had not been long on board ere I found out the demon I had for a captain; he was a brute—ate, talked, and dressed coarse, and his lust and rapacity were unbounded. We had one passenger on board—a poor girl going out to join a married sister, and I need not say that she suffered from the persecutions of the wretch, until I could no longer control my rage, and one day I forgot our relative positions and struck him down. I was put in irons, and for a month confined in a rat-hole of a place. We touched at some place—I know not its name—where I was taken out by a gang of Spaniards when the crew were ashore, on pretence of being tried, and brought here. I would I knew the fate of that girl."

" I can tell you," rejoined Wantlake, gloomily ; " the ' Bulldog ' fell in with a pirate, and she was found to be without a captain. The pirate was curious, and inquired the cause. The men said that it was folly to lie—they had hung him at the fore-yard arm. Again the pirate was curious, and asked them why ; and one old man came forward, and said he had persecuted a girl until she had thrown herself into the sea; but they rescued her, and, acting upon the impulses of their hearts, they obeyed a prayer she made, to turn her adrift, and let her take her chance upon the wide ocean, they put some provisions and water in a boat, and one quiet night set her free "

" And why did they hang him ?" asked Cecil.

WILL STEADFAST'S DREAM.

"Because he was supposed to have murdered our friend here, who was a bit of a favourite with the men, and when they got to sea, took the law into their own hands. The pirate was rather touched by the story, and spared their lives—a strange act of mercy, considering the brute he was then."

Dick Thorn, who had been pulling up the weeds around him in a mechanical manner, like one in deep thought, looked up suddenly and said,—

"What became of Lucy?"

"Who?"

"Lucy—the poor girl sent adrift?"

"Goodness knows; it's impossible to say; the ocean is wide, my lad; but she may have escaped," added Mason, quickly, seeing tears fill into the boy's eyes.

"It was better than being at the mercy of that brute," sighed poor Dick, "but bad and sorrowful to the best."

"Patience and hope," muttered Cecil.

"I have had it," sighed the youth, "or I should not be alive now. You have no idea of the horror of the life yonder"—he pointed towards the mine—"how should you, for what are a few hours beneath its gloom to days, months, and for aught I know, years ? No day or night ; no changing of the fiery light of the sun to the pale soft light of the moon—no stars, no sky —no trees, flowers, or air alive with the song of birds, but one long, lingering everlasting cold and gloom. Oh, how I have suffered, and what sufferings I have seen ! Men who beat their heads against the stone wall, as if they sought to dash out an enemy's brains. One man imploring me to hack out his life with the pick I carried, another deliberately strangled himself, and one went mad."

"Fearful !" murmured his listeners.

"And then we had fevers and agues; these I had," continued Dick. "Oh, the awful horror of that time. The sun was darkened, and seemed to suffer some mysterious eclipse; then came the noise of battle, and hurrying to and fro of figures unseen—the cries of innumerable fugitives, but whether fiends or angels I could not tell ; then the dark cavern was full of human faces, all in pain, such as one might fear to meet at the gate of Hades ; all this and much more, repeated again and again, with shrieks and groans, and sighs, such as would be uttered when sorrowing spirits part for ever. Such is a fever in the mine, and the awakening has its horrors, too ; to awake, not to the light of day and kind loving friends, but to the scowling faces of cruel masters, and to the soul-depressing, awful, indescribable gloom of the bowels of the mountain. Let us, if attacked by numbers, die like men, but never return to that awful place."

"Never !" cried Cecil.

"Never !" echoed Wantlake.

CHAPTER LIV.

THE GOLD TRAIN.—DEATH OF THE MULE-
TEER.

DAY and night a watch was kept by the inmates of the little camp upon the cliff, but the sea remained clear, and there was no sign of life upon land.

Will Steadfast was the first to feel the monotony of the island. He made several excursions by himself, and on one occasion when he returned he vowed that he had seen a beautiful Indian maiden wading across an inlet from the sea.

This assertion, however true it might have been, was not credited by the rest, and although Will kept steadfastly to his yarn, his companions only laughed at him and vowed he had been dreaming.

This served them with some amusement for a time, but not for long.

The living grew monotonous, and the adventurous spirits chafed beneath the bodies, longing for a change of every description, no matter if accompanied with great peril, rather than passing away the time lounging beneath the hot sky by day and the stars by night.

Harold saw this, and, fearing to ruin the spirit of his men, organised a hunting party composed of himself, Will Steadfast, and Tom Furnace (we keep to the old names), Monkey Jack, Crikey, and about a score of the seamen.

The rest remained behind under the command of Mr. Stanchion, in charge of the camp and the "Crucible."

"We shall be absent about a week," said our hero to his lieutenant ; "should a tide serve meanwhile, get the 'Crucible' off and wait for us."

"Ay, ay, sir ; you return in a week ?"

"At the outside ; we shall not go far into the country, as we may find hostile tribes ; in seven days from this expect us."

The little band went forth cheered by the greater portion left behind, who envied their comrades' good luck, and were but little pleased with the promise of another week's inactive life.

Harold struck straight across a wood, cutting off a corner, with the object of reaching a plain he had often observed lying on the horizon, where he hoped to find buffaloes and other animals, to give them a day or two's hunting.

"The only thing we lack," he said to Will, "is horses; we are armed sufficiently, but I fear, without steeds, we shall make but poor sport."

"No horses wanted, sar," interposed Jack. "I show you great sport, sar, if we come across any ob dem bufflers."

"You have hunted before ?"

"In my native country, sar, I jes' about one ob de best ; I take buffler by de horns an' put him on him back."

"And I, sar, trow him clean ober my head."

It was Crikey who made this astounding vaunt, and he would probably have proceeded still further to use the long-bow but for Jack, who pushed him back, and said—

"What you mean, you dam Crikey, obtrudin' yourself 'mong de 'stocracy ?

o behind, sar, and look arter the cookin' peraters."

"No, no," interposed Will, "Crikey is y body-guard, let him be, Jack."

"Yes, let him be," responded Tom.

"He not wordy ob de post," growled ack.

"When I make dat will I ain't," said rikey, showing the whites of his eyes, but since dat I turn ober a new leaf. 'm jes' about a 'pentant sinner, dat I am."

Jack growled again, but he had no 1ore to say, and strode on beside his captain, who, although he said not a word, ras, judging by the twinkling of his eyes, ighly amused.

And thus Crikey became the body-guard f the young middies, and in that capacity ie was happy, with one drawback, he did 1ot consider his rough neck shirt and ailor's trousers fitting attire for the post, specially as Jack was so gorgeously appaelled, but he concealed his feelings, and ransacked his brain day and night to find a substitute.

"I lef' my chess behind," he muttered, more than once, "or dat white hat would be somewhar tharabouts, wid a yallar hank'chief round dis neck ob mine, but it no use tinkin' ob dem orn'ments now."

Harold found the stretch of wood greater than he expected, and night fell while they were still apparently in the heart of it, so he camped in the midst of a grove of huge trees, whose umbrageous foliage hid the sky from view.

Then, more for the sake of light than warmth, a huge fire was ignited, and the men lay around, spinning yarns and singing songs far into the night, while, a hundred yards away, the sentries slowly circled the camp.

The men had erected a rough tent for their officers, where Harold and the lads lay asleep, Crikey and Jack recumbent at the entrance, unwillingly thrown into each other's society for the night.

For an hour they both remained silent, but the agony they suffered no words can tell, for a nigger's tongue is like quicksilver, and must keep moving. At first they sat back to back, but gradually, like two mechanical figures, they worked round until their eyes met, their mouths opened, and they sat grinning at each other like a pair of Chinese mandarins.

"A lubly night, Jacky."

"Jes' so, Crikey—yah!"

"How you find yourself, Crikey?"

"S'lubrious, Crikey."

"You feel sleepy, Jack?"

"Debil a bit."

"No more do dis chile. How shall we pass de time? Hab a game ob snick?"

Snick is a negro game, somewhat similar to a rustic game called "morrice," a very rude form of draughts, and Jack, anxious to while away the time, readily consented. Crikey marked a piece of ground into squares, cut a certain number of short sticks, raked out a corresponding number of stones, and, by the light of the fire, the game began.

At first they played for a trifling coin, but Crikey's skill proving superior, the stakes were increased, but the luck remained the same, and the last piece of silver went over to Jack's brother.

Crikey then urged him to desist, but the demon of play had got hold of Jack, and he insisted upon risking certain little valuables, such as a pocket knife, a silk handkerchief, and so on; but through that night "snick" befriended Crikey, and by the morning's dawn a change had taken place in the brothers.

Jack had lost everything, even the cocked hat and laced coat of which he had been so proud, and while Crikey strutted to and fro in his unwonted attire, he, Jack, presented himself before his captain in the rough check shirt and nether garments of his brother.

"What now, Jack? Where are your clothes?"

"I lose dem all, sar, wid Crikey, at de game ob snick."

"You have been foolish, Jack," said Harold, with a smile, "but take warning by the lesson and gamble no more. It is the vice of idiots. But so-called wiser and better men than you have staked their all on the cast of a die, and lost it."

After a frugal meal, the little band proceeded on its way; not a little edified by the airs Crikey gave himself, under his unexpected prosperity, and although Jack carried his head erect, they saw that he grieved for the loss of his treasures, as the Arab mourns the loss of his steed.

But Jack, in the midst of sorrow, did not forget duty, and they had not proceeded a couple of miles on the way, when he suddenly asked the captain to call a halt.

"I hear somet'ing, sar," he said, and Harold bade the men keep still.

Jack remained motionless for a few moments, then asked Crikey if he heard anything.

"I hear de tinklin' ob bells," replied Crikey, promptly.

"Dat de sound," replied Jack, nodding his head approvingly, "you hear it, sar?"

Harold did not, nor any other of the white men, and Jack drew himself up proudly.

"Nigger can," he said, "hear eberyt'ing, we near de plain, and across dat dere am a gold train goin'."

A gold train? the words ran through the men like an electrical shock, even Harold was excited, and having ascertained from Jack the direction of the sound, he led them quickly on.

The plain was more than a mile away, and as they did not come upon it at once some of the men thought Jack had been mistaken, but he persisted, and at length it burst upon their view, and there some hundred yards out a long train of mules, with drivers to each, was approaching.

"Dem all laden," said Jack, eagerly, "see how de mule loll him tongue, tired wid de work, all gold from de Spanish mines."

"And all lawful property to capture," thought Harold: "now, men, steady; when that train is within fifty yards of us, I will advance and order the men to surrender; if they refuse, out upon them and shoot the Spanish dogs."

The Spaniards numbered about thirty in all, and appeared to be well armed, for each carried a pair of revolvers in his sash, besides various stilettoes, and a musket in his hand.

Smoking and gaily singing, they came within the distance named by our hero, unsuspecting danger.

"Halt!" cried Harold, in Spanish, advancing from the shelter of the wood, "lay down your arms and surrender."

In a moment, all was confusion; the men ran to and fro, some hiding behind the mules, others firing wildly in the air, startled by the apparition of our masked hero.

"Surrender," cried our hero again, but the Spaniards, partly recovered from their panic, answered with another ill-aimed volley.

"Forward!" shouted Harold.

And his band burst from the wood. Only for an instant did the Spaniards make a stand.

Just long enough to receive one volley in return, which laid four of their men low, and then they turned tail, and, springing upon the backs of their steeds, galloped across the plain, leaving the long string of mules at the mercy of the strangers.

Of the four who fell, three died outright, the fourth was writhing on the plain as Harold went up to examine his hurts.

"Diablo! let me be, signor," growled the man. "I've got my ticket for the next world. Have you a priest among you?"

"We have not," replied Harold.

"Then let me die in peace; or, if there is a true son among you, give me some water."

"We are all true sons," said Harold, kneeling down and tendering him some water.

The man drank with avidity, and then lying back, coolly watched the sailors as they quickly unloaded the mules.

"You've a rich booty there, my masked friend," he said.

"From whence came it?"

"From the mines down by the Corderillas."

"And whose was it?"

"It belongs to many," said the Spaniard, wearily, "but I am the servant of Don Tralu, and yon mule, with the white star upon its forehead, carried his share. Ah, the Don works his mine cheap."

"With slaves?"

"Ah, signor, white slaves. I can tell the secret now—it hath lain heavily on my soul for many a year. The Don trades in them, and they have made him rich."

"And where lives this monster?"

"Follow the sun," replied the muleteer, "and it shall bring you to a mountain, with a cleft in the top, as if a giant had rent it with his axe; on the east side of that lies the valley where Don Tralu and his mine shall be found. More water, senor."

"Who are the victims of this wretch?" asked Harold, taking a cup from the hand of Will. The muleteer drank ere he replied, and then the words came slowly—for he was sinking fast.

"It mattered little who they were," he said; "all fish that—came—to the Don's

—net. The last—was a pirate—he deserved no pity."

"And his name!" eagerly asked our hero, bending down to catch the voice of the dying man.

He moved his lips, and faint as the far-off murmur of a brook—came the one word "Wantlake," and then, after a brief spasm, as if he would have leaped to his feet, the muleteer fell back and died.

CHAPTER LV.

THE ROAD TO THE RENT MOUNTAIN.—A BARGAIN BETWEEN JACK AND CRIKEY.

THEY buried the muleteer and his comrades; and then search was made for those who had so precipitately fled, but none of those valiant gentry were in sight; and finally, the treasure they had captured was buried.

"We cannot take it with us," said Harold; "but we can hide it so that we may find it on our return—the mules will be useful."

When it was done, he called the men together, and told them that he should not be able to return to the camp in a week as promised; for he had a mission to fulfil—many days' journey from them; but he left it to them whether to follow him or not.

"I go for my own sake alone," he said, "to get the one connecting link required to restore my honour; say, will you go with me or shall I go alone?"

A great shout from strong lungs was the answer, and every man addressed felt that the captain's honour was his, and worthy of any amount of toil to restore.

"We will follow you to the end," said they, with a shout, and two tears, that did not disgrace his manhood, rolled down Harold's cheek.

"Thank you, my friends," was all he could say, and then he bade Will Steadfast see to the arrangements for their further progress.

All the utensils and extra luggage, hitherto carried upon the shoulders of the men, were transferred to the backs of the mules, and even then there were many animals at liberty, to carry live burdens, if required.

The sailors were therefore told off into squads, each to take its turn at riding and walking, and it was a sight to see the equestrian performances of the sons of the ocean.

They rode in every position—straight out as a soldier's, legs curled up like a French chasseur; on the shoulder, on the back, behind like a sandboy, but through it all, they clung like leeches, and kept on.

All thought of sporting was abandoned now.

Away to the mountains with the cleft, like the work of a giant's hatchet, was the sole thought of Harold, and as they crossed that plain, drove after drove of buffaloes were passed, and only two slain for culinary purposes.

On the evening of the third day the plain came to an end, and they reached a vast forest, stretching right and left, as far as they could see, and by its gloomy outskirts the cavalcade halted.

"The sun sets behind it," said Harold, "but who shall follow even his refulgence beneath the shade of these vast trees?"

"How black and solemn it seems," said Will.

"It might be the forest of the dead," added Tom.

"Be it what it may we must cross it," returned our hero, "but to-night we rest here."

The sun in the morning shone upon the forest, and gave it a brighter appearance; its gloom had been enhanced the night before by the golden orb setting behind it, and they entered it with hopeful hearts.

"Dis a great big forest," said Jack, as they entered, "de biggest eber I been in since I left ole Africa."

"What signs do you go by?" asked Harold.

"No signs," returned Jack, "but I feel him here, sar."

Jack meant that some unfathomable instinct warned him, but he had never been to school, and his vocabulary was limited.

Away into the gloomy depths of a forest, unknown to our colder clime, our adventurers went, leaving no guide by which to retrace their steps but a tree notched here and there. They left the chattering birds on the borders, and as they penetrated deeper and deeper they felt they were diving into one of those awful places where nature seems absolutely silent.

The trees there, sheltered by the surrounding wood, neither rustled nor moved, each leaf hung listless in the dim twilight made by the massive foliage. The hot sun might have left the sphere for aught they could feel of it, the blue sky might have been wiped out of creation for aught their eyes could see.

Once they heard a wild shriek, as if some animal had fallen a prey to another of greater strength, but none could say what it was; even Jack was at fault, and Crikey only brought contumely on his head by suggesting it might be "a nippy poramus;" so on, on they went, with Jack at the head, trusting to his native instinct to lead them "with the sun."

They halted about noon, and, by the captain's directions, several skins carried by the mules were got ready to fill with water.

"At the first spring we come to," he said, "we will fill them. Who knows how much we may need them in such a place as this?"

Up sprang Crikey, who volunteered to go back a short way where he had seen the cool liquid bubbling from the earth as they came along, and Will Steadfast, who hated to be idle, volunteered, or rather insisted upon going with him.

"It's not far," he whispered to Harold, "and to lie still in this vast solitude gives me—I know not how or why—gives me the heartache."

And the two went, promising to return in half an hour at the outside, Harold warning them to note the peculiarities of the trees on their route, for a single wrong turn might be fatal.

Crikey carried the skins, and Will, hatchet in hand, cut a few extra notches on their route.

Crikey came to the point where he had marked the spring.

It lay in a small hollow, about fifty yards from their route, and was barely visible even to the keen eye of the negro; but, as before, he quickly discerned it, and pointed it out with a shout of joy to the middy.

"Dere him are," he cried, "a bubbling out ob de earth, jest as if him say— 'Come an' lick me. I jes' de sort ob t'ing to stop your thirst,' dat what him say to me."

"You are undoubtedly a poet," rejoined Will, laughing. "Fill the skins, Crikey; I will remain in the highway, we shall not miss our route then."

Crikey grinned assent, and went dow into the hollow, singing.

His first care was to wash and rinse th skins well, and while thus occupied Wil sat down upon the turf, idly watching him

While yet the task of Crikey was scarc begun a grim array of savages stole fortl from the trees behind Will, and silent as th Grim Destroyer fell upon him and held hin fast.

No chance of struggling, no time to cry for help, he was gagged and borne away with scarce a trace of the violence that had been done left on the mossy turf.

Stunned and prostrated by the unfore-seen calamity Will felt incapable of thought, his brain whirled round, and closing his eyes he lay back to recall his scattered senses.

When he opened them again he found himself surrounded by the gaunt savages, who moved onward as clouds float about the sky, without a sound, and as he looked at their remorseless, hideous faces, his heart sank within him.

"What is my fate now?" he muttered and feeling resistance useless he calmly awaited it.

After a time they released his feet, and by signs intimated that he must walk with them. His arms were still bound, he could not disobey, and with a heavy fore-boding in his breast he obeyed the signs, and plunged with his savage captors deeper into the forest.

Meanwhile Crikey, unconscious of his loss, filled the skins, and slinging them across his brawny shoulders, returned to the spot where he had left the middy.

"Dis berry good water, sar," he said, "like diamond, it taste better dan—eh! you not here, Massa Will, ha! I see, you hide up to frighten ole Crikey. I see you, sar."

And Crikey, putting on an immense cunning look, keenly glanced around; there was, of course, no sign of the boy.

"It berry good joke, Massa Will," he continued, "but the cap'en tell me to make haste; if you not come out, sar, I mus' go away alone."

He made a pretence of moving off, hoping to see Will emerge with a ringing laugh from some hidden place, but all re-mained as still as the depths of the Pyra-mids, then Crikey became alarmed.

"Massa Will, ole Crikey break him heart if him lose you."

No reply, and the negro fairly wept.

"What come to him?" he wailed, "ha! I know, dis 'chanted ground, an' some big giant fly up wid him in de air. Ho! Massa Will, dis break eberybody's heart. Massa Will, Massa Will, if you hide up, do come out, for ole Crikey am full ob sorrow."

Not a rustling leaf or broken twig responded to the darkey's call, and half mad between grief and terror, he sped back to the camp, and threw himself before the startled captain's feet.

"O, Massa Will—Massa Will!" he sobbed.

"What is the matter?" inquired Harold, sternly, "is he wounded?"

"No—no—sar."

"Have you lost him?"

"I no lose him, sar—I jes' stoop down to fill de skins; when I look up, him gone clean away. O, Massa Will!"

Tom Furnace, hearing the name of his friend uttered in such a tone, hurried forward, and the captain hurriedly informed him that something had happened—but what, he could not tell.

"Get up, man," he cried to Crikey, who was grovelling on the earth in abject sorrow, "and let me know what it is?"

"I berry soon make him speak," cried Jack, seizing his brother by the collar, and jerking him to his feet. "Now, you dam villain, speak up quick afore I choke you; where am Massa Will?"

"I tell de trufe," moaned Crikey; "I jes' stoop down to fill de skins, and when I get him I find him gone; first I tink him him hab a lark, but when I call him he not answer; den I 'plore him to speak, but him not come out, and den I come here."

"Something very strange in this," said Harold, pacing to and fro, "he must have strayed away. Jack, I must rely upon your instinct; come back with me, and you, Tom. Crikey, I shall want you also, to show me the precise spot where you left him."

CHAPTER LVI.

WE FOLLOW THE FORTUNES OF WILL STEADFAST.—MONKEY JACK EARNS THE REWARD.

THE four went back to the spot, and Crikey faithfully pointed out the exact spot where he had left the boy. As a bloodhound searches for scent, so Jack kneeled down and examined the ground.

"One, two, tree, four, dere a lot ob 'em, sar," he said, looking up at our hero, "and dey come upon him sudden, for dere hab been no struggle."

"Did they kill him?" asked Tom, hastily.

"Dere no signs ob it, no blood at all," replied Jack.

"Thank heaven."

"Go back to the camp, Jack," said Harold, " and bring up the men. We will all follow and either rescue him or know his fate."

Jack was not long bringing up the eager men, who with weapons prepared, were ready for anything, and fully resolved to rescue one of their heroes or avenge his death.

"What have you done with the mules?" asked Harold.

"Tethered them head to head, sir, replied one of the men; "they cannot stray."

"Good; Jack, get on, my lad."

As Jack prepared to obey, Crikey crept up to his side, and whispered in his ear— "You find the lilly Massa Will, Jack, and I gib you back you your hat and coat."

"Dat a true bargain," returned Jack, "and I find him as sure—as sure as you lost him."

A long delay had necessarily taken place, and when they started Will and his mysterious captors had been some two hours on their way, but the pursuers were swifter, having willing feet and no incumbrance, and rapidly gained ground.

Without a halt or turning for a moment aside, Jack, closely followed by Crikey, led them on through the depths of the vast silent forest, seeing what none but he saw, and following the signs with unerring instinct.

The pace was rapid, and at the end of two hours told upon them, and compelled a halt to be called.

"We gettin' nearer," said Jack, casting himself on the roots of a tree, "we halfway on them."

"Den yon earn 'arf de money," rejoined Crikey, "Jacky, take de hat."

Jack, with an eye kindling with admiration, put his regained treasure upon his head, and said—

"Crikey, you 'bout de only honest nigger dat I know; you are my brudder."

"How far are we from the wretches and poor Will?" asked Tom, sidling up to the two negroes.

"Massa Tom," replied Jack, "I tell you the trufe, dey good tree mile ahead."

"And night coming on," cried Tom, despairingly.

"No, for tree hours, Massa Tom, 'fore dat I cum up wid 'em. Dere's the cap'en rising, hark! for'ard agin, Massa Tom."

No delay now, all had got their second wind, and in determined silence the band sped upon the track.

Oh! the anxiety of those loving hearts, as they pictured a thousand awful things happening to their lost friend. What pictures of Indian cruelty, of devilish torture, uprose before their view, and spurred them on to increasing action.

Jack, of all the others, was confident of success. He had seen and recognised the footfall of Will, but he kept this much to himself for the present, rather than raise false hopes. Any moment might bring them in sight of a mangled corse, upon which the last devilish torture had been exercised, and that, after a hope of recovery, would give double pain.

And then, with hope and fear rising alternately in their breasts, the friends of Will Steadfast sped onward in their errand, while Will himself and his strange captors kept steadily on their way.

. . . .

We left Will Steadfast in the heart of the wood, in the power of his grim and silent captors, who maintained the terrible monotony of silence for several hours, the only sound uttered being an angry "Ugh!" as one of them trod upon a sleeping snake.

At length they halted for a few moments, and his arms were unbound.

Then the handkerchief was taken from his throat and passed round his eyes, and they once more moved on.

Not in a straight line, but hither and thither, as if to puzzle him.

And when at last the chief, in a loud voice, commanded them to halt, and the bandage was removed, Will felt certain that he was not, in reality, far from the spot where the bandage had been applied.

He expected, he hardly knew why, to to find himself in some strange place, surrounded by the horrible idols of savages and uncouth temples of their erection.

But he was disappointed: he was still in the forest, and not even a wigwam was in sight.

The chief then spoke to Will in a Spanish language he had acquired some years before, and perfected during talks with Harold Greystone.

"What brings my pale brother to our home?" he asked. "Is there not land enough where the sun rises that he must come hither?"

"We but seek to pass through the country," replied Will, firmly; "we have no war with you."

"So has said every pale-face," rejoined the chief, cunningly; "but he always lies. He comes and loves our land; then he brings his deadly fire-tube to destroy, and, when we are dead, he puts up his wigwam."

"Chief," said Will, "I assure you that you are mistaken; we are bound for a land far away from here."

"Your brothers will never reach it," replied the chief, coolly; "we come and go as the wind, and, as you have been stolen from your brothers, so we will take them, one by one, until none shall be left."

"You would not slay those who never harmed you," urged Will.

"We do," replied the chief; "our race knows no mercy. The Spaniards call us the 'Nameless Tribe,' for we have the blood of three races in our veins—the Ethiope, the Spaniard, and the Indian; we have the strength of one, and the cruelty and ferocity of the others; from us expect no mercy, and prepare to die."

"Let the blow be silent and swift, then," cried Will, between his set teeth; "do not add torture to the crime."

"It must be done according to our rites," was the reply. "My children will now lead you to the place of sacrifice."

Obeying a signal from his hand, several of the savages laid hold of Will, and, forcing him through a fringe of bushes, showed a hollow in the earth, bowl-shaped, about a hundred yards across, and, in the centre a rough sort of altar, made of unhewn rock, bearing the traces, as Will with a shudder perceived, of fire.

There the chief took up his stand, and his people, numbering about a hundred in all, slowly assembled to the sound of a chant, sung by those who had captured Will.

It was a dirge of death.

A strange wild wail of anguish it seemed to Will, and, awed by the fearful fate impending, his spirit for a moment flagged and he buried his face in his hands.

When he did this, the savages changed

their monotonous chant to a song of triumph, and this brought the boy to a sense of what was due from him.

He dashed the solitary tear from his eye, and drawing himself erect, cast an undaunted look upon his executioners.

The chief again used his hand, and a number of the savages sped into the wood; they quickly returned with roughly-bound faggots, and cast them by the altar.

"Pale-face," said the chief, "behold your fate—dost tremble now?"

"No!" replied Will, firmly, "you can but destroy my body—my spirit is beyond your reach."

"Madman and fool," said the chief, scornfully, "to talk of the spirit. Who has ever seen it?—who knows that it lives?"

"Every true heart," replied Will, firmly; "but spare your further words and do your work quickly."

"Are you tired of life?" asked the chief, with a grim smile—"have you no pleasure in the sunshine—no love for the green woods?"

"Do your work," was all Will said, and folding his arms he refused to speak again.

They taunted and reviled him, they danced before him, and snapped their fingers in derision in his face, and at last one old savage spat at the boy.

The next moment he lay grovelling on the earth, writhing under a well-planted blow delivered by the sturdy youth.

The savages saw their comrade fall, and uttering shouts of rage, ran at Will, clawing the air with their talon-like fingers.

He stood his ground, and sent the first two reeling; but it would have fared ill with him, but for the timely helping hand that was near.

A cheer responded to the shouts of the savages, a cheer Will had oft heard on board the "Crucible," and his heart leaped with joy, when his eyes were gladdened with the sight of Harold, Jack, and Crikey, followed by the gallant tars, who scattered the savages like chaff before the wind.

The pistol and cutlass did their work; but few escaped, and they fled shrieking into the wood, and crying to their senseless idols for help.

"In the nick of time, Will," said Harold, grasping the boy's hand.

"In another moment you might have found my remains—but not me," replied Will, faintly smiling; "but I never doubted you would save me."

"Thank Jack, not me," rejoined Harold; "his sagacity brought us to your rescue."

Will looked around for the sable hero, but he was at that moment behind some bushes changing attire with his brother.

"Now, you Crikey," he said, as soon as Will was saved, "you jes' take orf dem ere coat and trunks, and gib them back to de only chile as look well in 'em, an' dat's me, as sure as dere's a lumenary called de moon."

And Crikey, true to his word, resumed the check shirt and the unassuming pantaloons he had worn before.

"Such am de ups and downs ob dis ere life," he said; "one day a nigger swell about in cock hat an' lace coat, de next he got no hat or coat, an' only cubber him hunks wid an ole check shirt.

"Strange am de strife,
Ob dis ere life."

Sung Crikey as he followed Will and Harold on their return journey.

CHAPTER LVII.

THE END OF THE SPANIARD'S HOME.

WE left Dick Thorne, Cecil Warren, and and Mason Wantlake lying among the bushes waiting for the night, fully resolved to exercise their vengeance upon the Don, and put an end to his iniquitous establishment for ever.

"Nothing is too bad for them," said Dick, "for they make this paradise a hell with their wanton outrages upon their victims. Have you seen the senora?"

"I heard her voice," replied Mason.

"And I have seen her face," rejoined Dick, "the face of an angel. She is the daughter of Don Tralu. Strange that so fair a flower should spring from so coarse a tree."

"She must be spared," said Cecil.

"I would not harm a hair of her head, returned Dick; "a fair vision was her face to me."

"Poor Lucy," said Cecil, with a sly look.

"Nothing of the sort." smiled Dick. "Lucy is part and parcel of my nature, the senora was a beautiful vision—a picture I admired and revereneed, nothing more."

"Did you see much of her?"

"I will tell you," replied Dick. "It wants yet an hour to dark, and my narrative will pass away the time.

"I was not always in a mine; when they brought me here, I was stationed to watch against the prowling of wild beasts, for the Don had many rich herds of cattle.

"My watch hut was on the outskirts of the Don's garden, in which during the day-time I was free to roam.

"I cannot recollect how long I led this life. Time slipped away, the seasons varied very little, save for about two months of winter, and then spring came with a suddenness that left me to doubt that the winter had really passed.

"I employed my leisure time in the garden, in weeding the flower beds, cleaning the walks, and tending the grass plots that had been long neglected.

"This occupation made me sometimes forget that I was a slave; indeed, sometimes I even felt happy in the paradise in which I was Adam, and sighed for nothing but companionship.

"Don Tralu's daughter very seldom walked in the garden, nor did she appear even then to see the changes I had wrought in it.

"I would have given anything to have spoken to this lovely girl, but then I was her slave, a dog in her eyes.

"I bethought me of writing a humble epistle, setting forth my utter solitude, but I feared the consequences, and again, where were writing materials to come from?

"My next device was to place a small bouquet of flowers in a bower, in which la senora would be sure to pass during her walk.

"I returned about two hours afterwards, and saw, to my intense joy, that the bouquet was gone. I could have cried for very joy, and then the thought came that some servant might have passed the spot and purloined it; or even should la senora have received it, she would probably be ignorant of the donor.

"While I thus stood ruminating I heard a light footstep on the path behind me, and turning my head I saw la senora a few paces from me.

"She carried my bouquet, and smiled as she approached me.

"'I am indebted to you for these flowers,' she said, speaking the Spanish language; 'am I not?'

"I stammered out some reply in the affirmative. I could not speak, for at the sound of her gentle voice long dried up sources of emotion opened out afresh, and my eyes filled with tears.

"'You are an Englishman,' she said, after a pause, and adding in a tone of pity, 'and a slave.'

"I bowed my head, and remained silent; indeed, I dare not trust myself to look at her face.

"'Listen to me,' she said; 'they would punish you severely, if it were known that you had spoken to me, or presented these flowers.'

"'I am aware of that, senora,' I replied, 'and yet I could bear the punishment twice over for your sake.'

"She turned, and walking a little way up the pathway, glanced about as if to see that no one was about, and then returning, said—

"'Think not of me, but yourself. You are an Englishman; one of that nation whose people abhor the very name of slavery. Do you wish to escape from hence?'

"'Do I wish!' I cried, falling on my knees. 'Oh! senora—'

"'Silence,' she said. 'Listen, but do not speak. I will this night provide you with the means of escaping from your horrible life. You will find a mustang, a musket, some ammunition, and a map. Ride for the mountains. You may be overtaken, but sell your life dearly, for if you are taken, a fate more horrible than the worst of deaths awaits you; but, above all, do not betray me.'

"'I swear it,' I cried passionately.

"'I am satisfied,' she said, touching my hand; 'and now I must leave you. You will never see me again; but should you ever again see your country, think sometimes of me.'

My eyes became blinded with tears of gratitude.

I was about to speak, when I was prevented by an exclamation of terror from la senora, and to my horror I heard the voice of our overseer.

"La senora fled, and before I could rise, the overseer seized me by the throat, and bore me to the ground.

"He let go my throat, and rising to his feet, seized the heavy whip.

"The lash curled in the air, and fell across my face.

"It was like the sting of a serpent; and maddened by pain and rage, I rose to my feet, and was about to rush upon the fiend in human guise, but the next instant was pinioned behind, and again hurled to the ground.

"I was bound, and for several days closely watched, each day receiving a number of lashes from our brutal overseer.

"A few days after I heard my fate; I was to be sent to the mines, and for daring to address la senora, the daughter of Don Tralu."

The shades of night were deepening fast as Dick Thorne concluded, and, rising to his feet he said—

"The hour has come. I am no longer weak; let us go forward and settle this hornets' nest."

Silently they trod the springy turf between the trees, heedless of the thousand fireflies, illuminating the dark branches above their heads, heedless of the stars peeping through the foliage, of the moon rising in wondrous glory, heedless of all except their object, to destroy the home of the villanous Don.

Presently they came to the borders of the flower garden, with its fountains and its gorgeous masses of bloom, and there before them was the house, lit up, and the sound of music floating in the air.

The dusky forms of the friends, crawling all fours, approached the house.

Keeping carefully in the shade, they peeped through the intersections of the bamboo walls, and saw that their time was come.

The Don and about half-a-dozen other Spaniards were seated together, smoking, while the senora, lounging voluptuously on a pile of cushions, played and sang.

"She is beautiful," muttered Mason, "and must be spared. Cecil, to work."

Their plan was this: the house had but two entrances, and the only windows were too high from the ground for a leap, while any other loophole offered escape; our friends, therefore, designed to block up one of the outlets with brushwood, fire it, and wait at the other for the treacherous Don and his friends.

"The bamboo will burn quickly," said Mason; "and the Spanish curs, rushing out in mad affright, will be at our mercy. Slay them as you would wild beasts."

Something of his old passionate nature had returned to him, and as he drew a pistol from his belt and loosened the long, keen knife from its sheath, Cecil Warren thought with a shudder, of what crimes such a nature, when fully aroused could be capable.

But this was no time to stay his hand.

Don Tralu was unworthy of mercy, and he obeyed the commands of Wantlake, his leader for the time.

Brushwood, dried thoroughly by the sun, they found in great quantities, and piled up quickly a mass before one of the outlets.

Mason, with an old tinder-box brought from the mine, then knelt down and ignited the material.

This done, the three young fellows took up their stand opposite the other door, and waited patiently for the issue.

It quickly came, first a little wreath of smoke, then a volume, a flash of flame, and a shriek—

"Fire!"

Forth from the house came the cowardly Spaniards, leaving the senora to her fate; the first fell by the hand of Dick Thorne, but the others, quickly perceiving their danger, drew their rapiers, and an indiscriminate fight ensued.

Mason Wantlake wrenched the weapon from the side of the slain Spaniard, and furious with rage, lunged here and there like a madman.

The Spaniards had no chance; they were not prepared for this onslaught, and all were slain except Don Tralu, who lay upon the turf, stunned with a blow from the butt-end of a pistol.

It was only then that our friends became conscious of the presence of the senora, who, kneeling down by the fire-illumined doorway, was gazing at them, her large dark eyes distended with horror.

"Who and what are you?" she cried, as Mason approached her.

"A friend to you, lady, but a foe to such men as these," he replied.

"But why have you murdered them?" she urged.

"Senora," rejoined Wantlake, "we had wrongs to avenge, future sufferings of others to prevent. We were the slaves of Don Tralu—we are the destroyers of his ill-gotten home; now, lady, he lies there; he is your father, he is not slain."

She buried her face in her hands, and for a time made no reply.

The fire raged furiously, and many thousand sparks were floating around, some falling on the kneeling lady.

"Senora," he said, gently, "you are in danger; come further away"

She pressed back the dark locks from her face, and looked at him as if she did not comprehend him.

"Come away," he said, again.

"No, no," she replied, shrinking back with a shudder, "I know you not—I cannot—dare not trust you—my home is here."

At that moment her eyes for the first time fell upon her father, and throwing herself upon his breast, she called him a thousand endearing names. Mason Wantlake and his friends stood by, looking on, strangely touched to find the rough man loved so well by that beauteous Spaniard.

Dick Thorne brought some water from the fountain and sprinkled it over his face. The Don opened his eyes and saw his daughter's face. Every hard line on his countenance faded out as he drew her tenderly to him.

"Amina, daughter of my heart," he murmured, and then catching sight of the conflagration, he rose upon his elbow with an angry look.

"Where are the knaves?—ha! but you shall not live in their power."

He felt hastily in his sash, but every weapon had been removed, and he sank back with a groan.

"Fear not," said Wantlake, "your daughter is safe. She has not wronged us."

The Spaniard again rose up and looked eagerly into Mason's face.

"Can an Englishman suffer so much wrong and forgive?" he asked.

"Is there not vengeance enough here?" replied Wantlake, pointing to the slain men and the blazing house.

"They were carrion," said the Don, contemptuously, "let them lie, for my home I care not. The shelter of the trees is enough for me if I have Amina by my side."

"Don Tralu," said Mason, "I came here to kill you; but, for your daughter's sake, I spare your life, thank her, and not me."

Amina, with a quick, graceful gesture, intimated that she thanked the speaker, but disclaimed the merit of saving her father's life.

"See here, Don," continued Wantlake, "those victims of your vile traffic. Think of the power they hold now; and how amply they could avenge the wrongs you have heaped upon them; but enough and more than enough has been done—of all who called this their home, you and your daughter alone still remain."

The Spaniard started, and gave one look towards the mine. Mason shook his head

"Not one alive there," he said; "taskmasters and slaves—all are dead."

"All?" groaned the Spaniard.

"All," was the reply, "and let the accursed spot rest—leave it at once and for ever."

"But how shall I, unarmed and with such a charge, find my way across this land?" urged the Spaniard.

"Come with us, if you can trust us" interposed Cecil.

Don Tralu looked from one to the other as if he would read their inmost hearts, and then he said,—

"I will go with you; Amina, my soul, we will trust them."

Amina turned her lustrous eyes upon the young men, and, touching Mason's arm gently, rejoined,—

"I will trust your friends, senor, but, above all, I trust you."

A thrill ran through the frame of her listener, and his head sank upon his breast, as he thought how little worthy he was of trust from man or woman.

"Senora," he said, "I do not deserve your trust."

"You are kind to me," she said, simply "and therefore I trust you."

They were silent after this, and the group stood watching the fire, as it quickly lapped the light structure, roaring and leaping, as if it rejoiced in the destruction.

"I never parted with aught more willingly," said the Don, as the flames sank into a heap of glowing ashes. "It was built from the proceeds of a vile traffic, and has had a fitting ending."

"And, with the dying ashes, let all perish that has gone before, and begin the world anew," said Mason.

That night they buried the dead Spaniards in the garden, among the sweetest flowers; and, at early dawn, the five companions, so strangely banded together, set forward towards the coast.

And, coming towards them is another band of faithful hearts, bound together by a love for the gallant Harold Greystone.

The time draws nigh when he will cast aside that mask, and show his face to the world once more.

"MASSA, I HAB KILLED HIM."

CHAPTER LVIII.

FOUND AT LAST.

For two days longer Harold and his followers journeyed through the vast forest, and then the monotony of trees and turf was broken, and they came upon a plain.

A sandy arid plain, flat as the surface of a table, and blank as a sheet of untouched paper.

Harold asked the men if the sight daunted them, and whether they would go on.

Their reply was "We will follow you."

The water-skins were filled, and the mules burdened with nuts, prickly pears, and other fruits growing in abundance on the borders of the forest.

They set forward in the cool of the evening, and walked throughout the night.

In the morning the rising sun revealed other travellers on the plain.

Five in all, four men and a woman, all gaunt and worn with fatigue, and struggling with tottering steps over the sandy soil.

When first seen they were about a mile away, but even at that distance their painful mode of travelling was apparent, starvation was their in gait, and Harold hastened forward to give them what assistance lay in his power.

As he drew near, he put a white handkerchief upon his sword, to show that they need not fear, for he perceived that they halted in perplexity, and evidently made arrangements for resistance in case of foes.

"Fear not," cried Harold, "we are friends."

One of the five, the tallest of all, shading his eyes with his hand, gazed earnestly at our hero, then, whispering a few words to one who stood near him, turned his back.

"We are friends," again cried Harold.

"Welcome," replied one; "we have need of them."

"Whence come you?"

"From the interior, and a weary journey it has been."

Harold was now close upon him, and the man who had turned his back suddenly wheeled round, and faced our hero.

"Good Heaven!—Mason Wantlake!"

"Aye, Harold, it is I," replied the wretched man; "strike at once, and avenge your wrongs, but strike deep."

"I cannot kill you thus," returned Harold; "I never murdered in cold blood; you wronged me much, but I will not be your executioner."

"Ever generous," murmured Mason; "of all I know most noble, can you forgive me?"

"Eat and drink now," replied Harold, "and we will talk of that anon."

When the cravings of nature were satisfied, Cecil Warren introduced Don Tralu and the senora, and Dick Thorne introduced himself to the middies and the rest, while Harold and Mason Wantlake walked apart.

"Hear me first," said the latter; "I wronged you much, Harold, under the influence of a mad passion, and I have done other deeds that Heaven alone can pardon; but I have suffered, oh, how bitterly, how terribly! such as I alone, or those, my young companions there, can tell."

"How have you suffered?"

"I have been a slave, Harold, and there stands the man who was once my master. It is true; we were all slaves, doomed to a life of perpetual darkness in the gold mines of the Spaniard. How we escaped, and why the Don is here, I will tell you another time; for the present, hear the truth, and judge me accordingly. I was on my way to make such restitution to you at I could, purposing then to retire into some lone spot, and yon Spaniard and his daughter—I love her, Harold, and she is to be my wife—and with them found a home."

"Then you have repented?" said Harold, looking at him keenly.

"Repented sorely," replied Wantlake; "and with it came the hope of a better life. Amina is to be my guiding star; she loves, why it would be difficult to tell, but her heart is with me, and together there is a bright and happy future before us if you will have it so. I have wronged you bitterly, and my life is in your hands, take it, if you will."

"I sought for justice, not revenge," replied Harold; "and now that you are truly sorry for the past, your words carry conviction with them—Heaven forbid that I should mar your happiness. I have but one thing to demand of you, and then go forth with my best wishes."

"Ask what you will," cried Wantlake, eagerly, "and I will obey."

"Then journey back with me to the 'Crucible,' replied Harold, "and there I will prepare a document of confession, which you, in the presence of witnesses, shall sign; that done, you may go, and God speed you."

Mason Wantlake's head sank upon his bosom.

He was overcome.

At length he raised his head, and held forth his hand.

"Harold, will you touch it?"

"With all my heart."

And then their hands touched for the first time with the grasp of friendship—the grip of him who forgave, and he who was forgiven.

Then followed a short series of explanations appertaining to matters with which our readers are already acquainted, and the whole party returned across the plain to the forest.

They camped on the borders for the night, Mason swinging a rude hammock for Amina, and lying beneath it, as a faithful dog would do to its master.

Will and Tom Furnace knew all, and they urged Harold to remove his mask.

"No," he said, "not here; it shall be removed in the presence of my accusers only. The time has not yet come."

"The lads found congenial companion-
ip in Cecil Warren and Dick Thorne,
ho seemed to have recovered from their
itigue by magic, and a merry party lay
own by the camp-fire that night.

Crikey and Jack were admitted to the
ircle, the latter again in full fig, and
rikey in his check shirt and canvas
rousers, happy as ever, and literally over-
lowing with songs such as only a nigger
ould compose.

It was very late when the two brothers
eft the circle, to seek a clump of bushes
rhich they had pitched upon as a desirable
lace of rest.

"Jacky," said Crikey, stretching out
iis huge frame," "do you t'ink ole Chloe
ive long?"

"What for you arx dat question, Crikey?"

"Acause she my lawful wife, Jacky,
in' de sooner she die de better for me?"

"You let Chloe alone, she tuf enuf to
live a shentry."

"Den I git a diworsk," said Crikey,
deliberately.

"What dat for?"

"Cawse I'm guin' to marry agiin."

Jack opened his eyes to their utmost
limits, and rising up, looked at his brother,
whose grinning face was discernible in the
light of the fire.

"You gone mad, sar; hab you rolled
off your chump, Crikey?"

"I am sane as any man," replied Crikey,
"but I'm goin' to marry ag'in."

"And who am de piccaninny dat you
fix your affections on?"

"De Spanish girl dat swinging in de
tree."

This astounding announcement floored
Jack for awhile, and he lay gazing at the
stars, twinkling through the latticed boughs,
utterly speechless.

"Jacky?"

Jack groaned.

"You hear me?"

"I hear you, sar; you gone mad."

"No, Jacky, I marry dat girl. Yah!
golly, in no time, double quick. She berry
fond ob me. I smile at her dis mornin',
she smile ag'in at me. I open my mouf
wide, she open hers, and show her pretty
teef. It all right, Jacky, she berry fond
ob me."

"Crikey," replied Jack, impressively,
"you all wrong; you allers wus wrong
wid de ladies, 'specially ole Chloe, from
de berry fust hour you marry dat sweet

creetur, you lib in de berry buzzum ob
flyin' crockery, an' de neighbours come to
see fight atween you as dey go to de fair.

"Why de reason ob dat, Crikey? I tell
you dis, you don't know de signs ob woman. If she frown, scratch, an' spit like
wild cat, she lub you dearly; but if she
smile, she mean to scratch you; and when
she open her lily mouf, she mean to bite;
so leave de Spanish lady alone."

Jack, having concluded this peroration
on the qualities of the fair sex, lay down
and fell asleep, leaving the powerfully-
impressed Crikey to think it over.

CHAPTER LIX.

THE "CRUCIBLE" AFLOAT.—MASON WANT-
LAKE CHOOSES A HOME.

MR. STANCHION, left with the remnant of
the crew, lost no time in preparing the
"Crucible" for the hour when she would
be again afloat.

He saw with pleasure that every suc-
ceeding tide was higher than the last, and
personally he examined the hull of the
vessel to see if she had any signs of a
leak, but so sound was the work that no
damage of a material character could he
find.

On the fourth day after the departure
of our hero, the tide washed round the
"Crucible," and rose against her side to
the height of three feet. She moved restlessly like a lion slightly aroused from its
slumbers; but the waters went down, and
left her recumbent on the sand.

The next tide she righted, everything
was ready, and at the proper moment, the
boats towed her into deep water, and anchored there.

What a shout they gave! but their labours did not end there, for Mr. Stanchion
was determined to get her beyond the line
of rocks while the tides ran high, and having found a narrow opening between two
coral reefs, the "Urucible" was piloted,
with the utmost care, outside the line of
danger.

"All that now is needed," he thought
"is our gallant captain, and he will be here
to-morrow."

But the day appointed came and passed,
and Harold did not return.

"He is engrossed with his hunting,"
thought Mr. Stanchion; "but he will come
to-morrow,"

The morrow brought no better luck,

the next day and the next the same, and the spirits of the men fell quickly.

"He has been set upon by some accursed tribe," they said, "and killed. If Mr. Stanchion will lead us on we will seek him."

"Patience," said the lieutenant, "we cannot leave the 'Crucible.' Besides, where should we go, and in what direction? If misfortune has befallen him, one or more of the men will surely return to tell the tale."

Patience they had for two more days, and still the land before them was clear, no footsteps save their own, or shouts of returning comrades broke the stillness.

Then the men grew sad indeed, and those on shore lay listlessly about the cliff, with no heart for song or story, wondering what mishap had befallen their beloved leader, and those on board the "Crucible" watched from the masthead night and day.

Added to this, a huge fire was kept burning throughout day and night as a beacon to the wanderers should they be uncertain of their route; but the watchers watched, and the fire burned in vain.

"Is this to be his fate?" thought the lieutenant; "after the life of a hero, to perish miserably in the heart of a strange land, to lie rotting in the forest or find an unknown grave, to be hoped and longed for, and leave no record of his fate? It is pitiful, terrible."

But our hero came back at last, as all heroes must and should do, came back with every soul safe, and five additional friends in his train.

They had lost their way in the vast forest, and wandered about for several days, but Jack's sagacity worked them out in the end.

" But for him," said Harold, as he shook hands with his lieutenant, "we might have wandered hither and thither until utterly worn out, and then, like a large family of fully-grown babes, laid down and died."

This was the first time Harold had ever uttered the semblance of a joke in the presence of Mr. Stanchion, and he looked at his leader in surprise.

"I can laugh and joke now," added Harold, "for my task is done. The sole link of the evidence required is here, and my honour is restored."

That night, in the presence of Don Tralu. Mr. Stanchion, Tom Furnace, Will Steadfast, and Cecil Warren, Mason Wantlake signed a full confession of his crime, and Harold filled a loving cup with wine, and bade all drink.

"With this," he said, "I wash away all that man ought to forget, where fully atoned for—the wrongs he has suffered. Mason, you are my comrade in arms again."

"I am more worthy of the name," said Mason, with a sad smile, "but I shall never fully deserve it."

"But you may live to be worthy of it," urged Harold, "come with me and I will assure your safety in the world."

"No—no," rejoined Mason, "henceforth my home is here. This coast will not be frequented by man for many, many years, and this long line of rocks will keep away intruders. Here I choose my home, with this dear one for my wife."

He drew Amina to his side, and she looked up lovingly into his face.

"You will not think the life lonely, dearest?" he said.

"I have always lived in solitude," she replied, simply; "now I shall have a father and a husband, what more can I desire?"

The answer was sufficient, and Harold gave them his best wishes.

"Marriages are made in Heaven," he said, "so runs the old saying, and yours will really be so."

"I shall be true and faithful," said Mason, with a smile, "in this great wilderness my wife need not fear to lose my love."

The next morning Don Tralu, his daughter, and Mason went ashore, and having selected a spot for the erection of a house, numbers of the sailors were set to work under the superintendence of Duncan, Jack's one time mortal foe.

Jack's services were also in requsition, for he told them how to build it so as to withstand the hurricane that came sometimes to the coast, and Crikey's services were not to be despised, for he chopped down young trees as if they were sugar canes, and performed other feats of work of a prodigious nature.

The mules our friends had with them during their wanderings were turned over to the settlers, and a row of huts erected for them in the rear of the main house, stores of various natures were put ashore, fire-arms, powder, lead, &c., and then when all was done, came the final adieu.

It was brief, but it came from the heart, and the "Crucible," unfolding her white wings, went over the sea in the evening sunlight, watched by three figures on the cliff, until hull, spars, and sails sunk below the ocean.

"Farewell," said Mason. "Farewell, dear Harold, in you I have lost what would have been the dearest friend of my life; but I must not mourn," he added, turning to Amina, "for I have still one great treasure left—my loving wife."

They returned to their home, and as they entered its rough but strong portal, the sun dipped suddenly below the waves, and darkness fell upon the scene.

CHAPTER LX.

THE FRATRICIDE.—MOURNING ON BOARD THE "CRUCIBLE."—A GHOST.

A GOOD ship, wind fair, and a cargo of light hearts, go far towards making life on shipboard a happy one, and truly a happier captain and crew than those on board the "Crucible" never flitted over the ocean.

The guns were cleaned and burnished for a future life of ease; the cutlasses of the crew hung over their hammocks; and the men between watch and watch sang and danced to the sound of Crikey's fiddle; while the captain, the heroic youthful leader, kept much to his cabin, and dreamt of happiness to come.

As if designing to help him homeward, the wind blew steadily towards his destination, Honour Bay, from whence Harold intended to sail with all his captures, and thus add glory to the redemption of his name.

"When I have truly restored my name," he said to Will, "the 'Crucible' is yours; it is, I think, a fitting recognition of your fidelity and friendship. Ah, Harry," he added, calling the youth by his real name, "what a strength it has been to me during the darkness of dishonour to have one true heart by me, who knew me and loved me well."

"I have but done my duty to a dear friend," said Harry (or Will, as the reader pleases), in a low tone; "you would have done as much for me."

After this neither spoke for a time, but sat looking out at the stern ports at the yellow moon rising from the sea, her broad face smiling encouragement to the young privateer.

"How beautiful she looks," he said, at length, "so calm, so graceful. Harry, stay here awhile, I am going on deck for a few moments."

Ascending the companion, he walked aft, and leaning over the taffrail, thought of the varied incidents of his young life; but little more than a youth, he had gone through the varied incidents of an existence that would have done credit to a man grown grey—all ending, as Providence willed it, so happily.

While musing thus, he heard the voices of the two negroes, Jack and Crikey, growing loud in some dispute, but he heeded them but little, and his roaming fancy travelled on until a cry—half scream, half yell—arose from the lips of Jack.

"What's the matter?" he demanded, hastily.

"O, massa Cap'n," cried Jack, running forward and throwing himself upon his knees, "I murder my brudder."

Harold started, and ran his eye rapidly along the deck—Crikey was not to be seen.

"Him overboard, sar," groaned Jack, and grovelled on the ground in an ecstacy of repentance.

Harold at once gave orders for the "Crucible" to heave to, and a boat was lowered. Crikey was known to be a fair swimmer, and the men pulled about in all directions, calling him aloud by name.

No answer came; and it was not until two hours had expired, that the boat was hauled up, and the good ship pursued its way, all on board convinced that Crikey was lost to them for ever.

A sorrowing crew now, and Jack on parole, below with his captain, blubbering in the most violent manner.

"Now, Jack," said Harold, sternly, "tell me how it happened."

"How him happen, sar?"

"Yes, give me the truth."

"I will, sar; Crikey and I am brudders, and in consequench we quarrel, brudders allers do. Dis night I come on deck wid my heart full ob lub for him, and I see him walking the deck in a muddletative manner, sar, so I say to him, 'Dat you, Crikey?' an' him say 'Dat you Jacky?' after de manner ob salooting dat all true niggers do."

"Come to the great point, Jack."

"Comin' I am, sar; den I say to

Crikey, 'What am you t'inkin' ob jes' now?' He says, 'I t'ink ob de lubliest woman out, ole Chloe.' Den I rise up tif, an' I say, 'Crikey, don't you t'ink nuffin' ob dat woman, she ain't worf it.' No more she am, sar, for the moment she got married to Crikey she drag him out ob church by de wool acause him sneeze jes' as the parson say 'Amen.' "

"But about this unfortunate affair, Jack?"

"I am goin' on, sar; when I say dat Chloe ain't worf t'inkin' of, Crikey, a sittin' on de bulwark, an' look at me like tiger. 'Jack,' him say, 'don't you 'sult the wife ob my buzzum, she worf ten ob you.' Den my dander rise, an' I say, 'She ain't.' He say, 'She is worf' ten hunder t'ousand ob you.' I say, 'She am a trumpet.' He say, 'You tell big lie,' an' I hit him jes' whar de trowsers leave orf and de shirt begins, and ober he roll into de sea."

"Did you see him sink?"

"No, sar; I not look ober de side at all. I come straight to you, sar, an' 'fess my crime."

"Can Crikey swim?"

"Him jes' aboot lib in de water if dey bring him food."

"Did you hear a splash?"

"No, sar, him went quietly ober de side, where dam shark no doubt wait for him, and swallow him like pill."

"Jack," said our hero, gravely, "to strike a brother was a great crime; but to murder him was infamous."

"I neber t'ink to kill him," moaned Jack, "I jes' gib him one lilly blow in him stomach, and him trow up him long legs and go ober."

"To all intents and purposes you are a murderer," rejoined Harold, with a glitter in his eyes that might have represented either mirth or sorrow; "go to your cabin now, and wait for the sentence I may pass upon you. I must consider whether you are worthy of remaining on board the 'Crucible.' "

"Massa cap'in," cried Jack, wildly, "don't send me away—I lib an' die like a dog for ye—don't send me away, sar."

"Think of your crime, Jack!"

"I no t'ink to do him, sar."

"What will you say to the men?"

"Dey know I lub my brudder, sar."

"Ah! but they know how your love ended."

"I not kill him—it all a dream," cried Jack, tearing his hair. "Oh! I gib my life to bring him back. It all dam Chloe —she allers in de mischief."

"Go to your cabin, Jack," said Harold: "I will send for you presently."

Jack, weeping and wailing, crept deck and made his way forward. passed Will and Tom on the way, strange to say, looked very merry, neither spoke to him.

"I not mean to do it, Massa Tom and Will," groaned Jack, shaking his head, "it all a busteriferous axledent, and I nebber grow happy any more—can I hab dis lantern, sar?"

"Take it," said Will, briefly, making an effort to suppress some violent emotion.

Jack took the lantern, trimmed the candle with his fingers, and went below. He arrived at his cabin door, and was about to enter when a groan from the interior checked him.

"What dat?" he muttered, "not de wind, I sartain sure. Anybody dere?"

He tapped lightly on the panels, and receiving no reply, grew bold and threw open the door.

The light of the lantern fell upon a sight that froze the blood in his veins; tall and erect, as if in life, stood the form of Crikey, with a long white robe flowing down to the ground.

Jack dropped the lantern, but it still shed a light, and he stared aghast at the unexpected visitor, almost bereft of his powers of speech; opening his mouth and rolling his eyes with two hundred wax-work power.

"Jacky," began the ghost, "I am your brudder's spirit, dat's strue as pickle onions and molasses."

"Crikey," moaned Jack, recovering his speech, "it all an axledent."

"It dam rum axledent," replied the ghost, emphatically, "for you to take de breff out ob my body, which I nebber fetch agen until I two miles under de sea, and den it no use. Jacky, you nebber hab anoder brudder like me."

"I gib all I hab in de world to bring you back again," moaned Jack.

"What will you gib?" asked the ghost, with the air of one prepared to enter into a bargain.

"Anyt'ing."

"Will you gib dat pair ob high boots you keep in de locker?"

"JACKY," BEGAN THE GHOST, "I AM YOUR BRUDDER'S SPIRIT."

"I will," said Jack.

"An' de yaller silk handk'chief you wear in de warm wevver."

"Yes," acquiesced Jack, but not so readily as before.

"And gib Chloe's 'spectable characker."

"She am fair as a lilly, bright as de sun, and bootiful as de butterfly."

"Den de bargain's made," said the ghost; "you fetch dem boots an' han'kerchief, and I go back to de bottom ob de sea an' get Crikey."

"How long it take you?"

"'Bout two minits."

"All right."

Jack raised the lantern and went out in search of the boots and hankerchief; he returned quickly, and there, sure enough, was Crikey in the flesh. Jack put down the boots carefully in a corner, and then rushed into his brother's arms.

"You glad to see me, Jacky?"

"Dat so, Crikey."

"An' now gib me de boots an' silk handkerchief."

"Gib dem to you?" rejoined Jack; "what for I do dat? Dey not for you, I not make de bargain wid you, I make it wid de ghost, and when him come again him shall hab 'em, or somet'ing else dat do him more good."

CHAPTER LXI.
VIRTUE'S REWARD — MARTEN GRIP, THE PIRATE.

"CRIKEY."

"Yas, Jacky."

"Ain't de cap'in kind?"

"Him ginerally so, Jacky; what him doin' now?"

"I ax him to put in at Cuba, and him say, 'Jes' so, Jacky, I will.'"

"What for you go to Cuba?"

"To settle a corubial difficulty, Crikey."

"And who am de corubial parties, Jacky?"

"You an' Chloe."

"Yah! dat's good," grinned Crikey; "you go ashore wid me to put all square?"

"Dat so, Crikey."

"A true brudder am you, Jacky."

"But I do more, Crikey; you shall hab dem boots an' dat yaller hank'chief dat I promise to de ghost."

"You grow more ob de brudder ebery moment, Jacky."

"An' when ole Chloe put her eyes on dem boots an' dat hank'chief, I bet a dollar she fall round your neck and say—'Lubly Crikey, welcome home.'"

"Yah! golly! oh, scrumpers," grinned Crikey, "dat happiness too great for moral nigger."

"It corubial bliss, indeed, Crikey."

"It more dan dat, Jacky; it stacktasy."

"What dat word?"

"Stacktasy."

"Nebber heard him, afore," said Jack, pondering, "but I s'pose him all right."

"When us reach Cuba, Jacky?"

"In two days' time."

"Den I take de boots now," rejoined the cunning Crikey, striking while the iron was hot, "an' I put such a polish on 'em dat dey 'flect Chloe's lubly face, when I go in de door."

Jack, true to his word, brought forth the boots, with many encomiums upon their beauty, which were not altogether warranted, for the heels had long ago been run down by a sturdy wearer, and the tops would have been considerably improved by being fresh japanned.

"Who dese made for?" asked Crikey.

"I not know," replied Jack; "I found dem."

"Whar?"

"De purcise spot 'scape my mem'ry at dis moment," replied Jack, fibbing, for he remembered well the time when he discovered them on a heap of refuse at Havannah, doubtless thrown aside as no longer fit for wear.

"Dem berry good boots," said Crikey, slowly, "'specially if dey was made all ober agen."

"De man," responded Jacky, as he dived below, "who look at a brudder's gift in de mouf, ought to live a noutcas' to 'ciety, an' be debounced ebery war by him fellar man."

Harold had promised Jack to touch at Cuba, and he also determined to despatch from thence a communication for Captain Harloch, and another for Clara, telling them of his safety, and bidding them to expect him speedily after he had been to Honour Bay.

The "Crucible" arrived at Cuba shortly after noon, and Crikey and Jack were put ashore, each dressed in his best, and a very striking effect they made.

There was only one defect in Crikey's rig out, and that lay in his boots.

He had the true nigger's heel, as much of the foot behind the leg as he had before, and the boots had to be slashed for the purpose of wear, admitting his heel to public view, but in front they looked very well—very well, indeed.

A large party of men gathered at the bows to see them off, and at the quarterdeck stood Harold, Will, Tom, Cecil Warren, and Dick Thorne, all mightily amused with the brothers' rig out, whose gravity under the circumstances would have done credit to two gentlemen about to pay their respects at court.

"Worthy fellows both," said Harold, as the boat disappeared behind a schooner. "Well, gentlemen, you must excuse me for awhile, I have letters to write. If you wish to go ashore, the boats are at your service."

But nobody cared to go ashore, for they knew that the life ashore at such a place would have no charms for them, so they lounged upon the deck, watching the sinking sun, and talking of adventures of the past.

"We have done something to rid the sea of piratical scoundrels," said Will, with pardonable pride; "the gallant 'Crucible' can rest on her laurels."

"What blood-thirsty knaves they are," rejoined Dick Thorne; "my father died by the hand of one of the most atrocious of the race, Marten Grip, the pirate of the South Seas.

"He was taken prisoner by the crew of the wretch's vessel, with many others, all of whom, but my father, were at once butchered, and he was retained to give information, which they knew he possessed, of the course of other vessels they were in quest of."

"He never did it, of course?" said Will.

"No, he was a Thorn in their sides," replied Dick; "excuse the pun. Well, one day a large merchantman hove in sight. The pirates put out signals of distress, as they had sprung a leak; the merchantman hove to, and Grip commanded his men to hide their arms.

"This was done; the boats came alongside and all embarked in them.

"I hardly dare say what almost immediately followed. Enough that the unarmed, unsuspecting crew of the brig, fourteen or fifteen in number, were suddenly set upon and deliberately shot down—massacred by the miscreants.

"My father was so overwhelmed, horrorstricken by the butchery, that he for a time wholly lost his reason, or, at all events, all control over himself; furiously denounced Grip and all his brother villains, and madly swore to bring them all to the gallows.

"A brutal blow on the head with the butt-end of Grip's pistol felled him upon deck, as a pole-axe fells a bullock; and he remembered nothing more for many weeks —how many he had no means of judging.

"That blow it was, or, more correctly, the loss of blood occasioned by it, which caused my father's death.

"I say, 'caused his death,'" added Dick; "not that he died at once, for he lived to be saved by one of his Majesty's cruisers; but he never entirely recovered from the blow, and died shortly after being landed at Lima."

"Slavers are almost as bad," said Warren; "I had a run against one in the 'Cassandra,' off the coast of Africa.

"Cruising there, we heard of a slaver being fitted by Panama Bay, and at once set off in pursuit.

"We sighted her at daylight the next day: her peculiar build, the pitch of her bowsprit, the cut of her sails, minutely described to us, left no doubt whatever upon our minds as to who she was; and we urged the chase by every possible expedient to obtain speed.

"I was almost mad with excitement; for, though it was soon evident that we gained upon the chase, our advantage was not so great as to give hope of coming up with her before night fell; and during the darkness, which the state of the weather and absence of moon would no doubt render intense, she might easily give us the slip.

"An accident favoured us; it was blowing stiffly, and her maintopmast gave way, beneath the spread of sail she carried, in her efforts to shake off the 'Cassandra.'

The helm of the slaver was put sharply up (we were running before the wind), and she was steered stem on to the shore, then distant about two miles.

"The boats were then lowered, the crew hurried into them, cast off, and pulled lustily to the shore, preferring to take their chance with African savages than fall into our hands.

"No one being left at the helm, the ship broached to, and a minute or so afterwards fifty or sixty negroes rushed shouting and yelling from below upon the deck.

"No wonder they should shout and yell; the ship was rapidly sinking. The crew had scuttled her, calculating, and justly, that the 'Cassandra's' boats, the sea there shoaling so rapidly that the corvette herself dared not approach much nearer to the shore—that the 'Cassandra's' boats, instead of pursuing them, would be a sufficient time fully occupied in saving the negroes' lives. Another motive, no doubt, was to prevent so fine a vessel from becoming the British cruiser's prize.

"Of course the wretched Africans could not be permitted to perish before our eyes; and, by the time they had been brought off, pursuit of the pirates was hopeless; they had reached the shore, and night, dark as the inside of a tar-barrel, had fallen.

"We would not, however, leave the place. The wind was going down, there was excellent holding ground, and the 'Cassandra' anchored at about a mile and a half from the shore. It might be possible to organise, the next day, a land chase of the scoundrels.

"The slaves' place of refuge was a sort of horseshoe-shaped inlet, or miniature bay, scarcely half a mile wide, formed by two projecting tongues of land, low-lying and barren, running nearly parallel with each other, on each hand, and varying from fifty to one hundred yards in width, the narrowest and lowest part being nearest the shore.

"A few moments' thought sufficed to settle our plan of action. The crew of the 'Cassandra' numbered about one hundred and twenty men. Leaving fifty in her, we could man four boats; two of which, under the command of the lieutenant, would await the slavers off the end of one horn of the inlet—two, with me, off the other. We were quickly away; and having pulled, as I judged, to within half a mile of the shore, which none of us could, however, see, even at that distance, we rested on our oars.

"'A lantern in a boat, sir,' said the coxswain of the launch suddenly, in a low voice. 'And look, sir,' he added, peering in the direction of the shore, 'look, sir, it is seen and answered, the slavers show two lights; I can just make them out dim-like now.'

"No question that we were upon the threshold of a desperate encounter. I had but thirty-four men with me in the two boats; and I was sure that the crew of the slaver, who filled five boats when they abandoned their ship, were double the number.

"We might make up our minds, therefore to a desperate night encounter with eighty or ninety desperadoes, fighting with halters round their necks.

"The odds were fearful; and a sharp pang of self-reproach shot through me for having, in passionate pursuit of vengeance for a private wrong, placed the brave fellows entrusted to my guidance at such a disadvantage.

"Brolow, the coxwain, a first-rate seaman, in whom I had great confidence, either divined my thoughts, or I must have given muttered expression to self-accusing regrets.

"'All right, sir,' he said, in an undertone—all right, sir, the firing will bring up the lieutenant in just no time, we may be sure and certain.'

"'Excuse me, sir,' he added, 'but there must be no parley-vooing—no askin' who the infarnal warmints is that's a sneakin' out; we knows they are devilish cutthroats; that's enough. A musket-volley

from both boats, when least expected, will be half the battle, and a trifle over."

"The jerk of oars now became with each passing moment more distinct, and presently we could discern the boats, five in number, coming on in single-file, as a soldier would say, in the wake of the one which carried the lantern. Rather a bold thing to do, but the coast was dangerous.

"The moment of action quickly came; brain-fancies vanished, and, standing up in the stern-sheets of the launch, I challenged the leading boat, then scarcely one hundred yards distant. Though so near, we had not been seen, and the effect was that of a bombshell. Every oar was at once suspended, and a hubbub of curses and commands arose among the pirates. It was evident they were hurriedly snatching up and preparing their arms, and further parleying would have been madness.

"'Fire!' Every seaman's finger had been for some minutes on the trigger of a musket; and their volleys flew at once with deadly effect. We did not wait to re-load; and in about a minute were at death-grips with the villains, both pirates and slavers, as we knew; the weapons on both sides, pistols, tomahawks, cutlasses, wielded with unsparing fury. Recovered from their surprise, and finding that they had but two boats to contend with, the slaver and his men fought with ferocious energy. The launch, which I commanded, was assailed by three boats, one on each side, the third athwart her bow."

"The fight was not so long as we expected," added Warren, "for the lieutenant came up and the very sight of another boat cowed the villains. We captured a few and killed the rest. Those we captured were afterwards proved to be pirates, upon whose heads was a heavy price, and they suffered as every piratical dog should —they swung in chains."

"Hear, hear," cried Will, "but methinks I scent the dinner from afar, all those who are hungry, follow me."

CHAPTER LXII.

STRICTLY CONNUBIAL.

WE must now follow our two dark friends, Crikey and Jack, on their errand to pacify the neglected Chloe. Jack was sanguine as to the result, but dark thoughts arose in the bosom of Crikey, and he despaired.

"De last meetin' I had wid dat lubly

creatur'," he said, "was ob such a natur' dat I t'ink de corubial lub am broken orf for eber."

"Your ig'orance, Crikey, 'stonish me," returned his brother, "de apposite sex am cur'us, but a man, 'specially married man, ought to know dem well. De last meetin' you had wid Chloe was not fren'ly pr'aps, but you rile dat woman, an' she lub you. Wheneber a chap can rile a woman, dat woman lub you; if they don't lub, dey only larf at eberyting, and nebber, under no plobucation, clutch him wool."

"Where you gain dat 'sperience, Jacky?"

"In de plantation, where fust I cut de sugar cane; dere I see many married nigger, an' I watch 'em."

The two brothers had cleared the town by this time, and were on the high road to the abode of Chloe, where, a short time ago, Crikey resided also.

Presently the house hove in sight, a wooden log house on the summit of a hill, with a very pretty piece of ground around it. Both Chloe and Crikey had been free niggers for years, and they had worked well, the result was this very desirable piece of property.

"Jacky," said Crikey, in a voice broken with emotion, "stop a moment while I t'ink."

He paused, and wiped a few drops of perspiration from his brow; Jack paused also.

"De 'motions ob de human heart," said Crikey, "am ob a rum natur' at such a time as dis; mine is more dan dat, they dey is rummy. Jacky, will you go forrard an' see if Chloe am at home?"

"Suppose she am, Crikey, what am I to do?"

"Say dat Crikey am dead, dat he fell fighting like six wild cat, dat him last word as him t'row up him arms an' legs an' die, was 'Chloe.'"

"An' what den?"

"If she shed lily tear," said Crikey, dropping one himself, "say it only jolly lark, dat I'm down at de bottom ob de hill; but if she look sarcy——"

"What den, Crikey?" asked Jack, seeing he paused.

"Come away, Jacky, as quick as you can," replied Crikey, "if you hab any 'spect or your wool, an' we will go back to de Crucible,' an' trouble her no more."

Jack nodded sagaciously, and went forward, keeping the fence as much as possible between him and the house, so as to approach unobserved.

The evening was approaching, and the sun was already below the hill; the gloom, therefore, favoured our friend, and he reached the house unperceived.

Crikey, at a respectful distance, saw him kneel down and first put his eye, then his ear, to the keyhole, and, far off as he was, could distinctly mark his eyes rolling in an agitated manner.

Then he arose, and beckoned for Crikey to advance.

That sagacious negro, however, hesitated, and signalled for Jack to come to him.

It ended in each coming half way, and when they met Crikey saw that Jack was trembling.

"Chloe at home?"

"She am, Crikey."

"Am she well?"

"Her health am s'lubr'us, but——"

"Speak up, ole man," cried Crikey, clutching his arm.

"Crikey," moaned Jack, "Chloe's oder ole man is dere!"

For a moment neither spoke, and then Jack went on——

"I hab presimental 'bout dat nigger an' you meeting. Crikey, de hour am come, an' what will you do?"

"I'm getting ready," returned Crikey, rolling up his shirt-sleeves; "how's dat muscle, Jacky?"

"Hard as cocoa-nut?"

"How dat fist?"

"It's not a fist, Crikey, dat's a hammer."

"Den' come an' see me pound that nigger to nuffin," cried Crikey, waving his huge arms in an excited manner; come an' see it fall upon him like a t'underbolt. I put dat nigger out ob ebery worldly misery dis berry night."

"Crikey," said Jack, in a confidential tone, "git him head under your arm, dis way, den walk in and win de battle."

Crikey, boiling with rage, had no patience for further words, and hurried up the hill, closely followed by Jack.

They reached the house, and Crikey would have entered at once, but his brother held him back.

"Listen at de door a lilly bit."

Crikey bent down his head, and two voices fell upon his ear; one was the

..et-like utterance of Chloe, the other ..ceeded from some stranger, and, to .rikey's momentarily increasing wrath, he spake the tender words of love.

"Chloe, I always lub you; but ne'ber so much as dis moment. De oat-cake am scrumptious, an' de milk, with de lily rum in it, jolly—yah!"

"Glad you like it, Brutus," responded the sweet voice of Chloe. "I gib you de best ob de place, for I berry glad to see you."

"Chloe," said the stranger after a pause, "where am dat Crikey?"

"Him far enuf away," returned Chloe, laughing hysterically. Crikey ground his teeth and rolled up his sleeves a little tighter.

"Should him come back now—what den?" asked the stranger.

"He not come more; de last time he cum I drop on him hunks, and pull all de wool orf him head. Crikey nebber come agen," aud Chloe covered her face with her apron; but this Crikey, who was listening, could not see. He thought Chloe was enjoying his absence, and rolled up his sleeves still tighter.

"I nebber see Crikey," resumed the stranger, and Crikey, waiting to hear no more, threw open the door and entered.

"Den see him now," he cried.

Chloe arose with a scream that might have been either an expression of fear or joy, and the stranger sprang to his feet.

The next moment Crikey had him tight, his head well under his arm, and the huge fist pouring down a shower of blows upon the hapless nigger.

Chloe flew to the rescue, but Jack intervened, and threw his arms around her.

"No, Chloe," he said, "Crikey kill dat nigger first, then he talk to you."

"Kill him—what for?" screamed Chloe. "Leab dat chile alone, Crikey, or it be de worse for you. Jacky, you tell him he better stop."

"I stop in a moment," gasped Crikey.

And fairly tired out he administered a final blow, a stinger, and threw the nigger into a corner of the room, where he lay apparently dead.

"Oh, Crikey!" moaned Chloe, "what hab you done?"

"What hab I done?" repeated Crikey; "I kill your pallymore."

"No, no, Crikey," sobbed Chloe," dat my brudder."

Crikey stood aghast—he had upset t table, smashed all the crockery, and kill his wife's brother, and all for what?

He looked around in despair at the ce ing, at the floor, at Chloe, at Jack—an where but at his victim, who still lay m tionless.

"Jacky," he said in a hollow voice, "(mistake am yours."

"Him?" screamed Chloe, turning su denly upon Jack, who had leaped asi with the agility of a harlequin; "let n get hold ob him."

Jack prudently put Crikey between hir self and Chloe, and from that point vantage confessed his guilt.

"Yes, Chloe," he said, "I put dat in Crikey's head, and I sorry for it now. gib ten dollars to bring back your brudd to life agen."

The slain nigger opened one eye cat tiously, and listened intently.

"And I," added Crikey, "gib more, (cap'en gib me a gold dollar, dat I give t bring ole Brutus back."

Brutus opened the other eye.

"Ah! Chloe," moaned Crikey, "I gi all I hab in de world if him only lib agen.

Brutus sat up and groaned.

Jack and Crikey sprang towards hir with a cry of joy, the latter folded him i his arms.

"Don't smodder him," cried Jack "here, Brutus, taste dis."

Brutus took a tolerably large sip out c the flask presented, and declared himsel better, but he was still very weak, an rolled his eyes tremendously.

They helped him to his feet, and pu him into a chair.

Brutus groaned aloud, and requested second sip from the flask.

Jack tendered it, and this time it wa emptied.

"Berrer now," said Brutus, "dat 'bou de bes' rewiber I taste dis long time."

"It de cap'en's Cognac," returned Jack "I found a bottle just afore we come away.

"Dat so," grinned Brutus, who certainl had recovered in a most marvellou manner—"when nigger find a t'ing, h keep it."

During this, Crikey and Chloe had few words apart, and the former now ad vanced to the injured Brutus—

"Chloe's brudder," he said, "I ax you pardon."

"Dat freely giben, Crikey."

WILL LOST HIS FOOTING AND FELL INTO THE ARMS OF JACK.

"An' hope we shall be fr'ens?"

"I hope so, Crikey."

"Chloe say you run away, and she hide you."

"I came orf de plantation in de middle ob a cart," rejoined Brutus, "and I nearly die of stuffication, 'cause my head in de wrong way."

"It berry kind ob Chloe to hide you here," returned Crikey, "but it hardly safe; the officers here in no time, and den Chloe lose her freedom for hiding you."

"I can't go back, I die fust," cried Brutus, with manifest terror; "de master berry cruel, he pinch, and scratch dem as run away; he mark dem all like sheep wid hot iron."

"You not go back," said Crikey, with dignity; "Jacky and I lick all Cuba fust. When you run away?"

"Dis mornin'."

"And when will dey miss you?"

"'Morrow morning, when dey 'spect me back from de dykes."

"We am safe, den, for de night," said Crikey. "Chloe, put out some supper and

17

fresh crockery on de table—we hab broke some afore atween us, and we soon get ober dat."

Crikey grinned at his own joke, and Chloe positively smiled. Matters were decidedly mending.

"You like oat-cake, Crikey, dear?"

The voice was Chloe's, there was no doubt of it, and Crikey reeled under this sudden rush of affection.

"I like oat-cakes, Chloe——lub!"

The last word came out slowly, as if Crikey was not accustomed to pronounce it; but when it did come Chloe's face positively beamed. She mixed some oat-cakes in the twinkling of an eye, and put them upon the hearth to bake.

Then from the cupboard she produced a bottle containing a spirituous compound, and putting mugs upon the table—glasses were luxuries in those days—to match the company—bade them drink and be merry.

They drank and were merry. Crikey came out tremendously strong in poetry and songs. Jack spun yarns, and Chloe and Brutus listened with unaffected delight.

The oat-cakes were delicious; and when the meal was over, the mugs and bottle again stood upon the table. After several applications to both, Brutus drew Crikey aside, and whispered in his ear,—

"You t'ink you hurt me some time ago."

"I hit you berry hard, Brutus."

"Ah! but you not hurt my head, Crikey—Massa knock it about wid billets ob wood for years, and it tough as hickory."

CHAPTER XLIII.

A DILEMMA.—CRIKEY DISPOSES OF BRUTUS.

"WHAT am to be done wid dis chile, Brutus?" asked Crikey, the next morning.

"He must be put away," rejoined Jack, "for if dey nab him, dey tickle him back frightful."

"Dat sartain, sure," said Brutus, with a wriggle and a grin.

"Dey better not come har arter him," said Chloe, looking up from her cooking.

"Nobody do dat who know what Chloe can do in dis way," whispered Crikey to his brother, holding up his ten fingers in a significant manner.

"Yet you come back, Crikey."

"Yes so, Jacky," returned Crikey,

"but I came back to whop dat oder ole man who nebber turn up."

"Oh!" said Jack, "is dat it? Wal, what us do wid dis 'ere Brutus?"

"I jest run down to the dock while Chloe finish de oat cakes," replied Crikey, "if a ship goin' out I get him on board sure."

He was gone about an hour, and came back with the intelligence that two coasting vessels were going to Havannah; the steady trade winds having set in, and that either of them would take the negro refugee on board at once.

"But you must be sharp," said Crikey, "for dey go wid de next tide."

Brutus was accordingly very sharp, and disposed of a standing breakfast with the utmost dispatch.

That done, Crikey brought out an old cotton gown of Chloe's, and a few other articles of female wearing apparel, with which he proposed to disguise the refugee.

Brutus had no resource but to consent, and being duly invested, he took an affectionate leave of Chloe, and accepted Crikey's arm, who was to be his escort.

Crikey saluted his wife, and promising to return in an hour and report proceedings, hurried his charge down to the dock, where two luggers were getting ready for sea.

Brutus was smuggled on board of one, the sails were spread, and the lumbering old coaster tumbled out of port and Brutus was safe.

"Dat all right," said Crikey, with a sigh of relief, "now I jest run back to ole Chloe and say a few words to her, den come back agen."

"No time for dat," rejoined Jack, "de 'Crucible' got de return flyin' at de fore."

"I must say one word to her, Jacky."

"Den you lose de 'Crucible.'"

"I not do dat, Jacky."

"It one or de oder—you cannot lub 'em bofe; send message to Chloe, and take de boat back at once."

Crikey thought for a moment, scratching his head with a puzzled air, and then fell in with the proposition.

Hailing an old nigger, who was lying on his back on a bale of goods, Crikey thus addressed him—

"I say, you nigger, sar."

The nigger opened his mouth and yawned, but paid no further heed to him

"I say, you sar, move dat hunks ob yours dis way."

Another yawn, and a stretching of the limbs.

"Do you know a dollar when you see him?"

These words had a magical effect, the nigger was up, bowing and scraping like a dancing-master.

"Yes, sar, I know de dollar."

"What you do for him?"

"Anyt'ink, sar."

"Berry good," said Crikey; "now, do you know ole Chloe?"

"Jis out ob town? yas, sir."

"Den go to dat lubly woman an' tell her dat I gone on board ob de 'Crucible'—you t'ink ob dat, sar?"

"I t'ink dat an' more for a dollar."

"Den go 'mediate——"

"An' de dollar?"

"Chloe gib you dat," returned Crikey, with a lofty air, adding to himself, "or sumfin' else."

The nigger, after a quick, doubtful glance at Crikey, set off, having apparently derived confidence from the calm, candid appearance of Chloe's husband.

"Jacky," said Crikey, as the dark messenger disappeared, "I sorry for dat nigger, but some year ago he borror dollar ob me, and nebber pay it. Yah! it a dam ebil day when he do dat wid dis chile; I t'ink I see Chloe going round about him hunks. Yah golly!"

It was apparently an amusing picture to both the brothers, for they roared and rolled their eyes in concert as they sought the boat to return to the "Crucible."

It was there, but the men to whom she belonged were absent, and half an hour elapsed ere they could be found. This was done at last, and Jack was about to enter the boat in his usual dignified style, when Crikey hurriedly whispered—

"Make haste, Jacky."

"What for?" demanded Jack.

"Dere's dat nigger coming back."

It was true; the messenger, waving his arms in a furious manner, was rushing towards them.

Jack stepped hastily into the boat and the men gave way.

"Hi! you, stop, sar," shouted the infuriated nigger, rushing down to the water's edge; "you gib me my dollar, sar."

"You see him, Jacky?" asked Crikey, who had his back towards the shore.

"I see him, Crikey."

"How do him look—about de wool?"

"Him nearly bald."

"Chloe got him, den," chuckled Crikey, "dat a berry bad dollar he borrow ob me."

"You come back, sar," again shouted the nigger on the shore.

Crikey laughed aloud.

The next moment some missile was whirled through the air, and caught him on the back of the head. Crikey clapped his hand on the afflicted part—it was streaming.

"Jacky," he said, faintly, "it all ober wid me, I bleed to def."

"Yah, golly, him bleed to def," grinned Jack, "when him only hit wid de rotten melon."

Crikey recovered instanter, and having relieved his feelings by shaking his fist at the grinning nigger on shore, wiped the juicy contents of the melon from his neck.

They were welcomed on their return to the "Crucible;" that Jack was prepared for, but he was not prepared to see about two hundred additional hands, men of all nations, crowding the deck and undergoing inspection.

Harold was reviewing them in person, singling out men here and there, and putting questions to them. He was attended by Mr. Stanchion, and a seaman who entered the names of the majority in a book, the rest stood aside as they were told off, one by one, about twenty in all.

"What am de cap'in's game?" asked Jack, addressing Will Steadfast—"fight again."

"We may have one more brush at the mounseers," returned Will, indifferently, "but that is not his object with these men. Jack, you remember the ships stowed away in Honour Bay?"

"Golly!—jes' so, Massa Will—the prizes."

"The same. Well, our noble captain intends to man them all with sufficient to work them as far as Havannah. He was called a coward, Jack—who will dare to call him so, when his fleet, captured by him, in many a glorious fight, shall rise before them?"

"I know de story ob de cap'in's life," said Jack, in a low voice, "an' it strike me dat he confusilate some ob dem dat open dere moufs too wide some time ago.

"For every enemy he made then," rejoined Tom Furnace, "he will now gain ten thousand friends—England will ring with his fame."

"Ireland and Scotland will shout for joy," said Will; "how I long for the glorious hour."

Cecil Warren and Dick Thorne had been standing by, listening intently to the former conversation—the former now struck in.

"What prizes," he asked, "has the Captain in Honour Bay?"

"About sixteen in all, French, Spanish, and pirate craft," replied Will. "When first my friend set forth upon his mission, he, hoping for the glorious hour when he should return home triumphant, sailed along the westward African coast to find some depot for his prizes on its romantic shores. He found a nook, far away from the haunts of man, and well hidden by the natural formations from the sea, and this nook he christened 'Honour Bay.' 'Here,' he said, 'I will make my home until my hour for return shall come. Here I will store up proofs of my prowess, to cast back into the teeth of the liars who call me coward, and unless it falls to my lot to retrieve my name here, I will live and die apart from all the world, but those who have given it up for my sake.' That's what he said," added Will, "and he kept his word."

"But these men will not man that number of craft."

"There are many at the bay," returned Will, "besides a numerous body of negroes, who, in our absence, have been taught naval duties. Time after time we have sent off prizes, and re-manned the "Crucible" to a certain extent from the willing crews of captured ships, all of which we hope to find there."

The men who had been put aside by our hero were now passed over the side into a jolly-boat, and were pulled ashore, rejected on the score of ill-health, or some equally substantial reason.

Harold then joined the youngsters, and catching sight of the modest Crikey, hoped he had found all well at home.

"More dan well, sar," replied Crikey, "much berrer dan could be expected."

"I half expected to lose you," rejoined Harold, with a smile; "the temptation of a quiet domestic life, after a rough sojourn at sea, might have been too much for you."

"De quiet 'mestic life, sar," said Crikey, "am a great temptashun to dem as get it —Chloe's 'mestic life rader noisy."

"O, that's it—is it?" laughed Harold; "then you should have brought her on board."

"She much berrer away," returned Crikey, "much berrer, sar, in time ob peace."

The significant tone of the latter part of Crikey's remarks raised a general laugh, and the jolly-boat now returning, the group broke up, and all gave a hand to run her out to sea.

Out flew the willing sails, and like a racehorse she sped o'er the waves on her last voyage to Honour Bay.

Jack's way of assisting the sailors with their work was to strut about and look on in a good-humoured patronizing manner, which mightily suited him, and amused them.

He was strutting on the deck after his own fashion, a few minutes after the men who set the sails had descended, when a cry from above startled him.

Looking up he beheld the form of Will Steadfast falling through the rigging; the lad had lingered above, and, owing to an act of carelessness, the result of long usage, had lost his foothold.

The boy, as he turned in the air, made several frantic clutches at the rigging without avail, and down he came into the arms of Jack with such velocity that both fell upon the deck and lay stunned.

There was a great outcry, and Harold came rushing aft, his heart wildly throbbing as he looked upon the pale face of the senseless boy.

"What is it—who did it?" he cried.

"Mr. Steadfast lost his footing," replied one of the men, touching his forelock; "he stopped aloft, sir, to have what we call a last spy at old Cuba."

Restoratives were administered, and a rapid examination assured them all that no bones were broken. Then they turned to Jack, who was lying in Crikey's arms, staring in a bewildered manner at the scene.

"Are you hurt, Jack?"

"Not much, sir," gasped Jack; "but golly, am de ship safe?"

"The ship's right enough—what makes you inquire after her?"

"When Massa Will tumble down, and my head go bang ag'in de deck, I t'ought it struck fire."

"Dat," explained Crikey, "was de lumerosity ob de blow which come ober de boplics at de time."

"All's well that ends well," said Harold, "but we are indebted to you, Jack, for another bold deed. Few men would have had the nerve or courage to catch the lad, and, trust me, it won't be forgotten."

CHAPTER XLIV.

THE BREAKING UP OF THE CAMP AT HONOUR BAY.

BOOM!

The echoes of the gun roll far away as the anchor of the "Crucible" runs smartly out and holds that good ship in tow.

Immediately the shore is alive with men, mostly of sable hue, and boats and canoes of every shape and size put off to bid the young hero captain a hearty welcome.

The blue flag runs up to the mast-head and flutters in the breeze—the men man the yards as the cutter puts off with Harold Greystone and his faithful friends.

Hurrah! the cry rivals the roar of the gun, and floats away, finding ten thousand echoes in the depths of the vast forest, and is answered by another with which is mingled the peculiar negro yell—terrible to hear, although it speaks of peace and welcome—not death and war.

As the cutter proceeds, the boats cluster like a swarm of bees around the queen, and as the men bend to their oars they chant a rude song of welcome:—

Hail to our hero captain,
Who comes from over the sea,
Who has fought for his honour so nobly,
And bled for the brave and free.

When they left off, the negroes began a composition after their own heart :—

De "Crucible" is lyin' dere,
Her colours all a-flyin',
De enemy is berry green,
Him now all dead or dyin'.

Yah—golly—yah!
Dat's de way we do it,
And dem dat cross de "Crucible"
Am jolly sure to rue it.

When within a hundred yards of the land, all the shore boats and crews made a spurt ahead, and the men, both white and black, formed a semicircle to receive our noble hero.

As he stepped upon the land, the white men cheered again, but many of the negroes prostrated themselves in the dust as they would before their king, for to him they owed an escape from a life of slavery.

"Thanks, friends," said Harold, in a husky tone, and could say no more.

Leaning on Will's arm, he passed through the throng, followed by Jack, Crikey, and other heroes, down to old Duncan, who had the previous evening signed a lasting bond of peace with Crikey and his brother Jack.

"As de cap'en hab done with it," Jack had said, "let us follow him egsample, and make it up wid ole Duncan," and it was accordingly done.

"We will have such a feast to-night," said Harold, when he had somewhat recovered, "as these old woods never saw before, and may probably never see again. Jack, to you I entrust its preparation—the big tent for myself and friends; and as all here are my friends, throw open its folds, and prepare tables, so that all may join."

Jack immediately went to work, calling to his assistance some two hundred of the negroes, who, strange to say, worked with a will to a man, for your negroes are, as a whole, an idle chattering race, who seldom retain a fit of industry for more than half an hour, although there are, of course, many exceptions to the rule, as witness Crikey and Jack.

The big tent, which, our readers will remember, appeared in an earlier chapter of this story, was opened on one side, and the canvas supported on a series of posts, cut from the neighbouring trees.

The tables used in the huts by the residents at the bay, were brought out, and put together, thus affording seats for all who had shared the danger and trouble of the masked hero's life.

Wine and bread were brought from the "Crucible," and meat and fruit were abundant on shore, and two hundred ready hands made rapid progress towards the feast.

Harold lay under a banana tree, surrounded by those whom our readers are most intimately acquainted, smoking a fragrant cigar, while he watched the busy scene before him.

"To live this life is life indeed," he said, "and but for one dear voice that calls me to a life perhaps more worthy, I would ask no more than to remain here during the short span of my life. Here nature abounds in luxuries, the sun is seldom darkened by a cloud; the glorious sea is a deeper blue than I've seen elsewhere, and the woods have a thousand nooks, each a little paradise."

"But storms must arise at times," said Cecil Warren.

"But seldom," rejoined our hero; "but when they sweep by, the place is ruined for half a century; trees are laid low, rocks are cast down, the very courses of the rivers are changed; but well man learns what a storm is here, and then he knows no more."

"And yet who could dream it, looking on this scene?" murmured Will.

"But few," said Harold. "Jack, who reads nature as we more civilized men read a book, says that for many thousand moons the blasting storms of this huge continent have left this place untouched, and thus it is so beautiful. I am loth to leave it now, but love calls me away. My life of adventure is over, and I go to play the part of man in civilized life. I know that age will come upon me—friends would die off here, and this sweet life, so like a dream of youth, must pass away. So let it be."

He spoke mournfully, as if he regretted the termination of his wandering life; but there was a tinge of joy mingled with his sorrow as he thought of the happy after days in store.

"It's been a jolly time," said Will, "and when we get back to old England won't we spin some yarns, Tom—won't we put some of the stay-at-homes on their backs. I think I see Jeremiah Piper (he was the goody boy of the school)—I think I see him as we tell him how we slipped into some of the pirates, and tickled the Frenchmen."

"Piper," said Harold—"Piper! I think I knew the fellow—a lubberly-headed muff!—what became of him?"

"He's as old as you, you know," rejoined Will, "and, having a turn for street preaching and literature, his father put him into the office of a paper called the "Pretty Mess," a high class tea-meeting journal and general scandalizer. Jerry writes the leaders in the week time, and goes forth on the Sunday to spout on the commons."

"Let him go his way," said Harold, with a smile—" wallowing in his own mire. You need not step out of your way to astonish him."

"Dinner, sar," interposed Crikey, bowing until his nose came into close proximity with his heels.

"All ready, Crikey?"

"Yas, sar."

"So are we; bid the boatswain pipe all hands."

Mr. Stanchion now appeared, followed by the men who had remained to make all taunt on board the "Crucible," and for once that gallant little craft was left alone.

"There is no danger," Harold had said; "so bring all ashore. I would not have one of all my heroes absent."

So they all came and gathered around their leader, more than five hundred strong.

It was growing dusk, for the sun was rapidly declining towards the ocean, so, ere they began, some hundred lamps, of all shapes and forms, hanging from the trees, were lighted, and inside the tent the illumination was worthy of the old Vauxhall.

Add to this glorious landscape around, the mighty trees, the gleaming stars coming out as soon as the sun dipped into the sea, the many happy faces gathered round the tables, and there was such a scene as Harold, as he looked upon it, never hoped to see again.

He had fought for his honour and had proved victorious, by the aid of those who were gathered around him, and, unlike many heroes, he was grateful, as we shall presently see.

The feast began and the wine cup passed merrily round, rough sailors drank from golden flagons captured from the haughty don, negroes sipped from delicate glasses, fragile as flowers, the spoil of the volatile Frenchman.

Hush—the captain is up—and a toast is to be drunk.

"Comrades in arms," he said, "for three years I have been an outlaw, with a stain upon my name. He who caused the wrong has atoned for it, and therefore let it pass. By this time the authorities know how falsely I was accused, and the stain of outlaw is removed from my name. I am a loyal man again, and I propose a loyal toast—his Majesty the King, God bless him!"

"The King! the King!" resounded on all sides with a hearty cheer.

Harold sat down, and Mr. Stanchion was on his feet in a moment.

"My friends," he said, "I am a sailor, and the only tackle a sailor doesn't know

"CHLOE, I LUB YOU, BUT NEVER SO MUCH AS DIS MOMENT."

about is jawing tackle; therefore, I shall say in a few words what I have to say, and have done with it. Friends and comrades, we have fought and bled, and conquered, with a hero and a man. Up, lads, and drink his health—a bumper."

What a shout arose; every man was on his feet, mad with enthusiasm.

Crikey got upon the table, but Jack had him off again in a twinkling, and the two brothers hugged each other with enthusiastic joy.

"De health ob de cap'en," shouted Crikey, draining a bumper. "Anoder health for him," he yelled, tossing off another, and he was filling a third when Harold rose again to his feet.

"Comrades," he said, and those near him could detect a quaver in his voice. "I thank you. No words could tell the emotions of my heart this night, and therefore I bid you imagine them. Accept my heartfelt thanks."

He could say no more, and sank down overwhelmed with emotion; and, respecting his feelings, those around him left him awhile to himself.

After a lapse of some minutes it was

discovered that Crikey was on his legs, supported by Jack, upon whom he leaned, who in his turn clung to the table.

"Ladies an' genelmen," Crikey began.

"Hear, hear; hole up, ole chap," said Jack.

"All right, Jacky," returned Crikey. "Ladies an' genelmen, de cap'en's health bein' drunk, I rise—— wurra you doin', Jacky? hole up; de capen's health bein' drunk, I rise to gib you 'noder tose,—

> "Of all de lubly lily gals
>   Dat lib since de days of Noah.
> Dere one dat lick the bilin' lot,
>   And de name of her am Chloe.

Dat de tose, genelmen, an' de hunks dat don't want to drink him better come roun' hyar an' say so."

Nobody had any inclination to deny the virtues of the lovely Chloe, and that lady's health was drank with enthusiasm and much laughter, and so the night went on amidst feasting and laughter until the dawn of the morning.

With the rising of the sun the tent was struck, never to be pitched again; the valuables were taken on board the "Crucible," the huts were emptied of their household goods, and every man was told off to one of the vessels homeward bound.

One by one they were towed out of the bay, where they had rested too long, and anchored out in the open sea.

Then it was that Harold went ashore for the last time, with Will, Tom, Jack, and a dozen men, bearing with them a heavy package.

Arrived at the landing-stage, the package was carried to a point overlooking the bay, and there, breaking it open, a small plain marble monument was revealed.

They fixed it there with a short inscription on its face—turned towards the sea—

HONOUR BAY,

NO MONUMENT TO THE DEAD IS THIS, BUT ERECTED IN MEMORY OF

A LIFE RESTORED!

And they left it to tell its simple story to some castaway—perchance sitting by it and wondering if his poor existence shall also be saved.

"A royal salute to the old place," signalled Harold, when he again reached the deck, and a hundred and one guns sent their thunder across the blue waters.

There was little more to be done, the captured vessels—seventeen in all—had each as many men as could be spared told off to work it; and to Mr. Stanchion, Will Steadfast, Tom Furnace, Cecil, and Dick Thorne a separate command was given; the rest of the vessels were entrusted to the most experienced hands on board.

Nothing more could be done, the weather was fortunately fair, and the glass still rising, and the wind was favourable.

"Should winds or currents divide us," were Harold's final instructions, "make straight for Havannah—that shall be your rendezvous as it is mine, with Lord Sancroft and other friends, who, by this time, have restored my good name."

"You must not outsail us in your haste," said Will, with a knowing smile.

"If I outstrip you," rejoined Harold, "it will be at the last moment to announce your arrival. Keep well together; guard the prizes well, for they are all your own."

"Our own!" exclaimed his hearers, half incredulously.

"Your own," repeated Harold, emphatically. "What need have I of wealth? I had enough and to spare from the first. You have fought and gained these prizes —they are yours. At present the men know naught of this; keep it a secret within your hearts until we arrive in port."

They promised to do so, and each went to his vessel more and more imbued with a love for their gallant leader.

Now, with white sails spread, the strange fleet speeds on its way with colours flying —the Union Jack at every mast but one, and that carries a blue flag with the motto in gold letters "For Honour We Fight!"

CHAPTER XLV.

CRIKEY'S GHOST STORY.

ON board the "Crucible" there were joyous hearts that night.

In twenty-four hours Havannah would be in sight, and every man's heart beat high at the thoughts of the reception their gallant captain would receive.

The men were assembled in the forecastle, and under the influence of a double allowance of grog, were singing songs in praise of their wives and sweethearts, and it was not until every man had strained his vocal powers to the utmost, that the singing ceased.

Then it was that a dance was proposed, and Jack obliged the company with a second edition of the "toe-and-heel corker," accompanied on the violin by his brother Crikey, and elicited thunders of applause from his admiring audience.

Jack having danced himself both giddy and blind, fell upon his back to recover his breath, which having done, he rose to his feet, and said,—

"We hab had singin' and dancin' enuf. I call upon my brudder Crikey to gib us a yarn. Him done nothin' yet but scrape de fiddle an' drink him grog."

"Hear, hear! bravo!" cried the men, laughing. "Silence for Crikey's yarn."

The individual thus appealed to, looked round with a very solemn face, and without a word commenced:—

"When I was twelve years old, I was sold at New Orleans to slaveowner, Massa Jabez Hyam. Him berry great man in him way. Had large plantations, plenty ob niggers, and lots ob money. Massa bought seven oders besides me, and as soon as de sale was ober, we was chained togeder and sent off to Massa's plantation. De oberseer him berry bad man, and kept de whip at work de whole journey, an' when we got to plantation, we all fit to die ob thirst; but nigger stand ten times more den white man, and after little time we get ober it.

"Massa came dat night and looked at us, as we sat in de hut.

"'I don't stand any nonsense wid my niggers,' he said, crackin' him whip ober our heads. 'I don't stand any humbug, I can tell you. So don't let us hab any whimperin', or look out for squalls.'

"I was berry young at dat time, and as Massa shut the door, I threw myself upon de floor, and burst out cryin' an' wishin' myself dead.

"'Dat no use,' I hear some one say, 'Dat no use. Dere is ebery hope ob escape if we all stick togeder.'

"I raised my head, and saw one ob de niggers dat Massa had put wid us for de night sittin' up an' talkin' to de niggers dat had come wid me.

"'My name am Hambal,' he said. 'I hab been here fourteen years, but I neber lost hope dat one day I shall escape. De nigger make de whips to flog himself, an' den grumble 'cause him back smart. Massa berry cruel man. Him kill nigger last week in a fit ob passion, an' him flog all day long, but him no flog me more. I use dis,' he said, gettin' up an' holdin' up big knife.

'I suffer a def ebery day, but de next time shall be de last.'

"I went to sleep, thinkin' ob what I heard, an' woke de next mornin' jest as de niggers were goin' to work.

"De oberseer came an' tole me dat I was to work in de house, an' dat if I was good boy I get plenty to eat, but if not I get nuffin' but de whip, an' plenty ob dat.

"Massa's house was berry grand, and de carpets cubered wid such beautiful flowers, dat it seem almost pity to walk upon dem. Dere was beautiful looking-glasses, and lubly couches, such as make de legs ache to look at.

"I find Hambal dere, and he show me what I hab to do, and he gib me fedder brush to dust de furniture.

"Massa call me shortly afterwards, and tell me to wait at breakfast, and dere I see Missus and de lilly boy, dat Massa call George.

"De Missus was a nice-lookin' lady, but her face was pale, an' de lilly boy looked berry ill. Massa took on dreffal, cause I awkward de first time, and throwed de crockery at my head.

"I feel berry miserable until Missus came out and patted my head, and tole me to be a good boy; den I say dat I would for her sake, and dat I would be glad to die to serve her. Massa George come running out and call for Hambal, who I afterwards hear was berry fond ob de lilly boy.

"De next mornin' I get up early, and go to work wid lighter heart, but I slipped on de carpet and fell ag'in de table, knockin' down a beautiful glass vase, which broke in a thousand pieces.

"Massa heard de noise, and ran down. I could not mobe, and I stood lookin' from Massa to de pieces ob glass upon de table.

"'How you do dat?' he said, him eye glistening wid rage.

"I tole him how de accident happen.

"Massa call de oberseer, and tell him to tie me up, and gib me a couple o' dozen wid de cat. I fell on my knees and beg him pardon; but he no listen to me, and de oberseer drag me away, and call Hambal to tie me up.

"'What hab him done?' he asked, 'him only come yes'erday.'

"'What dat to do wid you?' said de oberseer. 'Tie him up, unless you want a dose yourself.'

SELECTING THE CREWS FOR THE PRIZES IN HONOUR BAY.

"'I no tie such a chile up," said Hambal, walking away; 'he no hurt me, and I no hurt him.'

"De oberscer him just speechless wid rage. Him foam at the mouf, and stamp de ground, and at last rush off to Massa's house, leabin' me alone.

"I see de Massa come out, and look about for Hambal; but him nowhere to be found. De day passed and he not come near, and Massa get in frightful rage, and swear to hang him when him catch him.

"Howeber, no Hambal turn up, and Massa order de oberseer to take de bloodhounds, and hunt de nigger down.

"I see de dogs start, an' in about four hours de oberseer come back—but alone.

"De dogs had got ahead, and de oberseer had lost all trace ob dem.

"Massa was jus' blind with rage, and tole de oberseer him fool, an' dat he belieb he help Hambal to 'scape.

"De oberseer put him hand on the handle ob him knife, but walk away.

"Dat night I sleep in de house—on de floor in Massa George's room.

"De wedder was hot, and de windows all open.

"I had been to sleep about two hours, when I wake as if someone call out for help.

"I listen for a few minutes, and den I hear a voice cry—

"'Massa George! help! Massa George!'

"Massa George was 'sleep, and I dare not wake him; so I go to de window and look out.

"De moon was shinin' brightly, and I could see eberything in de garden in front ob de house.

"Dere was nobody dere, and I was jes' goin' to sleep ag'in, t'inkin' dat I had been dreamin', when I hear de same voice cry out—

"'Help! Crikey! Massa George! De dogs will kill me!'

"De blood seem to leab my body, an' I stood at de foot ob Massa George's bed, too frightened to speak or go to de window ag'in.

"It was Hambal's voice, an' yet it had a peculiar sound, such as neber come from nigger's lips.

"Jus' as I was about to call out, Massa George spoke—

"'I thought I heard someone call my name,' he said; 'but I s'pose I must hab been dreamin'. Crikey, are you dere?'

"'Yes, Massa George,' I said; 'but it am no dream ob yours. I hear de voice quite plain. It call me as well as you. It am de voice of Hambal. Dere——'

"'Help, Massa George! Help!'

"Massa George burst out crying, and call for light, an' Massa rush upstairs an' ask reason ob de uproar; and when him hear, him punch my head, an' say dat I frighten young Massa.

"We no hear de voice ag'in dat night, but de next mornin' we hear dat de body ob Hambal was found, wid de bodies of de two dogs which he had fought an' killed.

"Poor Hannibal was brought back an' buried; and a lilly time after, Massa George died, den his mudder, an' den Massa blow him brains out; and de house an' niggers all sold.

"I don't ask you to belieb dis story," said Crikey, in conclusion; "but it am ebery word de trufe; an' I not forget dat night and dat voice to my dyin' day."

"A very likely story," growled Duncan; "why didn't you see the ghost?"

"'Cause nigger black, and how you see him when it dark?"

After a few more yarns and songs, the men retired to their hammocks, and after a few hours' rest tumbled out to find the sun rising in a cloudless sky.

There was very little breeze stirring, but the "Crucible" bowled along merrily, as if aware of the mission she was on, and the brave hearts she bore

"The "Crucible" had outstripped the prize fleet, and was now within six miles of land.

Every man was on deck, and Jack had adorned himself to the best advantage, adding an immense white shirt collar, which somewhat eclipsed the renowned cocked hat.

Crikey was also in holiday attire, a blue striped shirt; a pair of pantaloons to match, and a blue cotton handkerchief bound round the head in turban fashion.

The masked captain paced the deck in company with Mr. Stanchion, and the men, except those on duty, stood talking in groups.

Every face was turned towards shore, and every heart towards home.

Suddenly, the slight breeze dropped, and the sails of the "Crucible" flapped lazily to and fro.

This vexed Harold, as he knew that the "Crucible" had received the last of the breeze, and that his fleet would not be able to come up in time.

Harold was watching the shore when he saw emerging from a creek a proa, manned by about, as far as he could judge, fifty men.

This was followed by about twenty more, and it did not take long for the captain to see that their intention was to board the "Crucible."

He called Mr. Stanchion, and gave orders for every man to be armed for the fight.

The men, who had been laughing and talking before, received their arms, and awaited the next order, silence reigning fore and aft.

Jack hearing the order was about to rush below, when he was arrested by Crikey, who said,—

"Jacky, why you go below? you forget de cap'en."

"I go to take off de shirt collar, and den come up to pepper dem debils."

In a few minutes he appeared divested of this ornament, and took his usual station by the side of Harold. The cocked hat was pulled over the eyes, and he held a huge cutlass in one hand, and a pistol in the other.

"Dere's plenty ob dem," said Jack, "but we gib em pepper."

"I am certain," said Harold, "that you will all do your duty, but I fear we shall be outnumbered."

As he spoke the savages set up a hideous yell, which was answered by a cheer from those on board the "Crucible."

"Give it them, lads," shouted Harold, which order was echoed by the lieutenant.

A volley of musketry and a broadside did material damage, but still the proas came on, rowed by hands that longed to be stained with blood.

As the roar of the cannons subsided, a breeze sprung up, and, filling the sails of the "Crucible," bore her from the pirate craft, and almost at the same instant, a lateen sail ran up the slender mast of every proa.

"We shall cheat them yet," cried Harold, "give it to them, boys."

Jack, who had not left the captain's side, suddenly cried out,—

"A sail, cap'en! a sail! It am de fleet. De 'Crucible' am saved."

The savages, who were too intent their murderous design to observe thing else but the "Crucible," came uttering the most horrible yells, but were met by volley after volley, and an oar dropped rowerless into the sea

The prize crafts came up rapidly, hemmed the proas in.

The fight was soon over; nothing left but a floating mass of broken tim the sea was tinged with red.

The savages had, without except gone to learn the great secret.

The crew of the 'Crucible' had suffered much — several were slig wounded, but none killed.

This was the last peril; the crew of noble vessel had done their work no and with three British cheers they sa into Havannah, with the proofs of t prowess following in their wake.

That night, in the middle watch, a fie red glare was observed to rise up sudde from the distant horizon, and the cr "A ship on fire!" brought the crew the "Crucible" on deck.

Harold, surrounded by his offic stood on the weather quarter, night-g in hand—and after some moments' sur he exclaimed bitterly—

"It is the fiendish work of a pira There, can you not see her stealing aw from the burning ship?"

As he spoke, he pointed out a d object, in which an experienced eye l no difficulty in tracing the outlines o vessel gliding swiftly away under ev stitch of sail.

Harold's first thought was to give ch to the fiendish marauder, but on matu reflection he abandoned the idea.

In all probability he might not ov take the pirate, and his own little fle might need his protection.

So with beating heart he bore down the burning wreck to see whether the was a chance of saving any of the su vivors, and then shaped his own course before.

CHAPTER XLVI.
REWARD AT LAST.

OUTSIDE the town of Havannah, and fa ing the sea, stood a charming residenc with a well-kept garden in front, whe bloomed the cactus and the prickly pea

All the plants were tropical, and of grea beauty, but their arrangement was esser

HAROLD'S RETURN.

ally British, the flower beds being well kept, and the paths arranged with mathematical accuracy, in lieu of the slovenly gardening peculiar to the native residents of the place.

There resided Captain Harloch and his daughter.

The noble old man had not yet recovered entirely from the physical and mental distress following the loss of the "Curlew," and although the court martial of inquiry had acquitted him of all blame, and another command had been offered him, he resolved to take the needful rest, and taste the sweets of life on shore for a little while.

There was, however, more than the loss of the "Curlew" on his mind—he remembered and regretted the injustice done to Harold Greystone, when his enemy, Mason Wantlake, so fatally triumphed for a time, and when the doubts which soon began to dawn became certainties, he pined for the hour when he should be able to make all the atonement in his power to the young sailor so foully wronged.

Lord Sancroft had called upon him with

the messages sent by our hero, and the nobleman added something of his own very flattering to the youth who had been fighting so long and well for Honour's sake.

But Clara had been the greatest sufferer throughout; her faith had never swerved for a moment, and when the news of the exculpation of her lover came she only smiled sadly.

It was not that she wanted—her heart had never thought otherwise—Harold himself must come.

"And when will that be?" she would often ask; "can Lord Sancroft say?"

"His lordship has told us all he knows," Captain Harloch would reply, "'tis but a question of time."

"But there are storms at sea, and enemies afloat," urged Clara; "if he does not come shortly, I shall die."

But love is strong, and although months dragged their weary length along, without our hero appearing, she lived and hoped, rising almost with the sun to watch for the coming of the "Crucible."

Other vessels—great and small—came into the narrow neck of the harbour, but none brought tidings of the missing hero, until the coasting trader came with Brutus, the brother of Chloe, and that darky having talked loudly of his "Crucible's" connections, the reports reached Captain Harloch's ears, who summoned Brutus straightway to his home.

The account given by the son of Ham was none of the clearest, but the captain and his daughter managed to elicit from his garbled stories the fact that Harold was but gone to Honour Bay, and would quickly return.

From that time Clara knew no rest, and as each day dawned she was at her window, with an eager gaze turned towards the blue waters, and when night came without a sign of Harold, she returned, sighing—

"Not yet!—not yet! Will he never come?"

One evening Captain Harloch returned from a visit on board a Government craft, whither he had been in uniform, with a countenance very much perturbed.

Unbuckling his sword, he laid it on the table, and ringing the bell, desired the servant to bid his daughter come to him.

When Clara entered, she saw the alteration in his face, and flew to his side.

"Father, your news?—bad news, is it, for me?"

"Bad news for all," replied the captain, gravely. "Clara, we live in troublesome times—peace to-day and war to-morrow. There's a strong foreign fleet lying in the offing."

This was serious intelligence indeed. Clara turned pale.

"It's a mixed fleet of French and Spanish," pursued her father, "as far as we could make out; but it was nearly dark when they came in and dropped anchor. The forts are manned, and the few craft we have in harbour are ready to go out and fight, but what can they do against such odds?"

"If we are conquered, what follows?" asked Clara.

"Disgrace to the old country, and captivity for us," rejoined the captain, despairingly. "Where were our cruisers, that this lot of sharks have come down upon us without warning and without sign?"

He sank into a chair with a despairing gesture, to leap again to his feet as the door opened, and the servant announced,—

"Mr. Harold Greystone."

For an instant both father and daughter doubted the evidence of their senses, and neither spoke nor moved; but the vision did not melt away.

Harold, in the uniform of a midshipman of his Majesty's navy, stood before them, with the velvet mask he had worn so long grasped in his left hand.

"At last, sir, I can look again upon you without a blush."

It was his voice, and both the Captain and Clara sprang forward at the same moment—his right hand was given to the father, his left winded round Clara.

A happy moment for all—too deep for words. Tears of joy coursed down their cheeks, and convulsive hands bespoke their emotion.

"This atones for all," whispered Harold, at length. "Clara, my darling, for this I would go through thrice the peril I have passed."

She could not speak; but clung to him as if she besought him to leave her no more; but the captain replied, his voice husky by emotion.

"Harold—my boy—my son, henceforth —this is the happiest moment of my life."

By-and-by they became calmer, and so

own together; then came back the memory of the peril impending over the little own.

"You arrive in time, Harold," said the captain, "to do your country service."

"He must fight no more," broke in Clara, "I cannot part with him."

"He must do his duty with other good men and true," rejoined the captain, gravely.

"What danger threatens us?" asked Harold, with a dawning smile upon his face.

"A foreign fleet lies in the offing, my lad, of some sixteen sail."

"I saw them as I journeyed here," returned Harold, indifferently—"we need not fear them."

"My boy, what power can we bring against them?"

"I, single-handed, will reduce them to submission," returned our hero, coolly.

Captain Harloch stared — thinking Harold's brain was turned. Our hero hastened to relieve him from all apprehension.

"That fleet is passive in my hands," he said, "for it is mine—or, rather, my country's."

The captain stared harder, more puzzled than before.

"They are but prisoners of war," continued Harold, "the results of three years' fighting."

"Yours?"

"And my gallant men's," returned Harold.

Captain Harloch could not repress a shout of joy, and walked to and fro, rubbing his hands.

"The Admiralty were already prepared to atone for the wrong you have suffered," he said; "but this will make the country ring with your fame. I am proud of you, and Clara—"

The beautiful girl looked up at her father, then laid a hand upon her lover's shoulder.

The act expressed her feelings towards the noble fellow.

"I found the harbour in commotion," pursued Harold; "and, perceiving that the forts were preparing to honour me with a shower of grape, I landed with a flag of truce. A few words to the officer commanding sufficed, and I came hither at once—"

"To relieve our fears?"

"To behold those I so dearly love and respect."

Then followed certain needful explanations, Harold relating how he had lingered to obtain a full confession from Mason Wantlake, which he produced from the inner lining of his belt.

"The last link wanting," he said; "guard it for me, Captain Harloch, until I stand before my judges."

"You will stand before none but friends," was the captain's reply, "and they will not judge you, but only confirm their late decision."

"One question more," rejoined our hero; "how will it fare with Harry Carlton?"

"As with you—all is well; you are both promoted."

"I have done my work," said Harold, with a wave of his hand toward the sea, and fight no more. And here," turning to Clara, "is my harbour of rest, with your kind leave."

"The proudest of England's nobles should not take her from you," replied the captain.

"I have passed through a night of sorrow," said Harold, "and the dawn is here."

That night the port was full of gaiety.

All the vessels were illuminated as if for a royal gala, and far out at sea the line of prizes could be distinguished with the lanterns hanging around their hulls gleaming like huge glowworms.

Boats passed to and fro; guns were fired, rockets spurted into the air, and shed their brilliant light around; and the streets beyond the docks were full of gay people of the various castes residing there.

Many of the great potentates — the port-admiral, his followers, and so forth—called upon Captain Harloch, and were introduced to the hero of the hour.

So full of adventure had Harold's life been, that these men, accustomed as they were to adventures on land and sea, would have doubted them but for the all-convincing evidence rocking on the bosom of the deep.

Harold was modest, but they drew him out, and Harry, Tom, Monkey Jack, and Crikey were sent for, all of whom received their share of adulation, sufficient to turn their heads, had they been weaker.

After a brief interview with the great men, Jack and his brother went down into the kitchen, where the maid servants showed them so much attention that the various men in plush, who had come with their respective masters, were driven to a state bordering on frenzy.

One—a little weazen Frenchman—the valet of the commissioner of the Port, was disposed to be rude, and addressed Crikey as "Mr. Niggar," intending to arouse the ire of that sable hero.

Crikey looked at him for a moment, as a mastiff surveys a yelping cur, then stretched forth his mighty arm, seized him by the collar, and coolly seated him upon a shelf in the midst of certain iron utensils devoted to the art of cookery.

"Dere, you Frenchman, sar," he said, "you jes' 'pologize, or, by de ' Crucible,' I keep you dere for a munf."

The Frenchman looked around for an ally, but every face wore a broad grin of derision.

He glanced at the negro's muscular form, and gave in.

"I beg your pardon, sar," he said.

"Call me Mister Crikey, 'Squire, sar."

The Frenchman did so, and Crikey lifted him down again, and gave him as a parting piece of advice, the recommendation, "to be sure he 'sulted common nigger, and not true African, when him open him ugly mouf."

It was Liberty Hall with everybody that night, so they had a dance, in which both the dark heroes of the " Crucible " shone mightily, especially when they performed together their native dance of triumph, for which the kitchen had to be cleared of everything, and the spectators stood upon the staircase.

There was a certain pretty mulatto girl, Clara's waiting-maid, who took very kindly to Jack, and after the first dance refused the hand of every other suitor.

This Jack wisely accepted as an amatory sign, and devoted himself to the improvement of their acquaintance.

He succeeded so far to his satisfaction that more than once during the mazes of the dance, their heads came together, and a sound like the smacking of a carter's whip resounded through the room.

After each report the eyes of Jack rolled towards the ceiling in ecstacy, so we may conclude that, whatever was the real result of that contact of head, he enjoyed it to the fullest extent.

The observant Crikey marked this, and anxious to keep pace with his brother's gallantry, showed signs of gallantry towards the cook, a negress, whose weight was equal to that of a small elephant ; but the cook was very circumspect, and declined the honour without a certificate of character

"'Afore you do dat, sar," she said, "answer me one t'ing."

Crikey expressed himself willing to do so.

"Am you single man, or hab you entered into corubial bliss ?"

"I got one wife," rejoined Crikey, after a pause, "but she a berry little one."

While yet these words lingered on his lips the door of the kitchen opened, and Brutus entered, leading—can it be—the lovely Chloe, magnificently attired in a yellow cotton gown, and a handkerchief, like Joseph's coat, of many colours, about her head.

She advanced with stately mien, regardless of the company, her eye fixed upon the petrified Crikey's face, who looked as pale as any nigger could hope to be.

"So, sar, you am here ?" she said.

"Yas, Chloe," returned Crikey, feebly, " dis chile am here."

Chloe glared upon him—the outraged cook glared, and the company—especially the Frenchman—grinned.

"You run away from your lawful wife, sar."

A noise, as when a butcher smites a steak with the flat of his cleaver, followed this address, and Crikey reeled over, to be restored to his equilibrium by a similar salute on the other side from the cook.

This was a fortunate thing for him, it diverted the ire of Chloe, who, after demanding "why she gib her ole man dat blow?" fell upon the cook without further preliminary.

All the company lent a hand to separate the combatants ; but they clung fiercely to each other, and it was not until the apparel of both was in a condition for Rag Fair that they were got again upon their feet.

Then it was that Jack became oil upon the troubled waters. Mounting the dresser, he called the attention of the company to himself, by rattling his heels thereon, and began—

" Am dis de night for rumbustifications. Shall it be said by de genelmen above dat de peace an' 'armony of dis night was blowed upon by two ob de lubliest ob de nigger sext? Let de peace ob sisserly lub shine in 'em, and I pay for two new yaller gowns to-morrer " here he caught an angry glance from the eye of the pretty Mulatto girl, and added—"in addition to anoder present dis chile am goin' to make."

Negroes readily forgive. Chloe and the cook became friends. Crikey retired with his wife into a corner, and by some means peculiar to himself, made peace. This done, the dancing and merriment were renewed, and kept up until a young bantam cock in the rear announced the morning.

CHAPTER XLVII.
LAST SCENE OF ALL THAT ENDS THIS STRANGE EVENTFUL HISTORY.

THE story of our hero is almost over. The precious jewel—honour—for which he had fought and suffered, was regained, and the adventure part of his life was ended.

He only waited at Havannah for the prizes to be duly adjudged, and the money divided among his men—for his own part, he had fought for honour alone, and having obtained that, would have none of the spoil.

There were men who shrugged their shoulders at his dainty notions. Captain Harloch pressed him to maintain his rightful claim, but Harold said, "No, I fought for my good name—it is mine again, let the rest go. Without it I am rich, and need no more."

While they smiled and argued against this resolution, men admired it, and a whisper went abroad that our navy had lost the prospect of a noble admiral in the retirement of Harold Greystone, one who was bound in time to "put his mark" where the world could not easily forget it.

This was hinted to him, but Harold smiled, and declared himself tired of glory already, he would leave it to other men who loved and needed it.

His appearance before a court-martial for deserting from the "Curlew" was merely a friendly meeting, and in five minutes his acquittal of all charges made out, and a high eulogy upon his past and present conduct appended.

Then came a round of dissipation—night after night one or the other of the great dignitaries gave an entertainment, at which our hero and the lovely Clara were the observed of all observers, and truly they looked a gallant pair.

Then, of course, came also Lord Sancroft and his son—no longer Tom Furnace, but the Honourable Algernon—and Harry Carlton, his nom de plume, Will Steadfast, dropped for ever. And Mr. Stanchion was not forgotten.

But all this drew nigh to an end, for our hero and his friends were bound for England, where Harold and Clara were to be married, and then the question arose, "Who should accompany them?"

Lord Sancroft was going, and his son; Harry Carlton, also, for a time; but it was a question whether Jack and Crikey would care for the old climate, so Harold resolved to put the question to them at once.

On their way to a masquerade ball, he descended from the carriage and entered a small house where the darkies had taken up their abode for the time to taste the pleasures of a life ashore.

His sudden appearance threw them into commotion, but Jack quickly recovered, and did the introductory honours.

"Massa Brutus, sar; Chloe, dat am Crikey's much berrer arf; Crikey, you know, sar—he too orfen been dam nu'-sance on board ship, for you not know him, sar."

"I never forget old friends," rejoined Harold, pleasantly; "you have both been faithful to me, and I shall now remember you with gratitude. Jack, I am going to England in a day or two, will you go?"

"Sure you not leave dis chile behind, sar."

"No, Jack; but the climate is very cold, and you are a child of the tropics."

"I guess I'm berry big chile," grinned Jack. "No, Massa Cap'in, you no go widout me, unless you wish to break dis heart dat frob for you for eber and eber—Amen!"

"Well, be it so, Jack, and, now you, Crikey—what do you say?"

"Sar," rejoined Crikey, evidently labouring under great restraint. "I married man."

"So it seems," returned Harold, smiling at Chloe.

"And dat bein' de case," pursued Crikey, "it am my dooty to stand by de wife ob my bosum. I took her for wheels an' woes, sar, an', derefore, I tick to Chloe."

"But why leave her?—bring her with you."

"Will you go, Chloe?" asked Crikey, of his much better half.

"I ready dis moment," promptly responded Chloe.

Harold then bade them good night, and was about to depart when Brutus advanced and, with a bow worthy of a dancing-master, begged leave to speak to him.

"What is it?" asked Harold.

"Sar," began Brutus, "I am a chile ob misfortin'. I hab two mas'rs in six munf, 'cause one ob 'em kill hisself wid drink, an' den knock me 'bout de head wid ring bolt till I see lot ob moons runnin' 'bout like loose cheeses on board de ship. De second mas'r worse, for he nebber get drunk, but take pleasure in whoppin' dis air nigger wid a whip-wire 'bout de legs, until him all ober lines, and but for lady present sar, I gib you rocklar damnedstratim ob de fac,."

This peroration, listened to by Jack, Crikey, and Chloe as an almost unrivalled piece of eloquence, caused Harold considerable surprise.

Seeing that Brutus paused, he rejoined—

"I am sorry to hear that you have been the victim of barbarous cruelty. What can I do for you?"

"Sar," returned Brutus, "you can do much. Arter bein' cut up to small pieces, sar, seberal times, I walk into the breakfast room ob my massa, whar him sleep in all unsconshus innersense ob Brutus bein' round 'bout him hunks, I gib dat mas'r one whack ober de head wid coffee-pot, an' run away."

"You killed him?"

"No, sar, I t'ink not, for when I come 'way, sar, him roll him eyes frightful, jus' like possum in de trap. He offer two hundred dollar reward for dis chile, so him 'live an' kickin'."

"And what are you aiming at, to accompany your friends to England?"

"Dat my objec', sar; you take me an' I your slabe, you may do what you like, sar, but don't leab me to de marcy ob my massa. When him catch me he flay me 'live—skin me by inches."

"Jack," said Harold, as he turned to leave, "get on board the "Crucible" to-night or early to-morrow, you and your friends, for in her I sail with my friends to England.

"Brutus too, sar?"

"Certainly, all of you."

Brutus fell upon his knees to bless his benefactor, but Harold was gone, and he was obliged to content himself with a long-winded discourse upon the merits of our hero, which was heartily endorsed by Jack, Crikey, and Chloe.

It was a great day when the "Crucible" left. The harbour was gay with flags, and fort and ships sent forth a parting salute. There lay the prizes for which Harold had so gallantly fought, manned by his men, and the noble tars ran up the rigging to give him a parting cheer, his eyes were wet with tears.

One vessel sailed out a few miles with the "Crucible," and when it turned at last, and fired a final salute, Mr. Stanchion was seen to wave his hat, and a lusty cheer rang out over the sea, the last ever heard by our hero from his lips.

So away over the broad ocean sailed the "Crucible" with its freight of living happiness, and, leaping from wave to wave as if conscious of its burden, and longing to discharge it on the cliff-girt isle, their future home.

Favouring breezes wafted them on their way, the sun and moon smiled upon them, and Harold and Clara, happy in their love, talked of the happiness of the future, while Captain Harloch looked upon them, and thanked Heaven for giving him such blessings to cheer his old days.

There was Jack, too, and Clara's maid, the pretty mulatto, with whom Duncan, the carpenter, fell in love, and rashly proposed to. Jack could afford to be kind, so he let it pass, and laughed each time he passed his old foe, wearing the only woe-begone face on board.

Crikey, Chloe, and Brutus, all happy, but Chloe especially amiable, and bestowing such attentions upon her spouse as he had never received before—making for him the most prodigious collars, supplying neckties of the most startling colours from her wardrobe, making especially for him, in her capacity as cook, eatables rich and rare, until the hearts of Jack and Brutus ached with envy.

And who was captain? Harry Carlton —just growing into manhood; for from the hour they left Havannah the "Crucible" was his—a noble gift from his noble friend, Harold Greystone.

They reach home at last, and find that the news of their coming has landed before them. There are great men in the land who have come down to receive them, and if the eulogies of the rich and great are rewards for valour, Harold and his friends were amply repaid.

BRUTUS IS INTRODUCED TO THE CAPTAIN.

There was one reward especially in store for our hero, he is sent for from court—goes, and returns Sir Harold Greystone, an honour he had not sought, but welcome, because it shows to him that royalty on its pinnacle can find time to cast its eyes on merit struggling in the turbulent world at its feet.

It was good, simple, old George the Third who dubbed him, and the kingly grace was not lessened when he took the young sailor by the hand and praised him for his deeds.

Before marriage Harold purchased an estate in beautiful Devonshire, within easy distance of the bright blue sea he loved so well, and there he installed Jack and Crikey in a comfortable little home, and Brutus was installed in the livery of the house.

Jack married the pretty mulatto, and Clara found another maid. The ceremony took place at the village church close to Harold's estate, and the novel nature of the bride and bridegroom brought a large assemblage of people from the houses for miles around.

Then came Harold's union, and his fame filled the church with the better classes of the country round—who came to do him honour. Clara, beautiful as an angel, charmed them all, and many a heart envied her gallant husband as he led her from the church.

There were dancing and fireworks at night, and Crikey was master of the peasant ceremonies, and how he filled that post we need not tell—our readers know him thoroughly.

And thus, with those he loved around him, Harold lived happily. Harry Carlton came back at times; but he lived mostly on the sea, where his name almost rivalled that of the hero of his boyhood. Step by step, from the privateer the "Crucible," he rose to command a three-decker of his Majesty's fleet, and so on to one of the highest posts in the service.

Harold was proud of his friend, and always gave him hearty welcome at the hall, where several little likenesses of our hero were growing up. Among them, a little fellow, who rolled about in a little sailor's dress, and talked of the time when he should be "big enough" to go to sea, and would spend hours with certain negro friends not far away, who told him of his father's deeds, and fought "his battles o'er again."

One Christmas Eve, when Harry Carlton, grown a bearded man, was with his friend, Sir Harold, a servant said a woman was at the gate, and desired to speak with them.

She was admitted, and throwing back a cloak she wore, exhibited the Spanish lady who had married Mason Wantlake.

"I come," she said, "to tell you of the man you saved."

Harry handed her a chair, and she proceeded—

"He is dead, and marvel not that my eyes are dry, for many months have passed since I buried him with these hands of mine by the home you left us in. My father died first, then my only boy (here her voice faltered) fell sick and followed him. My husband alone was left to me. Three happy years we lived in Paradise, and then came the end. One day he returned from hunting, not with light footsteps and smiling face, but crawling step by step with a fearful wound in his side, from which the life blood was flowing. He had fought a bear and conquered, but at the cost of his own life.

"Ah! my noble friend, who shall tell the anguish of that moment! In an hour I was alone, with naught of human life

near me, and when I buried him, from that hour I kept a fire blazing day and night until a good ship, driven from her course, sent a boat ashore.

"It saved me," she concluded, after voyaging hither and thither, length landed me here, and I came to this house to-night, to do my husband's bidding, and tell you that he, dying, blessed your name."

Her mission done, she would have gone, but Sir Harold saw that she was poor, and bade her remain.

From that time she never lacked a home.

Time has rolled away since the deeds recorded here were done. England has had its heroes, Scotland its heroes and Ireland the same, and many, died out of the memory of leaving no friendly pen to their deeds to future gen none lived more dearly in all around him than our Greystone.

Some years have fled fought for his honour—and of his grandchildren are grey, a portrait of him in the old hall all love and venerate. It stands the huge fire-place, and when at Christmas they gather round the blazing to hear story, the children ask for a story of the first Sir Harold and the "Crucible," and they list with bated breath and voice tells them of the desperate fight upon the open sea, and the beauties of Honour Bay.

They laugh sometimes when Crikey and Jack are named, and think they should like Chloe; but all these have passed away, and slabs of stone speak of their old fidelity. Honest, simple, true, they died as they had lived, faithful to their hero.

And Harry Carlton had gone—long, long ago—leaving behind him a race of sailors who know no pleasure off the sea, men who have done, and are doing, much for their country.

Hark! the bell rings, and the curtain is falling upon our story, and as the light goes out so fade away the shadows of those who have been so long before us, the heroes of a hundred battles, who fought under the blue banner with the motto, "For Honour we Fight."

THE END.

www.ingramcontent.com/pod-product-compliance
Lightning Source LLC
Chambersburg PA
CBHW080839250626
47161CB00009B/3123